MARCEL PROUST

Finding Time Again

*Translated and with an Introduction
and Notes by Ian Patterson*

General Editor: Christopher Prendergast

PENGUIN BOOKS

PENGUIN BOOKS

Published by the Penguin Group
Penguin Books Ltd, 80 Strand, London WC2R 0RL, England
Penguin Putnam Inc., 375 Hudson Street, New York, New York 10014, USA
Penguin Books Australia Ltd, 250 Camberwell Road, Camberwell, Victoria 3124, Australia
Penguin Books Canada Ltd, 10 Alcorn Avenue, Toronto, Ontario, Canada M4V 3B2
Penguin Books India (P) Ltd, 11 Community Centre, Panchsheel Park, New Delhi – 110 017, India
Penguin Books (NZ) Ltd, Cnr Rosedale and Airborne Roads, Albany, Auckland, New Zealand
Penguin Books (South Africa) (Pty) Ltd, 24 Sturdee Avenue, Rosebank 2196, South Africa

Penguin Books Ltd, Registered Offices: 80 Strand, London WC2R 0RL, England

www.penguin.com

Le Temps retrouvé first published 1927
This translation first published by Allen Lane The Penguin Press 2002
Published in Penguin Classics 2003

009

Translation and editorial matter copyright © Ian Patterson, 2002
All rights reserved

The moral rights of the translator and editor have been asserted

Set by Rowland Phototypesetting Ltd, Bury St Edmunds, Suffolk
Printed in England by Clays Ltd, St Ives plc

ISBN-13: 978–0–141–18036–6

www.greenpenguin.co.uk

Contents

Translator's Introduction

The last volume of *In Search of Lost Time* begins, as the previous one ends, with the narrator staying with Gilberte de Saint-Loup at Tansonville. It is there that he is given a recently published volume of the Goncourts' journal to read in bed, a wonderfully accurate pastiche of the Goncourt style which leads on to a series of revisionary retrospects of his own life. Proust had written an earlier pastiche of the Goncourts' journal, in *Pastiches et mélanges* (1908), and various sorts of pastiche in fact crop up at different times in *Finding Time Again*, contributing implicitly to its continuing interest in questions of authenticity, reality and representation. This can be seen, for example, in more topical form in the pieces of fashion journalism, or in Charlus's comments on Brichot's newspaper articles. The journal extract that Proust reads provides a different perspective on his own past experience, since it deals with the Verdurins' salon and describes several figures – Swann, Elstir, Cottard – well known to him. His response to its ornate, mannered and precious style is significant: by focusing his attention on his own capacities, it allows him to work out his interest in general psychological features rather than in the specificities of visual and aural observation. This enables him to launch what is to be the central theme of the book, the question of how to write his book. Whether it should it be a novel or a philosophical essay was a question which had occupied him when he first considered the subject matter of *In Search of Lost Time*, and woven tightly into the complex folds of the narrative structure of *Finding Time Again* are many essayistic sequences in which the significance of the enterprise is gradually drawn out.

The pastoral prelude at Tansonville is interrupted by the war, the account of which, as experienced in Paris, is structured by the narrator's two brief returns to Paris from the sanatoriums where he is undergoing unsuccessful cures. The first visit coincides with the outbreak of war, in 1914, and provides him with an opportunity to discuss the tradition of strong, silent masculinity in relation to homosexuality, and to contrast Saint-Loup's courage with Bloch's false patriotism.

The second, in 1916, continues this theme at much greater length, with Baron de Charlus at its centre. The narrator has returned to the capital for a while and, in a conversation with Robert de Saint-Loup about the progress of the war, evokes the abstract aesthetic pleasure of aerial warfare above the darkened streets, described as a Wagnerian extravaganza of Zeppelins, biplanes and searchlights. Then, picking his own way through the pitch-black maze of small streets, he comes to the boulevard and runs into Charlus. We learn of the Baron's exclusion from society, his vilification by Mme Verdurin, and his relative unconcern for the external affairs which had plunged the world into war. Proust's clear-sighted depiction of a Paris in which war throws moral behaviour into a sharper focus is the backdrop for the narrator's most surprising discovery, when he takes shelter unwittingly in a sado-masochistic homosexual brothel owned by the Baron, and is witness to the Baron's own pleasures and to the comings and goings of a varied and well-connected clientele. For all this, the episode takes its place in Proust's extended meditation on love, as the narrator reflects that Charlus's 'desire to be chained and beaten betrayed, in its ugliness, a dream just as poetic as other men's desire to go to Venice or to keep a mistress'.

The war represents a watershed, and the narrator's final return is marked by a quality of retrospection that culminates in the recapitulatory sequence of involuntary memories that makes up the substance of the episode in the library of the Prince de Guermantes. In these epiphanic moments, from his stumbling on the paving-stones in the courtyard, through the sound of the spoon to the starch in the napkin and the copy of *François le Champi*, he experiences a joy which prompts renewed investigation (or '*recherche*') into the meaning of these 'impressions' and the purposes to which they can be put in his attempt to write his book. But instead of offering memories for his disposal in the traditional way, their effect is so powerful as to make him start to doubt the coherence of his own sense of self, and it is this that now dominates his quest to turn the experience of lost time into a way of writing his book. The 'inner book of unknown signs', as he calls it, 'the most painful of all to decipher, is also the only one dictated to us by reality, the only one whose "impression" has been made in us by reality itself'. 'The writer's task and duty are those of a translator,' he writes, in what is a prolonged autobiographical essay on the role of writing and memory in making sense of a life; the material is all there, and only the framework, the work of selection and the sense of purpose need to be found. When he is finally ushered into the afternoon party, it is his first extended impression that all the guests are wearing make-up to make themselves look old. Only as it dawns on him that they really are old, and that he is too, does he gradually come to recognize the foundational importance of the element of time in his life and all the lives around him and, despite his age and poor health, is overwhelmed with the need to devote himself at last to the task of writing the book whose shape and purpose he can now finally discern. His only worry, as the last volume of this work comes to its close, is that he should have sufficient time to complete it, an anxiety which itself points up the significance of the place we all occupy in Time.

The title *Le Temps retrouvé* appears for the first time in a letter Proust wrote in the autumn of 1912, and at that time designated what was to be the concluding (second or third) part of the novel; the first was to be called *Le Temps perdu* (Lost Time). Between then and its first publication in 1927, five years after Proust's death, the projected novel underwent a series of changes, additions, alterations and rewriting, changing and developing almost out of recognition. Some things, however, did not change. The heart of this last volume, the chapters known as 'Perpetual adoration' and the '*Bal des têtes*', were already quite extensively drafted by 1910. When Proust died in 1922, the manuscript of *Le Temps retrouvé* was complete, and at least to some extent revised, but it had not yet been typed. It contained contradictions, mistakes, repetitions and omissions (some of which are indicated in the notes to this translation), as well as the immense difficulties created by Proust's corrections and alterations, both in the text and its margins and on the additional pieces of paper glued to the edges of pages, or interleaved between them. It fell to his editors – his brother Robert, and Jean Paulhan (who had succeeded Jacques Rivière as editor of the *Nouvelle Revue Française* in 1925) – to produce a coherent text for publication, which they achieved with a certain amount of cutting and pasting, omitting illegible passages, and adjusting many of the points where repetition or inconsistency occurred. Consequently, the text published in 1927, and translated into English in 1931, was not entirely an accurate presentation of what Proust had written. When Clarac and Ferré published their revised text in 1954, they made a number of changes and corrections, most noticeably in the starting-point for the book, which they moved back some seven pages to the beginning of the narrator's stay at Tansonville. (The 1988 Pléiade edition under the general editorship of Yves Tadié restores the original beginning, on both internal editorial and aesthetic grounds.) A massive and lengthy process of re-evaluation of all Proust's manuscript corrections, insertions, additions and probable intentions resulted in the 1988 edition of the text with its variants, along with a great number of preliminary draft sketches, and although this text itself is not uncontroversial, it has provided the basis for all editorial decisions in this translation.

The translation history of *Finding Time Again* differs considerably from that of the earlier volumes. C. K. Scott Moncrieff died before he was able to begin translating it, in 1930, and the task was taken on by Sydney Schiff, a wealthy patron of the arts, a novelist under the name of Stephen Hudson, and a friend of Proust. (His grief at Proust's death was so demonstrative, and his devotion to Proust's memory so well-known in Paris, that he was nicknamed '*la veuve Proust*', Proust's widow.) For copyright reasons, his translation, though, was not published in America, where a separate translation was made by Frederick A. Blossom, a professor of French. In 1970, Chatto published a new translation, based on the 1954 Pléiade edition, by Andreas Mayor, and it is this translation which was reprinted unrevised in the Terence Kilmartin edition, and again, lightly revised by D. J. Enright, in 1992. Mayor had planned to make a complete revision of Scott Moncrieff's translation, but died before he was able to do so: his preparatory notes provided the basis for Kilmartin's revision. Although the revisions were ostensibly done in order to take account of the 1988 Pléiade edition, there are numerous points at which no alterations were made, or where errors were allowed to stand uncorrected. The most noticeable difference is in the division between *The Fugitive* and the last volume, where both Mayor and his followers retained the 1954 division, beginning *Finding Time Again* with the narrator's visit to Tansonville, rather than dividing that episode in two, as the first edition did and as the 1988 edition, on persuasive evidence, also does. I have followed the 1988 edition in reinstating the original opening. Mayor also did quite a lot of unacknowledged editing of his own, transposing the order of sentences or omitting words or phrases, occasionally sentences. Enright did not correct all these. Another characteristic feature of Mayor's translation is that he persistently extends or enlarges what Proust actually wrote in order to interpret or clarify his sentences. Sometimes this entails inserting some explanatory reference, sometimes spelling out a metaphor, sometimes expanding a pronoun into a recapitulatory phrase, sometimes merely varying nouns or verbs where Proust uses the same one a number of times. There is hardly a sentence without at least a trace of the rewriting of Proust's text. Allusions are spelled out, lexical neutrality (Proust's frequent use of 'avoir' for example) abandoned in favour of greater specificity. While this can occasionally be helpful, the cumulative effect is to add a layer of rather pedantic information, often too ornately phrased, which obscures the idiosyncratic precision of Proust's own style. In this translation I have tried to aim for equivalence rather than explanation.

Equivalence is a mark of recognition of the endless possibilities of interpretation, a quality that is inherent in both the thought-processes and the writing of the novel. The narrator's encounter with the Baron de Charlus on his way to the Guermantes' stands at the gateway to the novel's climax. It marks his first profound encounter with the process of ageing, which, as Walter Benjamin pointed out, is the external counterpart to the interior process of remembrance. 'To observe the interaction of ageing and remembering means to penetrate to the heart of Proust's world, to the universe of convolution. It is the world in a state of resemblances, the domain of the *correspondences*;

the Romanticists were the first to comprehend them and Baudelaire embraced them most fervently, but Proust was the only one who managed to reveal them in our lived life.' He is filled with the insight that none of us has time to live the true dramas of the life that we are destined for. If it is the writer's task to translate his 'book of inner signs', it is the translator's task to render it correctly: Mayor, Kilmartin and Enright departed from earlier versions by turning those signs, quite wrongly, into 'symbols', but they have to be signs.

Questions of vocabulary are not, in the end, all that difficult to resolve. And much of Proust's curious syntax, with its sinuous sideways movements into a series of digressions, each one displaced by the next, reminiscent of his beloved *Arabian Nights* in miniature, can be more or less adequately imitated. What remains a constant frustration, for this translator at least, is the near-impossibility of conveying the more detailed pleasures of Proust's writing, its poetic features, alliterations, anagrams and paragrams, and everything that Malcolm Bowie has described as 'the rhythm of concentration and dispersal in which Proust's details are caught'. It would take another lifetime of translation to find a way of doing that.

Translator's acknowledgements

My first debt is to Jean-Yves Tadié and the editors of the Pléiade edition, for their meticulous scholarship: I have drawn on their work for some of the notes, and have made constant use of it in the process of translation. I would also like to thank Christopher Prendergast, and the other translators, and those who answered specific queries, especially Christine Adams, Martin Crowley and the late Tony Tanner. I would also like to thank Jenny Diski for her patience and her advice as I forced her to listen to drafts of paragraphs, pages and chapters when she had many better things to do.

Finding Time Again

All day long, in that slightly too bucolic residence, which looked like no more than a place for resting between walks or sheltering from a downpour, one of those houses where every sitting-room looks like a conservatory and where, in the bedroom wall-paper, either the garden roses or the birds in the trees are brought vividly before you and keep you company, in a rather isolated way it being of the old-fashioned sort in which each rose was so clearly delineated that if it were alive one could have picked it, each bird so perfect that it might have been caged and tamed, without any of the exaggerated modern décor in which, against a background of silver, all the apple trees of Normandy are arrayed in profile, Japanese-style, to turn the hours you spend in bed into a hallucinatory experience; all day long I stayed in my room, which looked out over the fine greenery of the park and the lilacs by the gateway, over the green leaves of the great trees shimmering in the sunlight beside the water, and over the forest of Méséglise. But really the only reason I was enjoying the sight of it was because I was thinking: 'It is nice to see so much green from my bedroom window,' until the moment when, within the vast verdant scene, I suddenly recognized, coloured a contrasting deep blue simply by virtue of being further away, the steeple of the church at Combray. Not a representation of the steeple but the steeple itself, which, setting thus before my eyes the full extent of miles and of years, had appeared in the middle of that brilliant green, a completely different colour, so dark that it looked almost as if it were only a sketch, and inscribed itself within the rectangle of my window. And if I went out of my room for a moment, at the end of the passage I saw, since it faced in another direction, like a band of scarlet, the wall-hangings of a small

3

sitting-room which were only a simple chiffon, but red, and liable to blaze into colour if a beam of sunlight should fall on them.

In the course of our walks Gilberte spoke to me of Robert as turning away from her, but in order to be with other women. And it is true that his life was somewhat cluttered with them and, as with some kinds of male friendships for men who love women, they had that sense of unavailing defensiveness and of space taken up to no purpose which in most houses characterizes useless objects. He came to Tansonville several times while I was there. He was very different from the man I had known. His life had not thickened him or slowed him down, like M. de Charlus, but, quite the reverse, by working the opposite change in him had given him the confident ease of a cavalry officer, to a far greater degree – despite his having resigned his commission upon his marriage – than he had ever attained before. And just as M. de Charlus had grown heavier, Robert (and he was of course infinitely younger but one felt that he could only approach even closer to this ideal state as he got older, like those women who determinedly sacrifice their face to their figure and after a certain point never leave Marienbad,[1] deciding that, as they are not capable of retaining a plurality of youthful features, their shape is the one best able to represent the rest) had become slenderer and swifter, a contrary effect of the same vice. The swiftness of his movements, moreover, had a number of psychological causes: a fear of being seen, the desire not to appear to have that fear and a febrility created by dissatisfaction with himself and by boredom. He was given to visiting various unsavoury places, into which, as he did not like to be observed entering or leaving them, he would suddenly dive in order to provide the ill-disposed glances of potential passers-by with the least possible visible surface, as if launching a military attack. And this habit of conducting himself like a gust of wind had stuck. It may also perhaps have represented the superficial intrepidity of someone who wants to show that he is not afraid and does not want to give himself any time to think. A full description would also have to take account of his desire, the older he grew, to appear young, as well as of the impatience characteristic of men who are always bored and blasé, being too intelligent for the relatively idle life they lead, in which their faculties are never fully stretched. In many cases this idleness may appear as listlessness. But, especially since physical exercise has come to enjoy such a vogue, idleness these days has taken on an athletic form, even outside the confines of sport, and has come to be expressed in a feverish vivacity that seeks to deny boredom the time or space to develop, rather than in listlessness or indifference.

My memory, even my involuntary memory, had lost all recollection of the love of Albertine. But it seems that there is also an involuntary memory of the limbs, a pale and fruitless imitation of the other kind, which lives on longer, rather as some non-intelligent animals or vegetables live longer than man. One's legs and arms are full of torpid memories. Once, when I had left Gilberte rather early, I woke up in the middle of the night in my room at Tansonville and, still half asleep, called out, 'Albertine!' It was not that I had been thinking about her or dreaming of her, nor that I had mistaken her for Gilberte; but a recollection suddenly burgeoning within my arm had made me reach behind my back for the bell, as if I had been in my bedroom in Paris. And, not finding it, I had called out: 'Albertine!', thinking my dead lover was lying beside me as she often used to in the evenings, and that we were falling asleep together, I relying, when I woke up, on the time it would take Françoise to get to my room, so that Albertine might without risk pull the bell which I could not find.

Becoming – during this troublesome phase at least – much less sympathetic, Robert no longer displayed to his friends, to myself for example, any real evidence of sensitivity. On the other hand, he affected a sentimentality towards Gilberte that bordered on the theatrical, which was quite distasteful. Not that Gilberte was really unimportant to him. No, Robert loved her. But he lied to her all the time; his duplicitous nature, if not the root cause of his lying, was permanently exposed. And he therefore thought that the only way to redeem the situation was by exaggerating, on a ridiculous scale, the real sadness he felt at upsetting her. He used to arrive at Tansonville obliged, he would say, to leave again the next morning in order to attend to some business with a country neighbour who was meant to be waiting for him in Paris and who, encountered by chance that evening near Combray, would unintentionally expose the lie which Robert had neglected to tell him about, by saying that he had come down to the country for a month's rest and would not be returning to Paris during that time. Robert would redden, see Gilberte's sad, disdainful smile, extricate himself with some harsh words to the blunderer, return ahead of his wife and send her a despairing note in which he would claim to have lied in order not to upset her, so that when she saw him leave for reasons he was unable to explain to her, she would not think he did not love her (all of which, despite being written as a lie, was actually true), and would then send to ask if he could come to her room, where, partly in real distress, partly out of exhaustion at his life, and partly in a pretence that grew daily more outrageous, he would sob, drench his face in cold water, speak of his imminent death and sometimes throw himself on to the floorboards as if suddenly taken ill. Gilberte never knew how far she ought to believe him, imagined that he was lying about each individual instance, but that in some general way she was loved, and worried about these forebodings of imminent death, thinking that he did perhaps suffer from some illness she was unaware of and therefore did not dare to oppose him or to ask him to forgo his trips.

I was even more at a loss to understand why it was that Morel had to be treated as the son of the house, like Bergotte, wherever the Saint-Loups happened to be, in Paris or at Tansonville. Morel could mimic Bergotte perfectly. In fact after a while there was no need to ask him to do his imitation. Like those hysterics who do not have to be put into a trance in order for them to become some other person, he would of his own accord suddenly take on all his characteristics.

Françoise, who had seen everything that M. de Charlus had done for Jupien and everything that Robert de Saint-Loup was doing for Morel, did not thereby infer that this was a trait that resurfaced in different generations of Guermantes, but rather – as Legrandin too did so much to help Théodore – she concluded, moralistic and set in her ideas as she was, that this was a custom rendered respectable by its universality. She would always say of a young man, whether it were Morel or Théodore: 'He's found a gentleman who's interested in him and has done ever so much to help him.' And since in such cases it is the protectors who love, suffer and forgive, Françoise did not hesitate, between them and the minors they seduced, to accord them the better part, to find them 'good-hearted'. She had no hesitation in blaming Théodore, who had played so many tricks on Legrandin, and yet it seemed almost impossible that she could have any doubt about the nature of their relationship, for she would add: 'The boy realized he had to do his bit too, and said, "Take me with you, I'll love you, I'll be nice to you," and, my goodness, the gentleman is so good-natured that Théodore is bound to be treated better than he deserves, because he's a bit wild, but the gentleman is so good that I've often said to Jeanette (Théodore's fiancée), "My dear, if you're ever in trouble, go and see the gentleman. He'd sleep on the floor and give you his own bed. He's been too fond of the boy (Théodore) to turn him out. Of course he won't ever abandon him."'

Théodore was now living somewhere in the Midi, and out of politeness I asked his sister what his surname was. 'But that must be the person who wrote to me about my *Figaro* article!' I exclaimed when I heard that he was called Sautton.

In the same way she thought more highly of Saint-Loup than of Morel and reckoned that, despite all the things the boy (Morel) had done, the Marquis would always get him out of trouble, because he was such a good-hearted man, or else something terrible would have to have happened to prevent him.

Saint-Loup was insistent that I should remain at Tansonville, and on one occasion let slip, although he gave no other visible indication of wanting to please me, that my arrival had caused his wife such joy that she was transported by it, so she had told him, for the entire evening, an evening on which she had been feeling so wretched that by arriving unexpectedly I had miraculously saved her from despair, 'or perhaps even worse', he had added. He asked me to try to persuade her that he loved her, saying that the other woman he loved, he loved less than her, and that he would soon break with her. 'And yet,' he added with such complacency and such a need to confide in me that I thought that at any moment the name 'Charlie', despite himself, was going to 'pop out' like the winning number in a lottery, 'I did have something to be proud of. This woman, who has shown her affection for me in so many ways, and whom I'm going to sacrifice for Gilberte, had never been attracted to a man, she thought she was incapable of being in love. I am the first. I was so deeply conscious of her having rejected everybody that, when I received the adorable letter telling me she could never be happy except with me, I couldn't get over it. Obviously I could have lost my head completely, except that I couldn't bear the thought of my poor little Gilberte in tears. Don't you think she's rather like Rachel?' he went on. And in fact I had been struck by a vague resemblance that one could, at a stretch, now see between them. Perhaps this lay in the real similarity of some features (due possibly to their Jewish origins, though these were not very evident in Gilberte) which had caused Robert, when his family pressed him to marry, to feel more attracted to Gilberte than to other women of comparable fortune. It may also have had something to do with the fact that Gilberte, having come across some photographs of Rachel, who had previously not even been a name to her, attempted to please Robert by imitating some of the actress's habits of dress, like always having red bows in her hair and a black velvet ribbon on her arm, and by dyeing her hair to make herself look darker. Then, realizing that her distress was making her look ill, she tried to remedy things. Sometimes she took this to extremes. One evening, when Robert was due to be spending twenty-four hours at Tansonville, I was astounded to see her take her seat at the dining-table looking so curiously different, not only from her former self but even from her habitual appearance, that I sat there in amazement, as if I were watching an actress, a sort of Théodora.[2] I sensed that, despite myself, I was staring at her in my curiosity to discover what it was about her that was so changed. This curiosity was, however, soon satisfied when she wiped her nose, despite all the precautions she employed. From all the colours which remained on the handkerchief, turning it into a rich palette, I saw that she was entirely made-up. It was this that gave her the blood-red mouth which she tried to keep curved in a permanent smile, in the belief that it suited her, while the approaching arrival time of the train, with Gilberte still not knowing whether her husband would actually be on it or whether he would send one of those telegrams which M. de Guermantes had wittily characterized as: UNABLE TO COME: LIE FOLLOWS, made her cheeks grow pale beneath the violet perspiration of the rouge and etched dark shadows around her eyes.

'Ah, you know,' he would say to me, with a consciously affectionate manner which contrasted powerfully with the spontaneous affection of earlier times, in the voice of an alcoholic and with the modulations of an actor, 'I'd give anything to see Gilberte happy! She's done so much for me. You simply can't know.' And the most disagreeable aspect of all this was, again, his vanity, as he was flattered at being loved by Gilberte and yet, without daring to say that it was Charlie he loved, still provided details of the love the violinist was supposed to have for him, details which Saint-Loup knew were heavily exaggerated, if not entirely invented, given that Charlie was daily demanding larger and larger sums of money from him. And thus, entrusting Gilberte to my care, he would leave once again for Paris.

I did once have an opportunity (to anticipate a little, as I am still at Tansonville) to observe him in Paris society, from a distance, and on that occasion his conversation, lively and charming despite everything, enabled me to recapture the past; yet I was struck by how much he was changing. He was looking more and more like his mother: the haughty, elegant manner he had inherited from her and which she, after the most thorough education, had brought to perfection in him, was now becoming exaggerated and rigidified; the piercing gaze characteristic of all the Guermantes made it seem as if he were inspecting all the places in which he found himself, but in an almost unconscious way, out of a sort of habit or animal trait. Even when he was standing still, the colouring, which was more pronounced in him than in any of the other Guermantes, as if he were nothing but a day of golden sunlight given solid form, gave him as it seemed such a strange plumage, turned him into a species so rare and precious, as to make him a desirable acquisition for any ornithological collection; but when, in addition, this light become bird started to move, to act, when for example I was at a party and saw Robert de Saint-Loup enter the room, the way he held his head, so silkily and proudly crested beneath the gold plumes of his somewhat thinning hair, and moved his neck with so much more suppleness, pride and daintiness than humans display, inspired in one a curiosity and admiration half-social, half-zoological, such that one began to wonder whether one were in the Faubourg Saint-Germain or the Jardin des Plantes,[3] whether one were watching an aristocrat crossing a drawing-room or a bird walking round its cage. Furthermore, this whole regression to the birdlike elegance of the Guermantes, with pointed beak and sharpened eyes, was now being employed by his new vice, which was using it to maintain his dignity. And the more he used it, the more of a queen, as Balzac would say,[4] he looked. It required only a slender act of imagination to see that his warblings lent themselves no less well to this interpretation than his plumage. He was beginning to speak in sentences which he believed sounded seventeenth-century, and in that was merely imitating the style of the Guermantes. But at the same time some indefinable inflection was causing them to develop into the manners of M. de Charlus. 'I must leave you for a moment,' he said to me during the course of the evening, when M. de Marsantes was standing a little way off from us. 'I have to pay my court to my mother.'

As for his love, about which he spoke interminably, it was not, it must be said, only love for Charlie, even though that was the only affair that meant anything to him. Whatever the nature of a man's love affairs, one is always wrong about the number of people with whom he is having liaisons, partly because one mistakenly interprets friendships as affairs, and gets the addition wrong, but also because one tends to believe that one proven affair precludes another, which is an error of quite a different kind. Two people may say: 'X——'s mistress, yes, I know her', utter two different names, and both be right. A woman whom we love seldom satisfies all our needs, and we deceive her with a woman we do not love. As for the type of love affairs that Saint-Loup had inherited from M. de Charlus, a husband who is that way inclined usually makes his wife very happy. This is a general rule to which the Guermantes managed to be an exception, since those who had this taste wanted it to be thought that, on the contrary, they desired women. They were seen everywhere with some woman or other and drove their wives to despair. The Courvoisiers behaved more sensibly. The young Vicomte de Courvoisier thought he was the only man on earth, since the beginning of the world, to be tempted by somebody of his own sex. Believing his inclination to come from the devil, he fought against it, married a very beautiful wife and gave her children.

Then one of his cousins taught him that this inclination is really quite common, and was kind enough to take him to places where he could satisfy it. M. de Courvoisier's love for his wife only intensified, he redoubled his prolific zeal, and he and she were cited as the happiest couple in Paris. Nothing of the sort was ever said of Saint-Loup's household, because Robert, instead of being content with his inversion, caused his wife agonies of jealousy by keeping mistresses from whom he derived no pleasure.

It may be that Morel, being very dark-complexioned, was necessary to Saint-Loup in the same way as shadow is necessary to a beam of sunlight. It is very easy to imagine, somewhere within that ancient family, a golden-haired aristocrat, intelligent, endowed with every distinction, concealing deep down, unknown to everybody, a secret taste for negroes.

Furthermore, Robert never permitted his type of love to come up in conversation. If I mentioned it: 'Oh, I don't know,' he would reply, with such complete detachment that he would let his monocle drop, 'I don't have the least idea about that sort of thing. If you want information about that, my dear fellow, I advise you to enquire elsewhere. I'm a soldier, full stop. I'm as uninterested in all that as I am passionate about following the Balkan war. That was something that interested you once, the etymology of battles. I told you then that we would see the typical battles again, under very different conditions, like that great exercise in strategic encirclement, the Battle of Ulm. Well now, even with all the special features of the Balkan wars, Lüleburgaz is Ulm all over again: strategic encirclement. These are subjects you can talk to me about. But the kind of things you were hinting at, I know as much about them as I do about Sanskrit.'

Although Robert thus affected disdain for the subject, Gilberte on the other hand, after he had left, was very willing to broach it in conversation with me. Not of course in connection with her husband, as she was not aware, or pretended not to be, of anything. But she would happily expatiate on it where others were concerned, either because she saw it as an indirect excuse for Robert, or because he, torn like his uncle between a stern silence on such matters and a need to unburden himself and run others down, had alerted her to many instances of it. M. de Charlus, in particular, was not spared, probably because Robert, without speaking to Gilberte about Charlie, could not refrain, when he was with her, from repeating, in one form or another, what the violinist had told him. And he constantly harried his former benefactor with his detestation. These conversations, for which Gilberte had a predilection, enabled me to ask her whether, in a similar way, Albertine, whose name I had first heard spoken by her, when they were classmates, had any such tastes. Gilberte was unable to give me any information about this. And anyway it had long since ceased to be of any interest to me. But I continued to enquire mechanically, like an old man who has lost his memory periodically requesting news of the son he has lost.

What is odd, which I cannot go into here, is the extent to which, around that time, all the people whom Albertine loved, and who might have been able to make her do what they wanted, asked for, implored, I may even say begged for, if not my friendship, then at least some sort of acquaintance with me. I should no longer have needed to offer Mme Bontemps money to send Albertine back to me. This unexpected turn in my affairs, occurring when it no longer served any purpose, saddened me deeply, not on account of Albertine, whom I would have received with no pleasure had she been brought back, not now from Touraine but from the other world, but because of a young woman with whom I was in love and whom I could not arrange to see. I told myself that if she died, or if I no longer loved her, everybody who might have been able to bring us together would be throwing themselves at my feet. In the meantime I tried in vain to influence them, not having been cured by experience, which ought to have taught me – if it had taught me anything – that love is an evil spell, like the ones in fairy-tales, against which one is powerless until the enchantment be broken.

'Actually, the book I'm reading at the moment is about that sort of thing', she said to me. (I had mentioned that mysterious 'We would have got on very well together' to Robert. He claimed not to remember saying it, and added that, in any case, he had not meant anything out of the ordinary by it.)

'It's an old Balzac I've been mugging up on, so as to know as much as my uncles, *La Fille aux yeux d'or*. But it's absurd and unrealistic, a complete fantasy. I mean, a woman might be kept under surveillance like that by another woman, but never by a man. – You're wrong, I once knew a woman who ended up completely shut away by the man who loved her; she was never allowed to see anyone, and could only go out accompanied by trusty servants. – But someone as good as you must have been horrified by that. In fact Robert and I were saying that you ought to get married. A wife would make you healthy again, and you would make her very happy. – No, I'm not a good enough person. – What an absurd idea! – No, I mean it. Besides, I was engaged once, but I couldn't make up my mind to marry her (and then she broke it off herself, because of my fussiness and indecision).' It was, indeed, in this over-simplified form that I regarded my adventure with Albertine, now that I could see it only from the outside.

As I went back up to my room, I reflected sadly that I had not even once been to revisit the church at Combray, which looked, amidst all the greenery, in that violet-tinted window, as if it were expecting me. I said to myself: 'Never mind, it'll have to wait for another year, if I don't die in the meantime,' seeing no obstacle to this other than my death, never envisaging that of the church, which seemed bound to endure long after my death, as it had endured for so long before my birth.

Nevertheless I did mention Albertine to Gilberte one day, and asked her whether Albertine had loved women. 'Oh! Not in the least. – But you said once that she behaved badly. – I said that? I'm sure you must be wrong. Anyway, if I did, but I'm sure I didn't, I must have been talking about involvements with young men. Besides, at her age, they probably didn't amount to anything.' Was Gilberte telling me this in order to hide the fact that, according to what Albertine had told me, she loved women too and had made suggestions to Albertine? Or did she know (for others are often better informed about our lives than we think) that I had loved and been jealous of Albertine, and (others being able to know more of the truth about us than we think, but also to take it too far and fall into the error of assuming too much, where we had hoped that they might have made the mistake of not assuming anything at all) did she imagine that I still was, and was she, out of kindness, placing a blindfold over my eyes, as one is always prepared to do for those who are jealous? At all events, everything Gilberte said, from the original 'behaved badly' to the present certificate of good conduct, followed an inverse sequence to the assertions of Albertine, who had finally all but admitted a certain intimacy of relations with Gilberte. Albertine had astonished me by this, as I had been astonished by what Andrée had told me, because, before I came to know them, I had believed all of that little gang to be involved in perversion; I later realized that my assumption was wrong, as so often happens when one finds a decent girl, practically ignorant of the realities of love, in circles one had wrongly believed to be completely depraved. Later I had followed the same path in the opposite direction, ending with a renewed belief in the truth of my original supposition. But perhaps Albertine had wanted to tell me that so that she would appear more experienced than she really was, and to dazzle me in Paris with the glamour of her perversity, as she had done, that first time at Balbec, with the prestige of her virtue. And quite simply, when I had spoken to her about women who loved women, so as not to seem not to understand what I meant, as in the course of conversation one adopts an air of comprehension if Fourier[5] or Tobolsk[6] are mentioned, even though one has no idea what is meant by them. She had spent her time, perhaps, close to Mlle Vinteuil's woman friend and to Andrée, separated by a watertight partition from them because of their belief that she 'wasn't one', and had only informed herself about the topic later – in the same way as a woman who marries a man of letters seeks to improve her mind – in order to please me by becoming capable of replying to my questions, until the day when she realized that they were inspired by jealousy, after which she had backtracked. Unless it were Gilberte who was lying to me. It even occurred to me that it was because of having learned from her, in the course of a flirtation he would have conducted with his own ends in view, that she was not averse to women, that Robert had married her, hoping for pleasures which, since he took them elsewhere, he must never have found with her. None of these hypotheses was absurd, for with women like Odette's daughter, or the girls of the little gang, there is so much diversity, such an accumulation of alternating, if not indeed simultaneous tastes, that they pass easily from a liaison with a woman to a passionate affair with a man, so that determining their real and dominant taste remains difficult.

I did not want to borrow Gilberte's copy of *La Fille aux yeux d'or*, as she was still reading it. But she lent me, to read before going to sleep that last evening I spent with her, a book which made a powerful but uneven impression on me, although it proved not to be a lasting one. This was a recently published volume of the Goncourts' journal.[7]

And when, before snuffing out my candle, I read the passage I transcribe below, my lack of an aptitude for literature, sensed long ago on the Guermantes way, and confirmed during the stay whose last evening this was – one of those evenings just before a departure when, with the imminent loss of the cocoon of regularity, one attempts to take stock of oneself – seemed to me something less regrettable, as if literature did not reveal any profound truth; and at the same time it seemed to me sad that literature was not what I had believed it to be. On the other hand, the state of ill-health which was about to confine me to a sanatorium also seemed less regrettable, if the fine things spoken of in books were no finer than those I had seen myself. Yet, by a curious contradiction, now that this book was talking about them, I had a longing to see them. Here are the pages that I read before tiredness closed my eyes:

'The day before yesterday Verdurin drops in here to take me off to dine with him; he used to be a critic for *La Revue*, wrote that book about Whistler in which truly the technique, the painterly handling of colour, of the eccentric American is frequently conveyed with considerable refinement by that *amateur* of all the subtleties, all the *delicacies*, of the painted surface that Verdurin is. And while I am dressing to go out with him he starts telling me a long story, parts of it in a timorous whisper almost like a confession, about his renunciation of writing immediately after his marriage to Fromentin's "Madeleine", a renunciation due, he tells me, to his morphine habit, and which resulted, by his account, in most of the habitués of his wife's drawing-room having not the least idea that her husband had ever written anything, and talking to him about Charles Blanc, Saint-Victor, Sainte-

Beuve, and Burty[8] as figures to whom they thought him utterly inferior. "But of course you Goncourts know – and so did Gautier – that my *Salons* were something altogether different from those woeful *Maîtres d'autrefois*[9] which my wife's family take to be such a masterpiece." Then, through a dusk in which the last flickering rays of light on the towers of the Trocadéro turn them into towers exactly like the ones glazed with redcurrant jelly that confectioners used to create, the conversation continues in the carriage that is taking us to the Quai Conti and their *hôtel*,[10] which its present owner claims was once the residence of the Venetian ambassadors, and where there is apparently a smoking-room which Verdurin talks about as having been transported, *Arabian Nights*-fashion, from a famous *palazzo*, the name of which I forget, but a *palazzo* with a well-head depicting a coronation of the Virgin which he maintains to be absolutely one of Sansovino's finest works, and which their guests use as somewhere to drop their cigar ash. And, by Jove, when we arrive, in a greenish, diffused, watery moonlight very reminiscent of that in which the Classical paintings shroud Venice, and above which the silhouetted cupola of the Institut recalls the Salute in Guardi's pictures, I do have a momentary illusion of being beside the Grand Canal. An illusion further fostered by the *hôtel*'s construction, as you cannot see the Quai from the first floor, and by the evocative remark of the master of the house as he asserts that the Rue du Bac takes its name – dashed if it had ever occurred to me before – from the "bac", or ferry, on which an order of nuns, the Miramiones, once used to travel across to services at Notre-Dame. The whole quarter is one I used to wander around as a child when my aunt de Courmont lived there, and I began to *re-love* it when, practically next door to the Verdurins' house, I discovered the sign-board of "Le Petit Dunkerque", one of the very few shops to have survived, other than as vignettes in the scumbled shadow of Gabriel de Saint-Aubin's pencil drawings, where eighteenth-century collectors came to spend their idle moments haggling over French and foreign trinkets and "all the last creations of the arts", as an old bill of sale from "Le Petit Dunkerque" puts it, bills which Verdurin and I are, I believe, the only ones to possess copies of, and which are among the ephemeral masterpieces of those embellished documents on which the world of

Louis XV made out their accounts, with a letter-head depicting a wave-tossed sea laden with ships, a wavy sea that could easily have been an illustration to "The Oyster and the Plaintiffs" in the Fermiers Généraux edition of La Fontaine.[11] The mistress of the house, next to whom I am to sit at dinner, tells me charmingly that she has decorated her table with nothing but Japanese chrysanthemums, but chrysanthemums arranged in vases which turn out to be exceedingly rare masterpieces, one of them in particular being made of bronze overlaid with reddish copper petals so lifelike they would seem to have fallen there from the flower itself. Cottard, the doctor, is there with his wife, and the Polish sculptor Viradobetski, Swann the collector, an aristocratic Russian lady, a princess with a name ending in '-ov' which I don't quite catch, and Cottard whispers in my ear that it is she who shot at the Archduke Rudolph at point-blank range, and that according to her I have an extraordinarily exalted reputation in Galicia and the whole of northern Poland, no young woman ever agreeing to an offer of marriage without first determining whether her fiancé is an admirer of *La Faustin* [12] "This is not something you Westerners can understand," is the princess's concluding challenge, who strikes me, I must say, as possessed of an altogether superior intelligence, "this insight by a writer into a woman's most private feelings." A man with clean-shaven chin and lips and a butler's side-whiskers, holding forth in the condescending tone of a fifth-form master joking with his favoured pupils during the Charlemagne Day celebrations, turns out to be Brichot, from the University. Upon my being presented by Verdurin, he has nothing to say that suggests any acquaintance with our books, arousing in me an irascible despondency at the conspiracy organized against us by the Sorbonne, importing even into the gracious home where I am so warmly entertained the discrepant unfriendliness of a deliberate silence. We go in to dinner and there follows an extraordinary procession of plates which are quite simply masterpieces of the porcelain-maker's art, an art which, in the course of an elegant meal, flatters the attentive ear of a connoisseur with the most agreeably artistic tinkle of its conversation, – Yung-chêng plates, with their nasturtium-coloured borders and the blue of their irises, tumid and leafless, and a wonderfully ornamented flight of kingfishers and cranes across a dawn sky, the dawn rendered with precisely those matutinal tones which greet my daily awakening in the Boulevard Montmorency – Dresden plates, more delicate in the grace of their technique, with the drowsy anaemia of their roses washed to violet, with the wine-dark laciniation of a tulip, with the rococo of a pink or a forget-me-not – Sèvres plates latticed with the fine guilloche of their white fluting, verticillated with gold, or knotted, on the creamy surface of the paste, with a gold ribbon raised in elegant relief – finally an entire service of silver chased with those myrtles of Luciennes that the Du Barry[13] would have recognized. And what is perhaps equally rare is the really quite remarkable quality of the things served on them, a meal exquisitely planned, a veritable feast, such as the Parisians, it must most emphatically be said, never have at their grandest dinners, and which reminds me of some of the great dishes at Jean d'Heurs.[14] Even the *foie gras* bears no relation to the insipid mousse normally served under that name, and I do not know many places where a simple potato salad is made, like this, out of potatoes with the firmness of Japanese ivory buttons and the patina of those little ivory spoons with which Chinese women sprinkle water over their freshly caught fish. In the Venetian glass I have before me, a rich profusion of jewelled reds glows from an extraordinary Léoville, bought at M. Montalivet's sale, and it is a delight for the eye's imagination, and also, I do not scruple to say it, for the imagination of what one used to call the chops, to see carried in a brill which has nothing in common with the far from fresh brill that are served at the most luxurious tables and which have had, in the slow course of their journey to the kitchen, the pattern of their bones impressed on to their back, a brill served not with the floury paste so many chefs in great houses prepare under the name of white sauce, but with a real white sauce made with butter costing five francs a pound – to see this brill brought in on a wonderful Yung-chêng dish striated by the crimson rays of a sunset above a sea wittily navigated by a band of lobsters, their gritty stippling so extraordinarily rendered that they seem to have been moulded from the live carapace, a dish whose border depicts a little Chinese boy catching with rod and line a fish, the azured silvering of whose belly is an enchantment of nacreous colour. When I observe to Verdurin what an exquisite pleasure it must be for him to eat this superb provender off a collection such as no prince currently possesses in his glass cabinets, "It is clear to see you don't know him," interjects sadly the mistress of the house. And she speaks to me of her husband as a cranky eccentric, indifferent to all these sophistications, "Cranky," she repeats, "there's no other word for it," a crank who would prefer a bottle of cider, drunk in the rather plebeian cool of a Normandy farm. And this charming woman, whose eloquence reveals her complete love of its regional colour, speaks with brimming enthusiasm of that part of Normandy where they once lived, a Normandy that seems to have been like a great English park, fragrant with stands of mature trees, as in a painting by Lawrence, fringed with the cryptomerian velvet of their natural lawns, porcelained with pink hydrangeas, with masses of crumpled sulphur roses tumbling above a rural gateway, against which the overlay of two interlaced pear trees seems to imitate some purely ornamental sign board, calling to mind the free-flowing lines of a flowering branch in the bronze of a Gouthière sconce, a Normandy completely undreamed of by holidaying Parisians, each *clos* protected by its gates, all of which gates the Verdurins confess to me they had no qualms about opening. At the day's end, amid a soporific fading of all the colours, when the only source of light was an almost curdled sea, tinged with the milky-blue of whey ("No, not like any sea you've seen," protests frantically my neighbour, in response to my saying that Flaubert had taken us, my brother and myself, to Trouville, "absolutely nothing like, you'll have to come with me, else you'll never know"), they would return home, through the veritable forests of pink tulle formed by the rhododendrons, utterly befuddled with the smell of the sardine fisheries, which gave her husband terrible attacks of asthma – "yes, she insists, I mean it, they were real asthma attacks." And there, the following summer, they returned, accommodating an entire colony of artists in a marvellous medieval building, part of an ancient monastery, which they rented for practically nothing. And, by Jove, listening to this woman who, moving among so many circles of truly distinguished people, has yet retained in her speech something of the vitality of language of a woman of the people, language which shows you things with the colour that your imagination sees in them, my mouth waters at the life she confesses to me that they led down there, each person working in his cell and, in the drawing-room so vast that it had two fireplaces, everybody gathering before luncheon for altogether elevated conversation, interspersed with parlour games, making me think of the kind of life described in Diderot's masterpiece, the *Lettres à Mademoiselle Volland*. Then after lunch everybody would go out, even on squally days, in a burst of sunshine, or the effulgence of a shower, of a shower outlining with its gleaming trickles the nodes of a magnificent sweep of centenarian beeches, which set before the entrance gate that vegetable idea of *the beautiful* so dear to the eighteenth century, and the arborescent shrubs which, in place of burgeoning buds, had, hanging from their branches, drops of water. They would stop to listen to the delicate dabbling of a bullfinch, entranced by the coolness, bathing in the dainty, minuscule Nymphenburg bath formed by the petals of a white rose. And when I mention to Mme Verdurin the landscapes and flowers of the region in Elstir's delicate pastels: "But I'm the one who introduced him to all that," she interjects with an angry toss of her head, "everything, do you realize, everything, the hidden nooks, every one of his subjects, I threw it in his face when he left, didn't I, Auguste, all the scenes he painted. To be fair, he was always aware of objects, I have to admit that. But he'd never seen the flowers, he couldn't tell a hollyhock from an althea. You won't believe this, but I even had to show him how to recognize jasmine." And one must admit that it is a curious thought that the artist held up by connoisseurs today as the leading flower-painter, superior even to Fantin-Latour, would perhaps never, without this woman sitting beside me, have been able to paint a jasmine. "Yes, honestly, jasmine. And all the roses he has done were painted at my house, or else brought to him by me. When he was with us, we never called him anything but Monsieur Tiche: ask Cottard or Brichot, or any of the others, whether we treated him as a great man here. He would have laughed if we had. I taught him how to arrange his flowers; he couldn't manage it at all, to begin with. He never learned how to make a bouquet. He had no natural sense of what to choose, I always had to say, 'No, don't paint that one, it's not worth it, paint this one.' Ah, if only he'd listened to what we said about arranging his life as attentively as he did about arranging his flowers, and hadn't made that rotten marriage!" And abruptly, her eyes fevered by absorption in a reverie of the past, and nervously plucking, as she distractedly flexes her fingers, at the floss of the sleeves of her blouse, she presents, in the anguish of her averted pose, a wonderful picture that has never, I think, been painted, one in which would be displayed all the contained revolt, all the enraged sensibilities of a female friend outraged in the refinement, in the modesty of womanhood. Thereupon she talks about the wonderful portrait Elstir did for her, the portrait of the Cottard family, which she gave to the Luxembourg at the time of her quarrel with the painter, confessing that it was she who gave the painter the idea of having the man in full evening dress in order to achieve all that lovely frothing swell of linen, and who chose the woman's velvet dress, a dress that provides a solid resting-place amidst all the flitter of bright colours in the carpets, the flowers, the fruit, the little girls' muslin dresses that look like dancers' tutus. It was she too, I gather, who gave him the idea of the woman brushing her hair, an idea for which the artist was subsequently much praised, and which simply consisted of painting the woman not as it were on display but surprised in a moment of everyday intimacy. "I used to say to him, 'In a woman doing her hair, drying her face, warming her feet, when she is unaware of being observed, there is a wealth of interesting movements, movements of a quite Leonardo-esque gracefulness!' "

'But at a sign from Verdurin, indicating that the re-arousal of this indignation was not good for the health of his wife, who is very highly strung, Swann invites me to admire the necklace of black pearls worn by the mistress of the house, and bought by her, in their original whiteness, at the sale of a descendant of Mme de La Fayette, to whom they were given by Henrietta of England, pearls which had become black after a fire which destroyed part of the house in which the Verdurins lived, in a street whose name I no longer remember, a fire from which the casket containing the pearls was recovered, but with the pearls now entirely black. "And I know the portrait of them, of these pearls, on the very shoulders of Mme de La Fayette, yes, I know their portrait very well," insists Swann, forestalling the somewhat amazed exclamations of the other guests, "the authentic portrait of them, in the collection of the Duc de Guermantes." A collection without equal anywhere in the world, declares Swann, and which I ought to go and see, a collection inherited by the famous Duc, who was her favourite nephew, from his aunt, Mme de Beausergent, afterwards Mme d'Hatzfeldt, sister of the Marquise de Villeparisis and of the Princess of Hanover, in whose house my brother and I had at one time grown so fond of him in the person of the charming little child called Basin, which as a matter of fact is indeed the Duc's forename. Thereupon Dr Cottard, with the subtlety which reveals him to be a man of genuine eminence, turns back to the story of the pearls, and informs us that catastrophes of this nature produce alterations in the human brain quite comparable to those observable in inanimate matter, and cites, in a manner considerably more philosophical than most doctors could command, the instance of Mme de Verdurin's own manservant, who, from the horror of that fire, in which he very nearly perished, had become a changed man, with a handwriting so altered that when his master and mistress, then in Normandy, received his first letter informing them of the occurrence, they imagined it to be the work of a practical joker. And not only an altered handwriting, according to Cottard, who maintains that from being abstemious this man had become such an abominable drunk that Mme Verdurin had been obliged to dismiss him. And this thought-provoking discourse adjourns, at a gracious signal from the mistress of the house, from the dining-room to the Venetian smoking-room, where Cottard tells us that he has witnessed veritable instances of dual personality, citing the case of one of his patients, whom he very kindly offers to bring to my house, and whose temples he has, apparently, only to touch to awaken him to a second life, a life during which he remembers nothing of the first, to such a degree that, although entirely honest in the one, he has several times been arrested for thefts committed in the other, in which he is quite simply a complete scoundrel. Upon which Mme Verdurin shrewdly remarks that medicine might furnish the modern theatre with a more truthful set of subjects, in which the convolutions of the imbroglio would be founded upon misapprehensions of a pathological nature, which, by a natural progression, leads Mme Cottard to relate that a very similar idea has been used by a story-teller who is the bedtime favourite of her children, the Scotsman Stevenson, a name which prompts Swann to the peremptory assertion, "But he's altogether a great writer, Stevenson, I assure you, M. de Goncourt, very great, equal to the greatest." And when, after having marvelled at the ceiling, with its escutcheoned coffers, taken from the old Palazzo Barberini, of the room in which we are smoking, I hint at my regret at the gradual darkening of a certain stone basin by the ash of our Havanas, and Swann having recounted how similar stains on books once belonging to Napoleon I, books which are now, despite his anti-Bonapartist opinions, in the possession of the Duc de Guermantes, testify to the Emperor's having chewed tobacco, Cottard, who shows himself to be interested to a quite profound degree in everything, declares that the stains do not come from that at all – "No, no, not at all," he insists with authority – but from the habit he had of always having in his hand, even on the battlefield, liquorice tablets, to allay his liver pains. "Because he had a disease of the liver and that is what he finally died of," concludes the doctor.'

I stopped there, because I was leaving in the morning; and besides it was the hour at which I was customarily claimed by the master, in whose service we spend, each day, a large part of our time. The work to which he compels us, we accomplish with our eyes shut. Each morning he returns us to our other master, knowing that if he does not, we will be reluctant to surrender ourselves again to his service. Inquisitive, when our intelligence has reopened its eyes, to know what we may have done in the house of this master, who has his slaves lie down before putting them so rapidly to work, the shrewdest of them, their task scarcely finished, try to steal a clandestine glimpse of it. But sleep races against them to dispel the traces of what they would like to see. And after so many centuries we still do not know very much about it.

So I closed the Goncourts' journal. The magic of literature! I would have liked to see the Cottards again, asked them so many details about Elstir, gone to look at that shop, 'Le Petit Dunkerque', if it still existed, asked permission to visit the Verdurin *hôtel* where I had been to dinner. But I felt a vague sense of unease. Certainly I had never concealed from myself the fact that I did not know how to listen, nor, as soon as

I was not alone, how to observe. My eyes would not notice what kind of pearl necklace an old woman might be wearing, and anything that might be said about it would not penetrate my ears. Yet I had known these individuals in my daily life, I had often dined with them, whether they were the Verdurins, the Duc de Guermantes, the Cottards, and each of them had seemed to me as ordinary as that Basin had appeared to my grandmother, who little suspected that he was the cherished nephew, the charming young hero, of Mme de Beausergent, to me they had all seemed insipid; I could recall the numberless vulgarities of which each of them was compounded . . .

Et que tout cela fasse un astre dans la nuit.![15]

I resolved provisionally to set aside the objections to literature aroused in me by the pages of Goncourt read on the eve of my departure from Tansonville. Even discounting the evidence of personal naïvety so conspicuous in the work of this memoirist, I could set my mind at rest on a number of other points. First, so far as my own personality was concerned, my incapacity to look attentively and to listen, which the quotation from the journal had so painfully illustrated to me, was yet not total. There was in me a character who knew more or less how to look, but this was an intermittent character, coming to life only when some general essence was revealed, something common to several things, in which it found its nourishment and its delight. Then the character looked and listened, but only to a certain depth, so that my observation did not benefit from it. Just as a geometrician, stripping things of their physical qualities, sees only their linear substratum, so what people said escaped me, because what interested me was not what they wanted to say, but the manner in which they said it, in so far as this revealed their character or their absurdities; or, rather, the object that had always been the aim of my researches, because it gave me a specific pleasure, was the point that was common to one being and another. It was only when I glimpsed this that my intelligence – thitherto sleeping, even behind the apparent alertness of my conversation, the animation of which masked from the others a complete intellectual torpor – set out joyously in pursuit, but what it was then pursuing – for example, the identity of the Verdurin salon in different places and at different times – was situated at a somewhat deeper point, beyond appearances themselves, in a zone set slightly further back. Thus the visible, reproducible, charm of individuals escaped me, because I did not have the ability to dwell on it, like a surgeon who will see, beneath the sleek surface of a woman's belly, the internal disease which is gnawing at it. How ever often I dined out, I did not see the other guests, because when I thought I was looking at them, I was in fact radiographing them.

It followed from this that, by combining all the observations I had been able to make of the guests at a dinner, the pattern of the lines I had traced formed a cluster of psychological laws in which a guest's personal stake in the conversation had almost no place. But did that remove all merit from my portraits, since I was not offering them as such? If, in the realm of painting, one portrait demonstrates certain truths relative to volume, to light, to movement, does this make it necessarily inferior to some other portrait, with no points of similarity, of the same person, in which a thousand details omitted in the first are minutely stated – a second portrait from which one would conclude that the model was ravishingly beautiful, while one would have thought him or her ugly in the first, something which may possess a documentary, and even historical, importance, but is not necessarily a truth of art.

Moreover my frivolousness, as soon as I was not alone, made me eager to please, more eager to amuse by chattering than to learn by listening, unless it were that I had gone out into society to enquire about some aspect of art, or some jealous suspicion which had earlier been occupying my thoughts. I was really incapable of seeing anything for which the desire had not been awakened in me by something I had read, anything of which I had not first outlined for myself a sketch which I then wanted to compare with reality. How many times, as I was well aware even without the Goncourt pages reminding me of it, have I remained incapable of bestowing my attention on things or people that subsequently, once their image had been presented to me in solitude by an artist, I would have travelled miles, risked death, to encounter again! Only then had my imagination started to work, begun to paint. And of something which a year before had made me yawn, I would say to myself anxiously, contemplating it in advance, desiring it: 'Will it really be impossible to see it? What I wouldn't give to be able to!'

When one reads articles about people, even just society people, described as 'the last representatives of a world to which no witness any longer exists', one may of course exclaim: 'To think that they should speak so generously and so fulsomely about such an insignificant person! That is what I should so have regretted not having known, if I had only read the newspapers and magazines and not met the man!' But I was tempted instead, reading such pages in the newspapers, to think: 'What a pity that – when I was solely preoccupied with my next meeting with Gilberte or Albertine – I did not pay more attention to this gentleman! I took him for a society bore, a stuffed shirt, but he was a *major figure!*'

The pages of Goncourt that I read made me regret this tendency. For it may be that I might have inferred from them that life teaches us to diminish the value of what we read, and shows us that the things which the writer commends to us were never worth very much; yet I might equally well have come to the opposite conclusion, that reading teaches us to place a higher value on life, a value which we did not know how to appreciate, and the true extent of which we come to realize only through the book. If need be, we may console ourselves for finding scant pleasure in the company of a Vinteuil, or a Bergotte. The middle-class prudishness of the one, the insufferable deficiencies of the other, even the pretentious vulgarity of an Elstir in his early days (for the Goncourts' journal had made me realize that he was none other than the 'M. Tiche' who had once held forth so exasperatingly to Swann, at the Verdurins' house), prove nothing against them, since their genius is manifested by their work. In their case, whether it is the memoirs or ourselves that are at fault when they make their society, which we disliked, seem attractive, is not an important problem, since, even if it were the writer of the memoir who was wrong, that would prove nothing against the value of the life that produced such genius. (After all, what man of genius has not adopted the irritating conversational mannerisms of the artists of his set, before achieving, as did

Elstir, and as happens all too rarely, a higher level of taste? Are not Balzac's letters, for instance, strewn with vulgar turns of phrase which Swann would have died a thousand deaths rather than employ? And yet in all probability Swann, discriminating as he was, so free of every dislikeable absurdity, would have been incapable of writing *La Cousine Bette* or *Le Curé de Tours*.)

At the other extreme of experience, when I considered how the most revealing anecdotes, which make up the inexhaustible substance of the Goncourts' journal, providing entertainment for the reader's solitary evenings, had been recounted to him by these dinner-guests whom we might, through his pages, have felt a desire to meet, and who had yet left me no impression of any interesting recollection, that also was not too hard to explain. Despite the naïvety of Goncourt, who inferred from the interest of these anecdotes the probable eminence of the men who recounted them, it could very well be that undistinguished people might have encountered during their lives, or heard related, noteworthy things, which they themselves retold in their turn. Goncourt knew how to listen, as he knew how to see; I did not.

Moreover, all these facts would have had to be judged one at a time. M. de Guermantes had certainly not impressed me as that adorable model of youthful graces whom my grandmother had so much wanted to know, and which she set before me as a standard I could never match up to, as described in the memoirs of Mme de Beausergent. But it must be remembered that Basin was then seven years old, that the writer was his aunt, and that even husbands who in a few months will be obtaining a divorce will endlessly eulogize their wives to you. One of Sainte-Beuve's prettiest poems[16] is devoted to the apparition before a fountain of a little girl crowned with every gift and every grace, the young Mlle de Champlâtreux, who could not then have been more than ten years old. Despite all the affectionate reverence which that poet of genius, the Comtesse de Noailles, bore for her mother-in-law the Duchesse de Noailles née Champlâtreux, it is possible that, if she had been obliged to portray her, the result might have contrasted quite sharply with the portrait that Sainte-Beuve drew of her fifty years earlier.

What was perhaps more unsettling were the cases in between, were those people of whom what is said implies that there was more to them than simply a memory that could retain a revealing anecdote, yet without allowing one, as one has with the Vinteuils, the Bergottes, the recourse of judging them on their work, as they have not created any: they have merely – to the great astonishment of us, who found them so ordinary – inspired it. It may chance that the salon which, in the museums, will give the greatest impression of elegance since the great paintings of the Renaissance might be that of the absurd middle-class woman whom, if I had not known her, I would have imagined, as I looked at the picture, approaching in reality, hoping to learn from her the most precious secrets of the painter's art, which his canvas would not yield me, and how her ceremonial train of velvet and lace could have become a piece of painting comparable to the finest works of Titian. Having long understood that it is not the man who is the wittiest, the best educated, or the best connected, but the one who can become a mirror and thereby reflect his life, however commonplace, who becomes a Bergotte (for all that his contemporaries may have thought him less witty than Swann and less erudite than Bréauté), might one not say as much, and with greater justification, of an artist's models? When the love of beauty stirs in the breast of an artist who could paint anything, the model for the elegance in which he will be able to find a fittingly lovely subject will be furnished him by people somewhat richer than he is, in whose surroundings he will find what is generally missing from the studio of an unknown man of genius who sells his pictures for fifty francs: a drawing-room with furniture covered in old silk, plenty of lamps, beautiful flowers, beautiful fruit, beautiful dresses – relatively unpretentious people, or so they would seem to really glittering society (which is unaware that they even exist), but people, consequently, who are more likely to make an obscure artist's acquaintance, to appreciate him, to invite him, to buy his canvases, than members of the aristocracy who have themselves painted, like the Pope or Heads of State, by academicians. Will not posterity find the poetry of an elegant home and the beautiful dresses of our time better represented in Renoir's painting of the publisher Charpentier's drawing-room, than in the portraits of the Princesse de Sagan or the Comtesse de La Rochefoucauld by Cot or Chaplin?[17] The artists who give us the greatest visions of elegance have gleaned the elements of them from the homes of people who were seldom the leaders of fashion of their epoch, for those seldom had themselves painted by an unknown carrier of a kind of beauty which they are unable to perceive in his canvases, concealed as it is by the interposition of a stereotype of outmoded charm, which floats before the eyes of the public like those subjective visions which a sick person believes are actually present in front of him. But that these commonplace models whom I had known should also have inspired and advised certain arrangements which had enchanted me, that the presence of one or other of them in the pictures might be not merely that of a model, but that of a friend whom a painter might want to put into his canvases, made me wonder whether all the people we regret not having known because Balzac depicted them in his books or dedicated his books to them in admiring homage, about whom Sainte-Beuve or Baudelaire composed their finest verses, still more whether all the Récamiers, all the Pompadours, might not have seemed insignificant to me in person, either as a result of a weakness in my nature, which made me angry at my being ill and unable to go back and see all the people whom I had failed to appreciate, or else because they owed their prestige only to the illusory magic of literature, which forced me to change my reading habits, and consoled me for having, at any moment, because of the progress my illness was making, to break with society, give up travelling and visiting museums, in order to enter a sanatorium and undergo treatment. Yet perhaps this deceptive aspect, this artificial light, exists only in memoirs when they are too recent, when reputations are evaporating so quickly, intellectual ones as much as fashionable ones (for however much erudition then tries to react against this entombment, does it ever succeed in destroying even once in a thousand times the oblivion which piles up so relentlessly?).

*

Thoughts like these, tending in some cases to diminish, in others to increase my regret at not having a talent for literature, never crossed my mind throughout the long years, during which I had anyway completely renounced the project of writing, which I spent being treated far away from Paris in a sanatorium, until the time, at the beginning of 1916, when it became impossible any longer to obtain medical staff.

I then came back to a Paris very different from the one to which I had already returned on an earlier occasion, as we shall see shortly, in August 1914, to undergo a medical examination, after which I had re-entered my sanatorium. On one of the first evenings after my return in 1916, wanting to hear people's views on the only matter that interested me at that time, the war, I went out after dinner to visit Mme Verdurin, for she was, with Mme Bontemps, one of the queens of that wartime Paris so reminiscent of the Directory.[18] Rather as if they had been sprinkled with a small quantity of yeast, apparently of spontaneous generation, young women went about all day with tall cylindrical turbans on their heads as a contemporary of Mme Tallien[19] might have done, and, out of civic responsibility, wearing straight, dark-coloured Egyptian tunics, very 'wartime', over very short skirts; on their feet they wore thong-laced boots, reminiscent of Talma's[20] buskins, or long gaiters, recalling those of our dear boys at the front; it was, they said, because they never forgot that they had to gladden the eyes of those boys at the front, that they still adorned themselves not only in (loose) dresses, but also with jewellery which by its decorative subjects suggested the army, if indeed its raw material did not come from, and had not been worked by the army; but instead of Egyptian ornaments commemorating the campaign in Egypt, they wore rings or bracelets made out of shell fragments or the bands from seventy-five-millimetre ammunition, or carried cigarette-lighters made out of two English pennies to which a soldier in his dug-out had managed to impart a patina so fine that their profiles of Queen Victoria might have been traced by Pisanello. It was also because they never stopped thinking about them, they said, that, when somebody close to them fell, they hardly ever wore mourning, on the pretext that their grief was 'mingled with pride', which permitted them to wear a bonnet of white English crêpe (to most graceful effect and 'justifying every hope' in the invincible certainty of final victory), to replace the traditional cashmere with satin and chiffon, and even to retain their pearls, 'while continuing to observe the tact and correctness of which Frenchwomen have no need to be reminded'.

The Louvre and all the other museums were closed, and when one read, above a newspaper article, 'A sensational exhibition', one could be sure this referred to an exhibition not of paintings but of dresses, and dresses moreover designed as 'those delicate artistic joys of which Parisian women had for too long been deprived'. It was in this form that elegance and pleasure had returned; elegance, in the absence of the arts, seeking to excuse itself in the same way as happened in 1793, the year when the artists exhibiting at the revolutionary Salon proclaimed that it would be wrong for it to seem 'strange to austere Republicans that we should concern ourselves with the arts when the coalition of European powers is laying siege to the land of liberty'. This is just what the couturiers did in 1916, in addition asserting, with a proud consciousness of themselves as artists, that 'seeking the new, eschewing the ordinary, emphasizing individuality, preparing for victory, and defining a new pattern of beauty for the post-war generations, was the ambition that drove them forward, the chimera they pursued, as would be appreciated by anybody visiting their delightfully appointed salons in the rue de la –, where the watchword seems to be, by striking a bright and cheerful note, to wipe away the heavy sorrows of the time, all the while observing, of course, the discretion that circumstances impose.'

'The sorrows of the time', it is true, 'might have overborne feminine energies had we not so many lofty examples of courage and endurance to contemplate. Therefore, as we think of our fighting boys in their trenches, dreaming of better comforts and finer dresses for the girl they left at home, let us not cease to be ever more inventive in our creation of dresses responsive to the needs of the moment. The vogue', understandably enough, 'is for the English fashion-houses, thus for our allies, and this year the barrel-dress is all the rage, the pleasant unconstraint of which gives us all an entertaining air of uncommon distinction. One of the happier consequences of this sorry war, added the charming chronicler, may even be' (and one expected 'the repossession of our lost provinces, the re-awakening of national sentiment') 'one of the happier consequences of this sorry war may even be that we have achieved some pleasing results in the way of fashion, without mindless and inappropriate extravagance, from the slenderest resources, that we have created stylish dresses out of almost nothing. Instead of a dress from a grand designer, produced in a number of copies, women at this time prefer dresses made at home, as asserting the intelligence, taste and personal preference of each individual.'

As for charity, given all the miseries caused by the invasion, and the numbers of wounded and disabled, it was quite natural that it should be obliged to become 'more ingenious than ever', which obliged the women with tall turbans to spend the late afternoons having 'tea' round a bridge-table, commenting on the news from the 'front', while outside the door their cars waited for them, with a handsome soldier on the seat who chatted to the footman. Nor was it only the headdresses crowning the faces with their unfamiliar cylinders which were new. The faces themselves were also new. These women in the latest hats were young ladies, one did not know quite from where, who had been the flower of fashion, some for six months, some for two years, some for four. These differences, moreover, had for them as much importance as had, at the time I first entered society, between two families like the Guermantes and the La Rochefoucaulds, three or four centuries of proven antiquity. The lady who had known the Guermantes since 1914 regarded the one who was introduced to them in 1916 as a parvenue, acknowledged her with the distant air of a dowager, stared at her through her lorgnette and, pursing her lips, declared that nobody really even knew whether or not the lady was married. 'It is all rather sickening,' concluded the lady of 1914, who could have wished the cycle of new admissions to have ended with her own. These new ladies, whom the young men found rather ancient, and whom, moreover, certain older men, who had not moved exclusively in the best circles, were sure that they recognized as being not so new as all that, did not provide society merely with the pleasures of political conversation and music in suitably intimate surroundings: it was also that they had to be the ones who provided them, because for things to seem new, even if they are old, indeed even if they are actually new, there must in art, as in medicine, as in fashionable society, be new names. (They were, in fact, new in some matters. Thus Mme Verdurin had visited Venice during the war, but, like those people who try to avoid talking about distressing or emotional matters, when she said that it was wonderful, what she was admiring was not Venice, nor St Mark's, nor the palaces, all of which had delighted me so much and for which she had cared very little, but the effect of the searchlights in the sky, searchlights about which she provided information supported by figures. Thus from age to age is reborn a certain realism as a reaction against the art previously admired.)

The reputation of the Saint-Euverte salon had faded, and the presence at it of the greatest artists, the most influential ministers, would have attracted nobody. On the other hand, people would rush to listen to the utterances of a secretary of the former, or an under-secretary in the office of the latter, in the homes of the new turbaned ladies whose winged and chattering invasion was filling Paris. The ladies of the first Directory had a queen who was young and fair called Mme Tallien. Those of the second had two, who were old and ugly and called Mme Verdurin and Mme Bontemps. Who could have continued to hold it against Mme Bontemps that her husband had played a role in the Dreyfus Affair which had been harshly criticized by the *Écho de Paris*? The whole Chamber having at a certain point become revisionist, it was necessarily from among the former revisionists, as from among the former socialists, that the party of social order, religious toleration and military preparedness had been obliged to draw its recruits. At one time M. Bontemps would have been reviled, because then the anti-patriots went under the name of Dreyfusards. But that name had been quickly forgotten and replaced by that of 'opponent of the Three Years Law'.[21] M. Bontemps, however, was one of the architects of this law, and consequently he was a patriot.

In society (and this social phenomenon is merely one application of a much more general psychological law), novelties, blameworthy or not, arouse horror only if they have not been assimilated and surrounded by reassuring elements. This was as true of Dreyfusism as it was of Saint-Loup's marriage to Odette's daughter, which initially produced such an outcry. Now that one met everybody 'one knew' at the Saint-Loups', Gilberte might have had the morals of Odette herself, and people would still have gone there and endorsed Gilberte's dowager-like condemnation of as yet unassimilated moral changes. Dreyfusism was now integrated into a range of respectable and normal things. As for wondering what intrinsic merit it had, nobody gave it any greater consideration now, in accepting it, than formerly, when they had condemned it. It was no longer *shocking*. That was all that mattered. People scarcely remembered that it ever had been, just as they no longer know, after a lapse of time, whether a girl's father was a thief or not. At a pinch one can say: 'No, you're thinking of the brother-in-law, or someone with the same name. Nobody has ever had anything to say against the father.' In the same way, there had unquestionably been Dreyfusism and Dreyfusism, and somebody who was received at the Duchesse de Montmorency's and was helping to pass the Three Years Law could not be bad. In any case, no sin but should find mercy. The forgiveness granted to Dreyfusism was extended, *a fortiori*, to Dreyfusards. Besides, there were no longer any Dreyfusards left in politics, since at one time everybody who wanted to be in the government had been one, even those who represented the opposite of all that Dreyfusism, in its shocking novelty, had incarnated (at the time when Saint-Loup had been on the slippery slope): anti-patriotism, irreligion, anarchy, etc. Thus the Dreyfusism of M. Bontemps, invisible and constitutive like that of all politicians, was no more evident than the bones beneath his skin. Nobody even remembered that he had been a Dreyfusard, partly because people in society are inattentive and forgetful, also because it had all been a very long time ago, a time which people affected to believe was even longer ago, as one of the most fashionable ideas was the claim that the pre-war period was separated from the war by something as deep, something seemingly as long-lasting, as a geological period, and Brichot himself, the great nationalist, whenever he made allusion to the Dreyfus case, would say: 'In those prehistoric times'.

(Truth to tell, this profound change brought about by the war was in inverse ratio to the quality of the minds affected by it, at least above a certain level. Right at the bottom of the scale the utterly foolish, the pure pleasure-seekers, took no notice of the fact that there was a war on. But at the top end, too, those who have made for themselves an environing interior life have little regard for the importance of events. What profoundly modifies the pattern of their thoughts is much more likely to be something that seems quite unimportant in itself but which reverses their experience of the order of time by making them contemporaneous with another period of their life. One may appreciate this in practice from the beauty of the writing this inspires: the song of a bird in the park at Montboissier, or a breeze heavy with the scent of mignonette, are obviously events of less consequence than the epoch-making dates of the Revolution and the Empire. They none the less inspired Chateaubriand to write pages of infinitely greater value in his *Mémoires d'outre-tombe*.[22]) The words Dreyfusard and anti-Dreyfusard no longer had any meaning, yet the very people who maintained this would have been dumbfounded and outraged if one had told them that probably in a few centuries, perhaps even sooner, the term Boche would have merely the same curiosity value as words like *sans-culotte* or *chouan* or *bleu*.[23]

M. Bontemps was unwilling to hear any talk of peace before Germany had been reduced to the same fragmented state as in the Middle Ages, the fall of the House of Hohenzollern pronounced, and Kaiser Wilhelm put up before a firing squad. In a word, he was what Brichot called a 'diehard', the highest warrant of good-citizenship that could be conferred upon him. For the first three days Mme Bontemps must have felt a little bewildered at being surrounded by people who had asked Mme Verdurin to introduce them to her, and it was with a note of mild asperity that Mme Verdurin replied: 'No, my dear, the Comte' to Mme Bontemps's comment 'That was the Duc d'Haussonville you just introduced to me, wasn't it?', whether out of complete ignorance and failure to associate the name Haussonville with any title at all, or, on the contrary, as a result of having been given too much information and associating it in her head with the 'Ducs' Party' in the Academy, of which she had heard that M. de Haussonville was a member.[24]

But by the fourth day she had begun to be firmly established in the Faubourg Saint-Germain. Occasionally one still saw around her the unrecognized fragments of an unfamiliar social world, but to those who knew the egg from which Mme Bontemps had hatched this was no more surprising than the debris of shell around a chick. After a fortnight, however, she had shaken them off, and before the end of the first month, when she said 'I'm going to the Lévis',' everybody understood, without her needing to be more specific, that she meant the Lévi-Mirepoix, and there was not a duchess who would have gone to bed without having learned from Mme Bontemps or Mme Verdurin, at least by telephone, the contents of the evening communiqué, what had been left out, how matters stood with Greece, what offensive was being prepared, in a word all the news that the public would know only the next day or later, and of which she thus had, as it were, a sort of dress rehearsal. In conversation, Mme Verdurin, when imparting news, would say 'we' when speaking of France. 'Now listen: we demand of the King of Greece that he withdraw from the Peloponnese, etc., we send him, etc.' And in all these stories the GHQ cropped up constantly ('I telephoned the GHQ'), an abbreviation which she uttered with the same pleasure that, a little while before, women who did not know the Prince d'Agrigente took in asking with a smile, when people were talking about him, to show they were in the swim: 'Grigri?', a pleasure which in less agitated times is known only to fashionable society, but which in great crises becomes available to all classes. Our butler, for example, if someone mentioned the King of Greece, was able, thanks to the newspapers, to say 'Tino?' like Kaiser Wilhelm; whereas his familiarity with kings had hitherto remained at the more vulgar level of his own invention, as when he once referred to the King of Spain as 'Fonfonse'. It was also noticeable that, as the number of socially glittering people making advances to Mme Verdurin increased, so the number of those she called 'bores' diminished. By a sort of magical transformation, every 'bore' who came to pay a visit and solicited an invitation instantly became somebody charming and intelligent. In short, by the end of a year the number of bores was proportionately so far reduced that 'the fear of being unbearably bored', which had occupied such a considerable place in Mme Verdurin's conversation and played such a large part in her life, had almost entirely disappeared. It seemed that, late in life, this intolerance of boredom (which anyway she claimed never to have suffered from in her first youth) afflicted her less, just as some kinds of headache or nervous asthma lose their power as one becomes older. And the terror of being bored would probably have deserted Mme Verdurin completely, in the absence of any bores, had she not, to some slight extent, replaced those who were no longer boring with others drawn from the ranks of the former faithful.

For the rest, to conclude the topic of the duchesses who now frequented Mme Verdurin's, they came there, though this never occurred to them, in search of exactly the same thing as the Dreyfusards had once done, that is to say a social pleasure constituted in such a way that its enjoyment both assuaged political curiosity and satisfied the need to discuss among themselves the incidents they read about in the newspapers. Mme Verdurin would say: 'Do come in at five o'clock to talk about the war,' just as she would once have said 'to talk about the Affair', or more recently: 'Do come and listen to Morel.'

Not that Morel ought to have been there, for the reason that he had not been rejected for active service. He had simply never joined up, and so was a deserter, but nobody knew this.

Things were so extremely similar that people quite naturally found themselves using the old terms: 'right-thinking, wrong-headed'. And because they appeared different, just as the former Communards had been anti-revisionists, the greatest Dreyfusards wanted to have everybody shot and had the support of the generals, as those at the time of the Affair had been against Gallifet.[25] To these gatherings Mme Verdurin would invite a few recently arrived ladies, renowned for their good works, who came the first few times in striking outfits, with great necklaces of pearls which Odette, who had one equally fine, the display of which she had formerly over-indulged, looked at, now that she was in 'war dress' in imitation of the ladies of the Faubourg, with a degree of severity. But women are very adaptable. After three or four times they realized that the outfits they had believed chic were precisely the ones proscribed by those who actually were, and they put their golden dresses aside and resigned themselves to simplicity.

One of the stars of the salon was the 'also-ran'[26] who, despite his sporting tastes, had managed to obtain a medical discharge. So completely had he become for me the author of a series of admirable works which were constantly in my thoughts, that it was only by chance, when I established a cross-current between two sets of memories, that it came into my head that he was the same person as had brought about Albertine's departure from my house. But again this cross-current led, as far as these residual memories of Albertine were concerned, to a train of thought that stopped in the middle of nowhere, several years away. Because I simply never thought about her. It was a train of memories, a line that I never went down any more. Whereas the works of the 'also-ran' were recent, and that line of memories in permanent and active use by my mind.

I have to say that the acquaintance of Andrée's husband was neither very easy nor very pleasant to make, and that any attempted friendship was destined to have a number of disappointments. He was, in fact, at this point already very ill and avoided tiring himself unless perhaps there was a prospect of pleasure to be had. But only meetings with people he did not yet know, and whom his ardent imagination probably thought of as having a chance of being different from the rest, fell into this category. So far as those he already knew were concerned, he knew too well what they were like and what they would be like, and they no longer seemed worth the bother of his becoming dangerously, perhaps even fatally tired. In short, he was a very poor friend. And perhaps his taste for new people retained something of the mad recklessness that he had shown in the old days at Balbec, at sport, gambling and all the excesses of the table.

Mme Verdurin, for her part, insisted, every time I went, on trying to introduce me to Andrée, being unable to accept that I already knew her. But Andrée rarely came with her husband. To me she was an admirable and sincere friend and, faithful to the aesthetic ideas of her husband, who had taken against the Russian Ballet, she would say of the Marquis de Polignac: 'He's had his house decorated by Bakst. How anyone can sleep in the middle of all that! I'd much rather have Dubufe.'[27] The Verdurins, too, as part of the inevitable fate of aestheticism which ends up eating its own tail, began to say they could not bear Art Nouveau (there was also the fact that it came from Munich) or white rooms; all they liked now was old French furniture set against dark colours.

I saw a lot of Andrée at that period. We did not know what to say to each other, and on one occasion the name of Juliette came to me, which had risen from the depths of the memory of Albertine like a mysterious flower. Mysterious then, but today it would no longer arouse any feeling in me: while I spoke of many subjects to which I was indifferent, on that one I was silent, not because it was less important than anything else, but there is a sort of supersaturation of matters one has thought too much about. Perhaps the period when I saw so much mystery in it was the true one. But as these periods do not last for ever, one cannot sacrifice health and fortune to the revelation of mysteries which one day will cease to be interesting.

People were very surprised at that period, too, when Mme Verdurin could have anybody she wanted to the house, to see her making indirect advances to a person she had completely lost touch with, Odette. It was generally thought that she could add nothing to the glittering circle that the little group had become. But an extended separation, at the same time as diminishing bitterness, sometimes reawakens friendship. And then the phenomenon which not only leads dying men to utter only the names they knew long ago, but old men to take delight in their childhood memories, also has its social equivalent. In order to succeed in her attempt to get Odette to return to her, Mme Verdurin did not of course make use of the 'ultras', but the less faithful members of her circle, who had kept one foot in each salon. She would say: 'I don't know why we don't see her here any more. She may feel that we've quarrelled, but I don't: after all, what wrong have I done her? It was in my house that she met both her husbands. If she ever wants to come back, let her know that my door is always open.' These words, which might have made the Patronne swallow her pride if they hadn't been dictated by her imagination, were relayed, but without success. Mme Verdurin waited in vain for Odette to appear, until the events we shall see later brought about for quite different reasons what the representations, zealous though they were, of the deserters had failed to achieve. So seldom do we meet either with easy success or with final failure.

Mme Verdurin would say: 'It's simply too bad, I must telephone Bontemps to get him to do the needful for tomorrow. They've *blue-pencilled* the whole of the end of Norpois's article, simply because he hinted that Percin had been *bowler-hatted*.' For the currently voguish silliness meant that everyone gloried in using currently voguish expressions, believing this showed them to be fashionable, like a

39

middle-class woman hearing people talk about de Bréauté, d'Agrigente or de Charlus and saying: 'Who? Babal de Bréauté? Grigri? Mémé de Charlus?' And this is exactly what the duchesses did, really, taking the same pleasure in saying 'bowler-hatted': for with duchesses – in the eyes of commoners with a little poetry in their hearts – it is only the name that sets them apart; they actually express themselves in ways that are typical of the category of minds to which they belong, the membership of which is overwhelmingly middle-class. Classes of the mind have nothing at all to do with birth.

All this telephoning of Mme Verdurin's, however, was not without its difficulties. Although we have forgotten to say so, the Verdurin 'salon', while it continued in spirit and in its essential nature, had been moved temporarily to one of the largest hotels in Paris, the shortage of coal and light making it increasingly difficult for the Verdurins to entertain in the very damp former home of the Venetian ambassadors. But the new salon did have its attractions. Just as, in Venice, a site delimited by water dictates the plan of a *palazzo*, or a scrap of garden in Paris gives more pleasure than parkland in the country, the narrow dining-room that Mme Verdurin had in the hotel, an unevenly shaped rhombus with dazzlingly white walls, became a sort of screen against which were sharply outlined every Wednesday, and almost every other day, a diversity of the most interesting men and the most elegant women in Paris, all more than happy to take advantage of the luxury of the Verdurins, which continued to increase with their wealth at a time when even the richest people, unable to draw their dividends, were economizing. The form of these receptions was thus modified, but Brichot's enchantment with them continued undiminished, and the more extended the Verdurins' web of acquaintances grew, the more new pleasures he found packed into a small space, like surprises in a Christmas stocking. In the end the diners were sometimes so numerous that the dining-room in the private suite was too small and the dinner was given in the huge dining-room downstairs, where the faithful, while hypocritically pretending to lament the loss of the intimacy of upstairs, as long ago the need to invite the Cambremers had led them to tell Mme Verdurin that they would be too crowded, were at heart delighted – while continuing to keep their group separate from the others, as they once had on the little railway – to be a focus and an object of envy for the neighbouring tables. Under normal peacetime conditions a note would probably have been sent to the social pages of the *Figaro* or the *Gaulois* to inform a more numerous society than the dining-room of the Majestic Hotel could hold that Brichot had dined with the Duchesse de Duras. But since the outbreak of war, the society columnists having cut out that sort of news (although they made up for it with funerals, mentions in dispatches and Franco-American banquets), self-advertisement could exist only in an undeveloped and restricted form, appropriate to an earlier age, before the coming of Gutenberg's invention: being seen at Mme Verdurin's table. After dinner people went upstairs to the Patronne's reception rooms, and the telephoning began. But many of the grand hotels at that period were full of spies, who noted down the news telephoned through by Bontemps with an indiscretion that was, fortunately, only matched by the unreliability of his information, which was always proved wrong by subsequent events.

Before the hour at which the afternoon teas came to an end, as dusk came on but while the sky was still light, one would see in the distance little brown dots that might have been taken, in the blue evening, for gnats or birds. Similarly, a mountain seen from far away can be taken for a cloud. At the same time, it is emotionally unsettling because one knows that the cloud is vast, solid and resistant. Thus I was moved by the knowledge that each brown dot in the summer sky was neither a gnat nor a bird, but an aeroplane crewed by men who were watching over Paris. (The memory of the aeroplanes which I had seen with Albertine on our last drive near Versailles did not play any part in this emotion, for the memory of that drive had become indifferent to me.)

By dinner-time the restaurants were full; and if passing in the street I saw a poor soldier, home on leave, having had six days' escape from the constant risk of death, and now ready to set off back to the trenches, allow his eyes to rest for a moment on the lighted windows, I suffered as I had in the hotel at Balbec when fishermen had watched us eating, yet this time the pain was greater because I knew that the misery of the soldier is worse than that of the poor, as it combines every variety of misery, and even more touching because it is more resigned and nobler, and because it was with a philosophical shake of the head, without hatred, that, ready to set off back to the war, he would say, as he saw the shirkers rushing to grab their tables: 'You'd never know there was a war on here.' Then at half past nine, even though nobody had yet had time to finish eating, all the lights were abruptly turned off because of the police regulations, and the new rush of shirkers snatching their overcoats from the attendants, in that restaurant where I had dined with Saint-Loup one evening when he was on leave, took place at 9.35 in a mysterious semi-darkness, as of a room during a magic-lantern show, or of the film-projection hall of one of the cinemas to which the men and women diners would soon be hurrying. But after that time, for those who, like me, on the evening I am talking about, had stayed at home to dine and were then going out to see friends, Paris was, at least in certain quarters, even darker than the Combray of my childhood; when people went to call on each other, it felt like a visit to a neighbour in the country.

Ah, if Albertine had been alive, how lovely it would have been, on evenings when I had dined out, to arrange to meet her out of doors, beneath the arcades! At first I would not have seen anything, I would have had the pang of thinking that she had failed to come, then suddenly I would have seen one of her cherished grey dresses take shape against the black wall, seen her smiling eyes which had already noticed me, and we would have been able to walk along with our arms round each other without anybody recognizing us or disturbing us, and then go back home. But alas, I was alone and I felt as if I were going to pay a visit to a neighbour in the country, like the visits Swann used to pay us after dinner, encountering no more people in the darkness of Tansonville, along the narrow tow-path as far as the rue du Saint-Esprit, than I now met in the streets, which had become like winding country lanes, between Saint-Clotilde and the rue Bonaparte. Moreover, since those remembered fragments of landscape borne to me by the changing weather were no longer thwarted by my surroundings, which had become invisible, on evenings when the wind was chasing a glacial squall, I had a much more powerful sense of being beside that angry sea I had once dreamed so much about than ever I had felt at Balbec; and other features of nature, too, previously non-existent in Paris, could make one imagine that, climbing down from the train, one had just arrived for a holiday deep in the country-side: for instance, the contrast of light and shadow that lay all around one on moonlit evenings. The moonlight created effects that are normally unknown in the city, even in the middle of winter; its beams spreading across the snow on the boulevard Haussmann that there was nobody now to shovel away, just as they might have done on a glacier in the Alps. The outlines of the trees were revealed, sharp and pure against the golden-blue snow, with all the delicacy of a Japanese painting or a Raphael background; as shadows, they stretched out over the ground from the very foot of each tree, as one often sees them in the country when the rays of the setting sun flood the meadows, creating reflections of their evenly spaced trees. But by a wonderfully delicate subtlety, the meadow over which these tree shadows, weightless as souls, extended was a paradisal meadow, not green but of a white so dazzling, by virtue of the moonlight which shone on to the jade snow, that it might have been woven entirely from the petals of flowering pear trees. And in the squares, the divinities of the public fountains holding jets of ice in their hands looked like statues made of some twofold material, for whose creation the artist had set out to make a pure marriage of bronze and crystal. On rare days such as these the houses were all completely dark. But in the spring, on the other hand, every now and then, in defiance of police regulations, a private town house, or just one floor of a house, or even just one room of one floor, not having closed its shutters, appeared, as if independently supported by the impalpable darkness, like a projection of pure light, like an apparition without substance. And the woman whom, lifting up one's eyes, one could make out in that gilded shadow, took on, in this night in which one was lost and in which she too seemed cloistered, the veiled and mysterious charm of an oriental vision. Then one walked on, and nothing else interrupted the monotonous tramp of one's constitutional in the rustic darkness.

It occurred to me that it was a long time since I had seen any of the people who have been mentioned in this work. Only in 1914, during the two months I had spent in Paris, did I catch a glimpse of M. de Charlus and meet Bloch and Saint-Loup, and the latter only twice. The second time was undoubtedly the one when he had seemed most himself, effacing all the disagreeable impressions of insincerity he had created during the stay at Tansonville which I have just recounted, so that I again saw in him all the fine qualities he had once displayed. The first time I had seen him after the declaration of war, which was at the beginning of the following week, while Bloch was parading the most chauvinistic opinions, Saint-Loup, once Bloch had left us, could not be sufficiently ironical about the fact that he himself had not re-enlisted, and I had been almost shocked by the violence of his tone.

Saint-Loup had recently returned from Balbec. Later, I learned indirectly that he had made unsuccessful advances towards the manager of the restaurant. The latter owed his position to his inheritance from M. Nissim Bernard. In fact he was none other than the young waiter whom Bloch's uncle had once 'taken under his wing'. But with wealth had come virtue. With the result that Saint-Loup attempted in vain to seduce him. Thus by some compensatory process, while virtuous young men abandon themselves, as they grow older, to the passions of which they have finally become conscious, promiscuous youths become men of principle, from whom the Charluses of this world, turning up on the strength of the old stories, but too late, receive a disagreeable refusal. It is all a matter of chronology.

'No, he exclaimed with blithe emphasis, if anyone doesn't fight, whatever reason they give, it's really because they don't want to be killed, because they're *afraid*.' And with an even more energetic reiteration of the gesture with which he had underlined the fear of others, he added: 'And that goes for me too. If I don't re-enlist it's quite frankly because I'm *afraid, so there!*' I had already noticed in several other people that the affectation of laudable opinions is not the only way of cloaking bad ones, and that an alternative is the open display of these disreputable sentiments, so that at least one does not appear to be concealing them from oneself. This tendency was further intensified in Saint-Loup by his habit, when he had committed some indiscretion or made a gaffe for which he was likely to be blamed, of broadcasting it and saying that he had done it deliberately. A habit which, I rather think, he must have picked up from one of the instructors at the École de Guerre whom he had been quite close to, and for whom he professed great admiration. So I had no hesitation in interpreting this sally as the verbal confirmation of an attitude which, as it had dictated Saint-Loup's conduct and his non-participation in the war that was just beginning, he preferred to make publicly known.

'Have you heard anything, he asked as he was leaving, about my aunt Oriane getting a divorce? I know absolutely nothing about it myself. People talk about it from time to time, and I've heard it predicted so often that I'll wait till it happens before I believe it. Mind you, it would be quite understandable; my uncle is a charming man, not just socially but to his friends and his family. He's even, in a way, got more heart than my aunt, who is a saint but who does make him very much aware of the fact. Only he is a terrible husband, who has constantly deceived his wife, and insulted her, ill-treated her, and kept her short of money. It would be so natural for her to leave him that it would provide a reason for its being true, but it might equally well not be, because it's one of those ideas which people talk about as soon as it occurs to them. And given that she's put up with him for so long! But of course I know perfectly well that there are plenty of things that are mistakenly announced, then denied, but which go on to become true later.' That reminded me to ask him if there had ever been any talk of his marrying Mlle de Guermantes. He started and assured me that there had not, that it had merely been one of those society rumours that appear from time to time for no good reason, and vanish in the same way, without their falsity making the people who believed them any more cautious, the next time a new rumour of an engagement or a divorce, or a political rumour appears, about giving it their credence and passing it on.

Forty-eight hours had not gone by before certain facts which I learned showed that I had been completely mistaken in my interpretation of Robert's words: 'If anyone isn't at the front, it's because they're afraid.' Saint-Loup had said that only in order to sparkle in conversation, to be psychologically original, so long as he was not certain that his enlistment had been accepted. But all the time he was working as hard as he could to ensure that it would be, being in this

less original, in the sense in which he believed the word ought to
be taken, but more profoundly a Frenchman of Saint-André-des-
Champs,[28] more in conformity with all that at this moment was best
in the Frenchmen of Saint-André-des-Champs, lords, burghers and
serfs whether respectful of their lords or in revolt against them, two
equally French divisions of the same family, the Françoise sub-branch
and the Morel sub-branch, from which two arrows pointed, to join
forces once again, in a single direction, towards the frontier. Bloch
had been delighted to hear the admission of cowardice of a 'nationalist'
(who in point of fact was hardly nationalist at all) and when Saint-Loup
had asked him whether he was having to go, he adopted a high-priestly
expression and replied: 'Short-sighted.'

But Bloch had completely changed his mind about the war a
few days later when he came to see me, panic-stricken. Although
'short-sighted' he had been passed fit for service. I was taking him
back home when we met Saint-Loup, who had an appointment at the
Ministry of War to be introduced to a colonel, with a former officer,
'M. de Cambremer,' he told me. 'Oh, but of course, I'm talking about
an old acquaintance of yours. You know Cancan as well as I do.' I
replied that I did indeed know him, and his wife, and that I did not
think terribly highly of them. However I had grown so used, since I
had met them for the first time, to thinking of the wife, none the less,
as a remarkable person, with a deep understanding of Schopenhauer
and, generally speaking, as having access to intellectual circles that
were closed to her uncouth husband, that I was at first astonished to
hear Saint-Loup reply: 'His wife is an idiot, I give up on her. But he
himself is an excellent man, who had great gifts and is still very good
company.' By the wife's 'idiocy' Saint-Loup must have meant her
desperate desire to move in high society, something about which high
society is most severely judgmental. By the husband's qualities, he
probably meant something of those that his mother recognized in him
when she said that he was the best of the family. He at least had no
interest in duchesses, but this, to be honest, indicates a kind of
'intelligence' which differs as much from that which characterizes
thinkers as does the 'intelligence' attributed by the public to some rich
man for 'having been clever enough to make his fortune'. Saint-Loup's

words did not, however, displease me, in so far as they reminded me that pretention is very close to stupidity and that simplicity has a less visible but still gratifying aspect. I had not, it was true, had an opportunity to savour that of M. de Cambremer. But it is precisely this sort of thing that means that a person is a number of different people, depending on who is judging him, quite apart from differences of judgment themselves. All I had ever known of M. de Cambremer was the outer shell. And his flavour, to which others attested, was unknown to me.

Bloch left us outside his front door, brimming with resentment against Saint-Loup, telling him that the 'favoured sons' in their braided uniforms, strutting around at headquarters, were running no risks, and that he, a private second-class, had no wish to 'get himself perforated because of William'. 'I gather that the Emperor William is gravely ill,' replied Saint-Loup. Bloch, who, like everyone who keeps a close eye on the Stock Exchange, was particularly prone to accept sensational news, said: 'A lot of people are even saying he's dead.' On the Stock Exchange any ill sovereign, whether Edward VII or William II, is already dead, every town on the point of being besieged already captured. 'They're only concealing it, Bloch added, so as not to lower Boche morale. But he died the night before last. My father has it from an impeccable source.' Impeccable sources were the only ones which M. Bloch senior took any notice of when, by the good fortune he had, thanks to his 'important connections', to be in contact with them, he came by the still secret news that Foreign Bonds were about to rise or that de Beers[29] were about to fall. Moreover, if at that precise moment there was a rise in de Beers or there was an 'offer' of Foreign Bonds, if the market for the first was 'firm' and 'active', that for the second 'cautious', 'weak', one in which nobody was 'committing themselves', the impeccable source did not thereby become any the less impeccable. Thus Bloch informed us of the Kaiser's death with an air of mystery and self-importance, but also angrily. He was particularly exasperated at the way Robert said: 'the Emperor William'. But I believe that even under the blade of the guillotine Saint-Loup and M. de Guermantes would have been incapable of saying anything else. Two men who moved in society, finding themselves the sole survivors on a desert island, where there was no need to demonstrate their good manners to anyone, would recognize each other by these marks of their upbringing, just as two Latinists would quote Virgil correctly. Saint-Loup could never, even under German torture, have said anything except 'the Emperor William'. And these social graces, whatever else they signify, are an indication of significant mental shackles. Anyone unable to cast them off will always remain merely a society man. Yet even this elegant mediocrity was exquisite – especially with all the hidden generosity and unexpressed heroism that accompanied it – beside the vulgarity, simultaneously cowardly and arrogant, displayed by Bloch, who shouted at Saint-Loup: 'Couldn't you just call him William and be done with it? The truth is you're scared, even here you're crawling belly-down at his feet! Oh, what fine soldiers we're going to have at the frontier, they'll be licking the Boches's boots. All you know how to do, in all your fancy braid, is to strut about the parade-ground, and that's that.'

'Poor old Bloch quite wants me to do nothing but strut about on parade,' said Saint-Loup to me with a smile when we had left our friend. And I sensed that parading about was not at all what Robert wanted to do, even though I was not so fully aware of his intentions then as I later became when, the cavalry continuing inactive, he obtained permission to serve as an officer with the infantry, and then with the light infantry, or when finally occurred the sequel which the reader will discover later. But of Robert's patriotism Bloch remained completely unaware, simply because Robert gave absolutely no expression to it. Although Bloch had given us some extreme anti-militarist declarations of faith once he had been passed 'fit', he had earlier, when he thought he would be rejected because of his shortsight, made the most chauvinistic declarations. Saint-Loup would have been incapable of making any statement of that sort, principally because of a kind of moral delicacy that prevents the expression of sentiments which are so deeply rooted that they seem a part of one's nature. There was a time when my mother would not only not have hesitated for a moment to die for my grandmother but would have suffered terribly if anybody had her from doing so. Nevertheless it is impossible for me retrospectively to imagine her uttering a sentence like: 'I would lay down my life for my mother.' Equally unspoken was Robert's love of France; at this moment he seemed to me much more a Saint-Loup (to the extent that I could imagine his father) than a Guermantes. He may also have been protected from expressing sentiments of that sort by, as it were, the moral quality of his intelligence. Among really serious and intelligent workers, there is a certain aversion towards those who advertise what they do by turning it into fine words. We had not been at the Lycée or at the Sorbonne together, but we did separately follow courses given by some of the same lecturers (and I remember Saint-Loup's smile) who, when they gave a particularly noteworthy course, as some of them did, tried to make themselves look like men of genius by giving an ambitious name to their theories. Whenever we talked about this Robert would laugh out loud. Naturally, our instinctive predilection was not for the Cottards or the Brichots, but we did have a certain respect for the men who had a thorough knowledge of Greek or medicine but did not believe themselves thereby entitled to behave like charlatans. I have said that while all Mama's actions rested at one time on the feeling that she would have given her life for her mother, she had never formulated this sentiment for herself and would anyway have found it not only pointless and ridiculous, but shocking and shameful to express it to others; similarly, it was impossible for me to imagine Saint-Loup uttering, in the course of talking about his equipment, the things he had to get, our chances of victory, the shortage of bravery in the Russian Army, what England would do – it was impossible for me to imagine him uttering even the most eloquent phrase spoken by even the most popular minister to an audience of Deputies standing and cheering with enthusiasm. Yet I cannot say that in this negative side, which prevented him from expressing the fine sentiments he felt, there was not an element of the 'Guermantes wit', of which we have seen so many instances in Swann. For although I took him to be more of a Saint-Loup than anything else, he was still a Guermantes too, which meant that, among the numerous motives which inspired his courage, there were some which were different from those of his Doncières friends, those young men so smitten with their profession with whom I had dined every evening and so many of whom went to their deaths at the battle of the Marne or elsewhere, leading their men into action.

Any young socialists who may have been at Doncières when I was there, but whose acquaintance I did not make because they were not part of Saint-Loup's set, were able now to see that the officers in that set were not in the least 'toffs', with the connotations of haughty pride and low hedonism that the 'plebs', the officers promoted from the ranks, or the freemasons gave to the term. And by the same token, moreover, the aristocratic officers discovered fully the same degree of patriotism among the socialists whom I had heard them accuse, while I was at Doncières at the height of the Dreyfus Affair, of being 'men without a country'. The patriotism of the career soldiers, profound and deep-seated as it was, had taken a distinct form which they believed to be inviolable and which they were outraged to see made an object of opprobrium, whereas the relatively unthinking, independent patriots, with no distinct set of patriotic beliefs, that the radical-socialists were, had been incapable of understanding the profound reality that existed behind what they took to be empty and hate-inspired phrases.

No doubt Saint-Loup, like them, had grown used to developing in his mind, as the truest part of himself, the search for and the elaboration of the best manoeuvres by which to achieve the greatest tactical and strategic successes, so that for him as for them the life of the body was something relatively unimportant which could be easily sacrificed to this inward part, this truly vital core within them, around which individual existence was valuable only as a protective skin. But in Saint-Loup's courage there were also more individual elements, in which it would have been easy to recognize the generosity which had constituted the initial charm of our friendship, as well as the hereditary vice which had surfaced in him later, and which, together with a certain intellectual level which he had not transcended, caused him not only to admire courage, but to carry his horror of effeminacy so far as to find any contact with virility intoxicating. He discovered, no doubt chastely, from living in the open with Senegalese troops who were sacrificing their lives at every moment, an intense cerebral pleasure into which was infused a great deal of scorn for the 'little musk-scented gentlemen', and which, contradictory though it might seem, was not so different from the pleasure derived from the cocaine he had taken too much of at Tansonville and of which heroism – as one remedy replaces another – was curing him. But the principal aspect of his courage was that twofold habit of courtesy which, on the one hand, led him to praise others but for himself made him content to do the right thing and say nothing about it, unlike a Bloch, who had said to him in the course of our meeting: 'Obviously you'd turn tail and run,' but who was doing nothing himself; and, on the other, drove him to disregard everything he possessed, his fortune, his rank, even his life, and be ready to give them away. In a word, the true nobility of his nature. But so many different sources come together in heroism that the changed preference that had manifested itself in him, and also the intellectual mediocrity he had never been able to overcome, had their part to play in it. By adopting the habits of M. de Charlus, Robert found that he had also taken on, albeit in a very different form, his ideal of masculinity.

'Do you think we're in for a long haul?' I said to Saint-Loup. 'No, I think it will be a very short war,' he replied. But here, as always, his arguments were bookish. 'Bearing in mind Moltke's prophecies, re-read', he said to me, as if I had already read them, 'the decree of the 28th of October 1913 on the command of large units, and you will see that the replacement of the peacetime reserves has not been organized, or even foreseen, something they would not have failed to do if the war was going to be a long one.' It seemed to me that the decree in question could be interpreted not as proof that the war would be short, but rather as a lack of foresight about its length, and about its nature, on the part of those who had drafted it, and who had not the slightest idea of the appalling waste of every sort of raw material that would occur in a war of consolidation, nor of the interdependence of the different theatres of operations.

Outside the homosexual world, among the people most constitutionally opposed to homosexuality, there exists a certain conventional ideal of masculinity, which, unless the homosexual is quite exceptional, is at his disposal, but not without his distorting it. This ideal – represented by certain soldiers, certain diplomats – is particularly exasperating. In its lowest form it is simply the unsophistication of the man with a heart of gold who does not want to betray any emotion, and who, at the moment of parting from a friend who is perhaps going to his death, feels a deep desire to cry which nobody suspects because he overlays it with a rising anger, ending in an outburst at the actual moment of leaving: 'Come on, damn it! Embrace me, you bloody idiot, and you'd better take this purse, I've got no use for it, don't be such a damn fool.' The diplomat, the officer, the man who feels that the only thing that matters is the great task of national importance, but who none the less felt a fondness for the 'kid' in the legation or the battalion who died from fever or a bullet, presents the same taste for masculinity in a form that is more adept and more skilful, but fundamentally just as obnoxious. He does not want to weep for the 'kid', he knows that soon nobody will be thinking about him, any more than the kind-hearted surgeon does, who yet, despite everything, on the evening when some little girl has died in an epidemic, feels a sadness he does not express. Even should the diplomat be a writer and describe the death, he will not say that he felt any grief: no; first out of 'manly decency', and second by virtue of the artistic skill which arouses emotion by concealing it. He and one of his colleagues will watch by the dying man's bedside. Not for a moment will they say that they feel grief. They will talk about legation or battalion business, perhaps even in greater detail than usual:

'B—— said to me: "Don't forget that we've got the general's inspection tomorrow, so make sure your men are properly turned out." He is normally so softly spoken, but his tone was sharper than usual, and I noticed that he avoided meeting my eyes. Mind you, I felt rather on edge as well.'

And the reader understands that this sharpness is just grief as it appears in men who do not want to appear to feel grief, a fact which would be simply ridiculous if it were not also ugly and terribly sad, because it is the way that people who think that grief does not matter, who think that there are more important things in life than partings, etc., experience grief, so that when somebody dies they give the same impression of dishonesty, of pointlessness, as the gentleman on New Year's Day who brings you some *marrons glacés* and says: 'With my very best wishes for your health and happiness,' giggling, but saying it all the same. But to finish the account of the officer or the diplomat watching beside the deathbed, his head covered because the wounded or dying man has been taken out of doors, a moment suddenly comes when it is all over.

'I was thinking I must go back and get my things ready for cleaning; when, I don't know why, just as the doctor let go of the pulse, it happened that B—— and I, quite independently of each other, the sun was beating down on us, maybe we were hot, standing there beside the bed, both took off our *képis*.'

And the reader knows perfectly well that it is not because of the heat of the sun but out of emotion in the presence of the majesty of death that these two masculine men, who never allow the words affection or grief to pass their lips, removed their caps.

The ideal of masculinity found in homosexuals like Saint-Loup is not the same, but it is equally conventional and equally dishonest. For them, the dishonesty lies in the fact of their unwillingness to admit to themselves that physical desire is at the root of feelings to which they attribute some other origin. M. de Charlus detested effeminacy. Saint-Loup admires the courage of young men, the intoxication of a cavalry charge, the moral and intellectual nobility of those friendships between men, entirely pure, in which one sacrifices his life for another. War, which renders capital cities, where only women remain, the despair of homosexuals, is at the same time a story of intense romance for homosexuals, so long as they are intelligent enough to invent chimeras to pursue, but not intelligent enough to be able to see through them, recognize their origin and pass judgment on themselves. So that at a time when some young men were joining up simply out of a sporting spirit of imitation, just as one year everybody seems to be playing 'diabolo', for Saint-Loup war was rather the very ideal he imagined himself pursuing in his much more concrete desires, clouded in ideology though they were, an ideal he served alongside the kind of people he liked best, in a purely masculine order of chivalry, far removed from women, where he could risk his life to save his batman, and die inspiring a fanatical love in his men. And thus, while there might be a number of other elements in his courage, the fact that he was a nobleman was part of it, as was, in an unrecognizable and idealized form, M. de Charlus's idea that it was of the essence of manhood to display no trace of effeminacy. Moreover, in the same way as in philosophy or in art two analogous ideas only acquire value from the ways in which they are developed, and may be quite different depending whether they are expounded by Xenophon or by Plato, so, while fully acknowledging how much they share in this regard, I admire Saint-Loup's asking to be sent to the positions where there was greatest danger infinitely more than M. de Charlus's avoiding wearing brightly coloured cravats.

I spoke to Saint-Loup about my friend the manager of the Grand Hotel in Balbec, who, it appeared, had claimed that at the beginning of the war, in some French regiments, there had been defections, which he called 'defectations', and had accused what he called the 'Prussian militarist' of having provoked them; he had even believed, at one point, that there had been simultaneous landing of Japanese, Germans and Cossacks at Rivebelle, threatening Balbec, and had said that there was nothing left to do but 'evaculate'. He thought that the departure of the authorities for Bordeaux was somewhat precipitate, and declared that they were wrong to 'evaculate' so quickly. This hater of Germans would laughingly say, of his brother: 'He's in the trenches, just twenty-five metres from the Boche!' until, having discovered that he was one himself, they put him in a concentration camp.

'Talking of Balbec, do you remember that lift-boy they used to have in the hotel?' asked Saint-Loup as he was about to go, in a tone of voice that suggested that he did not quite know who it was and was relying on me to clarify matters. 'He's joining up and has written to ask me to get him into the flying corps.' The lift-boy was doubtless tired of going up in the captive cage of the lift, and the heights of the staircase in the Grand Hotel were no longer enough for him. He was going to 'win his stripes' in some other way than as a porter, for our destiny is not always what we thought it would be. 'Obviously, I'll support his application, Saint-Loup said. I was saying to Gilberte only this morning that we'll never have enough aeroplanes. With them we'll be able to see what the enemy is preparing. They'll take away the greatest advantage of an attack, which is surprise, and the best army will perhaps be the one that has the best eyes.'

I had met the lift-boy airman a few days earlier. He had talked to me about Balbec and, curious to know what he would have to say about Saint-Loup, I led the conversation round to the subject by asking him if it was true, as I had been told, that where young men were concerned M. de Charlus had etc. The lift-boy seemed astonished, he knew absolutely nothing about it. But he did make an accusation against the rich young man who lived with his mistress and three male friends. As he seemed to be tarring them all with the same brush, and as I knew from M. de Charlus, who had told me, it will be remembered, in front of Brichot, that it was not at all like that, I told the lift-boy that he must be mistaken. He responded to my doubts with the most confident assertions. It was the girl-friend of the rich young man who was responsible for picking up young men, and they all took their pleasure together. So M. de Charlus, the most competent of men in these matters, was completely mistaken, the truth being so partial, secret and unpredictable. For fear of seeming to think in a bourgeois way, or of seeing Charlusism where there was none, he had completely missed the fact that the woman was making the pick-ups. 'She came to look for me quite often, the lift-boy told me. But she realized straightaway who she was dealing with, I refused categorically, I don't get involved in that kind of stuff; I told her I really hated it. It just takes one person to be indiscreet, word gets around, and then you can never find another job anywhere.' These last reasons rather weakened the virtuous declarations with which he had begun, since they seemed to imply that the lift-boy would have acceded if he had been assured of discretion. That had doubtless been the case for Saint-Loup. It is quite probable that even the rich man, his mistress and his friends had not been less favourably treated, because the lift-boy cited numerous conversations he had had with them at various times, which rarely happens after such a categorical refusal. For instance, the rich man's mistress had come to him to make the acquaintance of a bellboy he was very friendly with. 'I don't think you know him, you weren't here then. Victor, they called him. Naturally,' added the lift-boy as if with reference to some vaguely secret and inviolable law, 'one can't say no to a pal who's short of money.' I remembered the invitation which the rich man's noble friend had extended to me a few days before my departure from Balbec. But in all probability that had nothing to do with it, and was prompted simply by friendliness.

'Well, now, what about poor Françoise, has she managed to get her nephew exempted?' But Françoise, who had for some time been doing everything she could to get her nephew exempted and who, when someone had suggested a recommendation, through the Guermantes, to General Saint-Joseph, had replied in a voice of despair: 'Oh no, that wouldn't help at all, there's nothing to be had from that old bloke, he's worse than the rest of them, he's patriotic'; Françoise, as soon as there had been any question of war, however much it pained her to think it, decided that we could not abandon the 'poor Russians' as we were 'allianced' to them. The butler, who was anyway convinced that the war would only last ten days and would end in a stunning victory for France, would not have dared, for fear of being contradicted by events, and also did not even have enough imagination, to predict a long and indecisive war. But he tried at least to extract in advance from this total and immediate victory anything likely to cause suffering to Françoise. 'It could easily get very nasty, because it seems that lots of them don't want to go, lads of sixteen in tears.' And his telling her unpleasant things in order to 'vex' her, was what he called 'giving her the pip, telling her a thing or two, having a laugh'. 'Sixteen, Mother of God!' Françoise would say, then suspicious for a minute: 'But they said they were only taking people over twenty, they're still children. – Naturally the newspapers are under orders not to say anything about it. Anyway, all the young men will be up at the front, and not many of them will be coming back. In one way that will be a good thing, after all, a good blood-letting is useful from time to time, it's good for trade. Oh yes, if there are any soft-hearted kids who hang back, they'll be shot straight away, a dozen bullets in them, bang! It's the only way, really. After all, the officers, what does it matter to them? They get their screw, that's all they ask.' Françoise would turn so pale during each of these conversations that one was afraid the butler would give her a fatal heart attack.

For all that, she didn't lose her old faults. Whenever a young lady came to see me, however badly the old servant's legs were troubling her, if I happened to leave my room for a moment, I would see her up a ladder in the dressing-room, in the process, she would say, of looking out some jacket of mine to check that the moths had not got at it, though she was actually there to listen to us. Despite my criticisms, she retained her insidious way of asking questions indirectly, to do which she had for some time now had a way of using 'because probably'. Not daring to say to me: 'Does this lady own a town house?' she would say, her eyes timidly raised like those of a faithful dog: 'Because probably the lady has a town house . . .', avoiding blatant interrogation less out of politeness than in order not to appear curious.

In the end, just as the servants whom we love best – especially if they have almost abandoned giving us the service or the respect that go with their job – remain, alas, servants and show most clearly the limits of their class (which we would wish to remove) when they think they have most penetrated into our own, Françoise when she was with me often ('to needle me', the butler might have said) made strange comments, which someone of my own class would not have done: with a joy disguised, but as deeply felt as if a grave illness were involved, if I were hot and sweat – if I had not noticed – beaded my forehead: 'Oh, but you're dripping,' she'd say, as if in wonder at some strange phenomenon, smiling a little with the sort of scorn provoked by some impropriety ('you seem to be going out but you've forgotten to put a tie on'), but adopting that preoccupied tone of voice which is designed to make someone worried about their state of health. It was as if I were the only person in the universe who had ever sweated. Finally she quite lost the pleasant manner of speaking she used to have. For in her humility, in her kind-hearted admiration for people who were infinitely inferior to her, she adopted their ugly turns of phrase. Her daughter having complained to me about her and saying (I don't know who she got it from): 'She's always going on at me, saying I shut doors the wrong way, and so on and so forth ad infinitum,' Françoise must have thought that only her incomplete education had thitherto deprived her of that elegant usage. And from the lips where I had once seen blossom the purest French, I now heard several times a day: 'And so on and so forth ad infinitum.' It is a curious thing how little not only a person's expressions but also their thoughts vary. The butler having got into the habit of declaring that M. Poincaré's intentions were bad, not for monetary gain but because he had been absolutely in favour of war, he would repeat this seven or eight times a day in front of the same familiar and always equally attentive audience. He never altered a word, a gesture or an intonation. Although it only lasted two minutes, the performance was unvarying. His errors of French corrupted Françoise's language quite as much as those of her daughter. He thought that what M. de Rambuteau had been so hurt one day to hear the Duc de Guermantes refer to as 'Rambuteau conveniences' were called urals. In his childhood he must have failed to hear the *in*, and it had stuck. He therefore pronounced the word wrongly, although he used it all the time. Françoise, initially embarrassed, ended up using it too, so that she could complain that women, unlike men, had no such things. But her humility and her admiration for the butler meant that she never said urinals, but – with a slight concession to custom – urials.

She no longer slept, no longer ate, and had the communiqués, of which she understood nothing, read to her by the butler, who, scarcely understanding them any better and in whom the desire to torment Françoise was often overridden by patriotic enthusiasm, would say with a sympathetic laugh, speaking of the Germans: 'They're going to get a rocket under them soon, good old Joffre's preparing a big new plan.' Françoise had no idea what rocket he was talking about, but sensing only that the phrase was one of those pleasant and original eccentricities to which politeness requires a well-brought-up person to respond with good humour, with a gay shrug of her shoulders, as if to say: 'Isn't he always the same?' she would temper her tears with a smile. At least she was glad that her new butcher's boy, who despite his job was rather timorous (even though he had started in the abattoirs), was not old enough to be sent to fight. If he had been, she would have been quite capable of going to see the Minister of War to have him exempted.

The butler was unable to imagine that the communiqués were not wonderful, and that the army was not close to Berlin, whenever he read: 'We have repulsed, with heavy enemy losses, etc.', engagements which he celebrated as further victories. I, however, was alarmed at the speed with which the theatre of these victories was approaching Paris, and I was equally astonished that the butler, having seen in one communiqué that a battle had taken place near Lens, had shown no

anxiety when he read in the next day's paper that the subsequent
fighting had turned in our favour at Jouy-la-Vicomte, and that we
were firmly in command of its approaches. Yet the butler was familiar
with the name of Jouy-le-Vicomte, which was not all that far away
from Combray. But we read the newspapers in the same way as we
love, blindfold. We do not attempt to understand the facts. We listen
to the editor's soothing words as we listen to the words of our mistress.
We are beaten and happy because we think we are victorious, not
beaten.

At all events I did not stay long in Paris and fairly quickly returned
to my sanatorium. Although in theory the doctor's treatment involved
complete isolation, I was handed letters on two separate occasions,
one from Gilberte and one from Robert. Gilberte wrote (it was some
time around September 1914) that, despite her desire to stay in Paris
in order more easily to get news of Robert, the perpetual air-raids of
the *taubes*[30] over Paris had caused her such terror, especially for her
little daughter, that she had fled from Paris by the last train to leave
for Combray, that the train had not even got as far as Combray, and
that it was only thanks to a farm-worker's cart, on which she had had
a ghastly ten-hour journey, that she had been able to reach Tansonville!
'And what do you think your old friend found when she got there,'
Gilberte wrote in conclusion. 'I had left Paris to get away from the
German aeroplanes, supposing that at Tansonville I would be safe
from all that. I had only been there two days when you can't imagine
what happened: the Germans were invading the whole district after
beating our troops near La Fère, and the German commanding officers,
followed by a regiment, appeared at the door of Tansonville, and I
had to put them up, and there was no way of escaping, no train,
nothing.' The German commanding officers did, in fact, behave well,
or else one had to imagine from Gilberte's letter some contagious
effect of the spirit of the Guermantes, who came from Bavarian stock,
and were related to the highest levels of the German aristocracy, but
Gilberte went on at length about the perfect manners of the commanding officers, and even of the soldiers who had merely asked for
'permission to pick some forget-me-nots that were growing beside the
pond', good manners which she contrasted with the disorderly violence

of the French deserters, who had devastated everything as they passed through the property, before the German generals arrived. At all events, if Gilberte's letter was in some respects impregnated with the spirit of the Guermantes – some would say, of Jewish internationalism, which would probably not be fair, as we shall see – the letter I received a few months later from Robert was, by contrast, much more Saint-Loup than Guermantes, and displayed in addition all the liberal culture he had acquired: in short, it was entirely delightful. Sadly, he no longer talked about strategy, as he had done in our conversations at Doncières, and did not say how far he thought the war confirmed or invalidated the principles he had expounded to me then.

The furthest he went was to say that since 1914 there had in reality been a succession of wars, the lessons of each influencing the conduct of the next. So that, for example, the theory of the 'breakthrough' had been supplemented by the proposition that, before breaking through, it was necessary for the artillery completely to disrupt the ground occupied by the enemy. But then the opposite had been argued, that such disruption made it impossible for the infantry and artillery to advance across ground where thousands of shell-holes created as many obstacles. 'War, he said, is no exception to good old Hegel's laws. It is in a state of perpetual becoming.'

This was scant answer to all the things I would have liked to know. But what annoyed me even more was that he was no longer allowed to mention the names of the generals. All the more so as, from the little I was able to glean from the newspapers, it was not those whose likely valour in the event of a war I had been so preoccupied with discovering at Doncières who were now in command of this one. Geslin de Bourgogne, Gallifet, Négrier, were dead. Pau had retired from active service shortly after the outbreak of war. Of Joffre, of Foch, of Castelnau and Pétain we had never spoken. *My dear boy*, wrote Robert, *I do realize that phrases such as 'shall not pass' or 'we'll get them' are not very pleasant; they have stuck in my throat as much as 'poilu'*[31] *and the rest, and of course it is tedious to be making an epic out of terms that are worse than faults of grammar or failures of taste, that are in fact that dreadful, contradictory thing, vernacular affectation or pretentiousness of the sort we detest so much, like for example the people who think it is clever to say 'coke' instead of 'cocaine'. But if you saw everyone, especially the ordinary people, the workers, the small shop-keepers, who never dreamed of possessing the kind of heroism they have been displaying and would have died peacefully in their beds without ever having imagined it, running through the bullets to rescue a comrade, or to fetch a wounded officer and, when they are hit themselves, smiling just before they die because the medical officer has told them that the trench has been recaptured from the Germans, then I assure you, my dear boy, that it gives you a marvellous idea of the French and makes you begin to understand those periods of history which used to seem a bit implausible when we studied them at school.*

The epic is so marvellous that you would discover, as I have, that words no longer matter. Rodin or Maillol[32] *could make a masterpiece from some hideous raw material, transforming it out of all recognition. At the touch of this sort of greatness, a word like 'poilu' for me has become one where I no longer have any more sense of its originally having contained an allusion or a joke than we have when we read words like 'chouans'. I feel 'poilu' is ripe for great poets, like the words Flood, or Christ, or Barbarians, which were already steeped in grandeur before they were used by Hugo, de Vigny or the others.*

Ordinary people, workers, as I say, are the best of all, but everyone is good. Poor young Vaugoubert, the ambassador's son, was wounded seven times before he was killed, and every time he came back from a sortie without having copped it, he seemed to be apologizing and saying it was not his fault. He was a delightful soul. We were very close; his poor parents were given permission to attend the burial on condition they did not wear mourning, and did not stay longer than five minutes because of the shelling. His mother, a bovine woman whom you have probably met, may have been deeply upset, but she showed no sign of it. But his poor father was in such a state that I tell you I, who have now become totally impervious to feeling, having got used to seeing the head of a comrade suddenly smashed by a shell, or even torn from its body, while he was in the middle of talking to me, I could not contain myself when I saw the collapse of poor Vaugoubert, who was nothing but a poor shadow of himself. The general tried to tell him how his son's heroic conduct had all been in the service of France, but that merely intensified the sobs of the poor man, who was unable to drag himself away from his son's body. But in the end, and this is why one has to get used to 'shall not pass', all of these men, like my poor valet and like Vaugoubert, have prevented the Germans from passing. Maybe you think we have not advanced very far, but it is no good just being rational about it, there is some deep inner feeling that gives an army the sense of winning, just as a dying man knows when he has had it. We know that we shall win, and we want victory so that we can impose a just peace, and I don't only mean just to our side, but truly just, just to the French and just to the Germans.

Of course, the 'scourge' had not raised Saint-Loup's intelligence to a higher level. Just as heroes with ordinary, commonplace minds, writing poems during their convalescence, placed themselves, in order to describe the war, at the level not of events, which in themselves are nothing, but of the commonplace aesthetic whose rules they had followed thitherto, talking as they might have done ten years earlier about the 'blood-red dawn' and the 'trembling wing of victory' etc., so Saint-Loup, whose nature was much more intelligent and much more artistic, remained intelligent and artistic, and, while halted at the edge of some marshy forest, with characteristic good taste would note down descriptions of the landscape for me, in the same way as he would have done if he had been out duck-shooting. To help me understand how certain contrasts of light and shade had created 'the magic of the morning', he would make reference to paintings we both liked, and was not afraid to make allusion to a passage by Romain Rolland,[33] or even Nietzsche, with the independent-mindedness typical of men at the front, who did not suffer the same fear of uttering a German name as did the civilian population, and even with that touch of vanity in quoting one of the enemy which led Colonel du Paty de Clam in the courtroom during the Dreyfus Affair to recite in front of Pierre Quillard, a Dreyfusard poet of extremely powerful convictions whom he had never previously met, some lines from his Symbolist drama, *La Fille aux mains coupées*.[34] If Saint-Loup happened to mention a melody by Schumann, he would only give its title in German, nor did he have recourse to circumlocution to tell me that, when he had heard the first twitterings of the dawn chorus at the edge of the forest, he had been as intoxicated as if he had just been spoken to by the bird in that 'sublime *Siegfried*', which he very much hoped to hear performed after the war.

And now, returning to Paris for the second time, I had received, the day after my arrival, another letter from Gilberte, who must have forgotten the one, or at least the gist of the one I cited, because her departure from Paris at the end of 1914 is described retrospectively in it in a rather different manner. *You may not know perhaps, my dear friend*, she told me, *that I have been at Tansonville for two years now. I arrived at the same time as the Germans; everyone had tried to stop me leaving. They thought I was mad. 'Why on earth, they would say, are you leaving the safety of Paris for the occupied regions, at the very moment when everyone else is trying to escape from there?' I did recognize how much good sense there was in all this. But what could I do, I only possess one good quality, I'm not a coward, or if you prefer I'm loyal, and when I learned that my beloved Tansonville was under threat, I couldn't leave our old steward to defend it by himself. It seemed to me that my place was by his side. And it was because of that decision that I was able to do something at least to save the house, when all the other chateaux in the neighbourhood, abandoned by their panic-stricken owners, have almost all been destroyed from top to bottom, and not only to save the house but to save those precious collections my dear father set so much store by.* In short, Gilberte was now persuaded that she had not gone to Tansonville, as she had told me in her letter in 1914, to escape from the Germans to a place of safety, but on the contrary to find them and defend her house against them. They had not, in fact, stayed at Tansonville, but from then on her house had seen a constant coming and going of soldiers which exceeded by far that which drew tears from Françoise in the street at Combray, and she had not ceased, as she put it quite truthfully this time, to live life on the front line. So the newspapers spoke in the most laudatory terms of her admirable conduct, and there was talk of giving her a decoration. The conclusion of the letter was entirely accurate. *You have no idea what this war is like, my dear friend, and the importance that a road, a bridge or a hill can assume. How often I have thought of you, and the walks, which you made so delightful, that we took together through this now devastated countryside, where vast battles were fought just to win possession of one of the paths or slopes you used to love, where we so often walked together! You probably did not imagine, any more than I did, that humble Roussainville and boring Méséglise, where they used to bring our letters from, and where they went to find the doctor when you were ill, would ever be famous places. Well, my dear friend, they now share the same immortal fame as Austerlitz or Valmy. The battle of Méséglise lasted for more than eight months, in the course of which the Germans lost over six hundred thousand men and destroyed Méséglise, but they did not take it. The little path you used to like so much, the one we called the hawthorn climb, where you claimed you fell in love with me when you were a child, though I can assure you quite truthfully that it was I who was in love with you, I can't tell you how important it has become. The huge cornfield it led into is the famous Hill 307, whose name you must have seen crop up time and again in the communiqués. The French blew up the little bridge over the Vivonne which you told me did not remind you of your childhood as much as you would have wished, the Germans put up some new ones, and for the last year and a half they have held one half of Combray and the French have held the other.*

The day after I received this letter, that is two days before that evening when I was walking along in the darkness, listening to the echoing sound of my footsteps, chewing over all these memories, Saint-Loup, back from the front and about to return there, had paid me just a few moments' visit, the mere announcement of which had powerfully affected me. Françoise had wanted to pounce on him at once, in the hope that he might be able to get an exemption for the timid butcher's boy, whose class was to be called up in a year's time. But she was stopped by her own realization that there was no point in such a step, as the timid animal slaughterer had long since moved to another butcher's shop. And whether our butcher's wife was afraid of losing our custom, or whether she was telling the truth, she told Françoise that she did not know where the boy, who anyway would never make a good butcher, was now employed. Françoise had searched high and low for him. But Paris is large, butchers' shops are numerous, and despite visiting a great number of them, she had never been able to find the timid, blood-stained young man again.

When Saint-Loup entered my room, I had gone up to him with that feeling of shyness, that sense of eeriness which in fact all soldiers on leave made one feel, and which one experiences when one comes into the presence of someone suffering from a fatal illness, who none the less still gets up, gets dressed and goes for walks. It seemed (it had seemed most strongly to begin with, because for anyone who had not, as I had, lived away from Paris, habit had taken hold, which takes away from things we have seen a number of times the radically profound impression and thought which gives them their real meaning), it seemed almost as if there was something cruel in the leave granted to combatants. When the first of them came, people said to themselves: 'They won't want to go back, they'll desert.' And indeed it was not that they came simply from places that seemed unreal to us because we had only heard of them through the newspapers, and therefore could not imagine how these men could have taken part in those titanic battles and returned with nothing more than a bruised shoulder; it was from the shores of death, whither they were about to return, that they came to spend a moment among us, Incomprehensible to us, filling us with tenderness, dread and a sense of mystery, like the dead whom we evoke, and who appear to us for a second, whom we dare not question and who could anyway only reply: 'You could not even imagine.' For it is extraordinary how, both in those who have survived combat, which is what soldiers on leave are, and in the living or the dead hypnotized or invoked by a medium, the sole effect of contact with mystery is to increase, if that be possible, our sense of the insignificance of what is said. It was with this in mind that I approached Robert, who still had a scar on his forehead, more noble and more mysterious to me than the imprint left in earth by the foot of a giant. And I had not dared ask him a single question and he had addressed only a few simple words to me. Even these differed hardly at all from those he might have spoken before the war, as if people, in spite of it, continued to be what they were; the tone of the discussion was the same, only the subject matter was different, if that!

My sense was that he had found resources in the army which had allowed him gradually to forget that Morel had behaved as badly to him as to his uncle. Yet he still had a great fondness for him and would suddenly be overcome with a desire to see him again, which he always put off doing. I thought it kinder to Gilberte not to point out to Robert that if he wanted to find Morel he had only to go to Mme Verdurin's.

I told Robert apologetically how little the war impinged on us in Paris. He said that even in Paris it was sometimes 'pretty unbelievable'. He was alluding to a Zeppelin raid that had taken place the previous evening and he asked me whether I had had a good view of it, but in the same terms as he might once have talked about some spectacle of great aesthetic beauty. At the front, as one knows, there is a sort of affectation in saying: 'It's wonderful, look at that pink! and that pale green!' when at any moment they might be killed, but in Paris Saint-Loup showed no trace of that, as he talked about a raid which was insignificant, but which from our balcony, in the silence of a night which suddenly contained a *real* display with rockets that were both useful and protective, bugle calls that were not just sounding for parade, etc. I talked about the beauty of the aeroplanes as they climbed into the night. 'And perhaps they are even more so as they are coming down, he said. I agree that the moment after they take off is very beautiful, when they join together in star-like formation, and in doing so obey laws as precise as the ones that govern the constellations, for the thing that strikes you as a marvellous sight is the rallying of squadrons, the orders they are given, their setting off in pursuit, etc. But don't you prefer the moment when having finally come to seem like stars, they peel off individually in pursuit of something or return home after the all-clear, the moment of apocalypse, when even the stars no longer keep their places? And those sirens, weren't they Wagnerian? Though I suppose that is quite an appropriate way to salute the arrival of the Germans, it was just like the national anthem, with the Crown Prince and the Princesses in the imperial box, the *Wacht am Rhein*; one wondered whether they really were airmen and not Valkyries who were climbing into the night.' He seemed rather pleased with this comparison between airmen and Valkyries, and went on to explain it in purely musical terms: 'Yes, by Jove, the music of the sirens was a *Ride of the Valkyries*! Obviously the Germans have to come before we can hear Wagner in Paris.'

And in some ways the comparison was not a false one. From our balcony the city, which had seemed merely a place of formless, shifting blackness, suddenly passed from the depths of night into the glowing sky, where at the shattering sound of the sirens the airmen soared up one by one, while with a slower but more insidious and alarming movement, as their questing gaze suggested the still invisible object, perhaps already close at hand, which they were seeking, the searchlights moved ceaselessly across the sky, sniffing out the enemy, surrounding him with their beams until the moment when the aeroplanes were ready to shoot off in pursuit to strike him down. And, squadron after squadron, each airman was thus soaring up above the city, transported now into the sky, like a Valkyrie. But here and there on the ground, at the level of the houses, lights went on, and I told Saint-Loup that if he had been at home the previous evening he might, while contemplating the apocalypse in the sky, have been able to see on the ground (as in El Greco's *Burial of Count Orgaz*, where these different levels are parallel) a genuine farce played out by characters in their nightshirts, all of them celebrities whose names would have been worth sending to a successor of Ferrari,[35] whose Society Notes had so often entertained Saint-Loup and myself that we used to amuse ourselves by making up imaginary ones. And that is what we did again that day, as if there were no war on, even though the subject, the fear of Zeppelins, was very 'wartime': 'I spotted the Duchesse de Guermantes looking superb in a nightgown, the Duc de Guermantes simply priceless in pink pyjamas and bathrobe, etc., etc.'

– 'I am sure, he said to me, that in all the big hotels you would have seen American Jewish ladies in their night-dresses, clutching to their withered bosoms the pearl necklaces that would enable them to marry a penniless duke. On nights like that the Ritz Hotel must look like the *Hôtel du libre échange* of Feydeau's farce.'[36]

It must be said, however, that although the war had not increased Saint-Loup's intelligence, this intelligence, developing according to laws in which heredity played a major part, had taken on a polish that I had never before seen in him. What a difference there was between the fair-haired young man who was once courted by women of fashion, or women who aspired to be fashionable, and the talker, the theorist, who played with words all the time! In another generation, in another branch of the family, like an actor taking on one of the roles that Bressant or Delaunay[37] used to play, he was like a successor – pink, fair-haired and golden, where the other had been half very black and half pure white – to M. de Charlus. He would hardly have agreed with his uncle about the war, having aligned himself with that section of the aristocracy which put France above everything else, while M. de Charlus was a defeatist at heart, but he could still show anyone who had not seen the 'creator of the role' how it was possible to excel in dexterous argumentation. 'Hindenburg seems to be a revelation, I said to him. – An old revelation, he parried, or a future revolution. Instead of being soft on the enemy, we ought to have let Mangin get on with it, smashed Austria and Germany and Europeanized Turkey, instead of Balkanizing France. – But we'll have the help of the United States, I said. – In the meantime, all I can see here is the spectacle of disunited states. Why does the fear of dechristianizing France prevent us making broader concessions to Italy? – If your uncle Charlus could hear you now! I said. You really wouldn't mind going for the Pope a bit more, while he is in despair at the thought of the harm that may come to the throne of Franz-Josef. And he claims that when he says that, he's just following in the footsteps of Talleyrand and the Congress of Vienna. – The age of the Congress of Vienna is over, he replied; secret diplomacy must be replaced by concrete diplomacy. My uncle is basically an unrepentant monarchist who will swallow a silly carp like Mme Molé or an unprincipled carper like Arthur Meyer, so long as they are both cooked à la Chambord.[38] He hates the *tricolore* so much that I think he would rather line up behind a rag like the *Bonnet rouge*,[39] which he'd take in good faith for the white flag.' Of course, this was all just word-play, and Saint-Loup was far from having the sometimes profound originality of his uncle. But he was by nature as affable and charming as the other was suspicious and jealous. And he had remained charming and pink, as he had been at Balbec, beneath all his golden hair. The only aspect in which his uncle could not have surpassed him was that state of mind characteristic of the Faubourg Saint-Germain which leaves its mark on those men who think they are most detached from it and which gives them a respect for intelligent men of no pedigree (something which really flourishes only in the nobility, and which makes revolutions so unjust) mingled with an inane self-satisfaction. As a result of this mixture of pride and humility, of acquired intellectual curiosity and innate authority, M. de Charlus and Saint-Loup, by different paths, and with opposite opinions, had become, a generation apart, intellectuals interested in every new idea and talkers whom no interruption could silence. The result of which was that people with more commonplace minds tended to find them both, depending on the situation, either dazzling or a complete bore.

'You remember our conversations at Doncières, I said to him. – Ah! those were good times. What a gulf there is between then and now! Will those happy days ever surface again

> du gouffre interdit à nos sondes
> Comme montent au ciel les soleils rajeunis
> Après s'être lavés au fond des mers profondes?[40]

– Don't let's think about those conversations merely in order to recall how enjoyable they were, I said. I was trying, through them, to reach a certain sort of truth. So has this war, which has upset everything, especially, as you say, the idea of war, rendered obsolete what you used to tell me then about battles, for instance the battles of Napoleon which were to provide a pattern for wars in the future? – Not at all! he replied. The Napoleonic battle is still with us, especially in this war, since Hindenburg is imbued with the Napoleonic spirit. His rapid troop movements, his feints, whether in just leaving a thin cordon of troops in front of one of his enemies in order to fall with all his forces on the other (Napoleon, 1814), or in launching such a sustained diversionary attack that the enemy is forced to keep its forces committed to a front which is not its principal one (as for example Hindenburg's feint before Warsaw, as a result of which the Russians were misled into concentrating their resistance at that point, and were beaten at the Mazurian Lakes), or tactical withdrawals analogous to those with which Austerlitz, Arcole, Eckmühl all began, everything he does is Napoleonic, and it is not over yet. Let me also say, though, that if, when I am at the front again, you want to try to interpret the events of this war as it progresses, don't trust too exclusively in this particular side of Hindenburg to discover either the meaning of what he is doing, or the key to what he will do next. A general is like a writer who wants to write a play, or a book, but whom the book itself, with the unexpected options that it reveals at one point, the impasse it presents at another, causes to deviate extensively from his preconceived plan. Remember that a diversion, for example, should be made only at a point of sufficient importance, and imagine a diversion that is successful beyond all expectation, while the main operation ends in failure; then the diversion may become the principal operation. I am waiting for Hindenburg to try one typical Napoleonic battle strategy, though, and that's the one that consists in driving apart two of his opponents, the English and us.'

All the time I was recollecting Saint-Loup's visit, I had been walking and had come far out of my way; I was almost at the Pont des Invalides. The lamps, of which there were only a few (because of the Gothas[41]), had been lighted, slightly too early because the 'time change'[42] had been made slightly too early, when the night still came fairly quickly, but had been fixed then for the whole of the summer (just as heating-stoves are lit or turned off from a certain date) and, above the nocturnally illuminated city, in a whole section of the sky – the sky which was unaware of summer-time and winter-time, and which did not deign to know that half past eight had become half past nine – in a whole section of the bluish sky the day still lingered. Across all that part of the city dominated by the towers of the Trocadéro, the sky looked like a vast turquoise-coloured sea on the ebb, disclosing a whole slender line of black rocks, which might even perhaps have been a row of simple fishing nets, but which were really small clouds. Sea for that moment coloured turquoise, and carrying all mankind, unawares, away with it, swept up by the immense revolution of the earth, that earth on which they are mad enough to continue their own revolutions, and their pointless wars, like the one that was at that moment steeping France in blood. Then as I continued to gaze at the lazy and impossibly beautiful sky, which regarded it as beneath its dignity to change its time-table and above the illuminated city gently prolonged, in these shades of blue, the last moments of its day, vertigo seized me, it was no longer a level sea but a vertical progression of blue glaciers. And the towers of the Trocadéro which seemed so close to the turquoise steps must, in fact, be very far away from them, like the twin towers in some Swiss towns which, seen from a distance, seem almost adjacent to the sloping peaks. I started to retrace my steps, but by the time I had left the Pont des Invalides the daylight had vanished from the sky, there were scarcely any lights in the city, and stumbling here and there against rubbish bins, mistaking one way for another, I unexpectedly found that by having mechanically followed a maze of dark streets, I was out on the boulevards. There the impression of the Orient which I had felt earlier came back to me, though this time my vision of the Paris of the Directory was replaced by one of the Paris of 1815. Just as in 1815, there was a stream of disparate Allied uniforms; and among them some Africans in red skirts and Hindus in white turbans were enough for me to create out of the Paris through which I was walking an entire, exotic, imaginary city, in an Orient both minutely precise as to costumes and the colour of faces, and arbitrarily chimerical as to setting, in the same way as Carpaccio turned the town where he lived into a Jerusalem or a Constantinople by assembling a crowd whose marvellous pattern of colour was no more varied than this one of mine. Walking close behind two Zouaves[43] who appeared to be taking almost no notice of him, I noticed a tall, stout man, in a soft felt hat and a long greatcoat, to whose florid features I hesitated whether I should put the name of an actor or a painter, each of whom was well known for numberless sodomitic scandals. I was quite sure, at all events, that I did not know the walking figure, so I was very surprised, when his gaze met mine, to see that he looked embarrassed and deliberately stopped and came towards me like a man who wants to show you that you have not surprised him in an occupation he would prefer to have kept secret. For a moment I wondered who was greeting me: it was M. de Charlus. One might say that in his case the development of his illness or the revolution of his vice had reached that extreme point at which the earliest character of the individual, his ancestral qualities, had been entirely eclipsed by the transit across them of the generic weakness or illness that comes with them. M. de Charlus had reached the most distant possible point from himself, or rather he himself was so perfectly disguised by what he had become and which did not belong to himself alone but to many other inverts, that at first I had taken him to be just another one of them, strolling after those Zouaves down the open boulevard, just another one of them who was not M. de Charlus, not a great aristocrat, not a man of imagination and intellect, and whose only resemblance to the Baron was that expression common to all of them, which now in his case, at least until one had looked more closely, cloaked him completely.

So it was that having set out to visit Mme Verdurin, I had run into M. de Charlus. I would certainly not have met him, as once I might have, at her house; their quarrel had only grown worse and Mme Verdurin even turned current events to her advantage in order to discredit him further. Having long said that she thought he was worn out, finished, more dated in his supposed audacity than the most boring traditionalist, she had now summed up her condemnation, and alienated everybody from him, by pronouncing him 'pre-war'. Between him and the present, according to the little set, the war had created a gulf which left him stuck in a completely moribund past.

Moreover – and this was addressed more to the world of politics, which was less well-informed – she made him out to be just as 'bogus', just as 'out of touch' socially as he was intellectually. 'He sees nobody, nobody receives him,' she said to M. Bontemps, who was easily persuaded by her. And there was some truth in her words. M. de Charlus's situation had changed. Caring less and less for society, having fallen out with people because of his touchy nature, and having, out of a sense of his own social worth, disdained to be reconciled with most of the people who were the flower of society, he lived in a relative isolation which, unlike that in which Mme de Villeparisis had died, was not caused by the ostracism of the aristocracy, but which in the eyes of the public appeared for two reasons to be worse. The bad reputation of M. de Charlus, which was now widely known, made the ill-informed think that this was the reason why people did not associate with him, when in fact it was he himself who declined to associate with them. So that something which was the result of his atrabilious temper seemed to be contempt on the part of those people against whom it was exercised. And secondly, Mme de Villeparisis had had one great bulwark: the family. But M. de Charlus had multiplied the quarrels between his family and himself. In addition to this, it had seemed – especially on the old Faubourg side, the Courvoisier side – of no interest to him. And he who, out of opposition to the Courvoisiers, had made such bold overtures towards art, had not the least idea that what would have made somebody like Bergotte most interested in him was his kinship with the whole of the old Faubourg, and his capacity to describe to him the almost provincial life led by his female cousins, from the rue de la Chaise to the place du Palais-Bourbon and the rue Garancière.

Then taking up a position which was less transcendent but more practical, Mme Verdurin affected to believe that he was not French. 'What nationality is he, exactly, isn't he Austrian?' M. Verdurin asked innocently. 'No, absolutely not,' replied the Comtesse Molé, whose first reaction was always one of common sense rather than bitterness. 'No of course not, he's Prussian, said the Patronne. I know perfectly well what I'm talking about, he's told us often enough himself that he was a hereditary member of the Prussian House of Lords and a *Durchlaucht*. – But the Queen of Naples told me – But you know she's a dreadful spy,' cried Mme Verdurin, who had not forgotten the way that deposed sovereign had behaved at her house one evening. 'I know, and I have it on very good authority, that it has been her only source of income. If we had a more energetic government, people like that would all be in concentration camps. Goodness me! Whatever else, you would be well advised not to receive people like that, because I know that the Minister of the Interior has his eye on them, and your house would be watched. Nothing will persuade me that Charlus did not spend two years spying on my house.' And thinking probably that some people might have doubts about how far detailed reports on the organization of the little set would interest the German government, Mme Verdurin pronounced, with an air of quiet perceptivity, like someone who knows that what she has to say will seem only the more valuable for her not raising her voice to say it: 'Let me tell you, on the very first day I said to my husband: "I don't like the way that man has inveigled his way in here. There's something fishy about him." We used to have a house that was situated high up above a bay. I'm convinced the Germans told him to set up a base there for their submarines. There were things about him which surprised me then, and which now I understand. For instance, at first he did not want to travel by train with the rest of my guests. Then, in the nicest way, I offered him a room in the house. But oh no! he preferred to live in Doncières where there were all those troops. It all smelled very strongly of espionage to me.'

About the first of the accusations levelled against the Baron de Charlus, that he was out of date, society people were only too willing to agree with Mme Verdurin. Actually in this they were ungrateful, for M. de Charlus was in a sense their poet, the man who had been able to extract from the social world a sort of poetry, in which there were elements of history, of beauty, of the picturesque, of the comic and of frivolous elegance. But the people in society, incapable of understanding this poetry, could see none of it in their own lives, so sought for it elsewhere, and set far above M. de Charlus in their estimation men who were infinitely his inferior, but who pretended to despise fashionable society and instead professed theories of sociology and political economy. M. de Charlus used to delight in recounting the involuntarily characteristic remarks, and in describing the skilfully graceful outfits, of the Duchesse de Montmorency, making her out to be the sublime of womanhood, which resulted in his being regarded as little short of an imbecile by those fashionable women who thought the Duchesse de Montmorency a silly woman of no interest, and that dresses were made to be worn while looking as if no attention had been given to them, whereas they, being more intelligent, were always rushing to the Sorbonne, or going to hear Deschanel speak in the Chamber.

In short, fashionable society had become disenchanted with M. de Charlus, not because it had seen through, but because it had never begun to penetrate his uncommon intellectual worth. People thought him 'pre-war', old-fashioned, because the very people who are least capable of assessing merit are the ones who, in order to classify people, are quickest to follow the dictates of fashion. They have not exhausted, not even skimmed the surface of the men of merit in one generation, and suddenly they have to condemn them all *en bloc*, because now there is a new generation, with its new label, which they will not understand any better than the last.

As for the second accusation, that of pro-Germanism, the tendency of people in society to eschew extremes led them to reject it, but it had found a tireless and particularly cruel spokesman in Morel, who, having been able to retain, in the newspaper world and even in society, the position which M. de Charlus, both times at a great deal of trouble to himself, had managed to obtain for him, but not thereafter to have rescinded, harried the Baron with a hatred all the more blameworthy for the fact that, whatever his relations may have been with the Baron, Morel had known a side of him that he concealed from so many people, namely his profound kindness. M. de Charlus had shown the violinist such generosity, such delicacy, had been so scrupulous in keeping his word to him, that when he left him, the impression that Charlie took with him was not at all that of a man of vice (and anyway he regarded the Baron's vice as a sickness), but of a man with the most lofty principles he had ever encountered, a man of extraordinary sensitivity, a kind of saint. He was so far from repudiating him, even after their quarrel, that he would say to parents in all sincerity: 'You can entrust your son to him, he can have nothing but the best influence on him.' So when he tried to cause him pain by the articles he wrote, in his mind it was not his vice but his virtue that he despised.

Shortly before the war, certain pieces in the gossip columns, transparent to the so-called initiated, had begun to do serious harm to the reputation of M. de Charlus. Of one called 'The Misfortunes of a Dowager ending in -us, or The Last Days of the Baroness', Mme Verdurin had bought fifty copies to lend to her acquaintances, and M. Verdurin, declaring that Voltaire himself had not written better, used to read it aloud. But since the war, their tone had changed. Not only was the Baron's inversion denounced, but also his alleged German nationality. Frau Bosch, Frau van den Bosch, were the habitual nicknames of M. de Charlus. One rather poetic piece took its title from some of Beethoven's dance tunes: 'An Allemande'. And two short stories, 'American Uncle and Frankfurt Queen' and 'The Poop Deck, or The Strapping Young Man Behind', which the little set read in proof, delighted Brichot himself, who exclaimed: 'I do hope the most-high and all-powerful Anastasia[44] doesn't blue-pencil us!'

The articles themselves were better than their ridiculous titles. Their style derived from Bergotte but, as I shall explain, in a way which I was perhaps the only person to understand. Morel had not been influenced at all by Bergotte's writings. The fertilization happened in a most peculiar way, so rare that it is on that account alone that I record it here. I have indicated at an earlier point the special way Bergotte had, when he spoke, of choosing and pronouncing his words. Morel, who for a long time used to see him at the Saint-Loups', used to do 'imitations' of him, in which he mimicked his voice perfectly, and used exactly the same words as he would have done. And now, when he wrote, Morel would transcribe conversations in the manner of Bergotte, but without subjecting them to the kind of transposition that would have turned them into written Bergotte. Few people having spoken with Bergotte, nobody recognized the tone of his voice, which was different from his written style. This oral fertilization is so uncommon that I wanted to mention it here. It never produces anything, however, except sterile flowers.

Morel, who was in the Press Office, then discovered, the French blood boiling in his veins like the juice of Combray grapes, that working in an office during wartime was not very satisfactory, and in the end he enlisted, despite Mme Verdurin's doing everything she could to persuade him to stay in Paris. She was certainly indignant that M. Cambremer, at his age, should be on the General Staff, and was wont to say of any man who did not accept her invitations: 'Where on earth has he managed to hide himself away?' and if someone asserted that the man in question had been in the front line from the beginning, she would reply with no scruples about lying, or perhaps because she was so used to being wrong: 'No, no, he's never been out of Paris, he does something about as dangerous as taking a minister for walks, take my word for it, I'm telling you, I heard it from someone who saw him'; but for the faithful it was quite a different matter, she did not want to let them go, regarding the war as a great 'bore' which made them abandon her. Thus she did everything she could to get them to stay, which gave her the double pleasure of having them to dine and, before they arrived, or after their departure, castigating their inactivity. But the faithful also had to acquiesce in being found cushy jobs, and she was most upset to see Morel behave so recalcitrantly in this regard; it was to no avail that she kept on telling him: 'But you *are* serving your country in the office, more than you would be at the front. The important thing is to be useful, to be really part of the war, to be involved. Some people are involved and some people manage to wangle their way out of it. Now you, you're involved, and don't worry, everybody knows that, nobody's going to cast stones at you.' In the same way, in different circumstances, when men were not yet so scarce and she was not obliged as she now was to make do chiefly with women, if a man lost his mother she had not hesitated to persuade him that there could be no objection to his continuing to attend her receptions, 'We bear our grief in our hearts. If you were thinking of going to a dance' (she didn't give dances) 'I should be the first to advise you against it, but here at my little Wednesdays or in a box at the theatre, nobody will raise an eyebrow. We all know that you are grieving.' Men were scarcer now, and mourning more frequent, and not even needed to prevent men going to parties, the war being enough to do that. Mme Verdurin clung on to those who remained. She tried to persuade them that they were more use to France if they stayed in Paris, as she might formerly have assured them that the deceased would have been happier to see them enjoying themselves. Yet despite everything she had very few men; perhaps she sometimes regretted having set such an irrevocable seal upon her break with M. de Charlus.

But although M. de Charlus and Mme Verdurin no longer met one another socially, they nevertheless continued, Mme Verdurin to hold receptions, M. de Charlus to go about his pleasures, as if nothing had changed – apart from a few unimportant minor differences: Cottard, for example, came to Mme Verdurin's receptions in a colonel's uniform straight out of *L'Île du rêve*,[45] looking just like a Haitian admiral, with a broad sky-blue ribbon on his jacket reminiscent of those worn by the Enfants de Marie; and M. de Charlus, finding himself in a city where the grown men, who had hitherto been where his tastes lay, had disappeared, had done the same as some Frenchmen, who in France had loved women, but who now lived in the colonies: he had, out of necessity, developed first the habit of, and then a taste for, little boys.

Yet the first of these characteristic traits disappeared quickly enough, for Cottard soon died 'facing the enemy' as the newspapers said, although he had not left Paris and had in fact just worked too hard for someone of his age, followed soon afterwards by M. Verdurin, whose death upset only one person, that, oddly enough, being Elstir. I had been able to study Elstir's work from a point of view that was, in a way, untrammelled. But he, especially as he grew older, linked it more and more superstitiously with the society which had provided his models; and society, after having thus been transformed in his studio, by the alchemy of impressions, into a work of art, had given him his public, his spectators. Inclining increasingly to the materialist belief that a substantial part of beauty resides in objects themselves, as at the outset he had adored in Mme Elstir the type of the rather heavy beauty he had pursued and caressed in his paintings and tapestries, he saw vanish with M. Verdurin one of the last vestiges of the social framework, the ephemeral framework – as rapidly obsolete as the sartorial fashions which partly constituted it – which underpins an art, and certifies its authenticity, just as the Revolution, by destroying the elegance of the eighteenth century, might have desolated a painter of *fêtes galantes*,[46] or as the disappearance of Montmartre and the Moulin de la Galette distressed Renoir; but more than anything else, with M. Verdurin he saw vanish the eyes and the brain which had best been able to see his paintings, and in which his painting, as a cherished memory, had always in some sense continued to exist. Of course young people had come along who also loved painting, but another kind of painting, and they had not, as Swann or M. Verdurin had, received the lessons in taste from Whistler, or the lessons in truth from Monet, which would enable them to make a just assessment of Elstir. Thus he felt himself more alone after the death of M. Verdurin, even though he had fallen out with him so many years earlier; for him, it was as if a little of the beauty of his work had been eclipsed along with a little of what awareness there was in the universe of that beauty.

As for the change that had overtaken the pleasures of M. de Charlus, this remained intermittent: keeping up a plentiful correspondence with men at the front, he was not short of sufficiently mature soldiers when they came on leave.

At the time when I believed what people said, I would have been tempted, hearing first Germany, then Bulgaria and Greece protesting their peaceable intentions, to have given them credence. But since life with Albertine and Françoise had accustomed me to suspecting them of thoughts and plans to which they gave no expression, I allowed none of the fair-seeming words of William II, Ferdinand of Bulgaria or Constantine of Greece to deceive my instinct, which sensed what each of them was up to. My quarrels with Françoise and with Albertine, of course, had been merely private quarrels, of interest only to the life of that little intelligent cell that is a human being. But just like animal and human bodies, that is to say like collections of cells each of which in relation to a single cell is as big as Mont Blanc, there are huge organized agglomerations of individuals which we call nations; their life merely repeats on a larger scale the lives of its component cells; and anybody who is incapable of understanding the mystery, the reactions, the laws of such entities will utter nothing but empty words when he talks about the struggle between nations. But if he has mastered individual psychology, then these colossal masses of conglomerated individuals confronting one another will take on a beauty in his eyes more powerful than that of a struggle arising merely from the conflict of two characters; and he will see them in the same scale as the body of a tall man would appear to infusoria, more than ten thousand of which are required to fill one cubic millimetre. Thus for some time the great figure of France, filled to its perimeter with millions of little irregular polygons, and the figure, filled with even more polygons, of Germany, had both been engaged in such a quarrel. Seen from this point of view, the body Germany and the body France, and the other Allied and enemy bodies, were behaving to a certain extent like individuals. But the blows they were exchanging were governed by the multifarious rules of boxing, whose principles Saint-Loup had explained to me; and since, even if one thought of them as individuals, they were also giant agglomerations of individuals, the quarrel took on immense and magnificent forms, like an ocean rising up in millions of waves in an attempt to batter down an ancient line of cliffs, or like gigantic glaciers which by their slow, destructive fluctuations attempt to break down the mountain ranges that circumscribe them.

For all this, life continued almost unchanged for plenty of the characters who have figured in this narrative, not least for M. de Charlus and the Verdurins, just as if the Germans were not in fact so close to them, the permanent presence of a threat of danger, even if temporarily checked, leaving us completely indifferent as long as we do not think about it. People generally go about their pleasures without ever thinking that, if the moderating and etiolating influences should ever stop, the proliferation of infusoria would reach its maximum, that is, in the space of a few days would make a leap of many millions of miles, would change from occupying a cubic millimetre to become a mass a million times bigger than the sun, at the same time destroying all the oxygen and the other substances by which we live, and that there would no longer be any humanity, or animals or earth; and also without imagining that an irremediable and entirely probable catastrophe may be induced in the ether by the incessant and frenetic activity normally hidden by the apparent immutability of the sun: they carry on with their own affairs without giving a thought to those two worlds, the one too small, the other too big for them to perceive the cosmic dangers that hover all around us.

So the Verdurins continued to give dinners (then after a little while, Mme Verdurin gave them on her own, for M. Verdurin died shortly afterwards) and M. de Charlus went about his pleasures, never dreaming that the Germans – albeit immobilized by a bloody yet constantly replenished barrier – were an hour by car from Paris. The Verdurins must have thought about it, one would have imagined, as they held a political salon at which people every evening discussed the situation not only of the army but of the fleet as well. And they did, it is true, think about the hecatombs of regiments annihilated and passengers swallowed by the sea; but a reciprocal process both so far multiplies whatever concerns our own well-being, and divides by such a formidable number whatever does not concern us, that the death of millions of unknown people hardly troubles us, and we find it scarcely as disagreeable as a cold draught. Mme Verdurin, suffering from migraines again now that there were no more croissants to dip in her coffee, had finally obtained an order from Cottard allowing her to have them made for her at a certain restaurant we have spoken about. This had been almost as hard to obtain from the authorities as the appointment of a general. She received the first of these croissants on the morning when the newspapers reported the wreck of the *Lusitania*. As she dipped it in her coffee, and flicked her newspaper with one hand so that it would stay open without her having to remove her other hand from the croissant she was soaking, she said: 'How awful! It's worse than the most horrific tragedy.' But the loss of all those people at sea must have been a thousand million times reduced before it struck her, because even while she uttered, through a mouthful of croissant, these distressing thoughts, the look which lingered on her face, probably induced by the taste of the croissant, so valuable in preventing migraine, was more like one of quiet satisfaction.

As for M. de Charlus, his position was but slightly different, but even worse, because not only did he not hope passionately for a French victory, he hoped rather, without admitting it, that Germany should, if not triumph, then at least not be crushed in the way that everybody wanted. The reason for this was that in these quarrels the great gatherings of individuals called nations behave to some extent as if they were individuals. The logic they follow is completely internal, and perpetually recast by passion, just like that of people confronting one another in a domestic or amorous quarrel, like a son's quarrel with his father, or a cook's with her mistress, or a wife's with her husband. The one in the wrong thinks he is in the right – as was the case with Germany – and the one who is right sometimes offers, quite justifiably, arguments which seem irrefutable to him only because they correspond to his passion. In these quarrels between individuals, the best way to be convinced of the rightness of either party is actually to be that party, a spectator will never agree quite so completely. Within a nation an individual, if he is really part of the nation, is no more than one cell within the nation-individual. Brain-washing is a term that makes no sense. If the French had been told that they were going to be beaten, no one Frenchman would have been in despair any more than if he had been told he was going to be killed by a Big Bertha. The real brain-washing is what we tell ourselves because of hope, which is one form of the instinct of national self-preservation, if we are really a living member of the nation. The best way to remain blind to what was unjust in the cause of the Germany-individual and to be aware at every moment of what was just in the cause of the France-individual was not for a German to have no judgment and for a Frenchman to possess it, the best way for both was to be patriotic. M. de Charlus, who did have unusual moral qualities, who was susceptible to pity, generous, capable of affection and devotion, also, for a whole variety of reasons – among which having a mother who was a Duchess of Bavaria may have played a part – did not have a sense of patriotism. In consequence he was no more part of the France-body than of the Germany-body. If I had been devoid of patriotism, instead of feeling myself to be one of the cells of the France-body, I do not think that I could have judged the quarrel in the same way as I might have done in the past. In my adolescence, when I believed exactly what I was told, I would, I am sure, hearing the German government protesting its good faith, have been tempted not to doubt it; but for a long time now I had known that our thoughts and our actions are not always in accord; not only had I, one day, from the staircase window, discovered a Charlus I had never suspected, but more than anything else with Françoise, and then, alas, with Albertine, I had seen decisions and plans take shape which were so contrary to what they said that, even as a simple spectator, I could never have allowed any of the apparently honest pronouncements of the German emperor, or the king of Bulgaria, to deceive my instinct, which would have sensed, as with Albertine, what they were secretly plotting. But in the end I can only imagine what I would have done if I had not been a participant, if I had not been part of the France-participant, just as in my quarrels with Albertine my sad expression or the feeling of breathlessness in my chest were a part of my individual being that was passionately involved in my cause, so that I could never feel completely detached. The detachment of M. de Charlus was total. And, seeing that he was merely a spectator, everything was bound to make him pro-German from the moment when, although not truly French, he started living in France. He was very intelligent, and in all countries most of the people are silly; no doubt if he had been living in Germany he would have been equally irritated by the way the German fools defended, passionately and foolishly, an unjust cause; but living in France, he was no less irritated by the passionate and foolish defence of a cause that was just. The logic of passion, even if it is in the service of the right, is never irrefutable for somebody who is not passionately committed to it. M. de Charlus's keen mind seized on each instance of false reasoning on the part of the patriots. The satisfaction an imbecile derives from having right on his side and being certain of success is especially irritating. M. de Charlus was particularly irritated by the triumphal optimism of people who did not know, as he did, Germany's strength, and who each month believed that she would be crushed within the month, and a year later were making equally confident new predictions, as if they had never made wrong ones with such assurance, which anyway they had forgotten, saying, if they were reminded of them, that it was not the same thing. M. de Charlus, profound though in some ways his mind was, would perhaps not have understood that in art 'it is not the same thing' is what the detractors of Manet retort to those who tell them 'they said the same thing about Delacroix'.

Ultimately M. de Charlus's position was a compassionate one, the idea of a loser made him feel ill, he always took the side of the weak, he never read the judicial reports in the newspapers so as not to have to suffer in his own body the pain of the condemned man and the impossibility of assassinating the judge, the executioner and the crowd cheering the fact that 'justice had been done'. He was convinced in any case that France could not now be beaten, and he also knew that the Germans were suffering from famine, and would be obliged, at some time or other, to surrender. This idea was made the more disagreeable to him by the fact that he was living in France. Also, his recollections of Germany were very distant, while the French people who annoyed him by talking so gleefully about crushing Germany were the people whose weaknesses he knew, whose faces he disliked. In such situations we feel sorry for the people we do not know, those whom we imagine, rather than those who are close to us in the vulgarity of everyday life, unless we are completely the same as them and form one flesh with them; that is the miracle of patriotism, which

83

makes one take the side of one's country just as one takes one's own side in a quarrel between lovers.

So for M. de Charlus the war provided an unusually fertile ground for the growth of those hatreds of his which blossomed in an instant and, while lasting only a short time, took the most violent hold of him. Whenever he read the newspapers, the triumphal tone of the editorials, presenting a daily picture of Germany brought low, 'the Beast at bay, reduced to powerlessness', when the opposite was all too true, would intoxicate him with rage by their flippant and ferocious stupidity. The newspapers were partly written at that point by well-known figures for whom that was a way of 'continuing to be of service', by men such as Brichot, Norpois, Morel himself, and Legrandin. M. de Charlus longed to encounter them and devastate them with the most withering sarcasm. Always particularly well informed about sexual irregularities, he was aware of those of several people who, thinking that nobody knew about them, took pleasure in denouncing them in the rulers of the 'predatory empires', in Wagner, etc. He had a burning desire to come face to face with them, to rub their noses in their own vice in front of the whole world and to leave those who insulted a beaten opponent dishonoured and gasping for breath.

M. de Charlus also had more private reasons for his pro-Germanism. One was that as a man of society he had passed a great deal of his time among the people of society, among honourable people, men of honour, people who would not shake hands with a scoundrel, and he understood their sensitivity and their severity; he knew that they were impervious to the tears of a man they have had expelled from a club or with whom they refuse to fight a duel, even though their act of 'moral scrupulousness' might lead to the death of the black sheep's mother. Despite himself, whatever admiration he may have had for England, and for the admirable way she had entered the war, this impeccable England, incapable of lying, by preventing wheat and milk from entering Germany, smacked too much of the man of honour among nations, of the dueller's official second, of the arbiter in affairs of honour; whereas he knew that men of uncertain reputation, scoundrels, like some of Dostoyevsky's characters, may be better human beings, although I could never understand why he identified the

Germans with them, lying and trickery not being adequate evidence of a good heart, which the Germans do not seem to have displayed.

There was one last trait in M. de Charlus's pro-Germanism, which he owed, by a bizarre reaction, to his 'Charlusism'. The Germans, to his eyes, were very ugly, perhaps because they were too close to his own blood; he was mad about Moroccans, but most of all about Anglo-Saxons, whom he viewed as living statues by Phidias. But pleasure for him was never without a certain tendency to cruelty, though at that point I was still unaware of the full extent of it; any man he loved became a delicious torturer. He may have believed that taking sides against the Germans would be acting as he acted only during his periods of sexual pleasure, that is, in opposition to his compassionate nature, burning with desire for seductive evil, and crushing virtuous ugliness. It was like that, too, when Rasputin was murdered, a murder which surprised people by its decidedly Russian stamp, at a Dostoyevskian dinner (an impression which might have been a great deal stronger if the public had not been unaware of what M. de Charlus knew perfectly well), because life disappoints us so often that we end up by believing that literature has no connection with it, and so we are amazed to see the precious ideas which we have found in books on display, without fear of getting spoiled, gratuitously, naturally, in the midst of everyday life, amazed, for instance, to find that a dinner and a murder occurring in Russia should have anything Russian about them.

The war seemed to be continuing indefinitely, and those who had already announced several years earlier, from a reliable source, that peace negotiations had started, and even specified the clauses of the treaty, no longer bothered when they talked to you to apologize for their false reports. They had forgotten them completely, and were ready to spread new stories with equal sincerity, which they would forget with the same rapidity. This was the time when there were constant Gotha raids, the air crackled all the time with the sonorous and vigilant vibration of French aeroplanes. But sometimes the siren rang out like a heart-rending Valkyrie call – the only German music anyone had heard since the outbreak of war – until the moment the fire engines announced that the alert was over, while beside them the all-clear, like an invisible street-urchin, commented at regular intervals on the good news and let loose its cry of joy on the air.

M. de Charlus was astonished to see that even people like Brichot, who had been militarists before the war, and had criticized France in particular for not being sufficiently so, were not content to blame Germany for the excesses of her militarism, but even criticized her admiration of the army. In all likelihood, they changed their attitude as soon as there was any question of slowing down the war against Germany, and continued, quite rightly, to denounce the pacifists. Yet Brichot, for instance, having agreed, despite his failing eyesight, to give an account in his lectures of some books which had recently been published in neutral countries, praised a novel by a Swiss writer in which two children who evince symbolic admiration at the sight of a dragoon are ridiculed as embryonic militarists.[47] This ridicule may also have annoyed M. de Charlus for other reasons, as he considered a dragoon capable of being an object of great beauty. But principally he failed to understand Brichot's admiration, if not for the novel, which the Baron had not read, then at least for its attitude, which was so far removed from that which Brichot had professed before the war. Then, everything to do with soldiers was good, even the irregularities of General de Boisdeffre, the disguises and schemings of Colonel du Paty de Clam, or Colonel Henry's forgery.[48] What extraordinary volte-face (which in reality was simply another side of the same noble passion, the patriotic passion, obliged to turn from the militarism he displayed when he was fighting against Dreyfusism, the tendency of which was anti-militarist, to a position almost of anti-militarism, as he was now fighting against super-militaristic Germany) led Brichot to declare: 'Oh, fabulous spectacle, and most worthy to entice the youth of an age of brutality, which knows only the worship of force: a dragoon! We may readily judge what will be the vile soldiery of a generation raised in the worship of these manifestations of brute force. Therefore Spitteler, wanting to set him against the hideous concept of the all-mighty sword, has symbolically exiled to the depths of the forest, ridiculed, slandered and alone, the visionary character he calls the Student Fool, in whom the author has so delightfully incarnated all the sweetness, so sadly unfashionable and likely soon to be forgotten if the dread reign of their ancient god is not broken, all the adorable sweetness of times of peace.'

'Tell me now, M. de Charlus said to me, you know Cottard and Cambremer. Every time I see them they tell me about Germany's extraordinary lack of psychology. Between you and me, do you think they concerned themselves about psychology before, or even that they are capable of showing any competence in it now? I am not exaggerating, believe me. Even if he is talking about one of the greatest Germans, about Nietzsche or Goethe, you will hear Cottard say: "with the habitual lack of psychology that characterizes the Teutonic race". There are things about the war that give me greater pain, obviously, but you must admit it is irritating. Norpois is more intelligent, I know, although he has been wrong about everything since the beginning of the war. But what is one to say about those articles that arouse such universal enthusiasm? My dear sir, you know Brichot's worth as well as I do, I like him a great deal, even after the schism which has separated me from his little church, which means that I see a great deal less of him. I do have a certain regard for this schoolmaster, he is a good talker and he is highly educated, and I grant you it is very touching that at his age, and enfeebled as he is, for he has been quite noticeably so for some years, he should have come back, as he puts it, to "serve". But in the end good intentions are one thing and talent is another, and Brichot has never had any talent. I admit that I share his admiration for certain examples of greatness in the current war. Yet it is strange, to say the least, that a blind partisan of antiquity like Brichot, who could never be sarcastic enough about Zola's finding more poetry in a working-class household, or down a mine, than in historic palaces, or about Goncourt's setting Diderot above Homer and Watteau above Raphael, should tell us endlessly that Thermopylae, even Austerlitz, are nothing compared with Vauquois.[49] Besides, this time, the public which rejected the modernists of literature and art accepts the modernists of war, because it has become fashionable to think in that way, and small minds, too, are overwhelmed not by beauty but by the enormity of action. Kolossal may be spelled only with a *k* nowadays, but it is still in essence the colossal that people kowtow to. Speaking of Brichot, have you seen Morel? I am told he wants to see me again.

He has only to make the first move, I am the older, it is not up to me to initiate it.'

Unfortunately, the very next day, to anticipate for a moment, M. de Charlus found himself face to face with Morel in the street; in order to arouse his jealousy, the latter took him by the arm and told him some more-or-less true stories, but when M. de Charlus, driven to distraction, felt a need for Morel to stay with him that evening and not to go anywhere else, Morel caught sight of a friend across the street and bade M. de Charlus farewell, at which he, hoping that this threat, which of course he would never have put into practice, would make Morel stay where he was, said: 'Watch out, I shall have my revenge,' but Morel, laughing, left him, patting his astonished friend on the neck, and putting his arm around his waist.

No doubt the things that M. de Charlus had said to me about Morel were testimony to the extent that love – and the Baron's must indeed have been very persistent – makes us (as well as more imaginative and more touchy) more credulous and less proud. But when M. de Charlus added: 'The boy is mad about women, and never thinks about anything else,' he spoke more truly than he knew. He said it out of pride, and out of love, in order that other people should think that Morel's fondness for him had not been followed by other attachments of the same sort. I, of course, did not believe this at all, having with my own eyes seen Morel agree to spend a night with the Prince de Guermantes for fifty francs, something of which M. de Charlus was still unaware. And if, seeing M. de Charlus pass by, Morel (except on those days when, feeling the need to confess, he would bump into him in order to have the opportunity to say 'Oh, I'm sorry, I know I've been horrible to you'), sitting at a pavement café with some friends, joined in their jeers, pointed his finger at the Baron, and made the clucking noises with which people make fun of old inverts, I was convinced he did it to conceal his hand, and that if they were taken aside by the Baron, each of his public denouncers would do everything he asked of them. I was wrong. While a remarkable impulse had led people like Saint-Loup, who were at the furthest remove from it, to inversion – something that happens in every class – a contrary impulse had weaned away from those practices those in whom they had been most habitual.

In some, the change was brought about by belated religious scruples, or by the agitation they felt when certain scandals broke, or by a fear of non-existent diseases in which they had been made to believe, in all sincerity, by relatives who were often concierges or valets, or quite without sincerity by jealous lovers who thought thereby to keep for themselves a young man on whom in fact their words had a quite contrary effect, alienating him from them as effectively as from others. Thus it was that the former lift-boy at Balbec would no longer have accepted, for love or money, propositions which now seemed to him as dangerous as approaches from the enemy. For Morel, his refusal of everybody, without exception, about which M. de Charlus had unwittingly uttered a truth which simultaneously justified his illusions and destroyed his hopes, stemmed from the fact that two years after leaving M. de Charlus he had fallen in love with a woman with whom he was still living and who, being more strong-willed than he was, had been able to demand absolute fidelity from him. With the result that Morel who, at the time when M. de Charlus was giving him so much money, had spent a night with the Prince de Guermantes for fifty francs, would not have agreed to do so with him or anybody else, even if they offered him fifty thousand francs. In the absence of honour and disinterestedness, his 'wife' had inculcated in him a certain fear of what other people might say, so that he was not averse to maintaining, with ostentatious bravado, that all the money in the world meant nothing to him when it was offered with certain strings attached. Thus the interplay of different psychological laws contrives to compensate, in the flowering of the human species, for everything which, in one way or another, would lead by superabundance or scarcity to its annihilation. As Darwin has shown, a comparable wisdom is to be found among the flowers, governing the methods of fertilization by opposing them successively one to another.

'It's a funny thing,' added M. de Charlus in the shrill little voice he sometimes adopted. 'I hear people who look quite happy all the time, and drink the best cocktails, declaring that they won't last until the end of the war, that their hearts are not strong enough, that they can think of nothing else, that one day they will just drop dead. And the most extraordinary thing is that this does actually happen. It is very odd! Is it a question of nutrition, because none of the food they eat is properly prepared any more, or is it because they have to demonstrate their zeal by buckling down to some futile job which only destroys the habits of life that kept them going? What ever it is, I've noticed an astonishing number of these strange, premature deaths, premature at least from the standpoint of the deceased. I can't remember what I was saying to you about Norpois's admiration for the war. But what a peculiar way he has of writing about it! To begin with, have you noticed the proliferation of new expressions which, when they have finally become threadbare from being used day in and day out – for Norpois is truly indefatigable, I think the death of my aunt Villeparisis must have given him a new lease of life – are immediately replaced by further commonplaces? I remember in the old days you used to amuse yourself by noting down the fashionable phrases as they appeared, stayed in circulation and then disappeared: "who sows the wind reaps the whirlwind"; "the dogs bark, the caravan moves on"; "show me sound politics and I'll show you sound finances, as Baron Louis used to say"; "these are symptoms which it would be excessive to regard as tragic but wise to take seriously"; "to labour and to seek for no reward" (that one has been resuscitated, as it was bound to be). Alas, how many phrases since have come and gone into the dark! We have had "the scrap of paper", "the predatory empires", "the infamous Kultur that consists in murdering defenceless women and children", "victory belongs, as the Japanese say, to the side that can hold out a quarter of an hour longer than the other", "the Germano-Touranians", "scientific barbarism", "if we want to win the war, in Lloyd George's potent phrase", though that is out of date now, and "the fighting-spirit of the troops" and "the pluck of the troops". The war has even wrought as profound a change in the excellent Norpois's syntax as in the baking of bread or the rapidity of transport. Have you noticed how the good fellow, although he insists on proclaiming his wishes as truths on the point of realization, does not quite dare use the future tense, pure and simple, which would run the risk of being contradicted by events, but indicates it instead by his adoption of the verb "to be able to"?' I confessed to M. de Charlus that I did not entirely understand what he meant.

I should mention here that the Duc de Guermantes shared none of his brother's pessimism. Also, he was as anglophile as M. de Charlus was anglophobe. And he regarded M. Caillaux[50] as a traitor who infinitely deserved to be shot. When his brother demanded proof of his treachery, M. de Guermantes replied that if people were only to be convicted if they had signed a document saying 'I am a traitor,' then the crime of treason would never be punished. But in case I do not have an opportunity to return to this matter, I should also say that two years later the Duc de Guermantes, his anti-Caillautism undiluted, met an English military attaché and his wife, a remarkably cultivated couple with whom he made friends, as he had with the three charming ladies at the time of the Dreyfus Affair, and was astounded at their first meeting, when he talked about Caillaux, whose crime he regarded as undeniable and whose conviction he thought a foregone conclusion, to hear the cultivated and charming couple say: 'But he will probably be acquitted, there is absolutely no evidence against him.' M. de Guermantes tried to argue that M. de Norpois, when he had given evidence, had looked straight at the appalled Caillaux and said: 'You are the Giolitti[51] of France, yes, M. Caillaux, you are the Giolitti of France.' But the cultivated and charming couple had smiled, made fun of M. de Norpois, cited examples of his senility, and concluded by saying that although the *Figaro* had claimed that he had spoken those words in front of 'the appalled M. Caillaux', it was more likely to have been a cynically amused M. Caillaux. The Duc de Guermantes was not slow to change his opinions. Attributing this change to the influence of an Englishwoman is not so extraordinary as it would have seemed if it had been predicted even as late as 1919, when the English still referred to the Germans only as the Huns and called for savage penalties against the guilty parties. Now English public opinion had also changed, and they approved every decision which might discomfit France and be of benefit to Germany.

To go back to M. de Charlus: 'Ah, yes,' he responded to my confession that I did not entirely understand, 'ah, yes: "to be able to", in Norpois's articles, indicates the future, that is, it indicates what Norpois wishes for, and what we all wish for, come to that,' he added, perhaps not completely sincerely. 'You realize of course that if "to be able" had not become simply an indication of the future tense, one might just about understand that the subject of the verb might be a country. For instance, every time Norpois says: "America would not be able to remain indifferent to these repeated violations of 'law'"; "the Dual Monarchy would not be able to fail to see the evil of its ways", it is clear that such phrases express his wishes (which are also mine, and yours), but in those cases, in spite of everything, the verb can still retain something of its original meaning, because a country can "be able", America can "be able", the Dual Monarchy itself can "be able" (despite its eternal "lack of psychology"). But that ambiguity is no longer possible when Norpois writes: "These systematic devastations would not be able to persuade the neutrals", "the region of the Lakes would not be able to fail to fall very quickly into the hands of the Allies", "the results of these neutralist elections would not be able to reflect the opinion of the great majority of countries". It is undeniable that these devastations, these regions and the results of these votes are inanimate things which cannot "be able". By using this formulation Norpois is simply addressing to the neutrals the injunction (which I regret to say they seem not to have obeyed) to abandon neutrality, or to the lake regions no longer to belong to the "Boches"' (it cost M. de Charlus the same kind of effort to pronounce the word 'Boche' as it had long ago in the tram at Balbec to speak about men whose taste was not for women).

'Also, have you noticed the crafty way Norpois, since 1914, has begun all his articles addressed to the neutrals? He starts by declaring that of course France has no desire to meddle in the politics of Italy (or Romania or Bulgaria, etc.). It is the business of those powers alone to decide, completely independently, taking into account nothing but the national interest, whether or not they should abandon neutrality. But while these preliminary statements of the article (what might once have been called the exordium) are so notably disinterested, what follows is generally much less so. "Nevertheless", Norpois in substance continues, "it is quite clear that the only nations to derive any material benefit from the struggle will be those who have ranged themselves on the side of law and justice. It cannot be expected that the Allies will reward, by allocating them the territories from which for centuries has risen the cry of their oppressed brothers, those peoples who, adopting the line of least resistance, have not taken up arms in the Allied cause." Having once taken this first step towards advising intervention, nothing can stop Norpois, and he goes on to offer less and less guarded advice not only about the principle of intervention, but about its timing. "Of course, he says, 'playing the saint' as he would put it, it is for Italy and Romania alone to decide on the time and manner at which it is most appropriate for them to intervene. Yet they must be aware that by equivocating too long they risk letting the moment slip past. Already the hoofs of the Russian cavalry are sending shivers through a Germany that faces an unspeakable horror. It is very clear that those peoples who have done no more than rush to help in a victory whose resplendent dawn is already in sight will have no entitlement at all to the reward that they may yet if they hasten, etc.' It is like those notices you see at the theatre: "Only a few seats left Book now to avoid disappointment!" A line of argument which is all the more stupid as Norpois has to revise it every six months, periodically telling Romania: "The moment has come for Romania to decide whether or not she wants to realize her national aspirations. If she delays any longer, it may be too late." He has been saying that for three years now, and not only has the "too late" not yet come, but Romania continues to be offered greater and greater incitements. Similarly, he invites France, etc., to intervene in Greece as protective power, on the grounds that the treaty allying Greece with Serbia has not been observed. But do you honestly think that if France were not at war and did not want the support or the benevolent neutrality of Greece it would occur to her to intervene in the role of protective power, or that the moral feelings which impel her to express outrage at Greece's failure to honour her commitments to Serbia do not fall silent the moment it is a question of an equally flagrant violation on the part of Romania and Italy, who, quite rightly I believe, and this applies to Greece too, have not fulfilled their duties, albeit less imperative and extensive than people say, as allies of Germany? The truth is that people see everything through the eyes of their newspapers, and how could they do otherwise given that they are not personally acquainted with the people or the events concerned? During the Dreyfus Affair, which you were so curiously worked up about, at a time conventionally regarded as separated from us by centuries now that the war-philosophers have added their weight to the idea that all links with the past have been broken, I was shocked to see members of my family express the highest esteem for anticlerical former Communards whom their newspaper represented as anti-Dreyfusards, and revile a Catholic general of good family who was in favour of a retrial. I am no less shocked now to see all Frenchmen execrate the Emperor Franz-Josef whom they used to venerate, quite rightly I may say, I having known him well, and whom he is kind enough to treat as a cousin. Ah! I have not written to him since the war,' he added as if bravely confessing to a fault for which he knew he could not be blamed. 'No, I did, just once, in the first year. What else can one do? None of this alters my respect for him, but I have plenty of young relatives here fighting in our lines who would, I know, think it very wrong of me to maintain a regular correspondence with the leader of a nation that is at war with us. What can I do? Censure me if you like,' he added as if bravely inviting my criticism, 'but I have had no wish, at this time, for a letter signed Charlus to arrive in Vienna. The only serious criticism I would level at the old sovereign is that a nobleman of his rank, head of one of the oldest and most illustrious houses in Europe, should allow himself to be led by a petty country squire, very intelligent I grant you, but basically just a parvenu, like William of Hohenzollern. It is not the least of the many shocking anomalies of this war.'

And as, from the moment he returned to thinking about things in terms of the Peerage, which for him fundamentally dominated everything, M. de Charlus became extraordinarily childish, he told me, in the same tone of voice with which he might have spoken of the Marne or Verdun, that there were significant and very curious matters which ought not to be passed over by anyone who came to write the history of this war. 'For example, he said, everybody is so ignorant that no one has pointed out this remarkable fact: the Grand Master of the Order of Malta, who is a pure Boche, continues none the less to live in Rome, where, as Grand Master of our order, he enjoys the privilege of extraterritoriality. Rather interesting,' he added, as if to say: 'You see that you have not had a wasted evening, meeting me.' I thanked him, and he assumed the modest expression of someone requiring no payment. 'But what was I saying to you just now? Oh, yes, that people nowadays hate Franz-Josef because their newspaper tells them to. As for King Constantine of Greece and the Tsar of Bulgaria, the public has repeatedly oscillated between loathing and sympathy, depending on whether they were said to be about to take the side of the Entente or the side that Brichot calls the Central Empires. It is like Brichot telling us all the time that "Venizelos's hour is about to come". I do not doubt that M. Venizelos is a very capable statesman, but how do we know that the Greeks want him as much as all that? We are told that he wanted Greece to honour her commitments to Serbia. Yet we still ought to know what these commitments were and whether they were more extensive than those that Italy and Romania believed that they could violate. We exhibit a concern for the way in which Greece implements its treaties and respects its constitution which we would certainly not feel if it were not in our own interest. If the war had not happened, do you think that the "guarantor" powers would even have noticed the dissolution of the Chambers? All I can see is that one by one all the supports of the King of Greece are being removed so that he can be thrown out or locked up as soon as he no longer has an army to defend him. I was saying that the public's judgment of the King of Greece or the King of the Bulgars is informed solely by what they read in the newspapers. But how could they think about them in any other way but through the newspapers, since they do not know them personally? Whereas I myself have seen a great deal of them, I knew Constantine of Greece very well when he was the Diadoch,[52] and he is quite wonderful. I always thought the Emperor Nicholas had a very great fondness for him. It was all entirely honourable, naturally. Princess Christian used to talk openly about it, but she is a poisonous woman. As for the Tsar of the Bulgars, he is a complete nancy, a raving queer, but very intelligent, a remarkable man. He likes me very much.'

M. de Charlus, who could be so agreeable, became obnoxious when he started on topics like these. He brought to them a self-satisfaction as annoying as that which we feel in the presence of an invalid who is always pointing out how good his health is. I have often thought that in the Balbec train we used to call the Slow-coach, the faithful, who so longed for the admissions he always evaded, might perhaps not have been able to accept such an overt display of his compulsion and, ill at ease, breathing awkwardly as in a sickroom or when faced with a dope fiend who takes out his syringe in front of you, it might have been they who put a stop to the confidences they thought they wanted to hear. And one was indeed annoyed to hear everyone accused, often probably without any sort of evidence, by somebody who excepted himself from the special category to which one none the less knew that he belonged and to which he was so ready to consign others. For all his intelligence, he had in this area fashioned a narrow little philosophy for himself (at the bottom of which there was perhaps a touch of that sense of curiosity which 'life' aroused in Swann), explaining everything in terms of these special causes, and in which, as when anybody lapses into their characteristic weakness, he was not only unworthy of himself but also exceptionally self-satisfied. Thus it was that he, who was capable of such gravity and nobility, adopted the most inane grin as he completed this pronouncement: 'As there are strong presumptions of the same kind as for Ferdinand of Coburg[53] in the case of Emperor William, that might be the reason why Tsar Ferdinand has aligned himself with the "predatory empires". Well, really, it is quite understandable, one is indulgent towards a *sister*, one cannot refuse her anything. I think that would be very neat as an explanation of Bulgaria's alliance with Germany.' And at this stupid explanation M. de Charlus laughed at length, as thought he really thought that it was very ingenious, and which, even if it had rested on true facts, was as puerile as the reflections M. de Charlus offered on the war when he judged it from the standpoint of a feudal lord or a Knight of St John of Jerusalem. He ended with a more sensible remark: 'The astonishing thing, he said, is that the public that thus judges the men and the events of the war solely on the basis of newspaper reports is convinced that it is forming its own judgments.'

In that M. de Charlus was right. I have been told that one really had to see the moments of silence and hesitation that Mme de Forcheville used to have, just like those that are necessary not simply to the expression but to the very formation of a personal opinion, before saying, in the tone of voice appropriate to a deeply private feeling: 'No, I don't think they will take Warsaw'; 'I don't feel they can last a second winter'; 'what I don't want is a botched-up peace'; 'the thing that scares me, if you want to know, is the Chamber'; 'yes, I still believe we'll be able to break through.' And to say these things, Odette adopted a simpering expression which she exaggerated even further when she said: 'I'm not saying the German armies don't fight well, but they lack what we call pluck.' As she pronounced the word 'pluck' (and even when she merely said 'fighting spirit'), she made a moulding gesture with her hand and half-closed her eyes as if she were a student artist using a technical studio term. Her own way of speaking, though, even more than before, indicated her admiration for the English, whom she was no longer obliged to content herself with calling, as previously she did, 'our neighbours across the Channel' or at most 'our friends the English', but now could call 'our loyal allies'. Needless to say, she never missed a single opportunity to cite the expression *fair play* in order to show how the English thought that the Germans were unfair players, and 'the main thing is to win the war, as our brave allies say'. She used even rather clumsily to link the name of her son-in-law to anything involving English soldiers and the pleasure he derived from living in close contact with Australians and Scots, New Zealanders and Canadians. 'My son-in-law Saint-Loup now knows the slang of all the brave *tommies*, he can make himself understood by the ones from the furthest *dominions* and fraternizes with the humblest *private* as easily as with the general commanding the base.'

Let this parenthesis on Mme de Forcheville, while I walk down the boulevards side by side with M. de Charlus, serve as my excuse for another, even longer but useful for describing this period, on the relations between Mme Verdurin and Brichot. The fact is that, although poor Brichot was judged with severity by M. de Charlus (because the latter was both very intelligent and more or less unconsciously pro-German), he was treated still more badly by the Verdurins. They were chauvinistic, of course, which ought to have made them like Brichot's articles, especially since they were no worse than plenty of the writings which Mme Verdurin thoroughly enjoyed. But, first, it will perhaps be remembered that even at La Raspelière Brichot had become, instead of the great man he had seemed to them in the past, if not a whipping boy like Saniette, at least the object of their scarcely disguised mockery. But at least he still remained, at that point, one of the most faithful of the faithful, which ensured him a share of the benefits tacitly envisaged by the statutes for all the founding or associate members of the little group. But as, thanks to the war perhaps, or to the sudden crystallization of a long-delayed elegance, all the necessary elements of which, albeit invisibly, had long saturated it, the Verdurin salon had been opening itself to a new social world, and the faithful, at first the lures to attract this new world, had ended by being invited less and less, so a parallel phenomenon had been occurring in Brichot's life. Despite the Sorbonne, despite the Institut, his renown had not, before the war, extended beyond the limits of the Verdurin salon. But when he started writing almost daily articles adorned with the shallow brilliance which one has so often seen him dispense so munificently to the faithful, yet also rich with a quite genuine erudition which, as a true member of the Sorbonne, he never tried to conceal however exaggerated the form in which he couched it, 'high society' was literally dazzled. For once, it bestowed its favour on somebody who was far from being a nonentity, somebody who could retain its attention by the fertility of his intelligence and the resources of his memory. And while three duchesses would go to spend the evening with Mme Verdurin, three more would compete for the honour of having the great man to dine with them, one of which invitations he would accept, feeling the freer to do so since Mme Verdurin, exasperated by the success that his articles were achieving in the Faubourg Saint-Germain, now took care never to have Brichot to her house when he was likely to meet there some glittering woman whom he did not yet know and who would hasten to entice him away. Thus it was that journalism (in which Brichot was really doing nothing more in the end than belatedly providing, to general praise and in return for magnificent fees, what all his life he had squandered gratis and incognito in the Verdurin drawing-room, since his articles, so eloquent and knowledgeable was he, cost him no more effort than his conversation) might have led Brichot, even at one point seemed to be leading him, to undisputed fame . . . if it had not been for Mme Verdurin. Brichot's articles, of course, were far from being as remarkable as people in society thought them. The vulgarity of the man was constantly visible beneath the pedantry of the literary scholar. And alongside images which meant nothing at all ('the Germans will no longer be able to look Beethoven's statue in the face'; 'Schiller must have been turning in his grave'; 'the ink which had initialled Belgium's neutrality was hardly dry'; 'Lenin speaks, but his words are all gone with the wind of the steppes'), there were trivialities such as: 'Twenty thousand prisoners, that is quite a number; our command will know to keep an extra eye open; we want to win, and that's that.' But mixed in with all this, how much knowledge, how much intelligence, what telling arguments! Mme Verdurin, however, never started an article by Brichot without the prior satisfaction of thinking that she was going to find ridiculous things in it, and she would read it with the closest attention in order to be certain of not letting them escape her. And unfortunately there were bound to be some. They did not even wait until they had found them. The most felicitous quotation from an author who was genuinely little known, at least for the work Brichot was referring to, was taken as proof of the most unbearable pedantry, and Mme Verdurin would wait impatiently for dinner-time when she would be able to unleash peals of laughter from her guests. 'Well, what do you think of Brichot this evening? I thought of you when I read the quotation from Cuvier. Upon my word, I think he's going mad. – I haven't read it yet, Cottard would say. – What, you haven't read it yet? But you don't know what a treat you're missing. Honestly, you'll die laughing.' And secretly pleased that someone had not yet read the latest Brichot as it meant that she herself had an opportunity to point out its absurdities, Mme Verdurin would tell the butler to bring *Le Temps* and herself would read it aloud, giving to the simplest sentences a ring of grandiloquence. After dinner, for the rest of the evening, the anti-Brichot campaign would continue, but with a pretence of reserve. 'I shan't say it too loud because I'm afraid that over there', she would say, indicating the Comtesse Molé, 'they rather admire this stuff. Society people are more gullible than we think.' Mme Molé, whom they tried, by speaking fairly loudly, to ensure was aware that they were talking about her, at the same time as they did their best to show her, by now and then lowering their voices, that they did not want her to hear what they were saying, was cowardly enough to disown Brichot, whom in reality she thought the equal of Michelet. She agreed with Mme Verdurin and then, in order nevertheless to conclude on a note that seemed to her to be unquestionable, said: 'The one thing nobody can take away from him is that it is well written. – You really call that well written? said Mme Verdurin, personally I think it reads as if it was written by a pig,' a piece of daring which made her fashionable guests laugh all the more as Mme Verdurin, as if horrified by the word 'pig', had uttered it in a whisper, her hand clapped to her lips. Her rage against Brichot was increased even more by the way he naïvely paraded his pleasure at his success, in spite of the fits of bad temper aroused in him by the censors every time that they, as he put it with his habit of using new words to show that he was not too academic, 'blue-pencilled' a part of his article. In his presence, Mme Verdurin did not let it be too clearly seen, save by a peevishness that might have put a more perspicacious man on his guard, how little store she set by what Chochotte wrote. All she did was to tell him once that he was wrong to use 'I' as often as he did. And indeed he got into the habit of using it continually, first of all because out of pedagogic habit he constantly employed phrases such as 'I grant that' and even, when he meant 'I am happy to admit that', 'I am happy that', as in: 'I am happy that the enormous expansion of the fronts necessitates, etc.', but principally because, as a former militant anti-Dreyfusard who had scented the German preparations long before the war, he had very often had occasion to write: 'Since 1897, I have denounced'; 'I pointed out in 1901'; 'I warned in my little pamphlet, now extremely hard to come by (*habent sua fata libelli*[54])', and thereafter the habit had stayed with him. He blushed deeply at Mme Verdurin's comment, a comment which had been delivered with a note of asperity. 'You are right, madam. A man who was as little fond of the Jesuits as M. Combes, albeit he never had a preface from our gentle master of exquisite scepticism, Anatole France, who was, if I mistake not, my adversary . . . before the deluge, said that the self is always hateful.'[55] From then on, Brichot replaced *I* with *one*, but *one* did not prevent the reader from seeing that the author was speaking about himself, and indeed allowed the author never to stop speaking about himself, or commenting on the most insignificant of his sentences, or fabricating an article on the basis of a single negative statement, always shielding himself behind *one*. For example, if Brichot said, perhaps in another article, that the German armies had lost some of their power, he would begin like this: 'One will not here conceal the true state of things. One has said that the German armies have lost some of their power. One has not said that they do not still possess great power. Still less will one write that they have no power. Nor will one say that the ground won, if it is not, etc.' In short, simply by pronouncing all he would not say, by recalling everything that he had said some years before, and that Clausewitz, Jomini, Ovid, Apollonius of Tyre, etc., had said at various times over the centuries, Brichot could easily have gathered the material for a substantial volume. It is to be regretted that he did not publish one, as those well-directed articles of his are difficult to find now. The Faubourg Saint-Germain, admonished by Mme Verdurin, began by laughing at Brichot when they were under her roof, but continued, once they had come away from the little set, to admire him. Then, after a while, making fun of him became as much the fashion as admiring him had been, and even those whom he continued to dazzle in secret, for as long as they were reading his articles, checked their adulation and laughed as soon as they were no longer alone, in order not to seem less intelligent than the others. Brichot had never been so much talked about by the little set as he was at this period, but only with derision. It became the criterion of any newcomer's intelligence to ask what he thought of Brichot's articles; if he gave the wrong answer the first time, people were quick to instruct him in how it was that people's intelligence was recognized.

'Well, my poor friend, all that is terrible, and we have more than boring articles to lament. People talk of vandalism and of statues being destroyed. But isn't the destruction of so many marvellous young men, once incomparable polychrome statues themselves, also vandalism? Isn't a town which will no longer have any beautiful men in it like a town with all its statues smashed? What kind of pleasure will I be able to get from dining in a restaurant if I am to be waited on by moss-covered old buffoons who look like Père Didon, if not by women in mob-caps who make me think I've wandered into a Duval Restaurant?[56] That's how things are, my dear chap, and I think I have a right to speak like this because beauty is no less beauty when it is living matter. What a pleasure it is to be served by rachitic creatures wearing glasses, with the grounds of their exemption writ large on their faces! Contrary to what always used to happen in the past, if you want to rest your eyes on someone nice-looking in a restaurant, you have to look at the customers eating and drinking, not at the waiters who are serving. And then one could always see a waiter again, even though they often changed, but how is one to find out who this English lieutenant is, and when he will come back, when it is perhaps the first time he has been there and when he may be killed tomorrow? When, as we are told by the charming Morand, the enchanting author of *Clarisse*,[57] Augustus of Poland exchanged one of his regiments for a collection of Chinese vases, he made, in my opinion, a bad bargain. Just think, all those great footmen, six feet tall, who used to adorn the monumental staircases of our loveliest female friends, have all been killed, and most of them only joined up because they kept on being told that the war would last for two months. Ah! they didn't know, as I did, the strength of Germany, and the courage of the Prussian race,' he said, forgetting himself.

And then, noticing that he had revealed too much of his point of view: 'It is not so much Germany that I fear for France, as the war itself. Here behind the lines people imagine that the war is merely a gigantic boxing match, which they can watch from a distance, thanks to the newspapers. But it is not like that at all. It is an illness which, whenever it seems to have been warded off at one point, reappears somewhere else. Today Noyon will be recaptured, tomorrow there will be no more bread or chocolate, the next day the man who thought he was content, and who was ready, if necessary, to accept the idea of a bullet because he could not imagine it, will panic when he reads in the newspaper that his age-group is being called up. As for monuments, the disappearance of a masterpiece like Rheims, unique in its quality, does not appal me so much as the sight of the annihilation of so many of the groups of buildings which once made the smallest village in France both charming and edifying.'

I thought at once of Combray, but in the past I had thought I would lower myself in the eyes of Mme de Guermantes if I confessed the modest position which my family occupied in the village. I wondered whether it had ever been disclosed to the Guermantes and M. de Charlus, either by Legrandin, or by Swann, or Saint-Loup, or Morel. But even preterition of that sort was less painful to me than the prospect of retrospective explanation. I only hoped that M. de Charlus would not say anything about Combray.

'I do not wish to speak ill of the Americans, Monsieur, he continued, it seems that they are inexhaustibly generous and, as there has not been a conductor in this war, and each performer has joined in long after the last, and the Americans have come in when we are almost finished, they may have an enthusiasm which four years of war have somewhat dulled in us. Even before the war they exhibited a love for our country and our art, and paid high prices for our masterpieces. Many of them are now in their country. But this deracinated art, as M. Barrès would call it,[58] is precisely the opposite of what used to make up the exquisite charm of France. The chateau explained the church, which itself, because it had been a site of pilgrimage, explained the *chanson de geste*. I do not want to make too much of the illustriousness of my family origins and my connections, which in any case is not to the point here. But recently, in order to settle a financial matter, and despite there being a certain coolness between that couple and myself, I had to pay a visit to my niece Saint-Loup, who lives at Combray. Combray was just a small town, like so many others. But our ancestors were depicted as benefactors in some of the church windows, while others bore our coat of arms. We had our chapel there, and our tombs. The church was destroyed by the French and the English because it was being used as an observation-post by the Germans. The whole of that mixture of living history and art that was France is being destroyed, and the process is not over yet. Of course I am not so absurd as to compare, for reasons of family, the destruction of the church at Combray with that of Rheims cathedral, in which by some miracle the gothic cathedral seemed to have rediscovered, quite naturally, the purity of classical statuary, or with that of the cathedral at Amiens. I don't know whether the uplifted arm of St Firmin is now broken. But if it is, the highest affirmation of faith and energy has vanished from this world. – The symbol of it, Monsieur, I responded. I adore certain symbols as much as you do. But it would be absurd to sacrifice to the symbol the reality which it symbolizes. Cathedrals should be adored until such time as their preservation becomes dependent on our denying the truths that they teach. The arm of St Firmin, uplifted in an almost military gesture of command, said: Let us be broken, if honour demands it. Do not sacrifice men for the sake of stones, the beauty of which derives precisely from their having for a moment embodied human truths. – I understand what you mean, replied M. de Charlus, and M. Barrès, who has sent us, alas, on too many pilgrimages to the statue of Strasbourg and to the tomb of M. Déroulède,[59] was moving and generous when he wrote that Rheims cathedral itself was less dear to us than the lives of our infantrymen. An assertion which renders rather absurd the anger of our newspapers against the German general in command there, who said that Rheims cathedral was less precious than the life of one German soldier. In the end, what is so exasperating and distressing is that each country says the same thing. The grounds on which the associated industrialists of Germany declare the possession of Belfort indispensable for protecting their nation against our ideas of revenge are the same as those of Barrès when he demands Mainz in order to protect us against the recurrent wish of the Boche to invade us. Why should the return of Alsace-Lorraine have seemed to France an insufficient motive for waging a war, yet a sufficient motive to continue one, and to declare it anew each year? You seem to think that victory is now guaranteed to France, and with all my heart I hope that it is, don't doubt that. But now that, rightly or wrongly, the Allies believe themselves certain to win (for my part I should naturally be delighted by that outcome, but what I see mostly are numerous paper victories, Pyrrhic victories, at a cost that is never vouchsafed to us) and that the Boches no longer believe themselves certain to win, we see Germany trying to hasten peace and France trying to prolong the war, France which prides itself on justice, and is right to pronounce words of justice, but which is also gentle France, and ought to pronounce words of mercy, even if only for her own children, and so that the flowers when they bloom again may light up other things than tombs. Be honest, my friend, you yourself have propounded to me a theory about things existing only by virtue of a creation which is perpetually renewed. The creation of the world did not happen once and for all, you told me, it has to take place, necessarily, every day. Well, if you are sincere, you cannot make war an exception to this theory. Never mind that the excellent Norpois has written (wheeling out one of those rhetorical flourishes that he is so fond of, like "the dawn of victory" and "General Winter"): "Now that Germany has determined upon war, the die has been cast", the truth is that every morning war is declared anew. Thus those who wish to continue it are as guilty as those who started it, perhaps more so, for the latter may not perhaps have foreseen the full horror of it.

'There is, besides, nothing to say that such a prolonged war, even if it must have a victorious outcome, is not without its own dangers. It is difficult to talk about things that have no precedent, and about the repercussions on an organism of an operation being attempted for the first time. It is true, generally speaking, that innovations, alarming though people may find them, go off very well. The most sensible Republicans thought that it was mad to separate Church and State. It went through as easily as posting a letter. Dreyfus was rehabilitated, Picquart became Minister of War, both without a murmur from anyone.[60] Yet what may we not fear from the stress and fatigue of a war that has continued uninterrupted for several years? What will the men do when they come back from it? Will they have been broken or driven mad by exhaustion? The whole thing may turn out very badly, if not for France, then at least for the government, even perhaps for our form of government. You once made me read Maurras's admirable essay on the memoirs of Aimée de Coigny. I would be very surprised if some modern Aimée de Coigny was not expecting, as a consequence of the Republic's war, what the 1812 Aimée de Coigny expected from the war waged by the Empire.[61] If the modern Aimée exists, will her hopes be realized? That is not something I want to see.

'But to return to the war itself, was it really the Emperor William who first started it? I am very dubious about that. And if it was, what has he done that Napoleon, for example, did not do, something that I myself find abominable, but which I am astonished to see also inspiring such horror in worshippers of Napoleon, and in those people who on the day war was declared exclaimed like General Pau: "I have been waiting for this day for forty years. It is the best day of my life." God knows, nobody protested more forcefully than I did when society afforded such a disproportionate place to nationalists and military men, and when every friend of the arts was accused of being involved in things that would be fatal to the country, all civilization that was not bellicose being regarded as pernicious! A genuine member of the best society barely counted compared with a general. Some madwoman even once almost presented me to M. Syveton.[62] You will tell me that the rules I was endeavouring to maintain were only those of society. But despite their apparent frivolity they might perhaps have prevented many excesses. I have always respected those who defend grammar or logic. We realize, fifty years later, that they averted serious dangers. Now our nationalists are the most anti-German, the most die-hard, of men. But over the last fifteen years their philosophy has completely altered. It is true that they are pressing hard for a continuation of the war. But this is only in order to exterminate a war-mongering race, and out of a love of peace. Because a warlike civilization, which they thought so fine fifteen years ago, now fills them with horror. Not only do they criticize Prussia for allowing the military element to become predominant in their state, they think that in every age military civilizations have been destructive of everything they now hold precious, not only of the arts but even of courtesy towards women. If any one of their critics is converted to nationalism, that is sufficient for him to become by the same token a friend of peace. He becomes convinced that in all warlike civilizations women have been humiliated and have occupied an inferior position. One does not dare respond that the "ladies" of knights in the Middle Ages, and Dante's Beatrice, were perhaps placed on a throne as elevated as the heroines of M. Becque.[63] One of these days I fully expect to find myself seated at table below a Russian revolutionary, or simply below one of those generals of ours who wage war out of a horror of war and in order to punish a people for cultivating an ideal which they themselves, fifteen years ago, judged the only one capable of reinvigorating us. The unfortunate Tsar was still honoured only a few months ago because he had called the peace conference at The Hague. But now that people are hailing the free Russia, they forget that he ever had that claim to glory. So turns the wheel of the world.

'And yet Germany uses such similar expressions to France that one might think she was quoting her, she never tires of saying that she "is fighting for her existence". When I read: "We shall fight against an implacable and cruel enemy until we have obtained a peace which will guarantee us a future free from all aggression, so that the blood of our brave soldiers shall not have flowed in vain," or: "He who is not for us is against us," I do not know whether the sentence comes from the Emperor William or from M. Poincaré, because they have both, give or take a few variations, pronounced each one twenty times, although to be honest I must confess that the Emperor, in this instance, is echoing the President of the Republic. France might perhaps not have been so enthusiastic about prolonging the war if she had remained weak, but above all Germany would probably not have been in such a hurry to end it if she had not ceased to be strong. To be as strong as she was, for strong you will see she still is.'

He had developed the habit of almost shouting some of the things he said, out of excitability, out of his attempt to find outlets for impressions of which he needed – never having cultivated any of the arts – to unburden himself, as an aviator looses his bombs, if necessary in open country, in places where his words affected nobody, especially in society, where they fell equally randomly and where he was listened to out of snobbery or dependence, and, so much did he tyrannize his audience, one may say under obligation and even out of fear. On the boulevards this harangue was also a mark of his contempt for passers-by, for whom he no more lowered his voice than he would have moved out of their way. But it was out of place there, caused surprise, and above all rendered audible to the people who turned round remarks which might have had us taken for defeatists. I commented on this to M. de Charlus but succeeded only in arousing his mirth. 'That would be very funny, you must admit, he said. After all, he added, one never knows, we all run the risk every evening of being an item in the next day's news. Is there really any reason why I should not end up shot in the moat at Vincennes? After all, that is what happened to my great-uncle, the Duc d'Enghien.[64] The thirst for noble blood maddens a certain kind of rabble, and in that they are more discriminating than lions are. You know that for those animals it would take no more than a scratch on her nose for them to leap on to Mme Verdurin. A scratch on what in my youth we would have called her conk!' And he began to roar with laughter as if we had been alone in a drawing-room.

From time to time, seeing some rather shifty-looking individuals emerge from the shadows as M. de Charlus went by and cluster together a short distance away from him, I wondered whether he would prefer me to leave him alone or to remain with him. In the same way, somebody who meets an old man subject to frequent epileptic fits, and who sees from his inconsistent movements that an attack is probably imminent, wonders whether his company is more desired as a support or dreaded as a witness from whom he would wish to conceal the fit, and whose mere presence, when absolute calm might perhaps succeed in averting it, would be enough to hasten its onset. But the possibility of the event from which one does not know whether or not one should remove oneself is revealed, in the case of the sick man, by his meandering progress, like that of a drunk. Whereas with M. de Charlus these variously divaricating positions, the indication of a possible incident in relation to which I was not sure whether he desired or feared that my presence should prevent its occurrence, were occupied, as if by ingenious stage-management, not by the Baron himself, who was walking straight ahead, but by a whole circle of extras. All the same, I believe he wanted to avoid the encounter, because he dragged me into a side-street, darker than the boulevard, yet into which it was constantly disgorging, except for those who were flocking towards it, soldiers from every branch of the service and from every nation, a youthful influx which compensated and consoled M. de Charlus for the ebbing of all the men towards the frontier which had, as if pneumatically, created a vacuum in Paris during the early days of mobilization. M. de Charlus made constant admiring comments about the brilliant uniforms which passed about us, turning Paris into a town as cosmopolitan as a port and as unreal as the scenery in a painter's studio, where a few bits of architecture have been assembled simply as a pretext for him to gather together the most varied and glittering costumes.

He still retained all his respect and all his affection for some great ladies who were accused of defeatism, as he had once for those who had been accused of Dreyfusism. He regretted only that by stooping to the level of politics they might have laid themselves open 'to being talked about by journalists'. As far as he was concerned, nothing about them had changed. For his frivolity was so much second nature to him, that birth, combined with beauty and other forms of prestige, was the thing that endured – and the war, like the Dreyfus Affair, was merely a vulgar and passing fashion. If the Duchesse de Guermantes had been shot for trying to reach a separate peace with Austria, he would still have considered her as noble as ever, and no more demeaned by it than Marie-Antoinette seems to us today for having been condemned to decapitation. As he spoke then, M. de Charlus, with the noble guise of a Saint-Vallier or a Saint-Megrin, was upright, stiff and solemn, his voice was serious, and for a brief moment he displayed none of the mannerisms by which men of his sort reveal themselves. And yet, why is it that none of them can ever have a voice that sounds absolutely right? Even at this moment, when it was approaching its most serious, his still sounded slightly wrong, as if it needed tuning.

M. de Charlus literally did not know which way to look, and often he glanced upward, regretting that he did not have a pair of binoculars, although they would not have been a great deal of use, since, because of the Zeppelin raid of two days earlier which had made the authorities extend their vigilance, there were soldiers in larger numbers than usual, even in the sky. The aeroplanes which I had seen some hours earlier looking like insects, brown spots against the blue sky, now passed through the night, the darkness of which was further intensified by the partial extinction of the street-lights, like gleaming fire-ships. The greatest impression of beauty that these human shooting stars made us experience was perhaps to make us look at the sky, towards which normally we hardly ever raise our eyes. In this Paris, whose almost defenceless beauty, in 1914, I had seen awaiting the threat of the approaching enemy, there was, certainly, now as then, the ancient, unchanged splendour of a moon cruelly and mysteriously serene which poured over the still intact monuments the useless beauty of its light, but as in 1914, and to a greater extent than in 1914, there was also something else, different lights, intermittent beams which, whether they came from aeroplanes or from the searchlights on the Eiffel Tower, one knew to be directed by an intelligent will, by a friendly vigilance which gave one the same kind of feeling, inspired the same sort of thankfulness and calm as I had experienced in Saint-Loup's room, in the cell of that military cloister where so many eager-hearted and disciplined young men were in training for the day when, unhesitatingly and in the prime of their youth, they would consummate their sacrifice.

After the raid of two days earlier, when the sky had been more turbulent than the earth, it was now as quiet as the sea after a storm. But like the sea after a storm it had not regained absolute calm. Aeroplanes still climbed like rockets to join the stars, and searchlights cast slowly across the sky they transected what looked like a pale dust of stars, or wandering Milky Ways. Meanwhile the aeroplanes took up their places among the constellations and looking at those 'new stars' one might easily have believed oneself to be in another hemisphere.

M. de Charlus spoke to me of his admiration for these airmen and, as he could no longer prevent himself from giving as free a rein to his pro-Germanism as to his other penchants, while denying it as firmly as he denied the rest, continued: 'All the same, I must add that I have just as much admiration for the Germans who go up in their Gothas. As for the Zeppelins, think of the courage it must take! They are quite simply heroes. What difference can it make that their targets are civilians, when our batteries are shooting at them? Are you afraid of the Gothas and the artillery fire?' I confessed I was not, but I may perhaps have been wrong. No doubt, having developed the habit, out of idleness, of each day putting off my work until the day after, I thought that death could be dealt with in the same way. How can one be afraid of cannon fire when one is convinced that it is not going to hit one that day? Anyway, isolated thoughts about bombs being thrown, or about the possibility of death, added nothing tragic to the image I had formed of the passing German airships, until, from one of them, buffeted by winds and partly hidden from my gaze by the billowing mists of a troubled sky, from an aeroplane which, even though I knew it was murderous, I still imagined only to be stellar and heavenly, I had seen, one evening, the gesture of a bomb dropped down towards us. For the true reality of a danger is perceived only in that new thing, irreducible to what one already knows, which we call an impression and which is often, as in this instance, summed up in a line, a line describing an intention, a line which contains the latent potentiality of its distorting fulfilment, while on the Pont de la Concorde, all around the menacing, hunted aeroplane, as if they were reflections in the clouds of the fountains of the Champs-Élysées, the place de la Concorde and the Tuileries, the luminous water-jets of the searchlights curved across the sky, in lines equally full of intention, of the far-sighted and protective intentions of wise and powerful men to whom I was grateful, as I had been one night in the army quarters in Doncières, that they were prepared to use their might to watch over us with such beautiful precision.

The night was as beautiful as in 1914, when Paris had also been illuminated. The moonlight seemed like a soft, continuous, magnesium flare allowing one for a last time to take nocturnal pictures of these lovely groups of buildings like the place Vendôme or the place de la Concorde, to which the terror that I had of the shells which were perhaps about to destroy them gave by contrast a sort of fullness in their still-intact beauty, as if they were putting themselves forward, offering their defenceless architecture to be shot. 'Aren't you afraid?' repeated M. de Charlus. The Parisians don't realize. They say that Mme Verdurin has parties every day. I know that only from hearsay, I don't know anything about them myself, I have broken with them completely,' he added, lowering not only his eyes, as if a telegraph boy had passed, but also his head and shoulders, and raising his arm in the gesture that signifies, if not 'I wash my hands of them', then at least 'I can't tell you anything else' (even though I was not asking him anything). 'I know that Morel still goes there a great deal,' he said (this was the first time he had spoken about him again). 'It is said that he very much regrets the past, that he wants a reconciliation,' he added, demonstrating both the same credulity as the man of the Faubourg who says: 'A lot of people are saying that France is closer than ever to discussions with Germany, and even that the talks have already begun,' and the lover who fails to be convinced by the harshest rebuffs. 'In any case, if that is what he wants, he has only to say so, I am older than him, it is not up to me to make the first move.' And really there was no point in saying this, as it was so obvious. But also it was not even sincere, which is why one was so embarrassed for M. de Charlus, because one felt that by saying that it was not up to him to make the first move he was in fact making it, and was expecting me to offer to arrange the reconciliation.

Of course, I was familiar with the naïve or feigned credulity of people who love someone, or simply fail to be invited to someone's house, and impute to the person in question a desire which, despite tiresome solicitations, he has never manifested. But from the suddenly tremulous voice in which M. de Charlus uttered these words, from the uneasy look that flickered behind his eyes, I had the feeling that there was something other than ordinary insistence involved here. I was not mistaken, and I will recount straight away the two facts which subsequently showed me to have been right (I anticipate myself by a number of years for the second of these, which was posterior to the death of M. de Charlus. This did not occur until much later, and we shall have the opportunity of seeing him several times, considerably changed from the man we have known, at a time when he had completely forgotten about Morel.) As for the first of these events, it happened only two or three years after the evening on which I thus walked down the boulevards with M. de Charlus. About two years after this evening, I ran into Morel. Immediately I thought of M. de Charlus, and how pleased he would be to see the violinist again, and I pressed him to go and see him, even if only once. 'He has been good to you, I said to Morel, and now he is old, he may die, you ought to put your old quarrels aside and wipe out the traces of your feud.' Morel seemed to be entirely of my opinion about the desirability of making peace, but he none the less refused categorically to make even a single visit to M. de Charlus. 'You are wrong, I told him. Is it out of obstinacy, or laziness, or meanness, or misplaced vanity, or virtue (you can rest assured it won't be attacked), or coyness?' Then the violinist, his features distorted by an admission which must have been extremely hard to make, replied with a shudder: 'No, it's not anything like that; I don't give a damn about virtue. Meanness? On the contrary, I'm beginning to pity him. It is not coyness, there would be no point in that. Nor is it laziness, I have whole days with nothing to do but twiddle my thumbs. No, it's got nothing to do with any of those things, it's, don't mention this to anyone, I must be crazy to tell you, it's, it's . . . it's out of fear!' He began to tremble all over. I confessed that I did not understand him. 'No, don't ask me, let's not talk about it, you don't know him like I do, in fact I might say you don't know him at all. – But what harm can he do to you? And anyway he would be even less likely to do anything if there was no longer any bitterness between you. And you know that, fundamentally, he is very kind. – Good Lord, yes, I know how kind he is! And how considerate, and honest. But leave me alone, don't talk to me about it any more, I beg you, it makes me ashamed to say it, but I am afraid.'

The second event dates from after the death of M. de Charlus. I was brought a number of mementoes he had left me, along with a letter enclosed in three envelopes, written at least ten years before his death. At the time, he had been seriously ill, and had made his final arrangements, but then recovered his health, before later falling into the state in which we shall see him on the day of an afternoon party given by the Princesse de Guermantes – and the letter, placed in a strong-box with the objects he was bequeathing to various friends, had remained there for seven years, seven years in the course of which he had completely forgotten Morel. The letter, written in a fine, firm hand, took the following form:

My dear friend, the ways of Providence are inscrutable. Sometimes it uses the failing of a merely ordinary being to prevent a just man falling from his supereminence. You know Morel, whence he came, and the pinnacle to which I wanted to raise him, namely to my own level. You know that he preferred to return, not to the dust and ashes from which each man, for man is the true phoenix, may be reborn, but to the mud in which the viper crawls. His falling prevented worse befalling me. You know that my coat of arms contains the device of Our Lord himself: Inculcabis super leonem et aspidem,[65] *with a man represented as having beneath the soles of his feet, as heraldic support, a lion and a serpent. Now if I* *have been able thus to crush the lion that I am, it is thanks to the serpent and his prudence which a moment ago I too glibly called a failing, for the profound wisdom of the Gospel makes it a virtue, or at least a virtue for other people. Our serpent, whose hissings were once harmoniously modulated, when he had a charmer — himself much charmed, moreover — was not only musical and reptilian, he possessed to the point of cowardice this virtue, prudence, which I now take to be divine. It was this divine prudence that made him resist the appeals to come back and see me which I had others convey to him, and unless I confess this to you I shall have no peace in this world nor hope of forgiveness in the next. In this he was the instrument of divine wisdom, for I was resolved that he should not leave my house alive. One of the two of us had to disappear. I had decided to kill him. God counselled him prudence to save me from a crime. I do not doubt that the intercession of the Archangel Michael, my patron saint, played a large part in this and I beseech him to pardon me for having so neglected him over the years and for having responded so ill to the innumerable kindnesses he has shown me, most of all in my struggle against evil. I owe to this servant of God, and I say this in the fullness of my faith and of my understanding, the fact that the heavenly Father inspired Morel not to come. And so it is I now who am dying. Your faithfully devoted,* Semper idem,*

P. G. Charlus.*

Then I understood Morel's fear; the letter, of course, contained its share of literariness and pride. But the confession was true. And Morel knew better than I that the 'almost mad side' that Mme de Guermantes discerned in her brother-in-law was not confined, as I had previously thought, to those momentary exhibitions of superficial and ineffective rage.

But we must go back to where we were. I am walking down the boulevards beside M. de Charlus, who has just conceived the idea that I might be some sort of intermediary between himself and Morel. Seeing that I did not respond, he continued: 'Anyway, I don't know why he does not still play, people don't make music any more, on the grounds that there is a war on, but they dance, and go out to dine, and women invent things like "Amberine" for their skin. Parties fill up what may perhaps, if the Germans advance any further, be the last days of our Pompeii. And that is what will save it from frivolity. If the lava of some German Vesuvius (their naval guns are quite as terrible as a volcano) should come and surprise them at their toilet, preserving them for eternity in mid-gesture, children one day will learn from looking at pictures in their school-books showing Mme Mulé about to apply a final layer of powder before going to dine with a sister-in-law, or Sosthène de Guermantes finishing painting his false eyebrows. This will provide lecture material for the Brichots of the future, for the frivolity of a period, when ten centuries have elapsed, is a subject for the most serious erudition, especially if it has been preserved intact by a volcanic eruption or by the lava-like substances thrown up by bombardment. What documents for history in the future if asphyxiating gases like the fumes emitted by Vesuvius, or complete ruin of the sort that entombed Pompeii, should preserve intact all the imprudent households that have not yet sent their paintings and statues away to Bayonne! And, anyway, has it not been somewhat like that for the last year, fragments of Pompeii every evening, with people running to their cellars, not to fetch up some old bottle of Mouton-Rothschild or Saint-Émilion, but to hide along with themselves their most valuable possessions, like the priests of Herculaneum overtaken by death in the act of transporting the sacred vessels? Attachment to an object always brings death to its owner. Paris, I grant you, was not founded by Hercules, as Herculaneum was. But how many resemblances there are between them! And the ability that we have been granted to see these things so clearly is not unique to our epoch, every period has possessed it. While I may think that tomorrow we may meet the fate of the cities of Vesuvius, they in their turn felt threatened by the fate that befell the accursed cities of the Bible. On the walls of one house in Pompeii was discovered the revealing inscription: *Sodoma, Gomora.*' I do not know whether it was the name Sodom and the ideas it awoke in him, or the idea of bombardment, which made M. de Charlus for an instant raise his eyes to the heavens, but he soon brought them back to earth. 'I admire all the heroes of this war, he said. Think, my dear fellow, the English soldiers whom at the start of the war I rather thoughtlessly regarded as mere football players presumptuous enough to measure themselves against professionals – and what professionals! – well, in purely aesthetic terms they are quite simply Greek athletes, if you see what I mean, they are Greek, dear boy, they are Plato's young men, or better, Spartans. I have some friends who have been to Rouen where their camp is, and they have seen wonderful things, almost unimaginably wonderful. It is not Rouen any longer, it is another town. Obviously the old Rouen is still there, with the emaciated saints on the cathedral. And that is beautiful too, of course, but it is something different. And our *poilus*! I cannot tell you how delicious I find our *poilus*, the young lads from Paris, look, like that one walking along over there, with his knowing expression and his funny, wide-awake face. I often stop them and have a few minutes' chat with them, and how intelligent and sensible they are! And the country boys, how amusing and pleasant they are, with their rolled *r*s and their provincial dialects! I have always spent a lot of time in the country, sleeping in farmhouses, I can talk to them. But our admiration for the French must not make us disparage our enemies, that would only diminish us. You don't know what kind of soldier the German soldier is, you haven't seen him as I have marching past on parade, goose-stepping down *Unter den Linden*.' And returning to the ideal of manhood which he had outlined for me at Balbec, and which, over time, had taken on a more philosophical form in his mind, but also using absurd arguments which, at times, even when he had just been unusually intelligent, revealed the rather narrow outlook of a plain society gentleman, albeit an intelligent one: 'You see, he said to me, that superb, strapping lad, the Boche soldier, is a strong and healthy individual, who thinks only of his country's greatness. *Deutschland über alles*, which is not so stupid, given that we – while they were preparing themselves so manfully – we were mired in dilettantism.' For M. de Charlus, this word probably signified something analogous to litera-ture, for immediately, recollecting no doubt that I was fond of literature and had at one time intended to devote myself to it, he clapped me on the shoulder (taking the opportunity to lean on me so heavily that it hurt as much as did long ago, when I was doing my military service, the recoil of a '76 against my shoulder-blade), and said, as if to soften the criticism: 'Yes, we were mired in dilettantism, all of us, you too, you remember, like me you may say your *mea culpa*, we have been too dilettante.' Out of surprise at the reproach, lack of any quick repartee, deference towards my interlocutor and affection for his friendly kindness, I responded as if I also, as he urged, had reason to beat my breast, which was completely stupid, as I had not the least grain of dilettantism to reproach myself for. 'Well, he said, I must leave you' (the group which had escorted him at a distance having finally abandoned us), 'I must go and put myself to bed like a very old gentleman, especially as it seems that the war has changed all our habits, to use one of those foolish aphorisms that Norpois is so fond of.' I knew, however, that by going home M. de Charlus would not thereby be leaving the company of soldiers, as he had converted his house into a military hospital, and in doing this, I believe, had yielded far less to the demands of his imagination than to those of his kind heart.

It was a transparent night without a breath of wind; I imagined that the Seine flowing through its circular bridges, composites of the arches and their reflections, must look like the Bosporus. And, a symbol perhaps of the invasion predicted in the defeatism of M. de Charlus, or perhaps of the cooperation of our Muslim brothers with the armies of France, the moon, narrow and curved like a sequin, seemed to set the Parisian sky under the Oriental sign of the crescent.

For a few moments more, however, as he bade me farewell, he pressed my hand in a crushing grip, a peculiarly German habit among people of the Baron's sort, and continuing for several moments, as Cottard might have said, to knead my hand, it was as if M. de Charlus had wanted to restore to my joints a suppleness which they had never lost. In some blind men, touch compensates to some extent for the absence of sight. I am not quite sure which sense it was replacing here. He may have believed he was merely shaking my hand, as he doubtless believed he was merely seeing a Senegalese soldier who was passing in the darkness and did not deign to notice that he was being admired. But in both instances the Baron was mistaken, the intensity of contact and of gaze exceeding the bounds of propriety. 'Doesn't that embody all the Orient of Decamps, Fromentin, Ingres and Delacroix?' he asked, still immobilized by the passing Senegalese. 'You know, personally, things and people only ever interest me as a painter, or a philosopher. Besides, I am too old. But how unfortunate that, to complete the picture, one of us is not an odalisque!'

*

It was not the Orient of Decamps, nor even of Delacroix, that started to haunt my imagination after the Baron had left me, but the old Orient of the *Arabian Nights* which I had loved so much, and as I plunged deeper into the maze of these dark streets I thought of the Caliph Harun-al-Rashid seeking for adventure in the hidden quarters of Baghdad. The hot weather and my walk had made me thirsty, but all the bars were long since shut and, because of the petrol shortage, the few taxis I came across, driven by Levantines or negroes, did not even bother to respond to my signals. The only place where I might have been able to get a drink and to gather my strength for the walk home would have been a hotel.

But in the street where I found myself, some distance from the centre of the city, all the hotels, since the Gothas had started dropping their bombs on Paris, had closed. The same was true of almost all the shops, the shop-keepers, either because of a lack of staff or because they themselves had taken fright, having fled to the country, and left the usual handwritten notice announcing that they would reopen, although even that seemed problematic, at some date far in the future. The few establishments which had still managed to survive similarly announced that they would open only twice a week. The whole quarter exuded a sense of poverty, neglect and fear. I was therefore all the more surprised to see that among these abandoned houses there was one where life seemed, on the contrary, to have triumphed over fear and bankruptcy and where activity and wealth continued to flourish. Behind the closed shutters of each window the lights, dimmed on account of the police regulations, none the less revealed a total disregard for economy. And at every moment the door opened to allow some new visitor to enter or leave. It was a hotel which (because of the money its owners must have been making) must have aroused the jealousy of all the neighbouring shop-keepers; and my curiosity was also aroused when, some fifteen metres away from me, that is to say too far away for me to be able, in the profound darkness, to make out who it was, I saw an officer hurriedly leaving it.

Something about him struck me, all the same; it was not his face, which I did not see, nor his uniform, which was concealed under a heavy greatcoat, but the extraordinary disproportion between the number of different points through which his body passed and the small number of seconds it took for him to effect this exit, which looked like an attempted dash to safety on the part of somebody under siege. So that I was reminded, even if I did not actually recognize him – I will not say exactly of the frame, or the slenderness, or the gait, or the speed of Saint-Loup – but of the sort of ubiquity which was so peculiar to him. The soldier who was capable of occupying so many different positions in space in such a short time had disappeared down a side-street without seeing me, and I stood there wondering whether or not I should enter the hotel, the modest appearance of which made me doubt very much whether it was Saint-Loup who had left it.

Involuntarily I recalled that Saint-Loup had been unjustly implicated in a case of espionage because his name had been found on some letters captured on a German officer. He had, of course, been completely cleared by the military authorities. But in spite of myself I connected this memory with what I had just seen. Was this hotel being used as a meeting-place for spies? The officer had been gone only a few moments when I saw some private soldiers from various branches of the service, which added further to my suspicions. On the other hand, I was extremely thirsty. I would probably be able to find something to drink there, and I might also have an opportunity, despite my anxiety at the prospect, to try to assuage my curiosity.

I do not think, therefore, that it was curiosity about my encounter which made me decide to climb the short flight of steps, at the top of which the door to a sort of lobby was open, doubtless because of the heat. I thought at first that I would not be able to satisfy my new-found curiosity, for from the steps, where I remained in shadow, I saw several people come and ask for a room only to be told that there was not a single one left. There could be nothing against them, though, except that they were obviously not part of the nest of spies, for a common sailor who appeared a moment later was speedily given room number 28. From my unseen position in the darkness, I could observe several soldiers and two working-class men who were chatting peacefully in a stifling little room, brashly decorated with coloured pictures of women cut out of illustrated magazines and reviews. These men, chatting peacefully, displayed undeniably patriotic views: 'In the end it doesn't matter, you have to do what your mates do,' said one. 'Oh, you can be quite sure I don't intend to get killed,' another, who, from what I could gather, was leaving the next day for a dangerous position, replied to some expression of good wishes which I had not heard. 'Blimey, at twenty-two, after just six months, it would be a bit steep,' he exclaimed in a voice that revealed, even more than the desire to live for a long time, a consciousness of the justice of his reasoning, as if the fact that he was only twenty-two had to give him a better chance of not being killed, and as if it were quite impossible that such a thing might happen. 'It's amazing in Paris, said another; you wouldn't think there was a war on. What about you, Julot, are you still going to join up? – Of course I'm going to join up, I want to get in a few shots at those dirty Boches. – But that Joffre, he's just a man who sleeps with politicians' wives, he's never done anything himself. – It's awful to say things like that,' said a slightly older airman, and turning to the workman who had just made the statement: 'I'd advise you not to talk like that in the front line, you'd soon get done in by the *poilus*.' The banality of the conversation did not make me very keen to hear more of it, and I was about to go in or go back down the steps when I was jolted out of my indifference by an exchange which made me shudder: 'It's amazing the boss isn't back yet. Christ, I don't know where he'll find chains at this time of night. – But the guy's already tied up, isn't he? – Sure he is, up to a point. But if I was tied up like that I'd be able to undo my chains. – But they're padlocked. – Of course they're padlocked, but it's not impossible to open a padlock. What it is, the chains aren't long enough. – Don't tell me what it is, I was beating him all last night till my hands were covered in blood. – Is it you that's beating him tonight? – No, not me. It's Maurice. But it'll be me on Sunday, the boss promised me.' I realized now why the sturdy arm of the sailor had been needed. If they had turned away peaceable citizens, it was not because the hotel was a nest of spies. A terrible crime was about to be committed, unless somebody arrived in time to reveal it and have the culprits arrested. And yet the whole thing, in this peaceful but ominous night, had the appearance of a dream or a fairy-tale, and so it was both with the pride of a champion of justice and the delight of a poet that I resolutely entered the hotel.

I touched my hat lightly, and the people in the room, without getting up, responded more or less politely to my greeting. 'Could you please tell me who I should speak to? I should like a room, and something to drink sent up to it. — You'd better wait a minute, the boss has gone out. — But the owner's here, he's upstairs, put in one of the men who had been talking. — But you know he can't be disturbed. — Do you think they'll give me a room? — I should think so. — 43 must be free,' said the young man who was sure he would not be killed because he was twenty-two. And he moved a little way along the sofa to make room for me. 'Perhaps someone could open the window a bit, it's very smoky in here!' said the airman; and indeed each of them had a pipe or a cigarette. 'Yes, but then close the shutters first, remember it's forbidden to show any light because of the Zeppelins. — There won't be any more Zeppelins over. There was even something in the papers about them all being shot down. — Won't be any more over, won't be any more over, what do you know about it? When you've had fifteen months at the front like me, and shot down your fifth Boche aeroplane, then you can talk. You don't want to believe the papers. They were over Compiègne yesterday, they killed a mother and two children. — A mother and two children!' said the young man who hoped not to be killed, with fiery eyes and a look of deep pity on his lively, open and extremely likeable face. 'There's been no news of big Julot. His "godmother" hasn't had a letter from him for eight days, and that's the first time he's gone so long without writing. — Who is his "godmother"? — She's the woman who looks after the public convenience just past the Olympia. — Are they sleeping together? — What are you on about? She's a married woman, very respectable. She sends him money every week out of the kindness of her heart. She's really nice, she is. — So you know big Julot, do you? — Do I know him!' rejoined the young man of twenty-two with enthusiasm. 'He's one of my best and closest friends. There aren't many I'd rate as high as him, he's a good mate, he'd do anything for you. You're dead right, it'd be a disaster if something's happened to him.' Somebody suggested a game of dice, and from the feverish haste with which the young man of twenty-two threw the dice and shouted out the results, his eyes starting from his head, it was easy to see that he had a gambler's temperament. I did not catch the next thing that was said, but he exclaimed in a deeply pitying voice: 'Julot a pimp! You mean he says he's a pimp. But he couldn't pimp even if he tried. I've seen him with my own eyes paying his girl, actually paying her. I mean I'm not saying that Algerian Jeanne didn't use to give him something, but never more than five francs, and she was working in a brothel, she was earning over fifty francs a day. Giving him just five francs, how stupid can a guy be! And now she's at the front, it's a hard life, granted, but she can make as much as she wants. And she doesn't send him a thing. Huh, a pimp, Julot? There's plenty could call themselves pimps at that rate. Not only is he not a pimp, but if you want my opinion, he's a bloody fool.' The oldest of the group, whom, doubtless because of his age, the manager had charged with maintaining a degree of respectability, had gone to the lavatory for a moment, and heard only the end of this conversation. But he could not help looking over at me and appeared visibly upset at the effect it must have had on me. Without addressing himself specifically to the young man of twenty-two, although it was he who had just been expounding this theory of venal love, he said, in a general way: 'You're talking too much, and it's too loud, the window is open, and some people are asleep at this time of night. You know perfectly well that if the boss came back and heard you talking like that, he wouldn't like it.'

At that precise moment we heard the door open, and everybody fell silent, thinking it was the manager, but it was only a foreign chauffeur, who was warmly welcomed by everybody. But seeing a splendid watch-chain prominently displayed on the chauffeur's jacket, the young man of twenty-two threw him an interrogative and amused glance, followed by a frown and a severe wink in my direction. And I understood that the first look meant: 'What's that? Did you steal it? Congratulations.' And the second: 'Don't say anything, because of this bloke we don't know.' Suddenly the manager came in, carrying several metres of heavy iron chain, enough to chain up several convicts, sweating, and said: 'What a weight! If you weren't all so lazy, I wouldn't have to go and get them myself.' I told him that I wanted a room. 'Just for a few hours, I couldn't find a cab and I'm feeling a little ill. But I would like something to drink sent up. — Pierrot, go down to the cellar and get some cassis, and tell them to get number 43 ready. There's number 7 ringing again. They say they're ill. Ill my foot, I think they've been taking coke, they look half-shot. Better kick them out. Has 22 had clean sheets? Good. There goes 7 again, run and see to it. Come on, Maurice, what are you standing about for? You know someone's waiting for you, get up to 14b. And hurry up about it.' And Maurice left hastily, following the manager, who, a bit annoyed about my seeing the chains, disappeared with them. 'How come you're so late?' the young man of twenty-two asked the chauffeur. 'What do you mean, late? I'm an hour early. But it's too hot for walking about. I'm not meant to be meeting him until midnight. — Who have you come for then? — For the lovely Pamela,' said the oriental chauffeur, whose smile revealed his fine white teeth. 'Ah!' said the young man of twenty-two.

Soon I was taken up to Room 43, but the room was so unpleasantly airless and my curiosity was so great that, once I'd drunk my cassis, I went downstairs again, then, a new idea having struck me, I went back up, past the floor that Room 43 was on, as far as the top floor. Suddenly, from a room set apart from the others at the end of a corridor, I thought I heard stifled moans. I walked quickly in their direction and placed my ear to the door. 'I beg you, mercy, mercy, have pity, untie me, don't hit me so hard, said a voice. I'll crawl, I'll kiss your feet, I shan't do it again. Have pity. — No, you piece of filth, replied another voice, and if you scream and drag yourself about on your knees like that, you'll be tied to the bed, and there'll be no mercy,' and I heard the sound of a whip, probably one with nails to give it extra sharpness, for it was followed by cries of pain. Then I noticed that the room had a small round side-window and that somebody had forgotten to draw the curtain behind it; advancing stealthily through the darkness, I slid up to the window and there, chained to a bed like Prometheus to his rock, receiving the blows which Maurice was delivering with a whip which was indeed studded with nails, I saw, already running with blood, and covered in bruises which proved that the flogging was not happening for the first time, there, right in front of me, I saw M. de Charlus.

Suddenly the door opened and somebody came in who fortunately did not see me. It was Jupien. He approached the Baron respectfully and with a smile of complicity: 'So, you don't need me?' The Baron asked Jupien to send Maurice out of the room for a moment. Jupien did so without a second thought. 'Nobody can hear us, can they?' said the Baron to Jupien, who assured him that nobody could. The Baron knew that Jupien, although as intelligent as a man of letters, had no practical sense at all, and was always talking about people in their presence, dropping hints in ways which deceived nobody and using nicknames which everybody recognized.

'Just a second,' interrupted Jupien, who had heard a bell ring in room number 3. It was a Deputy from *Action libérale*,[66] who was leaving. Jupien did not need to look at the bell-board, for he recognized the ring, as in fact the Deputy came every day after lunch. He had been forced to change his time on this occasion, as his daughter's wedding had taken place at noon at Saint-Pierre-de-Chaillot. He had therefore come in the evening but was anxious to leave early because of his wife, who became worried very easily when he was late home, especially in these days of bombardment. Jupien liked to show him out himself in order to demonstrate his deference for the title of 'honourable member', but he had no personal interest in him. For although the Deputy, who repudiated the extreme positions of the *Action française*[67] (and anyway would have been incapable of understanding a word of Charles Maurras or Léon Daudet), was well in with the ministers, whom he flattered by inviting them to his shoots, Jupien would not have dared to ask him for the slightest support in his troubles with the police. He knew that, if he had taken the risk of mentioning it to the well-provided but pusillanimous legislator, he would not only not have avoided even the most harmless raid, but would instantly have lost the most generous of his clients. After having escorted the Deputy as far as the door, where he pulled his hat down over his eyes, turned up his collar, and glided away with the same slickness that he employed in his electoral addresses, hoping thereby to hide his features, Jupien went back upstairs to M. de Charlus, to whom he said: 'That was M. Eugène.' At Jupien's establishment, as in sanatoriums, people were known only by their first names, although to satisfy the curiosity of the regular visitors, or to enhance the prestige of the house, their real names were generally added in a whisper. Sometimes, however, Jupien was unaware of the real identity of a client, and would imagine, and say, that he was some stockbroker or nobleman or artist, short-lived mistakes that amused those who were given the wrong name, and in the end would have to resign himself to the fact that he still did not know who M. Victor was. So, to please the Baron, Jupien would habitually reverse the procedure proper to certain sorts of gathering. 'May I introduce M. Lebrun?' (then, in a whisper: 'He likes to be known as M. Lebrun but he is really a Russian Grand Duke'). Jupien, by contrast, felt that it was not quite enough to introduce M. de Charlus to a milkman. He would murmur to him with a wink: 'He works as a milkman, but really he's one of the most dangerous villains in Belleville' (the salacious tone in which Jupien said the word 'villain' was something to hear). And if these references were insufficient, he would attempt to add a few 'citations'. 'He's been convicted several times for house-breaking and theft, he's been in Fresnes for assaulting (the same salacious note) people in the street and practically crippling them, and he was in the punishment battalion in Africa. He killed his sergeant.'

The Baron even bore a slight grudge against Jupien because he knew that in this house, which he had instructed his factotum to buy for him and to manage through a subordinate, everybody, as a result of the tactlessness of Mlle d'Oloron's uncle, was more or less aware of his identity and his name (though many thought it was only a nickname, which they then distorted by mispronouncing it, so that their own stupidity, rather than Jupien's discretion, had become the Baron's protection). But he found it simpler to allow himself to be reassured by Jupien's assurances, and, soothed by the knowledge that they could not be heard, the Baron said to him: 'I did not want to say anything in front of that boy, who is very nice and who does the best he can. But he is not rough enough. I like his face, but when he calls me a piece of filth, it's as if he were just reciting a lesson. – Oh no, nobody has said a word to him,' replied Jupien, not seeing the improbability of this assertion. 'What's more, he was involved in the murder of a concierge at La Villette. – Ah! that's more interesting, said the Baron with a smile. – But I tell you what, I do have the ox-killer here, the slaughterhouse man, and he looks quite similar. He just happened to drop in. Would you like to try him? – Oh yes, I certainly would.' I saw the slaughterhouse man enter the room, and he did indeed look a little like Maurice, but the odd thing was that both of them possessed something which, although I had never consciously noticed it, I now recognized as being typical of Morel's appearance; they bore a resemblance, if not to Morel as I had seen him, at least to a face which somebody seeing Morel with eyes other than mine might have put together out of his features. The minute that I had formed, out of the features borrowed from my memories of Morel, this mental sketch of the way that he might appear to somebody else, I realized that both these young men, one of whom was a jeweller's assistant and the other a hotel employee, were in some vague way substitutes for Morel. Was I to conclude from this that M. de Charlus, at least in one aspect of his loves, was always faithful to a specific type and that the desire which had made him choose these two men one after another was the same as that which had made him stop Morel on the station platform at Doncières; that all three somewhat resembled the ephebe whose form, intagliated on the sapphire of M. de Charlus's eyes, gave his expression that curious quality which had alarmed me so much the first day in Balbec? Or that, his love for Morel having modified the ideal type he was searching for, to console himself for Morel's absence he sought out men who looked like him? One other possibility that occurred to me was that perhaps, in spite of appearances, there had never been anything but a relation of friendship between Morel and himself, and that M. de Charlus persuaded young men who bore some resemblance to Morel to come to Jupien's so that he could have the illusion, with them, of taking his pleasure with Morel himself. Thinking of everything that M. de Charlus had done for Morel, this possibility would admittedly have seemed unlikely, if one were not also aware that love not only drives us to make the greatest sacrifices for the person we love, but also sometimes drives us to the sacrifice of our desire itself, which moreover is all the harder to satisfy when the person we love senses that we love them with an unreciprocated intensity.

Another thing that makes this possibility less unlikely than at first it seems (even though it probably does not correspond to the reality)

lies in the nervous temperament and the profoundly passionate character of M. de Charlus, in which he resembled Saint-Loup, and which
may have played the same part at the outset of his relations with Morel,
in a more decent and negative way, that it did at the start of his
nephew's relationship with Rachel. Relations with a woman one loves
(and this also goes for the love of a young man) may remain platonic
for reasons other than the woman's virtue or the unsensual nature of
the love that she inspires. It may be that the lover, made over-impatient
by the extremity of his love, cannot wait with a sufficient pretence of
indifference for the moment when he will obtain his desire. He constantly returns to the attack, writes incessantly to the woman he loves,
tries all the time to see her, she refuses, he is in despair. At that point
she understands: if she grants him her company and her friendship,
these will seem such substantial blessings to him who thought he would
never attain them, that she can refrain from giving him anything else,
and take advantage of a moment when he can no longer bear not to
see her, when he wants to end the war at any price, to impose upon
him a peace whose prime condition will be the platonic nature of their
relationship. Furthermore, for the whole of the time leading up to this
treaty, the lover, always anxious, constantly waiting for a letter, or a
look, has ceased to think about physical possession, the desire for
which had tormented him to begin with, but which has become worn
out with waiting and been replaced by needs of a different sort which,
if not satisfied, are even more painful. Then the pleasure, which at the
outset one had hoped to obtain from caresses, one receives later recast
in the form of friendly words, promises of her presence, which, after
the pangs of uncertainty, sometimes simply after a look from eyes
clouded with coldness, making her seem so distant that one thinks one
will never see her again, bring with them a delicious easing of tension.
Women divine all this, and know that they can afford the luxury of
never giving themselves to men of whose incurable desire for them, if
they were too agitated to hide it from them at the beginning, they
have become aware. The woman is only too happy that, without giving
anything, she receives much more than she usually gets when she gives
herself. In this way, these temperamental men come to believe in the
virtue of their idols. And the halo they place upon them is thus a

product, albeit as we have seen an indirect one, of the extremity of their love. The woman then has something of the same effect as occurs in a mechanical way with unwittingly crafty drugs, such as morphine or the soporifics. It is not the people to whom they bring the pleasure of sleep or genuine well-being who find them absolutely necessary, not these who would pay anything for them or exchange them for all the sick person possesses, but those other sick people (who may indeed be the same individuals, having, after several years, become irretrievably altered), for whom the drug no longer brings sleep, to whom it gives no thrill of pleasure, but who, as long as they do not have it, are prey to an agitation which they want to end at any price, even if it means their death.

For M. de Charlus, whose situation, by and large, allowing for the slight differentiation due to identity of sex, falls under the general laws of love, it did not matter that he belonged to a family older than the Capets,[68] that he was rich, that he was sought after in vain by smart society while Morel was nobody, it would have been no use saying to Morel, as he had said to me: 'I am a prince, I have your interests at heart,' Morel still had the upper hand so long as he did not want to surrender. And for him not to want to, it was perhaps enough that he felt loved. The horror that grand people have for the snobs who strive so hard to make their acquaintance is also felt by masculine men for inverts, and by women for every man who is too much in love with them. M. de Charlus not only possessed every advantage himself, but would have offered enormous advantages to Morel. But it is possible that all this was unavailing against will-power. In which case there would have been a similarity between M. de Charlus and the Germans, with whom in fact by descent he belonged, and who, in the war as it was progressing at that moment, were indeed, as the Baron was rather too fond of repeating, victorious on all fronts. But what good were these victories to them when, after each one, they found the Allies more determined than ever to refuse the one thing that they, the Germans, had hoped to obtain, namely peace and reconciliation? Napoleon, too, entered Russia and magnanimously invited the authorities to meet with him. But nobody came.

I went back downstairs and into the little ante-room where Maurice, uncertain whether he would be called back, and whom Jupien had told to wait just in case, was in the middle of a game of cards with one of his friends. There was a great deal of excitement about a *croix de guerre* which had been found on the floor: nobody knew who had lost it and to whom it should be returned to prevent the owner's being punished. Then there was talk about the generosity of an officer who had been killed trying to save his batman. 'You see? Some rich people are all right. I wouldn't mind getting myself killed for someone like that,' said Maurice, who obviously performed his terrible fustigations of the Baron only out of mechanical habit, a neglected education, need of money and a preference for getting it in a way that was meant to be less trouble than working, but which may in fact have been worse. But, as M. de Charlus had feared, he was perhaps a kind-hearted young man, as well, it seemed, as admirably brave. He practically had tears in his eyes as he spoke of the officer's death, and the young man of twenty two was no less upset. 'Yes, they're good blokes all right. Poor sods like us haven't got much to lose, but a gentleman who's got loads of servants, who can go out for fancy drinks at six o'clock every day, that's pretty wonderful! You can laugh if you like, but when you see blokes like that dying it really gets to you. God shouldn't let rich blokes like that die, apart from anything else they're too useful to us workers. A death like that, you want to kill all the Boches, every single one; and as for what they did at Louvain, and cutting the hands off little kids! No, I don't know, I'm no better than anyone else, but I'd sooner refuse and get a bullet in the head than obey orders from barbarians like them; because they aren't men, they're just barbarians, there's no other word for them.' All these young men were patriots really. Only one, who had a slight arm-wound and was soon going to have to return to the front, was not quite so enthusiastic as the others, saying: 'It wasn't the right sort of wound, worse luck' (the sort that gets you discharged as unfit), in the same way as Mme Swann used once to say: 'I've somehow managed to catch this tiresome influenza.'

The door opened to re-admit the chauffeur, who had gone out for a moment to get a breath of fresh air. 'What, finished already? That didn't take long,' he said catching sight of Maurice, whom he had thought would still be busy beating the person they had nicknamed

The Man in Chains, an allusion to a newspaper that was appearing at the time.[69] 'It may not seem long to you, out there in the fresh air,' replied Maurice, ruffled at being seen to have failed to give satisfaction upstairs. 'But if you'd had to beat someone as hard as you could in this heat, like I have! If it wasn't for the fifty francs I get. – But he's well-spoken, you can see he's educated. Did he say it'll soon be over? – He says we'll never be able to beat them, it'll end without either side winning. – For God's sake, he must be a Boche then . . . – I told you before, you're talking too loud,' said the older man to the others, noticing me. 'Have you finished with the room? – Oh, shut up, you're not in charge here. – Yes, I've finished, I've come to pay. – It'd be better if you paid the boss. Maurice, go and find him. – But I don't want to put you to any trouble. – It's no trouble.' Maurice went upstairs and came back saying: 'The boss is just coming down.' I gave him two francs for his pains. He blushed with pleasure. 'Oh, thanks very much. I'll send it to my brother who's a prisoner. No, he's not too badly off. It depends a lot on what camp you're in.'

While this was going on, two very elegant clients, wearing white tie and tails beneath their overcoats – two Russians, I thought from their slight accent – were standing in the doorway and deliberating whether or not they should enter. It was clearly the first time they had been there, somebody must have told them about the place, and they seemed torn between desire, temptation and very cold feet. One of them – a good-looking young man – kept saying every few moments to the other, with a smile that was half enquiring and half intended to persuade: 'Well? After all, what does it matter?' But although he may have meant by that that after all the consequences did not matter, it is likely that it mattered more than he let on, for the remark was followed not by any motion of entering but by another glance towards his friend, followed by the same smile and the same *after all, what does it matter?* This *after all, what does it matter?* was a very good example of that wonderful language, so different from the one we normally speak, in which emotion deflects what we wanted to say and in its place brings into being a quite different phrase, which emerges from an unknown lake where all these expressions live that are unrelated to thought but which for precisely that reason reveal what we are thinking. I remember how once Albertine, just as Françoise, whom we had not heard, was coming into the room at a moment when my lover was completely naked in my arms, said without thinking, in an attempt to warn me: 'Oh heavens, here's the lovely Françoise!' Françoise, whose sight was no longer very good and who was merely going across the room at some distance from us, would probably not have noticed anything. But the unfamiliar words 'the lovely Françoise', which Albertine had never uttered before in her life, themselves betrayed their origin, she sensed that they had been garnered randomly by emotion, did not need to see anything to understand everything, and went out muttering in her dialect the word 'poutana'.[70] And another time, much later, when Bloch, by then a family man, had married off one of his daughters to a Catholic, an ill-bred gentleman said to her that he thought he had heard that she was the daughter of a Jew and asked her his name. The young woman, who had been Mlle Bloch since her birth, replied, pronouncing it in the German way, just as the Duc de Guermantes might have done, 'Bloch' (pronouncing the *ch* not as a *c* or a *k* but with a Germanic *ch*).

But to go back to the scene in the hotel (the two Russians having finally decided to take the plunge: 'after all, what does it matter?'), the manager had still not arrived when Jupien came in to complain that people were talking too loud and that the neighbours would complain. But when he saw me he stopped in amazement. 'Outside on the landing, all of you.' But as they were all jumping up, I said to him: 'It would be easier if these young men stayed here and you and I went outside for a moment.' He followed me, extremely flustered. I explained why I was there. Clients could be heard asking the manager whether he couldn't introduce them to a footman, a choirboy or a black chauffeur. Every occupation interested these old maniacs, as well as troops from every branch of the services, and from all the Allied nations. Some asked especially for Canadians, influenced perhaps unwittingly by the charm of an accent so slight that it is difficult to know whether it comes from an older France or from England. Because of their kilts, and because certain lacustrine dreams are often associated with these desires, the Scots were at a premium. And as every sort of madness derives its particular traits from circumstances, if indeed it is not intensified by them, one old man, whose curiosity had doubtless been assuaged on every other front, was insistently asking whether it might be possible for him to meet a disabled soldier. We heard slow footsteps on the stairs. With his natural indiscretion Jupien could not help telling me that it was the Baron who was coming down, and that whatever happened he must not see me, but that if I wanted to go into the bedroom adjacent to the lobby where the young men were, he would open the fanlight, a method he had devised so that the Baron could see and hear without being seen, and which, he said, he would turn to my advantage against him. 'Only don't move.' And having pushed me into the darkness, he left me. There was no other room he could give me, anyway, his hotel, despite the war, being full. The one I had just left had been taken by the Vicomte de Courvoisier, who, having managed to leave the Red Cross at —— for two days, had come to relax in Paris for an hour before going on to join the Vicomtesse at the Château de Courvoisier, where he would say that he had not been able to catch the fast train. He never suspected that M. de Charlus was a few metres away from him, any more than the latter suspected his presence, never having encountered his cousin at Jupien's establishment, where even Jupien was unaware of the Vicomte's carefully concealed identity.

The Baron soon came in, walking with some difficulty on account of his injuries, even though he obviously must have been used to them. Although he had had his pleasure and came in only to give Maurice the money he owed him, he let his eyes travel, with a tender and curious gaze, around the whole circle of young men, clearly intending to enjoy with each of them the pleasure of a few quite platonic but lovingly prolonged words. And once again, in the spirited frivolity he displayed in the face of this harem which seemed almost to intimidate him, I recognized that manner of moving his body and tossing his head, those rarefied glances, which had struck me on the evening of his first appearance at La Raspelière, graces inherited from a grandmother whom I had not known and which in his everyday life were concealed on his face by more masculine expressions, but which would be caused to blossom there coquettishly, in certain circumstances where he was anxious to please an inferior audience, by the desire to appear a *grande dame*.

Jupien had commended them to the Baron's good favour by swearing to him that they were all Belleville pimps and that they would sell their own sisters for a few francs. And in fact what Jupien said was simultaneously both untrue and true. Better, and less insensitive than he claimed to the Baron, they did not belong to a race of savages. But the people who believed them to be villains none the less talked to them with complete honesty, as if these terrifying beings were bound to do the same. A sadist may believe he is with a murderer, but his purity of mind is not thereby altered, and he will still be amazed by the way these people lie, who are not murderers at all, but simply trying to turn an easy 'buck', and whose fathers or mothers or sisters are alternately brought back to life and killed off again, as they contradict themselves in conversations with the client whom they are trying to please. The client, in his naïvety, and with his arbitrary conception of the gigolo, is stunned, for while he is delighted by the number of murders he believes him to be guilty of, he is horrified by each lie or contradiction he discovers in his words.

Everybody seemed to know him, and M. de Charlus paused for a long while with each one, talking to them in what he took to be their own language, both out of a pretentious affectation of local colour and because he took a masochistic pleasure in mixing with the world of villainy. 'You, you're disgusting, I saw you outside the Olympia with two scrubbers. Trying to get hold of a few readies, I expect. That's the way you cheat on me.' Fortunately for the man to whom these words were addressed, he did not have time to declare that he would never have accepted 'readies' from a woman, a fact which would have diminished the Baron's excitement, and reserved his protest for the concluding phrase, saying: 'Oh no, I don't cheat on you.' This remark gave keen pleasure to M. de Charlus, and as, in spite of himself, the kind of intelligence which was naturally his emerged from beneath the façade he affected, he turned to Jupien: 'It is nice of him to say that. And how well he says it! One might almost think it was the truth. Anyway, what does it matter whether it is the truth or not since he manages to make me believe it? What pretty little eyes he's got. Look, I'm going to give you two big kisses for your trouble, dear boy. You will think of me in the trenches. It's not too bad there, is it? – Blimey,

there are some days when a grenade goes past your ear . . .' And
the young man proceeded to imitate the sound of the grenade, the
aeroplanes, etc. 'But you just have to get on with it like everyone else,
we'll carry on right to the end, you can count on that. − To the end!
If only one knew what the end will be!' said the Baron melancholically,
being a 'pessimist'. 'You didn't see what Sarah Bernhardt said in the
papers: "France will go on to the end. The French will give up their
lives, down to the last man." − I do not doubt for a moment that the
French will fight bravely to the last man,' said M. de Charlus as if it
were the simplest thing in the world, and although he himself had no
intention of doing anything at all. But by saying it he was trying to
correct the impression of pacifism he made when he forgot himself. 'I
do not doubt it, but I do wonder how far *Madame* Sarah Bernhardt is
qualified to speak in the name of France. But I don't think I know this
charming, this delightful young man,' he added, catching sight of
another, whom he did not recognize or perhaps had never seen before.
He greeted him as he might have greeted a prince at Versailles, and,
in order to make the most of the chance of some free supplementary
pleasure, just as when I was little and my mother had completed an
order at Boissier's or Gouache's,[71] I would take, at the invitation of
one of the ladies behind the counter, a sweet from one of the glass jars
between which they held sway, taking the hand of the charming young
man and pressing it in his for several moments, in the Prussian manner,
gazing at him with a smile for the interminable length of time it once
took photographers to pose you when the light was bad: 'I am charmed,
Sir, enchanted to make your acquaintance. He's got lovely hair,' he
said, turning to Jupien. Then he went over to Maurice to give him his
fifty francs, but first, putting his arm round his waist: 'You never told
me that you'd knifed an old concierge in Belleville.' And M. de Charlus
moaned with rapture and brought his face close to Maurice's: 'Oh! M.
le Baron,' said the gigolo, whom they had forgotten to warn, 'how
could you think such a thing?' Either the story was in fact false, or, if
it were true, its perpetrator none the less thought it abominable and
something to be denied. 'Me lay hands on a fellow-creature? On a
Boche, yes, because that's war, but not on a woman, let alone an old
woman!' This declaration of virtuous principles affected the Baron like

a douche of cold water and he moved abruptly back from Maurice, still giving him his money, but with the disappointed look of a man who has been cheated, who pays because he does not want to make a fuss, but is not happy about it. The bad impression received by the Baron was further aggravated by the way in which the beneficiary thanked him, as he said: 'I'll send this to the old dears and save a bit of it for our kid at the front.' These touching sentiments disappointed M. de Charlus almost as much as their rather conventional peasant expression irritated him. Jupien did sometimes warn them that they ought to be more perverse. Then one or other of them, as if confessing to something diabolically evil, would venture to say: 'I tell you something, Baron, you won't believe this, but when I was a kid I used to look through the keyhole and watch my parents making love. Pretty wicked, eh? You look as if you think I'm having you on, but I swear to you it's the honest truth.' And M. de Charlus would be driven both to despair and to exasperation by this contrived attempt at perversity, which resulted only in revealing so much stupidity and so much innocence. In fact even the most determined thief or murderer would not have satisfied him, for they do not talk about their crimes; and anyway sadists – however kind they may be, in fact the kinder they are – have a thirst for evil which villains acting in pursuit of other goals are incapable of satisfying.

The young man, realizing his mistake too late, proclaimed in vain that he could not stand coppers and even dared say to the Baron: 'Give us a meet, then,' but the spell had vanished. It rang false, like passages in books where the author has tried to write slang. It was to no avail that the young man detailed all the 'filthy things' that he did with his wife. M. de Charlus was merely struck by how insignificant these filthy things were. Nor was this just insincerity on his part. There is nothing more limited than pleasure and vice. In that sense, changing the meaning of the phrase slightly, it can truly be said that we are always going round in the same vicious circle.

If M. de Charlus was thought to be a prince, there was equally a great deal of sadness in the establishment at the death of someone of whom the gigolos would say: 'I don't know his name, but it seems he is a Baron,' and who was none other than the Prince de Foix (the father of Saint-Loup's friend). Believed by his wife to spend long hours at his club, in reality he passed his time chatting at Jupien's, gossiping with the low-life about fashionable society. He was a tall, good-looking man, like his son. Strangely enough, M. de Charlus, probably because he had always encountered him socially, was unaware that he shared his tastes. It was even said that at one time they had been directed towards his own son, when he was still at school (and the friend of Saint-Loup), which was probably not true. On the contrary, very well informed about kinds of behaviour which most people are unaware of, he kept a close eye on the company kept by his son. One day, when a man, and a man moreover of humble origins, had followed the young Prince de Foix to his father's house, where he had thrown a note through the window, the father had picked it up. But the follower, although not, aristocratically speaking, part of the same world as M. de Foix the father, did share it from another point of view. He had no difficulty in finding, among their mutual accomplices, an intermediary who procured M. de Foix's silence by demonstrating that it was the young man who had himself provoked this bare-faced action by an elderly man. And this was quite possible. For the Prince de Foix had been able successfully to preserve his son from contact with bad company, but not from heredity. But this was an aspect of the young Prince de Foix, as of his father, of which the people in their circle remained ignorant, although in other circles he was as extreme as anybody.

'How natural he is! You'd never think he was a Baron,' said several of the regular customers after M. de Charlus had left, accompanied as far as the street by Jupien, to whom the Baron complained at length about the young man's virtuousness. From the displeasure evinced by Jupien, who ought to have schooled the young man in advance, it was clear that the make-believe murderer was about to receive a very severe telling-off. 'It is the complete opposite of what you told me,' added the Baron so that Jupien might learn the lesson for a future occasion. 'He seems very good-natured, he shows feelings of respect for his family. – He doesn't get on with his father, though, objected Jupien, they live together, but they work in different bars.' This was clearly an insubstantial crime compared with murder, but Jupien had been caught off-guard. The Baron said nothing more because, while he wanted his pleasures prepared for him, he also wanted to retain the illusion that they were not prepared. 'He really is a crook, he told you all that stuff to mislead you, you're too gullible,' Jupien added, in an attempt to vindicate himself which only hurt M. de Charlus's pride.

'They say he gets through a million francs a day,' said the young man of twenty-two, seeing nothing improbable in this assertion. Shortly afterwards, we heard, a short distance away, the sound of the car which had come to fetch M. de Charlus. At the same time, I noticed somebody whom I took to be an elderly lady, in a black skirt, stepping slowly into the room at the side of a soldier who had evidently emerged with her from an adjoining room. I soon realized my mistake: it was a priest. It was that very rare thing, almost unheard of in France, a rotten priest. The soldier was obviously teasing his companion about the fact that his conduct suited ill with his cloth, because the latter, with an air of gravity, raising a finger to his hideous face like a doctor of divinity, said sententiously: 'What can you expect, I'm no' (and I expected him to say 'saint') 'angel.' He was on the point of leaving, and said good-bye to Jupien who, having seen the Baron out, had just come back upstairs, but absent-mindedly the rotten priest forgot to pay for his room. Jupien, whose quick wit never deserted him, shook the collection box into which he put each client's contribution, rattling it, and said: 'Towards the expenses of worship, M. l'Abbé!' The ugly character apologized, dropped in his coin, and disappeared.

Jupien came to find me in the dark lair where I had been lurking, not daring to move. 'Come into the vestibule for a moment where my young men are sitting, while I go up and shut the room; you've taken a room, so it's perfectly natural.' The manager was there, and I paid him. At that moment a young man in a dinner-jacket came in and asked the manager, with an air of authority: 'May I have Léon tomorrow morning at a quarter to eleven instead of eleven o'clock, as I'm lunching in town? – That depends, replied the manager, on how long the abbé keeps him.' This response appeared not to satisfy the young man in evening dress, who seemed to be on the point of cursing the abbé, but his anger took a new course when he caught sight of me; going straight up to the manager: 'Who's that? What is the meaning of this?' he asked in a voice of quiet fury. The manager, very embarrassed, explained that my presence was of no significance, that I had taken a room. The young man in evening dress seemed to be entirely unappeased by this explanation. He continued to repeat: 'This is extremely disagreeable, things like this ought not to happen; you know I hate it, and you'll be lucky if I ever set foot here again.' The implementation of this threat did not however appear to be imminent, for he went off angrily, but still advising that Léon should try to be free at a quarter to eleven, or if possible at half past ten. Jupien came back to find me, and went down with me into the street.

'I wouldn't like you to think ill of me, he said, this house does not bring in as much money as you might think, I have to let rooms to respectable people, though it's true that if I had to rely on them and nothing else, I'd be throwing my money away. Here it's the opposite of the Carmelites, it's the vice that takes care of virtue.[72] No, I took this house, or rather I got the manager whom you have seen to take it, simply as a way of helping the Baron and amusing him in his old age.' Jupien was not talking only about scenes of sadism such as the ones I had witnessed, or to the actual practice of vice by the Baron. The latter now, even for conversation, for company, or for a game of cards, only enjoyed being with working-class people who exploited him. Low-life snobbery is no more difficult to understand than the other sort. And both had long since come together, the one alternating with the other, in M. de Charlus, who thought nobody smart enough for him to be socially acquainted with, nor enough of a hooligan to be known in any other circumstances. 'I detest half-hearted works, he would say, bourgeois comedy is stilted, I have to have the princesses of classical tragedy or else broad farce. *Phèdre* or *Les Saltimbanques*,[73] nothing in between.' Finally, though, the balance between these two kinds of snobbery had been broken. Perhaps because of the tiredness of age, perhaps because sensuality had started to affect even his most commonplace relationships, the Baron now lived only among his 'inferiors', thus following involuntarily in the footsteps of those great ancestors of his, the Duc de La Rochefoucauld, the Prince d'Harcourt and the Duc de Berry, whom Saint-Simon describes spending their lives with their lackeys, who extracted vast sums from them, sharing their entertainments, to the point where people who had to visit them were embarrassed on behalf of these great noblemen when they discovered them familiarly ensconced with their servants, playing cards or drinking. 'It is mainly, went on Jupien, to keep him out of trouble, because the Baron, you see, is just a great child. Even now, when he's got everything he could wish for here, he still goes out looking for whatever wickedness he can find. And with his generosity, that could easily lead to all sorts of problems these days. There was a hotel bellboy, just the other day, who nearly died of fright because of all the money the Baron offered him to go home with him. (To his own house, of all the reckless things!) The boy, who anyway is interested only in women, was reassured when he realized what was wanted of him. Hearing all those promises of money, he had thought the Baron was a spy. He felt a lot more comfortable when he realized he was not being asked to hand over his country, just his body, which may not be any more moral, but is less dangerous, and certainly easier.' Listening to Jupien, I said to myself: 'What a pity it is that M. de Charlus is not a novelist or a poet! Not so much in order to describe what he sees, but because the position in which somebody like Charlus finds himself in relation to desire gives rise to scandals around him, forces him to take life seriously, prevents him from separating emotions and pleasure, and from getting stuck in an ironic and externalized view of things, by constantly reopening a stream of pain within him. Almost every time he propositions somebody, he suffers a humiliation, if not the risk of being sent to prison.' It is not just children who learn from a clip on the ear, poets do too. If M. de Charlus had been a novelist, the house which Jupien had set up for him, by much diminishing the risks, at least (for there was always the danger of a police raid) the risks involved in an encounter in the street with a person of whose inclination the Baron could never be completely certain, would have been a disaster for him. But M. de Charlus was no more than a dilettante in matters of art, never dreamed of writing and had no talent for it.

'Anyway, I may as well admit, went on Jupien, that I don't really have any scruples about earning money this way. What actually goes on here, there's no point in trying to hide the fact now, is what I like doing, it's what I really enjoy. But I ask you, is there a law against getting paid for things you see no harm in? You're better educated than I am, and you'll probably tell me how Socrates believed he couldn't accept money for his lessons. But these days philosophy teachers don't think like that, nor do doctors or painters or playwrights or theatre managers. Don't think that I come into contact only with riff-raff in this job. Obviously the manager of an establishment of this sort, like a great courtesan, receives only men, but he receives men eminent in all walks of life and who are generally, in their own way, among the most intelligent, the most sensitive and the pleasantest in their professions. The house could easily, I assure you, be turned into a school of wit and a news agency.' I, however, was still preoccupied with the memory of the blows I had seen M. de Charlus receiving.

And to tell the truth, when one knew M. de Charlus well, with his pride, his satiety with the pleasures of society, his whims which so easily became passions for men of the lowest class and the worst sort, one could easily understand how the possession of that huge fortune, which would have delighted a self-made man, had it fallen to him, by enabling him to marry his daughter to a duke and to invite royalty to his shooting parties, pleased M. de Charlus because it enabled him to control and enjoy one, perhaps several, establishments where there was a permanent supply of the young men with whom he got on best. Quite possibly his vice may not even have been necessary for that. He was the heir to so many great noblemen, princes of the blood or dukes, of whom Saint-Simon tells us that they never associated with anyone 'who had a name' and spent their time playing cards with valets to whom they gave enormous sums of money!

'But meanwhile, I said to Jupien, this house is something else entirely, it is worse than a madhouse, because here the madness of the inmates is staged, it is played out, it is all on display. It is complete pandemonium. I thought at first that, like the Caliph in the *Arabian Nights*, I had arrived just in time to rescue a man who was being beaten, and then I found a quite different tale from the *Arabian Nights* being enacted in front of me, the one where a woman who has been changed into a dog deliberately lets herself be beaten in order to regain her original shape.' Jupien was clearly very disconcerted by my words, realizing that I had seen the Baron being beaten. He remained silent for a few moments while I hailed a passing cab; then suddenly, with that refreshing wit which had so often struck me in this self-educated man when, in greeting Françoise or me in the courtyard of our house, he would produce some elegant turn of phrase: 'You've mentioned several tales from the *Arabian Nights*, he said. But I can think of another one, not unrelated to the title of a book which I believe I've seen at the Baron's' (he was alluding to a translation of Ruskin's *Sesame and Lilies*[74] which I had sent M. de Charlus). 'If you were ever curious, one evening, to see, I shan't say forty, but a dozen thieves, you have only to come here; to know whether I'm in, you have only to look up at that window, I'll leave it open a crack so that the light shows, meaning that I'm there and you may come in; it's my own private Sesame. Only Sesame, mind. Because if it's lilies you're looking for, I'd advise you to look elsewhere.' And with a rather off-hand wave, for an aristocratic clientele and the piratical way he ran his band of young men had given him a certain familiarity of manner, he was on the point of taking leave of me, when the noise of an explosion, a bomb which had pre-empted the warning sirens, made him advise me to stay where I was for a moment. Soon the anti-aircraft barrage started up with such intensity that we realized that the German aeroplane's position was very close, just above our heads.

In an instant the streets became completely black. Just occasionally an enemy aeroplane flying very low would light up the spot where it wanted to drop a bomb. I was no longer sure of my way. I thought about the day when, on the way to La Raspelière, I had encountered an aeroplane and my horse had reared in terror as if confronted by a god. I was thinking that this time the encounter would be different and that the god of evil would kill me. I increased my pace to get away, like a traveller pursued by a tidal bore, going round and round dark squares from which I could find no way out. Finally the flames from a burning building lit up the surrounding area and I was able to find my way again, while the guns continued to crackle all the time. But my thoughts had turned to another subject. I was thinking about Jupien's house, now perhaps reduced to ashes, for a bomb had fallen very near me just after I had left it, the house on which M. de

Charlus might prophetically have written 'Sodoma' as had, with no less prescience or perhaps as the volcano was starting to erupt and the catastrophe had begun, the unknown inhabitant of Pompeii. But what did sirens or Gothas matter to men who had come looking for pleasure? The social framework or the natural setting that surrounds our love-making is something we hardly think about. The storm rages out at sea, the ship pitches and rolls, wind-torn sheets of rain fall from the sky, and, as we take steps to prevent it from discommoding us, we give perhaps a second's attention to this vast scene in which we are so insignificant, we and the body we are trying to get close to. The siren with its warning of bombs no more disturbed Jupien's visitors than an iceberg would have done. In fact the threat of physical danger freed them from the fear by which they had been morbidly persecuted for so long. For it is wrong to think that the scale of fear corresponds to the scale of the danger that inspires it. One may be afraid of not sleeping and quite unafraid of a serious duel, afraid of a rat, but not of a lion. But for these few hours the police would be concerned with nothing beyond such trivial matters as the lives of the city's inhabitants, and would be posing no threat to their reputations. Several, rather than rediscovering their moral freedom, were tempted by the darkness which had suddenly fallen on the streets. Some of these Pompeians on whom the sky was already raining fire descended into the passages of the Métro, dark as catacombs. They knew that they would not be the only ones there. And darkness, enveloping everything like a new element, has the effect, irresistibly tempting to some, of suppressing the first stage of pleasure and allowing us immediate access to a realm of caresses which normally we reach only after some time. Whether the object of desire be a woman or a man, even supposing the initial approach easy, and the eternal badinage of the drawing-room (at least in daylight) unnecessary, on an evening (even in the most dimly lighted street) there is at least a preamble in which the eyes alone enjoy the delights in store, and fear of passers-by, even of the creature in question, prevents us from doing more than looking and speaking. In the dark, the whole of this old-fashioned routine is removed, and hands, lips and bodies can go straight to work. There is still the excuse of darkness and the mistakes it engenders if we are not well received.

But if we are, the immediate response of a body which does not pull away, which presses closer, gives us an idea of the woman (or the man) whom we are silently addressing as being unprejudiced, dissolute, an idea which adds extra spice to the pleasure of being able to bite straight into the fruit without coveting it with our eyes and without asking permission. Meanwhile the darkness continues. Plunged into this new element, the men from Jupien's imagined themselves explorers, witnesses of a natural phenomenon like a tidal wave or an eclipse, and enjoying, instead of a carefully prepared, sedentary pleasure, that of a chance encounter in the unknown, celebrated, to the volcanic rumbling of the bombs, as it were in the bowels of a Pompeian house of ill fame, secret rites in the dark shadows of the catacombs.

In one large room were gathered a number of men who had not wanted to leave. They did not know one another, but one could see none the less that they came from more or less the same sort of world, rich and aristocratic. Each man's appearance had something repugnant about it, which must have reflected their lack of resistance to degrading pleasures. One, a huge man, had a face covered with red blotches like a drunkard. I learned, though, that he had not been one to begin with, and used simply to get his pleasure by making young men drink a lot. But terrified at the idea of being called up (although he certainly looked over fifty), and being rather fat, he had started to drink continuously in an attempt to increase his weight to more than a hundred kilos, the point above which one was rejected for service. And now, this calculated behaviour having become a passion, wherever he was left alone, he could always be found in a wine shop. But as soon as he spoke I saw that, ordinary though his intelligence may have been, he was a man of some knowledge, education and culture. Another man, of equally high social standing but very young and of great physical distinction, also came in. In his case there were as yet, it is true, no external marks of vice but, more disturbingly, there were internal ones. Very tall, with a charming face, his manner of speaking revealed an intelligence of quite a different order from that of his alcoholic neighbour, one that could without exaggeration be described as really remarkable. But everything he said was accompanied by an expression more appropriate to some quite different remark. As if, though possessing the whole wealth of human facial expressions, he lived in another world, he put on these expressions in the wrong order, seeming to shed smiles and glances randomly without any relation to the intended subject matter. I hope for his sake, if he is still alive, as he must be, that he was the victim of a temporary intoxication rather than any lasting disorder. If one had asked all these men for their visiting cards one would probably have been surprised to see that they belonged to the upper class of society. But some vice or other, as well as the greatest of all vices, the lack of will-power that prevented them from resisting any of them, brought them all together here, admittedly in isolated rooms, but, as I was told, every night, so that while their names were known to society hostesses, these had gradually lost sight of their faces, and never any longer had an opportunity to receive them as visitors. They continued to receive invitations but habit always brought them back to the composite site of depravity. They hardly made any secret of it, unlike the young bellboys and working men, etc., who provided their pleasure. And apart from all the other plausible reasons, there is one simple explanation for that. For an industrial worker or a man in service to go there would be like an apparently honest woman going into a brothel. The few who did admit to having gone there would defend themselves by saying that they had never been back, and Jupien himself, lying to protect their reputations or to avoid competition, would insist: 'Oh no, he doesn't come to my place, he'd never come *there*.' For men of standing it is not so serious, particularly since the other people in their circles who do not go *there* do not know anything about it and do not concern themselves with how you live. In an aircraft company, on the other hand, if certain of the fitters have been *there*, their mates who have been spying on them would never dream of going *there*, for fear of being observed themselves.

Approaching my house, I pondered the speed with which conscience ceases to play a part in our habits, which it leaves to their own development without having anything more to do with them, and consequently how astonished we would be if we observed simply from the outside, while supposing that they involve the whole person, the actions of men whose moral or intellectual qualities may be developing independently in a completely different direction. It was clearly a weakness in their education, or an absence of any education, combined with a fondness for earning money, if not in the least painful (for there must have been plenty of jobs that in the long run were easier, but then does not an invalid, with his fads, sacrifices and medicines, construct a far more painful existence for himself than would be required by the often mild illness which he thinks his measures are countering?), at least in the least laborious way possible, which had led these 'young people' almost innocently and for indifferent wages to do things which gave them no pleasure and must to begin with have inspired in them a deep disgust. On this basis one might have thought them fundamentally bad, but not only were they wonderful soldiers during the war, true 'heroes', they had just as often been kind and generous in civilian life, even model citizens. They had long ceased to pay any heed to the moral or immoral implications of the life they led, because it was the life that everybody around them led. Thus, when we study certain periods of ancient history, we are amazed to find men or women, good in themselves, taking part without scruple in mass assassinations, human sacrifices, which probably seemed entirely natural to them.

The Pompeian pictures in Jupien's house, moreover, were well suited, in so far as they recalled the final period of the French Revolution, to the age, rather similar to the Directory, which was about to begin. Already, in anticipation of peace, under the concealment of darkness so as not to infringe the police regulations too openly, new dances were being evolved and danced frantically all night long. At the same time, some artistic opinions less anti-German than those of the first years of the war were gaining currency, enabling suffocated minds to breathe again, but before daring to advance them one needed a certificate of civic responsibility. A professor would write a noteworthy book on Schiller and it would be reviewed in the newspapers. But before saying anything else about the book's author, they would register the fact, as if it were an imprimatur, that he had been at the Marne, or Verdun, that he had been mentioned five times in despatches, or that he had lost two sons. Only then would they praise the lucidity and profundity of his book on Schiller, whom it was now acceptable to call great as long as, instead of 'this great German', one said 'this great Boche'. That was the password for the article, after which it was free to proceed.

Our own epoch, to anybody who reads its history in two thousand years' time, will probably seem just as guilty of immersing certain pure and tender consciences in settings which then will look monstrously pernicious, but to which they managed to adapt themselves. I knew few men, for example, indeed I may even say I knew nobody, who in terms of intelligence and sensibility was as gifted as Jupien; for that wonderful 'accumulated wisdom' which provided the intellectual framework of his remarks was not the product of the school education or university training which might have made him a truly exceptional man, while so many fashionable young men derive no profit from it. It was simply his innate sense, his natural good taste, which had enabled him, from occasional reading, chosen at random, without guidance, in odd moments, to construct that precise and elegant way of speaking, in which all the symmetry of the language was revealed in its full beauty. The profession he followed, however, might justifiably be regarded, admittedly as one of the most lucrative, but as the worst there is. As for M. de Charlus, whatever the scorn his aristocratic pride may have given him for common gossip, how was it that some feeling of personal dignity and self-respect had not forced him to refuse his sensuality certain satisfactions for which the only excuse would seem to be complete insanity? But in him, as in Jupien, the habitual separation between morality and a whole order of actions (something which must also occur in a number of public offices, sometimes in that of a judge, or perhaps that of a statesman, and in plenty of others too) must have been established for so long that habit (no longer ever asking moral sentiment for its opinion) had grown stronger with every day that passed, until the day when this consenting Prometheus had himself nailed by Force to the rock of pure matter.

No doubt, as I sensed, this constituted a new stage in the sickness of M. de Charlus, which, for as long as I had been aware of it, judging by the different phases I had observed, had pursued its evolution with increasing rapidity. The poor Baron could not now be far away from the end, from death, if indeed that were not preceded, as Mme Verdurin predicted and desired, by a period of imprisonment which, at his age, could only hasten the final outcome. Yet perhaps my phrase 'rock of pure matter' is not exactly right. It is possible that in this pure matter there still subsisted a small quantity of mind. This madman was quite aware, despite everything, that he was prey to a kind of madness and, for those few moments, was just playing a part, since he knew perfectly well that the man beating him was no more of a villain than the small boy who draws the short straw in a game of soldiers and has to play the 'Prussian', and whom everyone chases in a fervour of genuine patriotism and mock hatred. Prey to a kind of madness, however, into which a little of M. de Charlus's personality also entered. Even in these aberrations, human nature (as it does in our love affairs or in our travels) betrays its need for belief by its demands for truth. Françoise, if I spoke to her about a church in Milan – a town to which she would probably never go – or the cathedral at Reims – or even just the one at Arras! which she would not be able to see since it had been more or less destroyed, would express her envy of the rich who could afford to go and look at such treasures, and exclaim, with nostalgic regret: 'Ah! how beautiful that must have been!' even though she, who had lived in Paris for so many years, had never had the curiosity to go and look at Notre-Dame. The reason for this, though, was because Notre-Dame was so much a part of Paris, of the town in which the everyday life of Françoise took place, and in which it was difficult for our old servant – as it would have been for me if the study of architecture had not in certain respects corrected in me the instincts of Combray – to situate the objects of her dreams. In the people we love there is, immanent within them, a dream which we cannot always perceive but which haunts us. It was my belief in Bergotte and in Swann which had made me love Gilberte, my belief in Gilbert the Bad[75] which had made me love Mme de Guermantes. And what a great expanse of sea had been hidden away in that most painful, jealous and seemingly most individual love of mine, for Albertine! Besides, precisely because of that individuality one is desperately in quest of, our love of specific persons is already something of an aberration. (And are not the diseases of the body themselves, at least those that have anything to do with the nervous system, instances of special tastes or special terrors contracted by our organs or our joints, which thus find that they have a horror of some climates as stubborn and as inexplicable as the fondness some men show, for example, for women who wear pince-nez, or for women who ride? Who can ever say what enduring and unconscious dream lies beneath the desire that is re-awakened by every glimpse of a woman on horseback, a dream as unconscious and mysterious as is, for example, to someone who has suffered all his life from severe asthma, the influence of a certain town, in appearance just like any other town, where for the first time he is able to breathe easily?)

Anyway, aberrations are like love affairs in which pathological defects have spread everywhere, have completely taken over. The presence of love can still be recognized, even in the maddest of them. The insistence of M. de Charlus on having his hands and feet fastened by shackles of proven strength, on begging for the rod of justice,[76] and, so Jupien told me, for other ferocious props which, even from sailors, were extremely difficult to obtain – they having been used for the infliction of punishments which have been abolished everywhere, even where discipline is at its most rigorous, on board ship – had its roots in M. de Charlus's whole dream of virility, attested if necessary by brutal acts, and in all that inner illumination, invisible to us, but glimpses of which he projected through these acts, of penal crosses and feudal tortures, which adorned his medieval imagination. It was the same sentiment that made him, each time he arrived, say to Jupien: 'I hope there will not be an alert this evening, for I can just see myself consumed by this fire from heaven like an inhabitant of Sodom.' And he would pretend to be afraid of the Gothas, not because he actually felt the least shadow of fear, but in order to have the pretext, as soon as the sirens started up, of rushing off into the shelters of the Métro, where he hoped for pleasure from casual contacts in the darkness, with vague dreams of medieval dungeons and oubliettes. In short, his desire to be chained and beaten betrayed, in its ugliness, a dream just as poetic as other men's desire to go to Venice or to keep a mistress. And M. de Charlus clung so tenaciously to the illusion of reality created by his dream that Jupien had to sell the wooden bed that used to be in Room 43 and replace it with an iron bed that was better suited to the chains.

The all-clear finally sounded as I was nearing my house. A boy in the street was adding his voice to the noise of the fire-engines. I met Françoise coming up from the cellar with the butler. She thought that I had been killed. She told me that Saint-Loup had dropped in, with apologies, to see whether, during the visit he had paid me that morning, he might have dropped his *croix de guerre*. He had only just realized that he had lost it and, before he rejoined his regiment the next morning, had wanted to see whether by any chance it was at my house. He had searched everywhere with Françoise but had found nothing. Françoise thought he must have lost it before coming to visit me, because, she said, she rather thought, in fact she could have sworn, that he had not had it when she saw him. On which point she was mistaken. So much for the value of evidence and memory! But in any case, it was of no great importance. Saint-Loup was as highly esteemed by his officers as he was loved by his men, and the matter could easily be sorted out.

However I felt immediately, from the unenthusiastic way in which they spoke of him, that Saint-Loup had not made a good impression on Françoise, or on the butler. Of course the butler's son and Françoise's nephew had made as much effort to get themselves safe jobs as Saint-Loup had done, successfully, with the opposite intention of being sent to the most dangerous posting. But that was something which, considering the matter with reference to themselves, Françoise and the butler were unable to believe. They were convinced that the rich were always given safe positions. And in fact, even if they had known the truth about Robert's heroic bravery, it would not have meant anything to them. He did not say 'Boches', he had praised the bravery of the Germans in their presence, and he did not attribute to treachery the fact that we had not been victorious on the first day. And that was what they would have liked to hear, that is what, for them, would have seemed a sign of courage. So, although they continued to look for the *croix de guerre*, I found them cool on the subject of Robert. Myself, having a pretty good idea where the cross had been left (although if Saint-Loup had indeed entertained himself during the evening in that way, it was only to fill in time while he was waiting, because, seized with the desire to see Morel again, he had used all his military connections to discover which regiment Morel was in, so that he could go and see him, but had thus far only received hundreds of contradictory replies), I advised Françoise and the butler to go to bed. He, however, was always loth to leave Françoise now that, thanks to the war, he had found an even more effective means of tormenting her than the 'expulsion of the nuns'[77] or the Dreyfus Affair. On this evening, and every time I was near them during my remaining few days in Paris, before I left for a new sanatorium, I would hear the butler say to a horrified Françoise: 'They're in no hurry, of course, they're waiting till the pear's ripe for plucking, but when the time comes they'll take Paris, and then they won't show any mercy! – Oh my Lord! Holy Mary! exclaimed Françoise, aren't they satisfied that they've conquered poor Belgium? They suffered enough, they did, when they were invasioned. – Belgium, Françoise? What they did in Belgium won't be anything compared with this!' And then, the war having given conversational currency among the working class to a quantity of terms which they had come across only visually, from reading newspapers, and consequently did not know how to pronounce, the butler added: 'I don't know how everyone can be so stupid . . . Look at this, Françoise, they're preparing a new attack using more battle-lions than ever before.' Unable to contain myself, if not in the name of pity for Françoise and strategic good sense, at least in the name of grammar, I told him that the proper pronunciation was 'battálions', but achieved nothing except to make him repeat the terrible phrase to Françoise every time I entered the kitchen, for the butler, almost as much as he enjoyed frightening his companion, enjoyed showing his master that, although he had once been a gardener at Combray and was still only a butler, he was none the less a good Frenchman according to the rule of Saint-André-des-Champs, and that the Declaration of the Rights of Man gave him a perfect independent right to pronounce it 'battle-lion' if he wanted to, and not to let himself be ordered about on a matter that had nothing to do with his service, and on which consequently, since the Revolution, nobody had a right to say anything to him, as he was my equal.

So I had the irritation of hearing him talk to Françoise about an operation using many 'battle-lions' with an emphasis which was meant to show me that this pronunciation was the effect not of ignorance but of a mature and considered choice. He lumped the government and the newspapers together in a single, distrustful 'they', saying: '*They* talk about the losses of the Boches, but they don't say anything about ours, which are apparently ten times larger. They tell us they're at their last gasp, that they've got nothing to eat, but I think they've got a hundred times more to eat than we have. They shouldn't be trying to brainwash us. If they didn't have anything to eat they wouldn't fight the way they did the other day, when they killed a hundred thousand of our young men, all under twenty.' He constantly exaggerated the triumphs of the Germans like that, just as he had once done with those of the Radicals; at the same time he recounted their atrocities, so that the triumphs would be even more painful for Françoise, who would constantly repeat: 'Oh! Holy Mother of the Angels! Oh, Holy Mother of God!', or sometimes, to be unpleasant to her in a different way, he would say: 'Anyway, we're no better than they are, what we're doing in Greece is no better than what they did in Belgium. We're going to set everybody against us, you'll see, and we'll end up fighting against all the other nations,' when the true situation was quite the opposite of that. On days when the news was good, he would get his revenge by assuring Françoise that the war would last for thirty-five years and, if there was any talk of peace, he would assure her that it would not last more than a few months and would be followed by battles that would make these ones look like child's play, after which there would be nothing left of France.

The victory of the Allies seemed, if not close, at least more or less certain, and it must be admitted, sadly, that the butler was very upset by it. For, having reduced the 'world' war, like everything else, to his own private war against Françoise (whom actually he liked, despite that, in the same way that one likes somebody whom one enjoys enraging every day by beating them at dominoes), whenever he imagined victory it took the form of the first conversation in which he would have to put up with hearing Françoise say: 'Well, that's over at last, and they're going to have to give us a lot more than we gave them in '70.' For all this, though, he was always convinced that the fatal day was about to dawn, for an unconscious patriotism made him think, like all Frenchmen, victims of the same mirage as me since the onset of my illness, that victory – like my recovery – was just round the corner. He tried to take the initiative by announcing to Françoise that victory might be coming, but that the thought of it made his heart bleed, as it would immediately be followed by revolution, and then by invasion. 'Oh, this ruddy war, the Boches will be the only ones to get over it quickly, Françoise, they've already made hundreds of billions out of it. But the idea that they'd cough up even a penny for us, that's just a joke! They may say that in the newspapers,' he added cautiously, so as to be ready for any eventuality, 'to keep people quiet, just as they've said for the last three years that the war will be over tomorrow.' Françoise was all the more disturbed by these words in fact because, having believed the optimists rather than the butler, she could now see that the war, which she thought was bound to be over in a fortnight despite 'the invasioning of poor little Belgium', was still going on, that no advances were being made, a consequence of the fixed fronts, something she could not really understand, and, finally, one of the countless 'godsons' to whom she gave everything she earned with us told her that they had concealed the truth about first one thing and then another. 'It's the working man who will have to bear the brunt,' concluded the butler. 'They'll take your field away, Françoise. – Oh, Lord save us!' But he preferred more immediate misfortunes to distant ones of that sort, and pored over the newspapers in the hope of finding a defeat to announce to Françoise. He waited for bad news like a child waiting for an Easter-egg, hoping that things would go badly enough to frighten Françoise, but not so badly as to cause him actual suffering. Hence the attraction of a Zeppelin raid, which allowed him to watch Françoise hiding in the cellars, but did not shake his conviction that in a city as big as Paris the bombs would never chance to fall quite on to our house.

Meanwhile Françoise was beginning to have occasional recurrences of her Combray pacifism. She almost started to have doubts about the 'German atrocities'. 'When the war started they told us that the Germans were murderers, brigands, complete bandits, B-b-boches . . .' (If she gave several *b*s to *Boches*, it was because the accusation that the Germans were murderers seemed quite plausible to her, whereas the idea that they might be Boches seemed so terrible as to be completely improbable. Only it was rather difficult to know what mysteriously terrifying sense Françoise gave to the word 'Boche', since she was talking about the beginning of the war, and also because of the dubious expression with which she uttered the word. A doubt about whether the Germans were criminals might have no factual foundation, but from the logical point of view it did not contain a contradiction. But how could she doubt that they were Boches, since the word, in popular speech, means, quite simply, German? Perhaps all she was doing was repeating, indirectly, the violent remarks she had heard at the time, in which the word *Boche* was given a particularly powerful emphasis.) 'I used to believe all that, she said, but now I wonder if we are not as rotten as they are.' This blasphemous thought had been slyly introduced into Françoise's mind by the butler, who, observing that his friend had a soft spot for King Constantine of Greece, had constantly pictured him to her as being starved of food until such time as he gave in to us. That ruler's abdication had therefore moved Françoise deeply, who went so far as to declare: 'We're no better than they are. If we were in Germany we'd be doing the same as they are.'

Anyway, I saw very little of her during these few days, as she was often at the house of those cousins of whom Mama had said to me one day: 'They are much richer than you are, you know.' People throughout the country during this period were often privileged to see some very fine behaviour, which, if there were a historian to perpetuate its memory, would bear witness to the greatness of France, her greatness of soul, her greatness according to the code of Saint-André-des-Champs, conduct displayed as much by the many civilians living in safety behind the lines as by the soldiers who fell at the Marne. Françoise had lost a nephew at Berry-au-Bac who was also a nephew of these millionaire cousins of hers, the former owners of a large café who had long since made a fortune and retired. The young man who had been killed, himself the poor owner of a very small café, had joined up aged twenty-five, leaving his wife to run the little bar which he thought he would be returning to in a few months. He had been killed. And then do you know what happened? Françoise's millionaire cousins, who were not related to the young woman, who was just their nephew's widow, left their home in the country, to which they had retired ten years earlier, and set about running a café again, without taking a sou for themselves; every morning at six o'clock, the millionaire's wife, a real lady, and her young lady daughter were dressed and ready to help their niece and cousin by marriage. And for nearly three years now, they had rinsed glasses and served drinks from first thing in the morning until half past nine at night, without a single day's rest. In this book, in which there is not one fact that is not fictitious, not one real character concealed under a false name, in which everything has been made up by me in accordance with the needs of my exposition, I have to say, to the honour of my country, that Françoise's millionaire relatives alone, who came out of their retirement to help their niece when she was left without support, that they and they alone are real, living people. And convinced as I am that their modesty will not be offended by it, for the simple reason that they will never read this book, and being unable to mention the names of the many others who must have acted in a similar way, as a result of whom France survived, I take a childlike and deeply felt pleasure, in transcribing their real name here: appropriately enough, they are called by the very French name of Larivière. Although there were a few worthless shirkers like the imperious young man in a dinner-jacket I had seen at Jupien's, whose only concern was to discover whether he could have Léon at half past ten the next day 'because he was lunching in town', these were redeemed by the countless masses of the Frenchmen of Saint-André-des-Champs, by all the sublime soldiers, and by those whom I regard as their equals, the Larivières.

To increase Françoise's anxieties even more, the butler showed her some old copies of *Lectures pour tous*[78] he had found, the covers of which (these numbers dating from before the war) depicted the imperial royal family of Germany. 'That's our new ruler to be,' the butler said to Françoise, showing her 'William': she stared open-eyed, then pointed to the female figure standing at his side and said: 'And that must be the Williamess!' Françoise's hatred of the Germans was extreme; it was tempered only by that which our own ministers inspired in her. I don't know which she wished for more passionately, the death of Hindenburg or the death of Clemenceau.

My departure from Paris was delayed by a piece of news which caused me such grief that for a while I was quite unable to set off. This was the news of the death of Robert de Saint-Loup, killed two days after his return to the front, while covering the retreat of his men. No man had ever felt less hatred for a nation than he did (and as for the Emperor, for reasons of his own, which may have been mistaken, he thought that William II had wanted to prevent the war rather than bring it about). Nor did he have the slightest hatred of Germanism: the last words I had heard him utter, six days earlier, were the opening words of a Schubert song which he had been singing in German on my staircase, so enthusiastically that I had to tell him to stop because of the neighbours. Accustomed by a faultless education and upbringing to expunging every trace of praise, invective or flowery language from his manner, he had avoided, in the face of the enemy, as he had at the moment of joining up, the one thing that might have safeguarded his life through that self-effacement that characterized the whole of his behaviour, right down to the way he would follow me out on the street bare-headed to close the door of my cab every time I left his house. For several days I remained shut up in my room, thinking about him. I remembered his arrival for the first time at Balbec, when, in an almost-white wool suit, his eyes greenish and changeable like the sea, he had crossed the hall beside the great dining-room whose windows gave on to the sea. I remembered the special being he had seemed to me then, the being whose friend I so much wanted to be. That wish had been realized to a greater extent than I could ever have imagined possible, although I derived little pleasure from it then, coming only later to understand the many great qualities, and other things too, which that elegant exterior concealed. All that, the good and the bad, he had given unstintingly every day, last of all by going forward to attack a trench, out of generosity and the devotion of everything he possessed to the service of others, just as one evening he had run along the backs of the banquettes in the restaurant so that I didn't have to move. And the fact that I had really seen him so seldom, in such diverse settings, in such different circumstances and at such long intervals, in that hall in Balbec, in the café at Rivebelle, in the cavalry barracks and at the military dinners at Doncières, at the theatre when he slapped the journalist, in the house of the Princesse de Guermantes, all this meant only that I had a sharper, more vivid picture of his life, and a clearer sense of grief at his death, than often one has for people more dearly loved but so regularly seen that the image we retain of them is no more than a sort of vague composite of an infinite number of subtly different images, where also, our affections being fully gratified, we do not have, as we may with those we have seen only for brief moments, in the course of meetings inconclusive despite the wishes of both parties, the illusion of the possibility of a greater affection thwarted only by circumstance. Only a few days after I had seen him in pursuit of his monocle in the hall at Balbec, when I had thought him so haughty, there was another living form which I had seen for the first time on the beach at Balbec, and which also no longer existed outside the state of memory: this was Albertine, trudging across the sand that first evening, indifferent to everything around her, as much at home there as a seagull. So quickly had I fallen in love with her that, in order to be able to go out with her every day, I had never gone over from Balbec to see Saint-Loup. And yet the history of my relations with him bore witness also to the fact that I did once stop loving Albertine for a while, since the reason for my going to live for a time near Robert, at Doncières, was my sadness at seeing that the feeling I had for Mme de Guermantes was not reciprocated. His life and Albertine's, discovered so late, at Balbec, and so swiftly over, had scarcely touched; it was he, I reminded myself as I saw how the nimble shuttles of the years weave slender connections between those of our memories which seem at first most independent of each other, it was he whom I had sent to Mme Bontemps's house when Albertine left me. And then it had turned out that their two lives each had a parallel, and unsuspected, secret. Saint-Loup's secret perhaps caused me more sadness now than that of Albertine, whose life had become so alien to me. But I could not get over the fact that her life, like Saint-Loup's, had been so short. Often, when they were looking after me, she and he would tell me: 'You're not well.' And now it was they who were dead, and they whose first and final images I could compare, separated as they were by such a short span of time, the final image of each, in front of the trench, floating in the river, set against the first image which, in the case of Albertine, was precious to me now only by its association with that of the sun sinking into the sea.

His death was received more sympathetically by Françoise than Albertine's had been. Straight away she adopted her role of hired mourner and expatiated on the memory of the dead man with sorrowful threnodies and lamentations. She flaunted her grief and turned her face away dry-eyed only when in spite of myself I let her glimpse mine, which she wanted to appear not to have noticed. For like many highly strung people she was exasperated by other people's emotional volatility, probably because it was too much like her own. These days, she was always keen to mention the slightest touch of stiffness in her neck, or a feeling of dizziness, or a knock she had given herself. But if I were to say anything about one of my ailments, she would resume her stoic and solemn air and pretend not to have heard.

'Poor Marquis,' she would say, although she was unable to persuade herself that he had not done everything he could to avoid going to the front and, once mobilized, to keep well away from any danger, 'Poor lady,' she would say, thinking about Mme de Marsantes, 'how she must have cried when she heard about the death of her boy! If only she could have seen him one more time, but perhaps it's better that she couldn't because his nose was split in two, he was all disfigured.' And Françoise's eyes would fill with tears, through which, though, shone the cruel curiosity of the peasant woman. No doubt Françoise pitied Mme de Marsantes's sorrow with all her heart, but she regretted not knowing the form that sorrow had taken and not being able to enjoy the distressing spectacle of it. And as she would dearly have loved to weep, and to have me see her weep, she said, as a stimulus to her tears: 'Oh, it's really affected me, this has!' And she watched for signs of grief in me with such avidity that I feigned a degree of brusqueness when speaking of Robert. And largely, I'm sure, out of a spirit of imitation and because she had heard other people say it, for there are clichés among servants just as there are in literary circles, she would repeat, not however without a poor person's note of satisfaction: 'All his wealth didn't prevent him from dying like anyone else, and it's no good to him now.' The butler took advantage of the opportunity to tell Françoise that it was sad, of course, but that it hardly counted beside the millions of men who were falling every day despite the government's efforts to hide the fact. This time, however, the butler did not succeed in increasing Françoise's grief as he had hoped to. For she replied: 'It's true they are dying for France too, but they're strangers; it's always more interesting when it's people you know.' And Françoise, who enjoyed crying, added: 'Do make sure to tell me if there's anything about the Marquis's death in the paper.'

Robert had often said sadly to me, long before the war: 'Oh, don't let's talk about my life, I've been condemned in advance.' Was he alluding to the vice which he had succeeded up to that point in concealing from the world, but of which he was aware, and whose seriousness he perhaps exaggerated, as children making love for the first time, or even before that seeking solitary pleasure, imagine that they are like plants, unable to scatter their pollen without dying immediately afterwards? Perhaps this exaggeration, for Saint-Loup as for children, stemmed as much from the idea of a sin with which one is still unfamiliar, as from the fact that an entirely new sensation has an almost terrible power which only time and repetition will diminish. Or did he really have, to be justified if necessary by his father's death at an early age, an intimation of his own premature end? Intimations of that sort would seem to be impossible, of course. Yet death does seem to be subject to certain laws. Often, for instance, it seems that children born to parents who died either very old or very young are almost forced to disappear at the same age, the former extending incurable sorrows and illnesses into their hundredth year, the others, despite a happy and healthy life, carried off at the premature but inevitable date by an illness so opportune and so accidental (however deeply rooted it may have been in their temperament) that it seems no more than the formality necessary for the achievement of death. And might it not be possible that even accidental death – like that of Saint-Loup himself, which may have been linked to his character in more ways than perhaps I have thought it necessary to describe – is also inscribed in advance, known only to the gods, invisible to men, but revealed by a sadness, half unconscious, half-conscious (and even, in this last respect, expressed to others with that complete sincerity with which we predict misfortunes which we believe in our heart of hearts we can escape, and which will happen nevertheless), specific to each person who is permanently aware that within himself, like a heraldic device, he carries the fateful date?

He must have been magnificent during those final hours. The man who throughout his life had seemed, even when sitting down, or walking across a room, to be keeping in check the impulse to charge, concealing behind a smile the indomitable will that lurked within his triangular-shaped head, had charged at last. Stripped of its books, the feudal turret had regained its military function. By dying this Guermantes had become more completely himself, or rather more completely part of his race, into which he melted, becoming simply a Guermantes, as was symbolically visible at his burial in the church of Saint-Hilaire at Combray, which was completely hung with black draperies on which stood out in red, under the sealed crown, without the initials of titles or forenames, the G of the Guermantes that in death he had once again become.

Before going to the burial, which did not take place straight away, I wrote to Gilberte. I ought perhaps to have written to the Duchesse de Guermantes, but I told myself that she would greet Robert's death with the same indifference that I had seen her display towards the deaths of so many others whose lives had seemed so closely bound up with her own, and that perhaps, with her Guermantes cast of mind, she would even seek to show that she was not superstitious about ties of blood. Besides, I was too unwell to write to everybody. I had thought, once, that she and Robert were fond of one another, in the sense in which the term is used in society, that is that they told each other affectionate things that they happened to be thinking at the time. But when he was not with her he had no hesitation in declaring her an idiot, and although she may sometimes have taken a selfish pleasure in seeing him, I saw her as quite incapable of taking the slightest pains, and extremely reluctant to use what credit she had in order to do him a service, or even to save him from trouble. The maliciousness she had revealed by refusing to recommend him to General Saint-Joseph, when Robert was going to have to leave for Morocco, showed that the devotion she had shown on the occasion of his marriage was no more than a kind of compensation, which had cost her nothing. I was therefore very surprised to learn that, as she had been unwell when Robert was killed, they had felt obliged for several days, on the most spurious of pretexts, to hide from her eyes the newspapers which might have apprised her of his death, in order to spare her the shock she would have felt. My surprise was even greater, though, when I learned that, when they had finally had to tell her the truth, the Duchesse cried for a whole day, fell ill, and for a long time – for more than a week, which was a long time for her – was inconsolable. When I heard about her grief, I was touched by it. It meant that the whole of society could say, and I can attest, that there was a great friendship between them. But then, when I remember how much malicious gossip and reluctance to help were wrapped up in this friendship, I cannot help thinking how little a great friendship means in society.

A little while after this, however, in circumstances of greater historical, though less personal importance, Mme de Guermantes showed herself, I thought, in a still more favourable light. She, who when she was a girl had shown such outspoken impertinence, if you remember, towards the Imperial Russian family and who, when married, had always spoken so freely to them that they had sometimes accused her of a lack of tact, was perhaps the only person, after the Russian Revolution, to show unlimited devotion to the Grand Dukes and Grand Duchesses. Just a year before the war, she had considerably annoyed the Grand Duchess Vladimir by referring continually to the Countess of Hohenfelsen, the morganatic wife of the Grand Duke Paul, as 'the Grand Duchess Paul'. But despite that, the Revolution had hardly broken out before our ambassador in St Petersburg, M. Paléologue (known as 'Paléo' in diplomatic circles, which have their witty abbreviations like any others), was harassed by telegrams from the Duchesse de Guermantes, who wanted news of the Grand Duchess Maria Pavlovna. And, for a long time, the only regular marks of sympathy and respect that this princess received came exclusively from Mme de Guermantes.

Saint-Loup caused, if not by his death, at least by what he did in the few weeks preceding it, greater grief than that of the Duchesse. On the day after the evening when I saw him, and two days after Charlus had told Morel: 'I shall take my revenge,' Saint-Loup's attempts to locate Morel met with success. That is, they were successful in that the general, under whose command Morel ought to have been, had learned that he was a deserter, had had him found and arrested and, in order to apologize to Saint-Loup for the punishment which someone in whom he took an interest was about to undergo, had written to Saint-Loup to tell him about it. Morel was convinced that his arrest had been provoked by the resentment of M. de Charlus. He remembered the words: 'I shall take my revenge', thought that this was indeed that revenge, and asked to make certain revelations. 'It's true, he declared, that I deserted. But is it altogether my fault if I've been led astray?' He recounted stories about M. de Charlus and M. d'Argencourt, with whom he had also quarrelled, in none of which he had actually been involved directly, but all of which they, with the twofold expansiveness of lovers and inverts, had told him, which led to the arrest of both M. de Charlus and M. d'Argencourt. The arrest itself was probably less distressing to each man than their discovery of the fact, previously unknown to them, that the other was their rival, while the preparation of the case also revealed a huge number of others, unknown, ordinary men, casually picked up in the street. But they were soon released. Morel was, too, because the letter the general had sent to Saint-Loup was returned bearing the legend: 'Deceased. Killed in action.' Out of respect for the dead man, the general simply had Morel sent to the front, where he showed great gallantry, survived every danger and came back, at the end of the war, with the medal that M. de Charlus had once vainly solicited for him, and which he owed indirectly to the death of Saint-Loup.

I have often thought since then, remembering the *croix de guerre* lost at Jupien's, that if Saint-Loup had lived he might easily have been elected a Deputy in the post-war elections, with all its froth of nonsense and the ray of glory that came in its wake, when a single missing finger, wiping out centuries of prejudice, was an entry permit into a brilliant marriage into an aristocratic family, the *croix de guerre*, even if awarded for clerical duties, was enough for entry, after a triumphant election, into the Chamber of Deputies, almost to the Académie française. The election of Saint-Loup, because of his 'holy' family, would have caused M. Arthur Meyer[79] to pour out floods of tears and ink. Perhaps, though, he was too sincerely fond of the people to succeed in winning the popular vote, although they would probably, on account of his noble pedigree, have forgiven him his democratic ideas. He would doubtless have expounded these with success to a chamber composed of aviators. Certainly those heroes would have understood him, as would the few very intelligent minds. But thanks to the pompous self-satisfaction of the National Bloc, the old political hacks were dug out, the ones who were always re-elected. Those who could not enter a chamber of aviators begged, at least in the case of entry to the Académie française, the votes of marshals, the President of the Republic, a President of the Chamber, etc. They would not have been in favour of Saint-Loup, but were enthusiastic about another of Jupien's regulars, the *Action libérale* Deputy, who was re-elected unopposed. He continued to wear the uniform of a Territorial, even though the war was long over. His election was greeted with rapture by all the newspapers that had 'united' to support his nomination, by rich and noble ladies who now wore nothing but rags, out of a sense of propriety, and a fear of taxes, while the men of the Bourse were ceaselessly buying up diamonds, not for their wives but because, having lost all confidence in the credit of any country, they were taking refuge in this tangible form of wealth, and incidentally sending up de Beers stock by a thousand francs. So much stupidity was somewhat annoying, but people were less hostile to the National Bloc when they suddenly saw the victims of Bolshevism, Grand Duchesses in rags, their husbands murdered by the barrow-load, while their sons were killed by the stones thrown down on them after they had been kept without food, made to work amidst jeers of scorn, then pushed down wells because people thought they had the plague and might pass it on. The ones who had managed to escape suddenly reappeared . . .

*

The new sanatorium to which I retired cured me no more than the first; and many years passed before I left it. During the train journey, when I eventually did return to Paris, the thought of my lack of literary talent, which, as I believed, I had discovered long ago on the

Guermantes way, of which I had become even more mournfully aware during my daily walks with Gilberte, before we returned to dine, very late, at Tansonville, and which I had almost identified, the night before I left that house, as I read those pages of the Goncourts' journal, with the pointlessness and falsity of literature, this thought, perhaps less painful now but more dismaying than ever, its subject being not an infirmity peculiar to myself alone, but the non-existence of the ideal in which I had for so long believed, this thought which for so long had not troubled my mind, struck me once again with a more lamentable force than ever. The train, I remember, had come to a halt in open countryside. The sun's rays illuminated the upper half of the trunks of a line of trees that followed the railway. 'Trees, I thought, you have nothing to say to me any longer, my heart has grown cold and no longer responds to you. Here I am, after all, in the middle of nature, my eyes noting the line which separates your glowing foliage from your shaded trunks, and I feel only coolness and boredom. If ever I could have thought of myself as a poet, I now know that I am not. Perhaps in this new era of my life which, however desiccated, is now opening, human beings may be able to inspire in me what nature no longer says to me. But the days when I might perhaps have been capable of singing its song will never come back.' Yet by consoling myself with the thought that social observation might come to take the place of vanished inspiration, I knew that I was just trying to find some consolation, and that I knew myself to be worthless. If I truly had the soul of an artist, what pleasure should I not experience at the sight of this screen of trees lit by the setting sun, these little flowers on the embankment that reached almost up to the carriage step, whose petals I could count, and whose colours I was careful not to describe, as so many good men of letters would, for could one hope to transmit to the reader a pleasure one has not felt oneself?

A little later I had seen with the same indifference the flecks of orange and gold with which it splashed the windows of a house; and finally, later still, I had seen another house, which looked as though it were built of some strange pink material. But I made these observations with the same absolute indifference as if, walking in a garden with a lady, I had seen a piece of glass and a little further on an object made of some alabaster-like substance, the unusual colour of which would not normally have been enough to rouse me from my languorous boredom but none the less, out of politeness to the lady, in order to say something and also to show that I had noticed the colour, I had pointed out in passing the coloured glass and the fragment of stucco. In the same way, to put my mind at rest, I pointed out to myself, as to somebody who might have accompanied me and might have been more capable than I of taking pleasure from it, the fiery reflections in the windows and the translucent pink of the house. But the companion to whom I had pointed out these curious effects was of a nature no doubt less enthusiastic than plenty of good-natured people who would be ravished by such a view, for he had registered the colours without a trace of pleasure.

My name being still on their lists, my long absence from Paris had not prevented old friends from continuing faithfully to send me invitations, and when upon my return I found, alongside one to a tea-party given for her daughter and son-in-law by La Berma, another for an afternoon reception to be held the following day at the house of the Prince de Guermantes, the melancholy reflections that had assailed me in the train were not the least of the motives advising me to go there. There is really no point in depriving myself of the life of a man of the world, I told myself, since the famous 'work' which I have so long hoped each day to begin the next day, is one that I am not, or am no longer, fitted to, and perhaps corresponds to no reality whatever. In fact this reasoning was entirely negative, and simply removed the value of the counter-arguments which might have put me off going to this society concert. The real reason I decided to go was the Guermantes name, for so long out of my mind that when I read it on the invitation card it re-awakened a ray of my attention which was to lift from the depths of my memory a section of their past, accompanied by all the images of seigneurial forest and tall flowers which had then accompanied it, and took on again for me all the magic and significance which I used to find at Combray when, as I passed by on my way home, in the rue de l'Oiseau, I would see from outside, like dark lacquer, the stained-glass window dedicated to Gilbert the Bad, ancestor of the Guermantes. For a moment the

Guermantes had once again seemed completely different from the rest of society, not to be compared with them or with any living being, even royalty, creatures sprung from the impregnation of the sour and windy air of the sombre town of Combray, where my childhood was spent, by the past, visible there in the narrow street, at the level of the stained-glass window. I had wanted to go to the Guermantes' house as if that might have been able to bring me closer to my childhood and to the depths of my memory in which I saw it. And I had continued to read and reread the invitation until the letters composing that name, at once so familiar and so mysterious, like that of Combray itself, rebelled, regained their independent life and reorganized themselves before my exhausted eyes into something like an unknown name. It just so happened that Mama was going to afternoon tea with Mme Sazerat, an event which she knew beforehand would be extremely tedious, so I had no scruples about going to the Princesse de Guermantes's party.

I took a cab to go to the house of the Prince de Guermantes, who was no longer living in his old *hôtel* but in a magnificent new mansion he had had built on the Avenue du Bois. It is one of the mistakes of society people not to realize that if they want us to believe in them they have to believe in themselves, or at least respect the essential elements of our belief. At the time when I believed, even though I knew that the contrary was true, that the Guermantes inhabited such a palace by an hereditary right, to penetrate into the palace of the wizard or the fairy, for the gates which open only when one utters the magic word to open before me, seemed to me as difficult a task as to obtain an interview with the wizard and the fairy themselves. Nothing was easier than to make myself believe that the old servant, in fact only just engaged, or supplied by the Potel and Chabot Agency, was the son, grandson or descendant of those who served the family before the Revolution, and I was only too willing to take the portrait, bought from Bernheim Jeune the previous month, to be a family portrait. But the spell of a place cannot be simply decanted or transferred, memories cannot be divided up, and of the Prince de Guermantes, now that he had himself destroyed the illusions of my belief by going to live in the Avenue du Bois, little of any note remained. The ceilings which I had been afraid would fall in on me when my name was announced, and beneath which much of the magic and fear of long ago might still for me have hovered, now looked down on parties given by an American lady in whom I had no interest. Of course, things have no potency in themselves, and since it is we who confer it upon them, some young middle-class schoolboy was probably at that very moment experiencing the same thoughts outside the mansion in the Avenue du Bois as I had once felt outside the Prince de Guermantes's old *hôtel*. He, however, would still be young enough to have these beliefs, but I had passed that age, and lost that privilege, as after early infancy one loses the power that babies have to divide the milk they ingest into digestible quantities. Which forces adults, out of more than prudence, to take milk in small quantities, while babies can suck indefinitely without pausing for breath. At least the Prince de Guermantes's change of residence had this advantage for me, that the cab which came to collect me, and within which I was having these thoughts, had to pass along the streets leading to the Champs-Élysées. They were, at that time, very badly paved, but from the moment I entered them, what actually distracted me from my thoughts was a sensation of extreme smoothness such as one feels when, suddenly, a car proceeds more easily, more smoothly, silently, as when, the gates of a park being opened, one glides along over fine sand or dead leaves. Materially, nothing was different; but I suddenly felt the elimination of those external obstacles because in fact I was no longer having to make the effort of adaptation or attention which we make, without even being aware of it, when we come across something new: the streets through which I was now passing were those, forgotten for so long, through which I had walked with Françoise on the way to the Champs-Élysées. The ground knew of its own accord where it had to lead; its resistance was overcome. And, like an aviator, who has up to that point travelled laboriously along the ground, suddenly 'taking off', I rose up slowly towards the silent heights of memory. In Paris, these streets will always stand out for me, as if made of a different material from the rest. When I reached the corner of the rue Royale, where once had stood the open-air vendor of the photographs of which Françoise had been so fond, I felt that the cab, carried forward by so many hundreds of previous turnings, would be unable to resist turning of its own accord. I was not passing through the same streets as those who were out walking along them that day, but instead moving through a shifting past, sad and gentle. Yet it was composed of so many different pasts that it was hard to define what was causing my feeling of melancholy, whether it was due to those walks on the way to see Gilberte, simultaneously fearful that she would not come, or to the proximity of a certain house to which I had been told that Albertine had gone with Andrée, or to the sense of philosophical futility that a route seems to emanate when one has travelled it a thousand times, with a passion that has died, and which bore no fruit, like the route over which after lunch I used to run so hastily, so feverishly, to gaze on the posters, their paste still wet, advertising *Phèdre* or the *Domino Noir*. When I arrived at the Champs-Élysées, not being particularly keen to hear the whole of the concert being given at the Guermantes' place, I had the cab stop, and was just about to climb down and walk about for a little while, when I was struck by the sight of another cab, also in the process of coming to a halt. A man, eyes fixed straight ahead, body bent, was placed, rather than seated, in the back, and was making the same sort of effort to sit upright as a child does when he has been told to be good. But his panama hat revealed an unruly forest of entirely white hair; a white beard, like those formed by the snow on the statues of river-gods in the public gardens, flowed from his chin. With Jupien, who was endlessly attentive, at his side, this was M. de Charlus, convalescing now from an attack of apoplexy, of which I had been unaware (I had been told only that he had lost his sight; but this had in fact been a temporary condition, and he could now see perfectly well again) and which, unless he had previously dyed his hair and had now been forbidden to continue doing anything so tiring, seemed rather, as if by a kind of chemical precipitation, to have rendered gleamingly visible all the metal with which the locks, now pure silver, of his head and his beard were saturated and which sprang out from them like so many geysers, so that the old, decayed prince now wore the Shakespearian majesty of a King Lear. His eyes had not escaped this upheaval, this metallurgical alteration of his head, but by some inverse phenomenon they had lost all their lustre. But the saddest thing was that one felt that this lost lustre represented his moral pride, and that this enabled the physical and even the intellectual life of M. de Charlus to survive the disappearance of the aristocratic pride that at one time had been part and parcel of it. Just at that moment, as if to illustrate this, also no doubt on her way to the Prince de Guermantes's, there passed a victoria in which was Mme de Saint-Euverte, whom the Baron used to regard as beneath his notice. And immediately, with infinite difficulty but with all the determination of an invalid who wants to show that, however difficult they may still be, he can perform all his movements, M. de Charlus raised his hat, bowed and greeted Mme de Saint-Euverte with as much respect as if she had been the Queen of France. Perhaps there was, in the very difficulty that M. de Charlus experienced in making this greeting, a reason for him to do it, knowing that he would be making a greater impression by an act which, painful to an invalid, would become doubly meritorious on the part of him who performed it and doubly flattering in the eyes of the person to whom it was addressed, invalids like kings being prone to exaggerate politeness. Perhaps also the Baron's movements still suffered from the lack of co-ordination which follows from problems with the spinal cord and the brain, so that his gestures went further than he intended they should. For myself, I saw something more like physical gentleness, and a detachment from the realities of life, characteristics so marked among those over whom death has already cast its shadow. The exposure of the silver-bearing lodes of his hair revealed a change less profound than that unconscious social humility which turned all social relations upside down, and humiliated before Mme de Saint-Euverte, as it would have humiliated in front of the latest American hostess (who might have been able finally to attain the polite attentions, hitherto beyond her reach, of the Baron), what once used to seem the proudest snobbery of all. For the Baron was still alive, still thinking; his intellect had not been extinguished. And more than any chorus by Sophocles on the humbled pride of Oedipus, more than death itself and any funeral oration on the subject of death, the humble and ingratiating manner in which the Baron greeted Mme de Saint-Euverte proclaimed the full fragility and perishability of the love of earthly greatness and the whole of human pride. M. de Charlus, who up to then would never have consented to dine with Mme de Saint-Euverte, now bowed down before her. He greeted her perhaps out of ignorance of the rank of the person whom he was greeting (the articles of the social code being just as susceptible of destruction by a stroke as any other aspect of memory), perhaps by a lack of co-ordination of the movements which transposed on to the level of apparent humility the uncertainty, which would otherwise have been haughty, that he might have felt about the identity of the woman who was passing. He greeted her with the politeness of a child coming timidly forward, at his mother's request, to say how do you do to some important people. And indeed a child, without a child's pride, was what he had become.

To receive the homage of M. de Charlus had been for her the apogee of snobbery, as it had been the essence of snobbery in the Baron to refuse it. And now the whole of that inaccessible and affected nature which he had succeeded in making Mme de Saint-Euverte believe lay at the heart of his character had been annihilated at a stroke by the painstaking timidity, the apprehensive zeal, with which he had raised a hat, from beneath which, for as long as he left his head deferentially uncovered, had tumbled, with the eloquence of a Bossuet,[80] the torrents of his silver hair. When Jupien had helped the Baron out of the cab, and I had greeted him, he spoke very rapidly, in a voice so imperceptible that I could scarcely make out what he was saying to me, which drew from him, when for the third time I made him repeat his words, a gesture of impatience which surprised me because of the impassivity his face had registered, due no doubt to some residue of his paralysis. But when finally I grew accustomed to this *pianissimo* of whispered words, I realized that the invalid's intellect had survived absolutely unimpaired.

There were, however, two distinct M. de Charluses, quite apart from any of the others. Of the two, the intellectual spent his time complaining that he was becoming aphasic, that he was constantly pronouncing one word or one letter instead of another. But whenever he happened to do this, the other M. de Charlus, the subconscious one, who wanted as much to be envied as the other did to be pitied, and had a degree of vanity and affectation despised by the first, stopped immediately, like an orchestral conductor when his musicians are floundering, in mid-sentence, and with infinite ingenuity substituted for what was about to follow the word actually spoken another word which none the less appeared to be one he had chosen. Even his memory was intact, from which moreover his vanity made him, not without the fatigue of extremely arduous concentration, dredge up this or that ancient recollection, of no importance, relating to me, in order to show me that he had retained or recovered all his clarity of mind. Without moving his head or his eyes, nor varying a single inflection of his delivery, he said to me, for example: 'Look, there's a poster on that telegraph-pole just like the one I was standing beside when I saw you for the first time at Avranches, no I'm wrong, at Balbec.' And it would indeed be an advertisement for the same product.

At first I had hardly been able to make out what he was saying, just as to begin with one can make out nothing in a room where all the curtains are drawn. But like eyes in the half-darkness, my ears soon grew accustomed to this *pianissimo*. I think also that his voice had gradually became louder as he continued speaking, either because the feebleness of his voice was in part the product of a nervous apprehension which gradually dissipated as he became distracted by the presence of another person and stopped thinking about it; or, on the contrary, because this feebleness corresponded to his true state and the momentary strength with which he spoke in the conversation was provoked by an excitement that was factitious, short-lived and rather doleful, making strangers think: 'He's much better, he must be careful not to think about his illness,' but which in fact aggravated the illness, which rapidly took hold again. Whatever the reason, the Baron at that moment (and even taking into account my own adjustment) was tossing out his words more forcefully, rather as the tide, on days when the weather is bad, flings down its twisted little waves. And the residue of his recent attack could be heard underneath his words, like the sound of pebbles dragging on the shore. Yet continuing to speak to me about the past, probably as much as anything else to show me that he had not lost his memory, he evoked it in a funereal manner, yet without any sadness. He enumerated at endless length all the members of his family or his social circle who were no longer alive, less, it seemed, with any sadness that they were no longer with us than with a sense of satisfaction at surviving them. Recalling their demise seemed to make him more aware of his own return to health. It was with an almost triumphal severity that he repeated monotonously, with his slight stammer and a faintly sepulchral resonance: 'Hannibal de Bréauté, dead! Antoine de Mouchy, dead! Charles Swann, dead! Adalbert de Montmorency, dead! Boson de Talleyrand, dead! Sosthène de Doudeauville, dead!' and, every time, the word 'dead' seemed to fall on the deceased man like a spadeful of earth, each one heavier than the last, thrown down by a gravedigger trying to pin them more securely in their graves.

The Duchesse de Létourville, who was not going to the Princesse de Guermantes's party as she was just recovering from a long illness, passed us at that moment on foot, and seeing the Baron, and unaware of his recent attack, stopped to say good-afternoon. But having been ill herself had not made her more understanding of the illness of others, indeed it had given her a greater impatience, a bad-tempered nervousness which may perhaps have concealed the fact that she felt sorry for them. Realizing that the Baron was having difficulty in pronouncing, even remembering, certain words, and in moving his arm, she looked at Jupien and myself in turn, as if asking us for an explanation of such a shocking phenomenon. As neither of us said anything, it was to M. de Charlus himself she addressed a long look full of sadness, but also critical. She looked as if she was about to reproach him for being out of doors with her in a state as unusual as if he had come out without a tie or shoes. When the Baron made yet another error of pronunciation, the Duchesse's annoyance and indignation both became too much to bear, and she said to the Baron: 'Palamède!' in the exasperated interrogative tone of those nervous people who cannot bear to wait a few minutes, and who, if one invites them to come in straight away, apologizing for not being quite ready, will ask in a tart tone of voice, more accusatory than apologetic: 'I'm not disturbing you, am I?' as if the person being disturbed was to blame.

He asked if he could sit down on a bench and rest while Jupien and I went for a stroll, and painfully pulled a book out of his pocket, one which looked to me like a prayer-book. I was not displeased to have this opportunity to learn more details from Jupien about the state of the Baron's health. 'I'm glad to have a chance to speak to you, sir, said Jupien, but we shan't walk any further than the Circus. The Baron is much better now, thank heavens, but I don't dare leave him alone for very long, it's always the same thing, he's too generous, he gives everything he's got to other people; and anyway that's not all, he's still as randy as a young man, so I have to keep my eyes open. – All the more, since he got his own sight back, I replied; I was very sad when I heard that he had gone blind. – Yes, that was a side-effect of his stroke, he lost his vision completely. Imagine, right through the cure, which did him so much good in every other way, it was as if he'd been blind since birth. – At least that must have made some of your surveillance unnecessary? – Don't you believe it! We'd hardly got to the hotel before he starts asking me what the various members of staff look like. I told him they were all ghastly. But he soon realized that they couldn't all be, and that I must be lying about some of them. You see what I mean, what a little monkey he is! And then he had a kind of nose for it, something in people's voices maybe, I don't know. So he'd arrange to send me off on some urgent errand. One day – excuse me telling you this, but you did once come to the Temple of Shamelessness by mistake so I've got nothing to hide from you (besides which, Jupien always obtained a rather unpleasant satisfaction from divulging the secrets he was privy to) – I was coming back from one of these so-called urgent errands, hurrying back in fact because I was fairly sure it'd been arranged on purpose, when, just as I had almost reached the Baron's bedroom, I heard a voice saying: "What? – Really? replied the Baron, you mean that was the first time?" I entered without knocking, and you can imagine my fright! The Baron, misled by the voice, which was in fact much lower than is usual at that age (and remember the Baron was still, at that point, completely blind), this man who used to have a taste for somewhat older men, was with a child who wasn't even ten years old.'

I had been told that during that time he had been subject almost daily to crises of mental depression, characterized not by any actual mental divagation, but by his avowal, at the top of his voice in front of third parties whose presence or severity he had forgotten, of opinions he had been accustomed to conceal, like his pro-Germanism. Even though the war was long over, he would groan about the defeat of the Germans, among whom he counted himself, and say with pride: 'And yet there is no doubt but that we shall have our revenge, for we have proved that it is we who are capable of the greater resistance and who have the better organization.' Or else his confidences would take another direction, and he would proclaim angrily: 'Lord X—— or the Prince den —— had better not repeat what they said yesterday, it was all I could do then not to reply: "You know perfectly well that you are as much one as I am."' Needless to say, when M. de Charlus thus uttered, at the times when, as one says, he was not 'all there', pro-German or other opinions, the members of his close circle who happened to be there, whether Jupien or the Duchesse de Guermantes, would as a matter of habit interrupt his incautious words and provide for the less intimate and more indiscreet listeners an interpretation of them which, while strained, was not dishonourable.

'But, heavens above! exclaimed Jupien, I was quite right not to want us to go too far. Look, he's already managed to get into conversation with a gardener's boy. Good-bye, sir, I'd better leave you, I can't leave my invalid alone for a second, he's nothing but a great baby.'

I got out of the cab again shortly before arriving at the Princesse de Guermantes's house and began to think once more about the lassitude and boredom with which, the previous evening, I had tried to note the line, in one of the most reputedly beautiful parts of the French countryside, that separated shadow from light on the trees. Certainly, the intellectual conclusions I had drawn from it did not affect my sensibility so cruelly today. They were still the same. But as happened each time I was wrenched out of my habits, going out at a different time, or to a new place, I felt acute pleasure. The pleasure today seemed to me to be a purely frivolous one, that of going to an afternoon party at the house of the Princesse de Guermantes. But since I knew now that I could never attain to anything more than frivolous pleasures, what point would there be in refusing it? I told myself again that I had not experienced, when I attempted that description, anything of the enthusiasm which, if not the only one, is one of the main criteria of talent. I tried now to extract from my memory other 'snapshots', particularly the snapshots it had taken in Venice, but the very word made it as boring as a photograph exhibition, and I felt that I had no more taste, or talent, for describing now what I had seen earlier, than yesterday for describing what I was observing, at that very moment, with a doleful and meticulous eye. Any moment now, hosts of friends whom I had not seen for such a long time would doubtless be asking me to give up this isolation and to devote my days to them. I had no reason to refuse them since I now had proof that I was no longer good for anything, that literature could no longer bring me any joy, whether through my own fault, because I was not talented enough, or through the fault of litera- ture, if it was indeed less pregnant with reality than I had thought.

When I pondered what Bergotte had said to me: 'You are ill, but one cannot feel sorry for you because you have the joys of the mind,' it struck me how wrong he had been about me. How little joy there was in this sterile lucidity! I could even add that if perhaps I did sometimes have pleasures – not of the intellect – I wasted them, and always on a different woman; so that if destiny had granted me another hundred years of life, free of infirmities, it would only have added successive extensions to a tediously protracted existence, which there seemed to be no point in prolonging thus far, let alone even further. As for the 'joys of the intellect', could I use that phrase for these cold observations which my perceptive eye or my precise reasoning picked out without any pleasure and which remained infertile?

But sometimes it is just when everything seems to be lost that we experience a presentiment that may save us; one has knocked on all the doors which lead nowhere, and then, unwittingly, one pushes against the only one through which one may enter and for which one would have searched in vain for a hundred years, and it opens.

Turning over the dismal thoughts which I have just set down, I had entered the Guermantes' courtyard and in my distraction had failed to see an approaching car; at the chauffeur's shout I had time only to step smartly aside, and as I retreated I could not help tripping up against the unevenly laid paving-stones, behind which was a coach-house. But at the moment when, regaining my balance, I set my foot down on a stone which was slightly lower than the one next to it, all my discouragement vanished in the face of the same happiness that, at different points in my life, had given me the sight of trees I had thought

I recognized when I was taking a drive round Balbec, the sight of the steeples of Martinville, the taste of a madeleine dipped in herb tea, and all the other sensations I have spoken about, and which the last works of Vinteuil had seemed to me to synthesize. Just as at the moment when I tasted the madeleine, all uneasiness about the future and all intellectual doubt were gone. Those that had assailed me a moment earlier about the reality of my intellectual talent, even the reality of literature, were lifted as if by enchantment.

Without my having started a new line of thought, or discovered a decisive argument, the difficulties which just now were insoluble had lost all their importance. This time, though, I had decided not to resign myself to not knowing the reason for it, as I had done on the day I tasted the madeleine dipped in herb tea. The happiness that I had just experienced was indeed just like that I had felt when eating the madeleine, and the cause of which I had at that time put off seeking. The difference, purely material, was in the images each evoked; a deep azure intoxicated my eyes, impressions of coolness and dazzling light swirled around me and, in my desire to grasp them, without daring to move any more than when I had tasted the madeleine and I was trying to bring back to my memory what it reminded me of, I continued, even at the risk of making myself the laughing-stock of the huge crowd of chauffeurs, to stagger, as I had done a moment before, one foot on the raised paving-stone, the other foot on the lower one. Each time I simply repeated the outward form of this movement, nothing helpful occurred; but if I succeeded, forgetting about the Guermantes' party, in recapturing the feeling I had experienced when I put my feet down in that way, then the dazzling and indistinct vision brushed against my consciousness, as if it were saying: 'Seize hold of me as I pass, if you are strong-minded enough, and try to solve the riddle of happiness I am offering you.' And almost at once I realized that it was Venice, all my efforts to describe which, and all the so-called snapshots taken by my memory, had never communicated anything to me, but which the sensation I had once felt on the two uneven flagstones in the baptistery of St Mark's had now at last expressed for me, along with all the other sensations associated with that sensation on that day, which had been waiting in their place, from which a sudden chance had imperiously made them emerge, in the sequence of forgotten days. In the same way, the taste of the little madeleine had reminded me of Combray. But why had the images of Combray and Venice given me at these two separate moments a joy akin to certainty and sufficient, without any other proofs, to make death a matter of indifference to me?

Still wondering what the answer was, and determined to find it that day, I entered the Guermantes' *hôtel*, because we always place less importance on the inner tasks we have to carry out than we do on the visible role we are playing, which, on this occasion, was that of a guest. But when I reached the first floor, a butler asked me to go into a small library-cum-sitting-room, next to the room where the refreshments were, and wait for the few moments until the piece being played was over, the Duchesse having ordered the doors to be kept closed during its performance. At that very moment, a second intimation occurred to reinforce the one which the two uneven paving-stones had just given me and to exhort me to persevere in my task. A servant, trying fruitlessly not to make any noise, had just knocked a spoon against a plate. The same kind of happiness I had felt from the uneven flagstones flooded over me; the feeling was again one of great heat, but quite different: mingled with the smell of smoke, alleviated by the cool fragrance of a forest setting; and I recognized that what I was enjoying so much was the same row of trees that I had found tedious to observe and to describe, and beside which, opening the bottle of beer I had had with me in the carriage, I had just for a moment, in a sort of dizziness, believed myself to be, so powerfully did the sound of the spoon against the plate give me, before I had time to pull myself together, the illusion of the sound of a workman's hammer doing something to one of the wheels of the train while we were halted beside the little wood. It seemed after that as if the signs which were, on this day, to bring me out of my despondency and renew my faith in literature were intent on multiplying themselves, for a butler who had long been in service with the Prince de Guermantes having recognized me, and having brought to me in the library, where I stayed in order to avoid going in to the refreshment room, a selection of petits fours and a glass of orangeade, I wiped my mouth with the napkin he had given me; but immediately, like the character in the

Arabian Nights who, without knowing it, performs precisely the ritual which makes appear, visible to himself alone, a docile genie ready to take him far away, a new vision of azure passed in front of my eyes; but it was pure and saline, and billowed into a bluish, bosomy swell; the impression was so strong that the moment I was reliving seemed actually to be the present; more stupefied than the day when I wondered whether I was really going to be welcomed by the Princesse de Guermantes or whether the whole prospect was about to dissolve, I thought that the servant had just opened the window on to the beach and that everything was inviting me to go down and stroll along the sea-front at high tide; the napkin which I had taken to wipe my mouth had exactly the same stiffness and the same degree of starch as the one with which I had had so much trouble drying myself in front of the window, the first day after my arrival in Balbec, and, now in this library in the Guermantes' *hôtel*, it displayed, spread across its folds and creases, the plumage of an ocean green and blue as a peacock's tail. And it was not just these colours which filled me with joy, but a whole moment of my life which aroused them, which had probably been an aspiration towards them, which some sense of fatigue or of sadness had perhaps prevented me from enjoying at Balbec, and which now, freed of whatever was imperfect in the external perception, pure and disembodied, filled me with delight.

The piece that was being played was about to end at any moment, at which point I would be obliged to enter the drawing-room. I therefore forced myself to try to see as clearly and quickly as possible into the nature of the identical pleasures I had just experienced three times in a few minutes, and then to isolate the lesson I was to draw from it. On the enormous difference between the true impression we have had of a thing and the artificial impression we give ourselves of it when we try by an act of will to represent it to ourselves, I did not pause; remembering too clearly with what relative indifference Swann had once been able to speak of the days when he had been loved, because beneath his words he saw something different, and the sudden pain that the little phrase of Vinteuil had caused him by bringing back those very days, just as he had felt them at the time, I understood only too well that what the sensation of the uneven flagstones, the stiffness of the napkin, the taste of the madeleine, had awoken within me bore no relation to what I was trying to remember about Venice, about Balbec and about Combray, with the help of a uniform memory; and I understood that life might be deemed dreary, even though at certain moments it may seem so beautiful, because for the most part it is on the basis of something quite different from it, on the basis of images which retain nothing of life itself, that we judge it and that we disparage it. At most I noted incidentally that the differences which there are between each of the real impressions – differences which explain why a uniform depiction of life cannot be a good likeness – was probably because the slightest word we have spoken at any point in our lives, the most insignificant action, was surrounded by, and was a reflection of, things which logically were not connected to it, were separated from it by the intelligence which had no need of them for its rational purposes, but in the middle of which – here, the pink reflection of the evening on the flower-covered wall of a country restaurant, a feeling of hunger, the desire for women, the pleasure of luxury – there, the blue scrolls of the morning sea enveloping the musical phrases which partially emerge from them like the shoulders of mermaids – the gesture, the simplest action remains enclosed as if within a thousand sealed vessels each one of which would be filled with things of a completely different colour, odour and temperature; quite apart from the fact that these vessels, arranged across the full length of our years, during which we have never ceased to change, even if only our thoughts or our dreams, are placed at quite different heights and give us the sensation of extraordinarily varied atmospheres. Admittedly, these are changes that we have accomplished imperceptibly; but between the memory which suddenly comes back to us and our current state, even between two memories of different years or places or times, the distance is such that it is enough, apart even from any specific originality, to render them incomprehensible to each other. Yes, if the memory, thanks to forgetfulness, has not been able to make a single connection, to throw up a single link between it and the present moment, if it has stayed in its place, at its date, if it has kept its distance, its isolation in the depths of a valley or at the very peak of a summit, it suddenly makes us breathe a new air, new precisely because it is an air we have breathed before, this purer air which the poets have tried in vain to make reign in paradise and which could not provide this profound feeling of renewal if it had not already been breathed, for the only true paradise is a paradise that we have lost.

And I noticed in passing that, in the work of art that I now, without having made any conscious resolution, felt close to undertaking, this would pose great difficulties. For I would have to execute its successive parts in slightly different materials, and would need to find one very different from that suited to memories of mornings beside the sea, or afternoons in Venice, if I wanted to depict the evenings at Rivebelle at the moment when, in the dining-room that opened on to the garden, the heat was beginning to break up, to subside and settle, when a last glimmer was still illuminating the roses on the walls of the restaurant, while the last water-colours of the day were still visible in the sky – in a different way, new, with a particular transparency and sonority, compact, cooling and pink.

I slid rapidly over all that, being more imperiously required to seek out the cause of this happiness and the nature of the certainty with which it imposed itself, an enquiry I had hitherto postponed. And I began to divine this cause as I compared these varied impressions of well-being with each other, all of which, the sound of the spoon on the plate, the uneven flagstones, the taste of the madeleine, had something in common, which I was experiencing in the present moment and at the same time in a moment far away, so that the past was made to encroach upon the present and make me uncertain about which of the two I was in; the truth was that the being within me who was enjoying this impression was enjoying it because of something shared between a day in the past and the present moment, something extra-temporal, and this being appeared only when, through one of these moments of identity between the present and the past, it was able to find itself in the only milieu in which it could live and enjoy the essence of things, that is to say outside of time. This explained why my anxieties on the subject of my death had ceased the moment when I unconsciously recognized the taste of the little madeleine, since at that very moment the being that I had been was an extra-temporal being, and consequently unconcerned with the vicissitudes of the future. It lived only through the essence of things, and was unable to grasp this in the present, where, as the imagination does not come into play, the senses were incapable of providing it; even the future towards which action tends surrenders it to us. This being had only ever come to me, only ever manifested itself to me on the occasions, outside of action and immediate pleasure, when the miracle of an analogy had made me escape from the present. It alone had the power to make me find the old days again, the lost time, in the face of which the efforts of my memory and my intellect always failed.

And perhaps, if just now I thought that Bergotte was wrong when he talked about the joys of the life of the mind, it was because at that moment what I meant by 'life of the mind' was the sort of logical reasoning which had no connection with it, or with what existed in me at that moment – exactly as I had been able to find life and society boring because I was judging them according to untruthful memories, whereas I had a considerable appetite for living now that a real moment of the past had just, on three separate occasions, been recreated within me.

Was it no more than a moment of the past? Perhaps it was a great deal more; something which, common both to the past and the present, is much more essential than either of them. So many times in the course of my life reality had disappointed me because at the moment when I perceived it, my imagination, which was my only organ for the enjoyment of beauty, could not be applied to it, by virtue of the inevitable law which means that one can imagine only what is absent. But now all the consequences of that iron law had suddenly been neutralized, suspended, by a wonderful natural expedient, which had held out the prospect of a sensation – sound of a fork and a hammer, same book title, etc. – both in the past, which enabled my imagination to enjoy it, and in the present, where the actual shock to my senses of experiencing the sound, the touch of linen, etc., had added to the dreams of the imagination the thing which they were habitually deprived of, the idea of existence – and, thanks to this subterfuge, had allowed my being to obtain, to isolate, to immobilize – for the duration of a flash of lightning – the one thing it never apprehends: a little bit of time in its pure state. The being which had been reborn in me when, with such a tremor of happiness, I had heard the sound common at once both to the spoon touching the plate and the hammer hitting the wheel, or felt the unevenness beneath my feet common to the stones of the Guermantes' courtyard and St Mark's baptistery, etc., this spirit draws its nourishment only from the essence of things, and only in them does it find its sustenance and its delight. It languishes in the observation of the present where the senses cannot bring this to it, in the consideration of a past where the intelligence desiccates it, and in the expectation of a future which the will constructs out of fragments of the present and the past from which it extracts even more of their reality without retaining any more than is useful for the narrowly human, utilitarian ends that it assigns to them. Yet a single sound, a single scent, already heard or breathed long ago, may once again, both in the present and the past, be real without being present, ideal without being abstract, as soon as the permanent and habitually hidden essence of things is liberated, and our true self, which may sometimes have seemed to be long dead, but never was entirely, is re-awoken and re-animated when it receives the heavenly food that is brought to it. One minute freed from the order of time has recreated in us, in order to feel it, the man freed from the order of time. And because of that we can understand why he trusts his joy, and even if the simple taste of a madeleine does not seem logically to contain reasons for this joy, we can understand how the word 'death' has no meaning for him; situated outside time, what should he fear from the future?

But this optical illusion which brought back to me a moment of the past incompatible with the present could not last. The scenes played out by our voluntary memory, of course, can be prolonged, as they require no more effort on our part than leafing through a picture-book. Long ago, for example, on the day when I had to go to the house of the Princesse de Guermantes for the first time, from the sun-filled courtyard of our house in Paris, I had idly gazed on images of my choice, of the place de l'Église in Combray, or the beach at Balbec, as if I had been leafing through an album of water-colours painted in the different places I had been to choose illustrations of each of these days, enabling me to say, with the selfish pleasure of a collector, as I catalogued the illustrations of my memory: 'I've certainly seen some beautiful things in my life.' My memory probably then affirmed the difference between these sensations; but all it could do was to rearrange homogeneous elements in different ways. The same was not true of the three recollections I had just had and in which, instead of giving me a more flattering idea of my self, I had on the contrary almost doubted that self's current reality. Just as on the day when I had dipped the madeleine in the warm herb tea, in the place where I happened to be, wherever that were, then in my bedroom in Paris, or today, at this moment, in the library of the Prince de Guermantes, or a little earlier in the courtyard of his *hôtel*, there had been within me, irradiating a small area around me, a sensation (taste of the soaked madeleine, the sound of metal, a feeling underfoot) which was common to the place where I was and also to another place (my aunt Octave's bedroom, the railway carriage, St Mark's baptistery). And at the moment I was working this out, the piercing noise of a water-pipe, just like those long cries that in summer the pleasure boats sometimes made in the evening off the coast at Balbec, made me feel (as I had already once at Paris, in a grand restaurant, at the sight of a luxurious dining-room half empty, summery and hot) much more than a sensation simply analogous to the one I had had at the end of the afternoon at Balbec when all the tables were covered with their cloths and their silverware, the vast bay-windows wide open to the beach, in one long space, a single wall of glass or stone, while the sun slowly descended over the sea where the ships were starting their cries, and all I had to do, to join Albertine and her friends who were walking on the sea-front, was to step over the wooden frame, scarcely higher than my ankle, into a groove in which, to let the air into the hotel, all the continuous panes of glass had been slid. But the painful memory of having loved Albertine was not a part of this sensation. The only painful memory is of the dead. And they rapidly decay and nothing remains, even around their tombs, save the beauty of nature, silence and pure air. Yet it was not just an echo, the duplicate of a past sensation, that the sound of the water-pipe had just made me experience, it was that sensation itself. In this instance, as in all the preceding ones, the shared sensation had sought to recreate the old location around it, while the actual location which now occupied the place used all the resistance of its substantiality to oppose this intrusion into an *hôtel* in Paris of a

Normandy beach, or a railway embankment. The seaside dining-room at Balbec, with its damask linen laid out like altar cloths to receive the setting sun, had tried to undermine the solidity of the Guermantes' *hôtel*, to force open its doors, and for a moment had made the sofas around me flicker, as on another occasion it had done to the tables in the Paris restaurant. Always, in resurrections of this sort, the distant location engendered around the common sensation would be meshed for a moment, like a wrestler, with the actual location. The actual location had always been the winner; and the loser had always seemed to me to be the more beautiful; so beautiful that I remained in ecstasy on the uneven paving-stones, as before the cup of tea, attempting to retain, when it appeared, and bring back, the moment it escaped me, this influx and rejection of Combray, or Venice, or Balbec, which surged up only to abandon me a few moments later in the midst of these new surroundings, permeated though they now were by the past. And if the current location had not immediately been victorious, I believe I would have lost consciousness; because these resurrections of the past, for the second they last, are so complete that they do more than simply force our eyes to stop seeing the room around them in order to look at the railway line bordered with trees or the incoming tide. They force our nostrils to breathe the air of places that are actually far away, our will to choose between the different plans they suggest to us, our whole person to believe itself surrounded by them, or at least to stumble between them and the present locations, in a dizzying uncertainty akin to that which one sometimes experiences through some ineffable vision at the moment of falling asleep.

So it began to seem that what the being which had now been resuscitated in me three or four times had just enjoyed might well have been fragments of existence which had escaped from time, but that the contemplation of them, while a contemplation of eternity, was itself fugitive. And yet I felt that the pleasure it had brought to my life, albeit at rare intervals, was the only one that was both real and fertile. The sign of the unreality of the others is surely shown clearly enough, either by the impossibility of their satisfying us, as for instance in the case of social pleasures, which at best result in discomfort caused by the ingestion of awful food, or friendship, which is a fiction because the artist who, for whatever reason, gives up an hour of work to spend an hour chatting with a friend knows that he is sacrificing a reality for something that does not exist (friends being friends only within the ambit of that mild eccentricity which accompanies our lives, and which we acquiesce in, but which in our heart of hearts we know is like the wanderings of a madman who believes the furniture is alive and talks to it), or else by the sadness which follows their satisfaction, as with the sadness I felt on the day when I had been introduced to Albertine, for the trouble I had gone to, slight though it was, in order to obtain something – the acquaintance of a young girl – which seemed a slight thing only because I had obtained it. Even a more profound pleasure, like the one I should have been able to experience when I loved Albertine, was in fact perceived only inversely, through the anxiety I felt when she was not there, because when I was sure that she would soon be with me again, as on the day when she came back from the Trocadéro, I had seemed to experience no more than a vague sense of worry, whereas I became more and more excited the more deeply I penetrated, with an increasing sense of personal joy, into the sound of the knife or the taste of the tea which had brought into my bedroom my aunt Léonie's bedroom, and with it all of Combray, and its two ways. I had therefore decided to cling on to this contemplation of the essence of things, to stabilize it, but how, by what means? Of course at the moment when the stiffness of the napkin had brought back Balbec, and for an instant had caressed my imagination, not only with the view of the sea as it had been on that day, but with the smell of the room, the strength of the wind, the desire for lunch, the uncertainty which walk to take, all of it tied to the feeling of the linen like the thousand wings of angels which revolve a thousand times a minute; and of course, at the moment when the unevenness of the two paving-stones had extended the thin, desiccated images I had of Venice and St Mark's, and all the sensations I had felt there, into every sense and each dimension, linking the square to the church, the canal to the landing-stage and, to everything the eye can see, the world of desires seen only by the mind, I had been tempted, if not, because of the time of year, to go back and float along the canals of Venice, for me associated principally with the spring, then at least to return to Balbec.

But I did not linger for an instant over this thought. In the first place, I knew that places were not the same as the pictures conjured up by their names, and that it was almost only in my dreams, in my sleep, that a place stretched out before my eyes in that pure materiality that is completely distinct from the ordinary things that we can see and touch, and which I always used to imagine them as possessing. But even when it came down to images of an altogether different kind, those of memory, I knew that the beauty of Balbec was something I had never experienced when I was there, and that the beauty it left me with, the beauty of memory, was something I was unable to discover when I went back there to stay for a second time. I had too much experience of the impossibility of making contact in reality with what lay deep within myself; it was not in St Mark's Square, any more than it had been in my second visit to Balbec or in my return to Tansonville to see Gilberte, that I would find Lost Time, and travel, which did nothing but offer me once again the illusion that these bygone impressions had an existence outside of me, in some corner of a particular place, could not be the means which I was looking for. And I did not want to let myself be taken in yet again, for what I wanted to do was to find out once and for all whether it was truly possible to reach that which, always disappointed as I had been in the presence of places and human beings, I had (even though that piece of chamber music by Vinteuil seemed to tell me the opposite) believed to be unreachable. I was therefore not going to attempt another experiment on a path that I had long known led nowhere. Impressions of the sort that I was trying to stabilize would simply evaporate if they came into contact with a direct pleasure which was powerless to bring them into being. The only way to continue to appreciate them was to try to understand them more completely just as they were, that is to say within myself, to make them transparent enough to see right down into their depths. I had been unable to know pleasure at Balbec, any more than the pleasure of living with Albertine, which had become perceptible to me only after the event. And the recapitulation I was making of all the disappointments of my life, as I had lived it, and which made me believe that its reality must reside somewhere else than in action, was not bringing the different disappointments together in a purely fortuitous manner in accordance with the circumstances of my existence. I felt very strongly that the disappointments of travel and the disappointments of love were not different disappointments, but the varied aspect taken on, according to the circumstances which bring it into play, by our powerlessness to realize ourselves in material pleasure or real action. And, thinking once again about the extra-temporal joy caused by the sound of the spoon or the taste of the madeleine, I said to myself: 'Was this the happiness which the sonata's little phrase offered to Swann, which he was unable to find in artistic creation and therefore mistook by assimilating it to the pleasure of love; was this the happiness I had felt as a presentiment, even more supra-terrestrial than the little phrase of the sonata, of the mysterious, glowing appeal of the septet which Swann had not been able to recognize, being dead like so many others before the truth made for them can be revealed to them? And anyway, it would not have been any use to him, for the phrase could easily symbolize an appeal, but not create the powers to make Swann the writer that he was not.'

Yet after a moment I realized, having given some thought to these resurrections of memory, that in another way, obscure impressions had sometimes, even already at Combray on the Guermantes way, attracted the attention of my thoughts, in the way these reminiscences did, but not then hiding a past impression but a new truth, a precious image that I sought to discover by efforts of the same kind as those which one makes to remember something, as if our most beautiful ideas were like tunes in music which come back, so to speak, to us without our ever having heard them, and which we do our best to listen to and to transcribe. I remembered with pleasure, because it showed me that I was already the same then and gave me back something that was fundamental to my nature, but also with sadness when I thought that I had not progressed since then, that in Combray already I used attentively to fix before my mind's eye some image which had impelled me to look at it, a cloud, a triangle, a church spire, a flower, a pebble, feeling that there might be something quite different beneath the signs which I had to try to uncover, some form of thought they translated like those hieroglyphics that people used to believe represented only material objects. Doubtless the effort of deciphering was difficult but it alone gave reading a degree of truth. For the truths that the intellect grasps directly as giving access to the world of full enlightenment have something less profound, less necessary about them than those that life has, despite ourselves, communicated in an impression, a material impression because it enters us through our senses, but one from which it is also possible to extract something spiritual. So in each case, whether we are dealing with impressions such as that made on me by the sight of the steeples of Martinville, or recollections like that of the unevenness of the two steps or the taste of the madeleine, I had to try to interpret the sensations as the signs of so many laws and ideas, at the same time as trying to think, that is to draw out from the penumbra what I had felt, and convert it into a spiritual equivalent. And what was this method, which seemed to me to be the only one, but the making of a work of art? The consequences of this were already thronging into my mind; for whether it was a matter of recollections of the sort characterized by the sound of the fork or the taste of the madeleine, or of those truths written with the aid of figures, the meaning of which I was trying to find in my head where, church steeples or wild grasses, they composed a complicated and elaborate book of spells, their primary character was that I was not free to choose them, that they were given to me just as they were. And I sensed that this was the mark of their authenticity. I had not been looking for the two uneven paving-stones in the courtyard where I stumbled. But the very fortuity, the inevitability of the manner in which the sensation was encountered, controlled the authenticity of the past that it resuscitated, the images it let loose, since we feel it striving towards the light, we feel the joy of the real, found again. It is also the control of the truth of the whole picture made out of contemporary impressions that it brings in its train, with this infallible proportion of light and shade, intensity and omission, memory and forgetfulness, of which conscious memory or observation will always be incapable.

As for the inner book of unknown signs (signs which seemed to stand out, as it were, in relief, and which my attention, exploring my unconscious, cast around for, stumbled over, and traced the shapes of, like a diver feeling his way underwater), for the reading of which nobody else could provide me with any rules, reading them becomes one of those acts of creation in which nobody can take our place or even collaborate with us. So many people are discouraged from writing because of this! There are almost no tasks they will not take on in order to avoid it. Every major event, from the Dreyfus Affair to the war, provided further excuses for writers not to decipher that book – they wanted to ensure the triumph of justice, to rebuild the moral unity of the nation, they were much too busy to think about literature. But these were simply excuses because they did not have, or no longer had, genius, or to put it another way, instinct. For instinct shows us the work we have to do and intelligence provides the pretexts for evading it. Excuses have absolutely no place in art, mere intentions do not count for anything, the artist has to listen to his instinct all the time, with the result that art is the most real thing there is, the most austere school of life, and the true Last Judgment. That book, the most painful of all to decipher, is also the only one dictated to us by reality, the only one whose 'impression' has been made in us by reality itself. Whatever the ideas that may have been left in us by our life, their material outline, the trace of the impression they originally made on us, is always the indispensable warrant of their truth. The ideas formed by pure intelligence contain no more than a logical truth, a possible truth; their choice is arbitrary. The book whose characters are forged within us, rather than sketched by us, is the only book we have. Not that the ideas which we form ourselves may not be logically right, but that we do not know whether they are true. Only the impression, however slight its material may seem, however elusive its trace, can be a criterion of truth, and on that account is the only thing worthy of being apprehended by the mind; it alone, if the mind can elucidate its truth, can bring the mind to a more perfected state, and give it pure happiness. An impression is for the writer what an experiment is for the scientist, except that for the scientist the work of the intelligence precedes it, and for the writer it comes afterwards. Anything we have not had to decipher, to bring to light by our own effort, anything which was already clearly visible, is not our own. The only things that come from ourselves are those we draw out of the obscurity within us, which can never be known by other people.

A slanting ray of the setting sun suddenly reminded me of a time in my early childhood which I had completely forgotten about, when, as my aunt Léonie had a fever which Dr Percepied was afraid might be typhoid, they put me for a week in the little bedroom Eulalie usually occupied, looking over the place de l'Église, where there was nothing but rush matting on the floor and thin percale curtains which were always buzzing with a sunlight that I was not used to. And, seeing how the memory of an old servant's little bedroom suddenly added such a different and delightful stretch of time to my past life, I contrasted this with the utter absence of impressions left on my life by the most sumptuous celebrations in the most princely mansions. The only slightly bad thing about this room of Eulalie's was that in the evenings, because of the proximity of the viaduct, one heard the hooting of the trains. But because I knew that these bellowings proceeded from properly regulated machines, they did not frighten me in the way that I might have been frightened, in prehistoric times, by the cries of a nearby mammoth on its wild and unpredictable path.

So I had already come to the conclusion that we have no freedom at all in the face of the work of art, that we cannot shape it according to our wishes, but that as it pre-exists us, and both because it is necessary and hidden, and because it is, as it were, a law of nature, we have to discover it. But is not this discovery, which art can cause us to make, the discovery, fundamentally, of the thing that ought to be most precious to us, and of which we normally remain unaware for ever, our true life, our reality as we have experienced it, which is often so different from what we believe it to be that we are filled with happiness when some chance event brings the real memory back to us? I found further support for this view in the falsity of so-called realist art, which would not be so untruthful if life had not given us the habit of expressing our experience in ways that do not reflect it, but which we none the less take in a very short space of time to be reality. I felt that I would not have to worry about the various literary theories which had troubled me now and then – notably those which critics had developed at the time of the Dreyfus Affair and which they had taken up again during the war, with the intention of 'bringing the artist down from his ivory tower' and encouraging the abandonment of frivolous or sentimental subjects in favour of the great workers' movements or, if crowds were not possible, at least of noble intellectuals or heroes rather than insignificant members of the idle rich ('I must admit that the depiction of these useless people leaves me rather cold,' Bloch would say).

But anyway, quite apart from their intellectual content, these theories seemed to me to indicate the inferiority of their supporters, in the same way that a really well brought-up child who hears the people with whom he has been taken to lunch saying: 'We don't hide anything here, we say whatever we think,' senses that this indicates a moral quality inferior to that inherent in good deeds, pure and simple, which do not need words. Real art has nothing to do with proclamations of this sort, and carries out its work in silence. Also, the people who indulged in this kind of theorizing used ready-made expressions which had a curious similarity to those of the idiots they were attacking. Indeed it may well be that quality of language is a better gauge of the level of moral or intellectual endeavour than aesthetic approach. Conversely, though, this quality of language (and the laws of character can be equally well studied in a frivolous subject and in a serious one, just as an anatomist can as easily study the laws of anatomy on the body of an imbecile as on that of a man of talent, the great moral laws, as much as those of the circulation of the blood or renal filtration, differing very little with the intellectual level of the individual), which the theoreticians think they can do without, those who admire the theoreticians believe simplistically that it shows no great intellectual worth, worth which they need, if they are to discern it, to see expressed directly and which they cannot infer from the beauty of an image. Whence the vulgar temptation for the writer to write intellectual works. Gross unscrupulousness. A work in which there are theories is like an object with its price-tag still attached. Even this latter only gives something a value, which, on the contrary, logical reasoning in literature diminishes. One reasons, that is one wanders off the track, each time that one does not have the strength of mind to force oneself to make an impression pass through all the successive states which will lead to its stabilization and its expression.

The reality to be expressed resided, I now realized, not in the subject's appearance but at a depth where appearance hardly matters, as in the case of its symbolization by the sound of the spoon on a plate, or the starched stiffness of the napkin, which had been more valuable for my spiritual renewal than any number of humanitarian, patriotic, internationalist or metaphysical conversations. 'No more style, was what I had heard people say in those days, no more literature, what we want is life.' It is easy to see how even M. de Norpois's simple theories in opposition to 'flute-players' had taken on a new lease of life since the war. For all those who do not have an artistic sense, by which I mean the submission to an interior reality, may still be endowed with the capacity to argue about art till the cows come home. And to the extent that they are also diplomats or financiers, deeply involved in the 'realities' of the present time, they are all the more willing to believe that literature is just a form of intellectual amusement destined to be gradually eliminated. Some even wanted the novel to be a sort of cinematographic stream of things. This was an absurd idea. Nothing sets us further apart from what we have really perceived than that sort of cinematographic approach.

On the subject of books, I had remembered as I came into the library what the Goncourts say about the fine editions it contains, and had promised myself that I would look at them while I was closeted here. So all the time I had been following my line of thought, I had been taking down the precious volumes at random until, absent-mindedly opening one of them, *François le Champi* by George Sand,[81] I felt unpleasantly struck by some impression which seemed to have too little in common with my current thoughts, until I realized a moment later, with an emotion which brought tears to my eyes, how much in accord with them this impression actually was. In a room where somebody has died, the undertaker's men are getting ready to bring down the coffin, while the son of a man who has done his country some service shakes hands with the last friends as they file out; if a fanfare suddenly sounds beneath the windows, he is horrified and thinks that some mockery is being made of his grief. At this, although he has until then remained in control of himself, he can suddenly no longer restrain his tears; because he has just realized that what he is hearing is the band of a regiment that is sharing his mourning and paying its last respects to his father's mortal remains. In the same way, I had just recognized how well suited my current feelings were to the painful impression I had experienced when I read the title of a book in the Prince de Guermantes's library; a title which had given me the idea that literature really did give us that world of mystery which I no longer found in it. And yet it was not a particularly outstanding book, it was only *François le Champi*. But that name, like the Guermantes' name, was not like all the other names I have come across since: the memory of what had seemed inexplicable to me in the subject of *François le Champi* when Mama was reading me George Sand's book was re-awoken by the title (just as the Guermantes' name, when I had not seen them for such a long time, contained the essence of the feudal system for me – so *François le Champi* contained the essence of the novel), and for a moment took the place of the generally accepted idea of what George Sand's rural Berry novels are about. At a dinner-party, where thought always remains close to the surface of things, I would probably have been able to talk about *François le Champi* and the Guermantes without either of them meaning what they had meant in Combray. But when I was alone, as at this moment, I was plunged down to a much greater depth. In those moments, the idea that some woman I had met in society was a cousin of Mme de Guermantes, that is, the cousin of a magic-lantern character, seemed incomprehensible, and it seemed equally incomprehensible that the finest books that I had read might be – I do not say better than, which of course they were – but even equal to the extraordinary *François le Champi*. This was an impression from long ago, in which my memories of childhood and family were affectionately mingled and which I had not immediately recognized. For a moment I had angrily wondered who the stranger was who had just upset me. But the stranger was myself, it was the child I was then, whom the book had just brought back to life within me because, knowing nothing of me except this child, it was this child that the book had immediately summoned, wanting to be looked at only by his eyes, loved only by his heart, and wanting to speak only to him. So this book which my mother had read aloud to me in Combray until it was almost morning had retained for me all the wonder of that night. It is true that the 'pen' of George Sand, to use an expression of Brichot's, who was so fond of saying that a book had been written 'with a nimble pen', did not at all seem to me, as it had seemed so long ago to my mother before she slowly began to model her literary tastes on mine, a magical pen. But it was a pen which, without meaning to, I had charged with electricity, as schoolboys often do for fun, and now a thousand insignificant details from Combray, unglimpsed for a very long time, came tumbling helter-skelter of their own accord to hang from the magnetized nib in an endless, flickering line of memories.

Some mystery-loving minds maintain that objects retain something of the eyes that have looked at them, that we can see monuments and pictures only through an almost tangible veil woven over them through the centuries by the love and contemplation of so many admirers. This fantasy would become truth if they transposed it into the realm of the only reality each person knows, into the domain of their own sensitivity. Yes, in that sense and that sense only (but it is much the more important one), a thing which we have looked at long ago, if we see it again, brings back to us, along with our original gaze, all the images which that gaze contained. This is because things – a book in its red binding, like the rest – at the moment we notice them, turn within us into something immaterial, akin to all the preoccupations or sensations we have at that particular time, and mingle indissolubly with them. Some name, read long ago in a book, contains among its syllables the strong wind and bright sunlight of the day when we were reading it. Thus the sort of literature which is content to 'describe things', to provide nothing more of them than a miserable list of lines and surfaces, despite calling itself realist, is the furthest away from reality, the most impoverishing and depressing, because it unceremoniously cuts all communication between our present self and the past, the essence of which is retained in things, and the future, where things prompt us to enjoy it afresh. It is this that any art worthy of the name must express, and, if it fails in this, we can still draw a lesson from its incapacity (whereas there is none to be drawn even from the successes of realism), namely that this essence is, in part, subjective and impossible to communicate.

More than that, a thing which we saw at a certain time in our lives, a book which we read, does not remain for ever a part solely of what there was around us; it remains just as faithfully part of what we then were, and can be re-experienced, rethought, only by the sensibility, the thought processes, the person that we then were; if in the library I take down *François le Champi*, a child immediately rises up within me and takes my place, the only one who has the right to read the title *François le Champi* and who reads it as he read it then, with the same impression of the weather outside in the garden, the same dreams as he formed then about other countries and about life, the same anxiety about the future. Or again, if I see a thing from another time, it will be a young man who rises up. So that my character today is nothing but an abandoned quarry, thinking everything it contains to be monotonous and identical, but out of which each memory, like a sculptor of genius, makes countless statues. I say each *thing* that we see again, because books in this respect behave as things; the way a book opened along the spine, the texture of the paper, may have retained within it as vivid a memory of the way I imagined Venice then, and of my wish to go there, as the book's actual sentences. More vivid even, for words sometimes get in the way, like those photographs of a person, looking at which one remembers him less well than if one had been content just to think about him. Certainly with many of the books of my childhood, even, sadly, some by Bergotte himself, if I happen to pick them up some evening when I am feeling tired, I do so only as I might take a train, in the hope of finding some repose by looking at different things and breathing the atmosphere of times past. But it sometimes happens that this sought-for evocation is hindered by prolonged reading of the book. There is, for instance, one of Bergotte's books (the copy of which in the Prince's library bore a dedication that was fawning and platitudinous in the extreme), which I read one winter day when I was unable to see Gilberte, in which I can never manage to find the phrases I used to love so much. Certain words almost make me believe that I've found them again, but it's impossible. Where could the beauty be that I used to find in them? Yet from the volume itself, the snow that covered the Champs-Élysées on the day I read it has not been removed: I can see it still.

And that is why, if I had ever been tempted to be a bibliophile, like the Prince de Guermantes, I should only have been a rather odd one, except that the beauty which accrues to a book for collectors, independently of its inherent value, when they know the libraries through which it has passed, or know that it was given by a particular sovereign on the occasion of some significant event to some famous man, when they have been able to trace its movements, from sale to sale, throughout its life, all the, so to speak, historic beauty of a book, would not be lost on me. But I would prefer to derive its value from my own life, rather than mere curiosity; and it would often not be the physical copy itself that I would associate with it, but the work itself, as in the case of *François le Champi*, revealed to me for the first time in my little room at Combray, during perhaps the loveliest and saddest night of my life, when I had, alas! (at a time when the mysterious Guermantes appeared completely inaccessible to me) obtained from my parents their first surrendering of authority, from which I would later come to date the decline of my health and my will, and my withdrawal, each day more complete, from a difficult task — and rediscovered today, appropriately, in the Guermantes' library, on this most glorious day, by which were illuminated suddenly not only the old fumblings of my thought, but even the purpose of my life and perhaps of art. As for individual copies of books, I could have been interested in them too, in a living sense. The first edition of a work would have been more precious to me than the others, but by that I would have meant the edition in which I had read it for the first time. I would look for the original editions, by which I mean those from which I had received an original impression of the book. Because subsequent impressions are not original. In the case of novels, I would collect old-fashioned bindings, the ones from the period when I read my first novels and which so often would have heard Papa telling me to 'Sit up straight!' Like the dress a woman was wearing when we saw her for the first time, they would help me to rediscover the love I had then, the beauty over which I have superimposed too many decreasingly loved images in my attempt to rediscover the first one, I who am not the I who saw it and who must give way to the I that I was then, if it calls up the thing it knew and that my I of today does not recognize at all. But even in this sense, which is the only one I could ever understand, I would not be tempted to be a bibliophile. I am too aware of how porous things are to the mind, and how they become saturated with it, for that.

The library which I would put together for myself in this way would be of an even greater value still; because the books I read long ago at Combray, in Venice, enriched now by my memory with vast illuminations representing the church of Saint-Hilaire, the gondola moored at the foot of San Giorgio Maggiore on the Grand Canal encrusted with glittering sapphires, would have become worthy of those 'illustrated books', illuminated bibles or Books of Hours, which the collector never opens to read but only to be enchanted once again by the colours which were added to it by some rival of Foucquet,[82] and which make these works as priceless as they are. And yet even to open these books read long ago just to look at the pictures which did not adorn them then would still seem so dangerous that, even in this sense, the only one I could understand, I would not be tempted to be a bibliophile. I know all too well how easily these images left by the mind are effaced by the mind. For the old ones they substitute new ones which do not have the same power of resurrection. And if I still had the *François le Champi* which Mama took one evening out of the parcel of books my grandmother must have given me for my birthday, I would never look at it: I would be too frightened of gradually inserting into it my current impressions until they had completely covered up the old ones, I would be too frightened of seeing it become at this point a thing of the present which, when I asked it to raise up once again the child who spelled out its title in the little bedroom at Combray, the child, not recognizing its accent, would no longer respond to its call, and would remain for ever buried in oblivion.

The idea of a popular art, like that of a patriotic art, seemed to me, if indeed not dangerous, certainly laughable. If it was a question of making it accessible to the people, by sacrificing the refinements of form, 'only good for the idle rich', I had spent enough time among society people to know that they are the real illiterates, not the electrical workers. Seen from this perspective, an art which was popular in form might have been destined for the members of the Jockey Club rather than for those of the Confédération Générale de Travail;[83] as for subject matter, popular novels are as boring to working people as books written specially for them are to children. When we read, we are seeking to be taken out of our surroundings, and workers are as curious about princes as princes are about workers. At the beginning of the war M. Barrès said that the artist (in that instance, Titian) had a duty above all else to serve the glory of his country. But he can serve it only by being an artist, that is, on condition, while he is studying these laws, instituting his experiences and making his discoveries, which are as delicate as those of science, that he does not think about anything else – even his country – except the truth which is before his eyes. Let us not be like the revolutionaries who despised the works of Watteau and de La Tour out of 'good citizenship', painters who do more honour to France than all those of the Revolution. Anatomy is perhaps not what the tender hearted would choose, if they had a choice. It was not his good-hearted benevolence (which was great) that made Choderlos de Laclos write *Les Liaisons dangereuses*, nor his fondness for the middle class, lower or upper, that made Flaubert choose as his subjects those of *Madame Bovary* and *L'Éducation senti-mentale*. Some used to say that art in a period of speed and haste would be brief, like the people before the war who predicted that it would be over quickly. The railway was thus supposed to have killed contempla-tive thought, and it was vain to long for the days of the stage-coach, but now the automobile fulfils their function and once again sets the tourists down in front of abandoned churches.

An image presented to us by life brings us in reality, in that moment, multiple and different sensations. The sight, for example, of the cover of a book already read has, woven into the letters of its title, the moonbeams of a distant summer night. The taste of our morning café au lait brings with it the vague hope of good weather which so often, long ago, while we were drinking it out of a creamy-white, rippled porcelain bowl which might almost have been made out of hardened milk, when the day was still intact and full, made us smile at the sheer uncertainty of the early light. An hour is not just an hour, it is a vessel full of perfumes, sounds, plans and atmospheres. What we call reality is a certain relationship between these sensations and the memories which surround us simultaneously – a relationship which is suppressed in a simple cinematographic vision, which actually moves further away from truth the more it professes to be confined to it – a unique relationship which the writer has to rediscover in order to bring its two different terms together permanently in his sentence. One can list indefinitely in a description all the objects that figured in the place described, but the truth will begin only when the writer takes two different objects, establishes their relationship, the analogue in the world of art of the unique relation created in the world of science by the laws of causality, and encloses them within the necessary armature of a beautiful style. Indeed, just as in life, it begins at the moment when, by bringing together a quality shared by two sensations, he draws out their common essence by uniting them with each other, in order to protect them from the contingencies of time, in a metaphor. Had not nature herself, from this point of view, set me on the way to art, wasn't she herself the beginning of art, she who made it possible for me, often after a long interval, to recognize the beauty of one thing only in another, noon at Combray only in the sound of its bells, mornings at Doncières only in the hiccuping of our water-heater? The relationship may not be very interesting, the objects ordinary, the style bad, but if no relationship has been established, there is nothing.

But that was not all. If reality were a kind of residue of experience, more or less identical for everybody, because when we talk about bad weather, a war, a cab-stand, a brightly lit restaurant, a garden in flower, everybody knows what we mean, if reality were just that, then no doubt some sort of cinematographic film of things would be enough and 'style' and 'literature' which departed from their simple data would be an artificial irrelevance. But was this really what reality was? When I tried to ascertain what actually happens at the moment when something makes a particular impression on us, whether as on the day when, crossing the bridge over the Vivonne, the shadow of a cloud on the water had made me exclaim 'Damn!' and jump for joy, or when, listening to a sentence of Bergotte's, the only part of my impression that I had been conscious of was the not particularly characteristic phrase 'That's marvellous', or when, annoyed by some piece of bad behaviour, Bloch uttered these words, which were completely unsuited to such a commonplace event: 'I can only say that such conduct b-b-beggars belief,' or when, flattered at having been made welcome at the Guermantes', and also a little drunk on their wines, I could not help saying, half out loud to myself as I was leaving: 'They really are terribly nice people, it would be lovely to spend all one's time with them,' I slowly became aware that the essential book, the only true book, was not something the writer needs to invent, in the usual sense of the word, so much as to translate, because it already exists within each of us. The writer's task and duty are those of a translator.

But while, in cases where the imprecise language of, say, vanity is involved, realigning interior indirect speech (which as it goes on moves further and further away from the original, central impression) until it coincides with the straight line which ought to have run directly from the impression, while this realignment is a difficult matter and something which our idle nature is reluctant to take on, there are other instances, where love is involved for example, where the same realignment becomes painful. All our pretence of indifference, all our indignation against those lies which are so natural, so like the ones we tell ourselves, in a word all those things we have not only, whenever we felt wretched or betrayed, said endlessly to our loved one, but even said over and over again to ourselves while we were waiting to see her, sometimes speaking aloud, breaking the silence of our bedroom with comments such as: 'No, really, that sort of behaviour is intolerable,' and: 'I consented to see you one last time, but I won't pretend it isn't painful,' to bring all that back to the truth of experience when it has moved so far away from it means putting an end to all that we value most, to everything that, when we have been alone with our over-excited plans for letters and approaches, has constituted our passionate dialogue with ourselves.

Even where the pleasures of art are concerned, although we seek them because of the impression they make on us, we contrive as quickly as possible to dismiss the specificity of this impression as being inexpressible, and to concentrate on whatever allows us to experience the pleasure of it without properly analysing it, and to think that we are communicating it to other art-lovers, with whom conversation will be possible because we will be speaking to them about something we have in common, the personal root of our own impression having been suppressed. Even at the moments when we are the most disinterested onlookers of nature, or society, or love, or art itself, since every impression comes in two parts, half of it contained within the object, and the other half, which we alone will understand, extending into us, we are quick to disregard this latter half, which ought to be the sole object of our attention, and to take notice only of the first, which, being external and therefore impossible to study in any depth, will not impose any strain on us: we find it too demanding a task to try to perceive the little furrow that the sight of a hawthorn or of a church has made in us. But we play a symphony again and again, we go back to look at the church until – in this flight from our own lives, which we don't have the courage to look at, which people call erudition – we know them as well, and in the same manner, as the most knowledgeable student of music or of archaeology.

Very many people, therefore, leave it at that, extracting nothing from their impressions, growing old useless and unsatisfied, like celibates at the shrine of art! They have the bitterness that goes with virginity and indolence, but which in those instances can be cured by pregnancy or work. They get more excited by works of art than real artists do, because their excitement, not being for them the result of hard introspective investigation, bursts outward, overheats their conversation and makes them go red in the face. They think they are accomplishing something by shouting 'Bravo, bravo' at the tops of their voices after the performance of a work they enjoy. But these demonstrations do not force them to clarify the nature of their enjoyment, and they remain unaware of it. Yet, untapped, it overflows even into their calmest conversations, makes them make grand gestures, and grimace and toss their heads whenever they talk about art. 'I went to this concert. I must say it didn't do anything for me. Then they started playing the quartet. Lord, what a difference!' (at this point, the music-lover's face expresses anxious concern, as if he was thinking: 'I can see sparks, there's a smell of burning, something must be on fire'). 'Damn it all, what I heard was exasperating, it's badly written, but it's astounding, though, mind you, it wouldn't be everyone's cup of tea.' The look is also accompanied by a worried tone of voice, head on one side, more gesticulation, the whole absurd pantomime of a gosling with half-grown winglets which has not solved the problem of wings but is none the less tormented with a desire to soar into the air. And so this barren music-lover spends his life going from one concert to the next, embittered and unsatisfied as his hair turns grey and he enters an unfruitful old age, the celibate bachelor of art, as it were. Yet there is something almost touching about this most unlikeable breed, though they reek of worthiness and though they have not received anything like their due share of contentment, because they are the first half-formed products of the need to pass from the shifting objects of intellectual pleasure to its permanent organ.

So, ludicrous they may be, but they are not totally to be despised. They are the first experimental efforts of nature's attempt to create artists, as ill-formed and unviable as the original creatures which preceded the animal species we now have, and which were not made to last. These weak-willed, sterile art-lovers are surely as touching as those early machines which could not get off the ground but which embodied, not the secret of flight, which was yet to be discovered, but the desire to fly. 'Also, old chap, adds the music-lover, gripping you by the arm, this is the eighth time I've heard it, and I can promise you it won't be the last.' And indeed, since they cannot take in the truly nourishing elements in art, they are permanently in need of artistic pleasures, victims of a bulimia which never lets them feel satisfied. So they go to concert after concert to applaud the same work, believing that by being there they are fulfilling a duty, an obligation, in the way that other people feel a duty to attend board meetings or funerals. Then, whether it be in literature, in painting or in music, new, even diametrically opposed, works start to appear. For the ability to launch new ideas and new systems, and more importantly the capacity to assimilate and reproduce them, has always been much commoner, even among those who produce art, than genuine taste, but it has become much more widespread now with the multiplication of reviews and literary journals (and concomitantly of factitious careers as writers and artists). Thus the best part of the younger generation, the most intelligent and disinterested of them, used to like nothing in literature so much as works that had an elevated moral and sociological, even religious, significance. They imagined this to be the criterion of a work's value, thereby repeating the error of artists such as David, Chenavard, Brunetière, etc. Instead of Bergotte, whose finest sentences did in fact require a much more profound consideration by the reader, they preferred writers who seemed more profound simply because they wrote less well. The complexity of his artistry was aimed at fashionable society, said the democrats, thus paying the people in society an unmerited tribute. Whenever the rational intelligence decides to start passing judgment on works of art, nothing continues to be fixed or certain, you can prove anything you like. While the reality of talent is a universal possession or acquisition, our primary responsibility being to establish its presence or absence beneath the surface fashions of thought and style, criticism in its classification of authors never goes beyond that surface. It hails a writer as a prophet, on account of his peremptory tone and his very public scorn for the school that preceded him, when in fact he has absolutely nothing new to say. These aberrations on the part of criticism are so constant that a writer might almost prefer to be judged by the general public (if they were not incapable even of recognizing what an artist has tried to achieve in an area of research which they know nothing about). For there is a closer analogy between the instinctive life of the public and the talent of a great writer, which is no more than an instinct religiously listened to while imposing silence on everything else, an instinct perfected and understood, than between it and the superficial verbiage and shifting criteria of the recognized arbiters of judgment. New battles of words take place in every decade (for the kaleidoscope is not only made up of fashionable groupings, but also of social, political and religious ideas which become widespread for a short while thanks to their refraction among ordinary people, but which are none the less still subject to the brief lifespan of ideas whose novelty has been able to seduce only those minds which do not require strict standards of proof). So one school or party had followed another, always winning ❯ adherents among the same minds, men with a limited amount of intelligence, always liable to become caught up with things which other minds, more scrupulous and more difficult to convince, keep away from. Unfortunately, precisely because the former are only half-minds, they need to supplement themselves by doing things, so they are more active than the better minds, and attract crowds of followers, and create around them not only exaggerated reputations and unjustified contempt, but civil and foreign wars, which a little Port-Royalist[84] self-criticism might have prevented.

As for the enjoyment the beautifully expressed thought of a master gives to a truly discerning mind or a spirit that is genuinely alive, it is probably entirely healthy but, however prized the men may be who can really appreciate it (and how many of them are there in twenty years?), it does reduce them to being no more than the complete consciousness of another. When a man has done everything he can to be loved by a woman who could only have made him miserable, but despite his best efforts over the years has not succeeded even in arranging a meeting with her, then instead of trying to give expression to his sufferings and the danger he has escaped, he reads and rereads this comment of La Bruyère's, adding to it his own 'million words' and some intensely moving recollections of his life: 'Men often want to love where they cannot succeed, they seek their defeat without being able to bring it about and so, if I may put it like this, they are compelled to remain free.'[85] Whether or not this is the meaning the comment had for its writer (for it to have done so, it would have had to read 'be loved' instead of 'love', which would have been better), there can be no doubt that, taking it this way, this sensitive and well-read man gives it new life, inflates it with meaning until it is ready to burst and cannot repeat it without brimming over with joy, so true and fine does he think it to be; yet despite all that he has added nothing to it, and it remains the thought of La Bruyère alone.

How could a purely descriptive literature have any value at all, when reality lies hidden beneath the surface of little things of the sort it documents (grandeur in the distant sound of an aeroplane, or in the outline of the steeple of Saint-Hilaire, the past in the taste of a madeleine, etc.) so that the things have no meaning in themselves until it is disentangled from them?

Preserved by our memory, it is the piecemeal sequence of all those inaccurate expressions, in which nothing of what we have really experienced remains, which constitutes our thought, our life, reality, and all that the so-called art of 'real life' can do is to reproduce that lie, in an art which is as simple as life, devoid of beauty, and such a tedious and pointless duplication of what our eyes see and our intellect records that one wonders where anyone who engages in it can find the joyous, dynamic spark capable of setting his task in motion and then keeping it going. The greatness of true art, on the other hand, the sort of art that M. de Norpois would have called dilettante amusement, lies in rediscovering, grasping hold of, and making us recognize this reality, distant as it is from our daily lives, and growing more and more distant as the conventional knowledge we substitute for it becomes denser and more impermeable, this reality which we run a real risk of dying without having known, and which is quite simply our life.

Real life, life finally uncovered and clarified, the only life in consequence lived to the full, is literature. Life in this sense dwells within all ordinary people as much as in the artist. But they do not see it because they are not trying to shed light on it. And so their past is cluttered with countless photographic negatives, which continue to be useless because their intellect has never 'developed' them. Our lives; and the lives of other people, too; because style for a writer, like colour for a painter, is a question not of technique but of vision. It is the revelation, which would be impossible by direct or conscious means, of the qualitative difference in the ways we perceive the world, a difference which, if there were no art, would remain the eternal secret of each individual. It is only through art that we can escape from ourselves and know how another person sees a universe which is not the same as our own and whose landscapes would otherwise have remained as unknown as any there may be on the moon. Thanks to art, instead of seeing only a single world, our own, we see it multiplied, and have at our disposal as many worlds as there are original artists, all more different one from another than those which revolve in infinity and which, centuries after the fire from which their rays emanated has gone out, whether it was called Rembrandt or Vermeer, still send us their special light.

This labour of the artist, this attempt to see something different beneath the material, beneath experience, beneath words, is the exact inverse of that which is accomplished within us from minute to minute, as we live our lives heedless of ourselves, by vanity, passion, intellect and habit, when they overlay our true impressions, so as to hide them from us completely, with the repertoire of words, and the practical aims, which we wrongly call life. To put it briefly, this art, complicated though it be, is actually the only art that is alive. It alone can express for others, and make us see for ourselves, our own lives, lives which are unable to keep a watch on themselves, and whose visible manifestations, such as they are, need to be translated and frequently to be read against the grain and painstakingly deciphered. The work carried out by our vanity, our passion, our imitative faculties, our abstract intelligence, our habits, is the work that art undoes, making us follow a contrary path, in a return to the depths where whatever has really existed lies unrecognized within us.

And of course it was very tempting to recreate real life and rejuvenate one's impressions in this way. But it called for all kinds of courage, including emotional courage. Because above all it involved giving up one's most cherished illusions, ceasing to believe in the objectivity of what one had elaborated oneself, and instead of comforting oneself for the hundredth time with the words: 'She was very nice,' reading what underlay them: 'I enjoyed kissing her.' Certainly what I had felt in these hours of love was what all men feel. One feels, but what one has felt is like those negatives which show nothing but blackness until they are held close to a lamp, and which also have to be looked at from the other side: one does not know what it is until it has been brought into contact with the intellect. Only when that has clarified it, when that has intellectualized it, can one make out, and even then only with difficulty, the form of what one felt. But I also realized that the suffering I had first known because of Gilberte, that our love does not belong to the creature who inspires it, is salutary. To a lesser extent as a means to an end (because, short as our life may be, it is only during suffering that our thoughts, in a sense shaken up by endless and shifting impulses, elevate, as in a storm, to a level at which it becomes visible, all that regulated immensity, which we, stationed at a badly placed window, do not normally see, because the calm of happiness leaves it smooth and at too low a level; perhaps only for some great geniuses does this movement of thought continue all the time without any need for the agitations of grief; yet we cannot be certain, when we contemplate the expansive and even development of their cheerful works, that we are not too inclined to infer from the happiness of the work that the life was happy too, when it may perhaps, on the contrary, have been permanently miserable) – but principally because, if our love is not only the love of a Gilberte (and this is what we find so hard to bear), this is not because it is also the love of an Albertine, but because it is a part of our soul, longer lasting than the various selves which die successively within us and which selfishly would like to hold on to it, and a part which must – whatever pain, and it may even be productive pain, this may cause – detach itself from individuals and recreate its general nature and give this love, the understanding of this love, to everyone, to the universal mind, and not first to this woman and then another in whom one or another of the selves that we have successively been has wanted to be dissolved.

I needed to restore to even the slightest of the signs which surrounded me (Guermantes, Albertine, Gilberte, Saint-Loup, Balbec, etc.) the meaning which habit had made them lose for me. And when we have attained reality, if we are to express it and preserve it we must eliminate everything that is not a part of it and which is constantly being introduced by the speed that accompanies habit. Most of all, I would eliminate all words which come from the tongue rather than the mind, humorous remarks of the sort we make in conversation and which after a long conversation with other people we continue to address artificially to ourselves and which fill our minds with untruths, these purely automatic remarks which, in the writer who sinks so far as to transcribe them, are accompanied by the little smile, the little grimace which constantly spoils, for example, the spoken sentence of a Sainte-Beuve, whereas true books must be the product not of daylight and chitchat but of darkness and silence. And as art exactly reconstructs life, an atmosphere of poetry will always hover around the truths that one has reached in oneself, a gentle sense of mystery which is merely the remains of the semi-darkness we have had to pass through, the indication, as precisely marked as on an altimeter, of the depth of a work. (For depth is not inherent in certain subjects as, not being able to go beneath the world of appearances, some materialistically spiritual novelists believe, all of whose noble intentions, like the virtuous tirades common among the sort of people who are incapable of the smallest act of kindness, should not prevent us from noticing that they have not even had the strength of mind to get rid of all the banalities of form they have acquired through imitation.)

As for the truths which the intellect – even of the finest minds – gathers in the open, in front of it, in broad daylight, their value may be very great; but their outlines are starker and they are featureless, without any depth, because no depths had to be negotiated in order to reach them, because they have not been recreated. It is often the case that writers in whose deeps those mysterious truths no longer appear write, after a certain age, only with their intelligence, which becomes increasingly powerful; because of this, the books of their mature years have greater power than those of their youth, but none of the same aura of sweetness.

I felt, however, that these truths which the intelligence derives directly from reality are not to be despised completely, for they could provide a setting, in a material less pure but still imbued with mind, for those impressions which are conveyed to us outside time by the essence common to both past and present sensations, but which, because they are more precious, are also too rare for a work of art to be composed from them alone. I felt thronging within me a crowd of truths relating to passions, characters and conduct, all capable of being used in that way. Their perception caused me joy; yet it seemed to remind me that I had discovered more than one of them in suffering, and others in very ordinary pleasures.

Each person who makes us suffer can be linked by us to a divinity of which he or she is only a fragmentary reflection at the lowest level, a divinity (or Idea) the contemplation of which immediately gives us joy in place of the pain we had before. The whole art of living is to use the people who make us suffer simply as steps enabling us to obtain access to their divine form and thus joyfully to people our lives with divinities.

Then, less dazzling no doubt than the one which had shown me that the work of art was the only means of finding Lost Time again, a new light dawned on me. And I understood that all these raw materials for a literary work were actually my past life; I understood that they had come to me, in frivolous pleasures, in idleness, in tenderness, in sorrow, that they had been stored up by me without my divining their ultimate purpose, even their survival, any more than a seed does as it lays up a reserve of all the nutrients which will feed the plant. Like the seed, I would be able to die when the plant had developed, and I began to see that I had lived for its sake without knowing it, without ever having realized that there should be some contact between my life and the books I had wanted to write and for which, when I used to sit down at my table, I could not find a subject. So all my life up to that day could, and at the same time could not, have been summed up under the title: A vocation. It could not have been, in the sense that literature had not played any role in my life. It could have been, to the extent that this life, the memories of its times of sadness, its times of joy, formed a reserve comparable to that of the albumen stored in the ovule of a plant and from which it draws the nourishment it needs to transform itself into a seed, before anybody is aware that the embryo of a plant is developing, despite the fact that it is the site of secret but very active chemical and respiratory phenomena. In the same way my life was linked to that which would bring about its maturation. And those who might subsequently draw nourishment from it for themselves would have no idea, any more than people do when they eat food grains, that the rich substances which they contain were made for its nourishment, had first nourished the seed and enabled it to ripen.

In this area, comparisons which are false if one takes them as a starting-point can be true if one ends up with them. The man of letters envies the painter, he would like to make sketches, to take notes, but if he does so it is a waste of time. When he writes, though, there is not one gesture of his characters, not one mannerism, one tone of voice, which has not been supplied to his inspiration by his memory, there is not one name of an invented character beneath which he cannot subsume sixty names of characters he has seen, one of whom has posed for the grimace, another for the monocle, this one for anger, that one for the conceited movement of the arm, etc. And then the writer realizes that while his dream of being a painter was not realizable in a conscious and deliberate manner, it has nevertheless been realized and that the writer, too, has created a sketch book without being aware of it.

For, driven by the instinct that was in him, the writer, long before he thought that he might one day become one, regularly failed to look at a large number of things that other people looked at, which caused him to be accused by other people of not paying attention and by himself of not knowing how to listen or look; during that time he was telling his eyes and ears to retain for ever things that to other people seemed puerile trivialities, the tone of voice in which a phrase had been said, and the facial expression and movement of the shoulders that at a certain moment, many years before, some person had made about whom perhaps he knows nothing else, and that because this tone of voice was one that he had already heard, or felt that he might hear again, that it was something that might be repeated, something durable; it is this feeling for the general which, in the future writer, itself selects things that are general and that will be able to be part of the work of art. For he has listened to the others only when, stupid or demented as they may have been, repeating like parrots all the things that other people of similar character say, they make themselves into birds of prophecy, mouthpieces of a psychological law. The only things he remembers are the general. It was by tones of voice like these, by such facial movements, even if seen in his earliest childhood, that the life of others was represented in his mind, and when later he comes to write, he will describe a common movement of the shoulders, as realistically as if it had been written in an anatomist's note-book, but in order here to express a psychological truth, and then on to those shoulders graft somebody else's neck-movement, each person having contributed his momentary pose.

It may well be that, for the creation of a work of literature, imagination and sensitivity are interchangeable qualities, and that the second may without any great disadvantage be substituted for the first, in the same way as people whose stomach is incapable of digesting pass that function over to their intestine. A man born sensitive but with no imagination might none the less write admirable novels. The suffering that other people caused him, his efforts to prevent it, the conflicts that it and the cruel other person created, all of this, interpreted by the intelligence, might make the raw material of a book not only as beautiful as it would have been if it had been imagined, invented, but also as unrelated to the daydreams the author would have had if he had been been happily left to his own devices, as surprising for himself, and as accidental as a fortuitous vagary of the imagination.

The stupidest people manifest by their gestures, their comments, their involuntarily expressed feelings, laws of which they are unaware but which the artist manages to catch in them. Because of observations of this sort, the writer is commonly thought to be malicious, wrongly so, because in an idiosyncrasy the artist sees a beautiful generality and no more holds it against the person observed than a surgeon would dismiss someone for suffering from a common circulation disorder; indeed, he is less likely than anyone to make fun of people's foibles. Unfortunately, he is more unhappy than malicious: where his own passions are concerned, even though he knows all about them in general terms, he has more difficulty is extracting himself from the personal sufferings they cause. Obviously, when some insolent person insults us, we would rather he had been singing our praises, so when a woman we adore betrays us, we feel even more intensely that we would have given anything for it to be otherwise! But the resentment at the affront, or the pain of rejection would then have been territories we would never have known, and discovering them, painful though it is for a man, is a valuable experience for an artist. Which is why the malicious and the heartless, despite both their wishes, feature in his work. The pamphleteer cannot help but share his fame with the riff-raff he has stigmatized. In every work of art one can recognize those the author hated most and also, alas! those whom he loved best. All they have done is to pose for the artist at the moment when, against his will, they were causing him the most suffering. When I was in love with Albertine, I had to recognize that she did not love me, and I was forced to resign myself to the fact that all she would do was show me what it was like to experience suffering, love and even, at the outset, happiness.

And when we try to extract the generalizable features from our grief, to write about it, we are perhaps slightly consoled by one other factor in addition to the ones I adduce here, which is that to think in terms of generalities, to write, is for the writer a healthy and necessary function, the fulfilment of which makes him happy, just as exercise, sweating and baths do men of a more physical bent. In truth, I was a little unwilling to accept this. I was prepared to believe that the supreme truth of life was in art, and, at the same time, I could see that I was no more capable of the effort of remembering that would be necessary if I were still to love Albertine than I was of continuing to mourn my grandmother; all the same, I wondered whether a work of art of which they were unaware would be a fulfilment for them, for the destiny of those poor dead creatures. My grandmother, whom I had with so much indifference watched as she suffered her last moments and died before my eyes! Oh, that I might, in expiation, when my work were finished, fatally injured, suffer for long hours, abandoned by everybody, before finally dying! In addition, I felt infinite pity even for less cherished beings, even for people I cared nothing about, and for all the human destinies, which my thought, in its attempt to comprehend them, had reduced to their suffering or even to their foibles. All those people who had revealed truths to me, and who now were no longer living, appeared to me to have lived lives which had profited only myself, and to have died for my benefit.

It was sad for me to think that my love, which I had prized so highly, would in my book be so detached from an actual person that the readers of all sorts would apply it in all its detail to what they had felt for other women. But ought I to be scandalized by this posthumous infidelity, or by the fact that some person or other might provide unknown women as objects of my feelings, when this infidelity, this division of love among a number of beings, had begun in my lifetime, and even before I started to write? I had indeed suffered one after another for Gilberte, for Mme de Guermantes, for Albertine. One after another, too, I had forgotten them, and only my love, dedicated to different beings, had lasted. The profanation of one of my memories by unknown readers was something I had already accomplished myself. I felt something close to horror at myself, as perhaps might some nationalist party in whose name hostilities had been fought out, and who alone would benefit from a war in which large numbers of noble victims had suffered and died, without even knowing (which for my

grandmother at least would have been some compensation) the outcome of the struggle. And my only consolation for the thought that
she did not know that I was finally setting myself to work was that
(such is the lot of the dead), while she was unable to enjoy my progress,
she had long since ceased to to be aware of my inaction, my failed life,
which had been such a source of unhappiness to her. And certainly it
was not only from my grandmother or from Albertine, but from many
others as well, that I had been able to incorporate a remark, a look,
although I might no longer remember them at all as individuals; a
book is a great cemetery where the names have been effaced from
most of the tombs and are no longer legible. Yet there are times when
one remembers a name perfectly well, but without knowing whether
anything of the person who bore it survives within these pages. That
girl with the very deep-set eyes and the drawling voice, is she here?
And if she really does repose here, then do we any longer know in
what part, or how to find her underneath the flowers?

But since we live our lives detached from individual beings, since
after a few years our strongest feelings, such as had been my love for
my grandmother and for Albertine, are forgotten, since they mean no
more to us than words we cannot understand, since we can talk about
these dead people with society acquaintances in houses we still frequent
with pleasure even though everything we loved is dead, then, if there
is a way for us to learn to understand these forgotten words, ought we
not to use it, even if it entails first transcribing them into a universal,
but at least therefore permanent, language, and thereby making out of
those who are no longer with us, in their truest essence, an acquisition
of lasting value for all human beings? Indeed, if we could succeed in
explaining the law of change which made these words unintelligible to
us, would not our weakness become a new kind of strength?

In addition to that, the work to which our sorrows have contributed
may be interpreted, so far as our future is concerned, both as a baneful
sign of suffering and as an auspicious sign of consolation. Indeed,
when we say that the loves and sorrows of a poet have been useful to
him, have helped him to build up his work, when unknown women
who never had the slightest idea that they might, by an act of malice
here, or a mocking remark there, each have brought their stone to the

construction of the monument which they will never see, we tend to forget that the writer's life does not come to an end with this work, that the temperament which has caused him to have these sufferings, the ones that have entered into his work, will still be his when the work is finished, will make him love other women in conditions which would be almost identical, if all the modifications which time brings to circumstances did not result in slight variations, in the subject himself, in his appetite for love and in his resistance to pain. From this first point of view, then, the work is to be regarded solely as if it were an unfortunate love which fatally presages more of the same, assuming that the life to come will resemble the work, and that the poet will have almost no further need to write, because for most of the time he will be able to find the shape of future events anticipated in what he has already written. Thus my love for Albertine, to the extent that it is different from it, would already be inscribed in my love for Gilberte, in the middle of which happy time I had first heard Albertine's name spoken, and her character described, by her aunt, without my having the slightest idea that this insignificant seed would grow, expand and one day spread its branches over the whole of my life.

But from another point of view, the work is a sign of happiness, because it shows us that in every love the general is to be found alongside the particular, and shows us how to pass from the latter to the former by means of exercises which fortify us against unhappiness by detaching our attention from its cause in order to focus on its essential qualities. Indeed, as I was shortly to discover for myself, even while you are in love and suffering, if you have finally achieved your vocation, then during the hours you are working you feel very strongly that the being whom you love is dissolving into a greater reality, and you start intermittently to forget her and, while you are working, suffer no more from love than from any purely physical illness that has nothing to do with the loved being, such as some sort of heart ailment. It is true, though, that this is a matter of timing and that the effect seems to be the opposite if the work comes more slowly. Because there are some individuals who, having managed, in spite of us, by their unkindness or their insignificance to destroy our illusions, have themselves been reduced to nothing and severed from the chimera of love we had conjured up in our minds; and if we then set to work, our mind raises them up again, identifies them, for the purposes of our self-analysis, with individuals who have loved us, and in such cases literature, reconstructing the demolished work of amorous illusion, gives a sort of afterlife to feelings which were no longer in existence.

It is true, then, that we are obliged to relive our private suffering with all the courage of a doctor who continues to give himself a dangerous course of injections. At the same time, though, we have to think about it in its general form, which enables us to some extent to escape its grasp, makes everybody sharers in our pain, and may even offer a kind of joy. Where life walls us in, the intellect cuts a way out, for although there may be no cure for love that is not reciprocated, the investigation of one's suffering does provide a way out, even if only by revealing its likely consequences. The intelligence does not recognize closed situations in life, with no way out.

So I had to resign myself, since nothing can last unless it is generalized, nor without the mind dying to itself, to the idea that even those who were dearest to the writer had done nothing in the end except pose for him like models for a painter.

In love, a favoured rival, in other words our enemy, is our bene-factor. To a being who was arousing in us nothing but an insignificant physical desire he immediately adds immense value, quite unrelated, but which we confuse with her. If we had no rivals, pleasure would not be transformed into love. If we did not have any, or even if we thought we did not have any. Because there is no need for them actually to exist. The illusory life which our suspicion, our jealousy, gives to non-existent rivals is enough for our needs.

Sometimes, when a painful section is still in rough draft, a new attachment, and new suffering, come along which enable us to finish it, to give it substance. One cannot really complain too much about these great but useful sorrows, because there is no shortage of them and they do not make us wait long for them. None the less we have to hurry if we are to profit from them, for they do not last very long: one finds consolation, or else, if they are too overwhelming, and if one's heart is no longer very sound, one dies. Because happiness alone is good for the body; whereas sorrow develops the strength of the mind. Moreover, even if it did not reveal a law to us each time this happened, it would be no less indispensable for returning us each time to the truth, forcing us to take things seriously, and uprooting each time the weeds of habit, scepticism, levity and indifference. Admittedly this truth, which is not compatible with happiness, or with health, is not always compatible with life either. Sorrow kills in the end. At each new, unbearable affliction, we feel yet another vein stand out, extending its deadly sinuosity across our temples, or under our eyes. And it is in this way that are gradually formed those terrible, ravaged faces of the old Rembrandt, and the old Beethoven, whom everybody used to laugh at. The bags under the eyes and the wrinkled forehead would not matter, of course, if there were not also suffering of the heart. But since forces can change into other forces, since accumulated heat becomes light and since the electricity in lightning can power a camera, since the dull pain in our heart can raise above itself, like a flag, the permanently visible image of each new sorrow, let us accept the physical damage it does to us in return for the spiritual knowledge it brings us; let us leave our body to disintegrate, since each new particle that breaks away from it comes back, now luminous and legible, to add itself to our work, to complete it at the price of the sufferings of which others more gifted have no need, to increase its solidity as our emotions are eroding our life. Ideas are substitutes for sorrows; the moment they change into ideas they lose a part of their power to hurt our hearts and, for a brief moment, the transformation even releases some joy. Substitutes only in the order of time, though, because it seems that the primary element is actually the idea, and the sorrow merely the mode in which certain ideas first enter our minds. But there are numerous families within the general group of ideas, some of which are joys from the start.

These reflections allowed me to give a firmer and more precise meaning to the truth that I had always felt, particularly when Mme de Cambremer used to wonder how I could abandon a man as remarkable as Elstir for Albertine. Even from an intellectual point of view I sensed that she was wrong, but I did not know what it was that she did not understand: which was the kind of lessons through which one serves one's apprenticeship as a man of letters. The objective value of the arts is hardly relevant to that; what we have to draw out, to bring to light, are our feelings, our passions, in other words the passions and the feelings of everyone. A woman whom we need, and who makes us suffer, arouses in us a series of feelings far more profound and far more intense than does an unusually gifted man who interests us. It remains to be seen, depending on the sphere in which we live, to what extent we regard some betrayal by which a woman has made us suffer as insignificant in relation to the truths which the betrayal has revealed to us and which the woman, happy to have made us suffer, would scarcely have been able to understand. But, whatever else, there will be no shortage of betrayals. A writer may start work on a lengthy task without any anxiety about that. Let his intelligence begin the work, plenty of sorrows will arise along the way and look after the business of finishing it. As for happiness, almost its only useful quality is to make unhappiness possible. We need, during periods of happiness, to form particularly pleasant and powerful bonds of trust and affection in order that their destruction can cause us the precious laceration called unhappiness. If one had not been happy, even if only in expectation, unhappinesses would be devoid of cruelty and consequently fruitless.

And more than the painter, the writer, in order to obtain depth and substance, generality, literary reality, just as he needs to have seen a number of churches in order to depict a single one, also needs a number of individuals for one single feeling. For if art is long and life short, one may also say that, while inspiration is short, the feelings it has to depict are not much longer. It is our passions which provide the outline of our books, the intervening periods of respite which write them. When inspiration returns, when we can take up work again, the woman who was sitting for us to illustrate some feeling has already lost the ability to make us experience it. To continue to depict her we have to use another model, and while this may be a betrayal of the individual, from the literary point of view, thanks to the similarity of our feelings, which means that a work is both the recollection of our past loves and the prophecy of our new ones, there is no real disadvantage to these substitutions. This is one reason why studies where people try to work out who an author is talking about are pointless. Because any work, even if it is directly confessional, is at the very least intercalated between a number of episodes in the author's life, the earlier ones which inspired it and the later ones which are no less characteristic, the details of subsequent love affairs being traced from the ones which came before. Because we are not so faithful even to the person we have loved the most as we are to ourselves, and sooner or later we forget her in order to be able – since this is one of our own traits – to start loving again. At most, this woman whom we have loved so much has given a particular form to our love, which will make us faithful to her even in infidelity. With the next woman we shall need the same morning walks, need to see her home in the same way in the evening, or to give her a hundred times too much money. (It is a curious thing, this circulation of the money we give to women, who because of that make us unhappy, that is, enable us to write books – one can almost say that books, as in artesian wells, rise to a height that is proportionate to the depth to which suffering has bored down into the heart.) These substitutions add something disinterested, something more general, to the work, something which at the same time is an austere lesson that it is not to individuals that we must attach ourselves, that it is not individuals who really exist and are consequently capable of being expressed, but ideas. So one has to hurry and lose none of the time during which one has the models at one's disposal; for those who pose for happiness do not generally have many sittings to offer, nor alas, as it too passes so quickly, do those who pose for grief.

All the same, even when that does not, by uncovering it, provide us with the raw material of our work, it is useful to us as a spur to doing it. Imagination and thinking can be admirable mechanisms in themselves, but they can also be inert. Suffering sets them in motion. And the individuals who pose to us for grief give us such frequent sittings, in the studio we go into only during those periods and which is within ourselves! Those periods are like an image of our life, with all its different griefs. For they in turn contain more griefs, and just when you think they have been quieted, a new one arises. New in every sense of the word: perhaps because these unpredictable situations force us come into closer contact with ourselves, and the painful dilemmas with which love is constantly presenting us instruct us and show us, little by little, what we are made of. So when Françoise, seeing Albertine having the run of my place like a dog, spreading chaos everywhere, ruining me, causing me so much pain, told me (for at that point I had already done a few articles and some translations): 'Ah, if only Monsieur, instead of this girl who makes him waste all his time, had taken on a nicely brought-up young secretary who would have sorted out all Monsieur's manuscribbles!' I was perhaps wrong to think she was speaking wisely. By making me waste my time, by causing me pain, Albertine might perhaps have been more useful, even from the literary standpoint, than a secretary who could have organized my 'manuscribbles'. But all the same, when a living creature is so badly constituted (and perhaps it is natural for man to be that creature) that he cannot love without suffering, and that he needs to suffer in order to learn truths, the life of such a creature must in the end be very tedious. Years of happiness are years wasted, waiting for a bout of suffering to make one work. The idea of this preliminary suffering then comes to be associated with the idea of work, and one is afraid of each new work because one thinks of the pain one will first have to endure in order to imagine it. And when one realizes that suffering is the best thing one can encounter in life, one thinks without terror, almost as of a release, about death.

Yet although I rather recoiled from this, I was still very much aware that writers have frequently not treated life as a game, and exploited individuals in order to use them for books, but quite the opposite. I did not, alas, have the nobility of young Werther.[86] Without for a moment believing in Albertine's love, I had twenty times wanted to kill myself for her, I had ruined myself, I had destroyed my health for her. Where writing is concerned, one is scrupulous, one examines things very closely, one rejects everything that is not the truth. But when it is only a matter of living, one ruins oneself, makes oneself ill, kills oneself, for lies. The vein that these lies come from may, it is true, still (if one has passed the age of being a poet) yield a small quantity of truth. Sorrows are obscure, detested servants, against whom one struggles, under whose influence one increasingly falls, unbearable, irreplaceable servants who lead us by devious ways to truth and to death. Fortunate are those who met the former before the latter, and for whom, however close together the two may be, the hour of truth struck before the hour of death.

I also understood that the most insignificant episodes from my past life had contributed towards giving me the lesson in idealism from which I was going to benefit today. Had not my encounters with M. de Charlus, for example, even before his pro-German attitudes taught me the same lesson, done more even than my love for Mme de Guermantes or for Albertine, or than Saint-Loup's love for Rachel, to convince me how utterly neutral matter itself is, and how thought can give it any characteristics it wants; a truth which is more profoundly emphasized by the widely misunderstood and pointlessly censured phenomenon of sexual inversion even than by that, which has already proved so instructive, of love? This latter may show us beauty deserting the woman we no longer love and taking up residence in a face which other people would find extremely ugly, and which once we might have disliked ourselves, as one day we shall again; but it is even more striking to see it, capturing the complete devotion of a great nobleman who instantly abandons a beautiful princess, migrate to a position beneath the cap of a bus conductor. And was not my astonishment each new time that I had seen, on the Champs-Élysées, in the street, or on the beach, the face of Gilberte, of Mme de Guermantes, or of Albertine, proof of the extent to which a memory persists only in a direction which diverges from the impression with which it originally coincided but from which it becomes increasingly remote?

A writer must not take offence when inverts give his heroines masculine faces. This mildly deviant behaviour is the only means by which the invert can proceed to give full general significance to what he is reading. For Racine to be able to give her full universal value to the Phaedra of antiquity, he had first for a moment to turn her into a Jansenist; similarly, if M. de Charlus had not given to the 'faithless one' over whom de Musset weeps in *La Nuit d'octobre* or in *Le Souvenir* the face of Morel, he would not have wept, nor understood, since it was by that narrow and circuitous way alone that he gained access to the truths of love. It is only out of a habit derived from the insincere language of prefaces and dedications that writers talk about 'my reader'. In reality each reader, when he is reading, is uniquely reading himself. The writer's work is only a kind of optical instrument which he offers the reader to enable him to discern what without this book he might not perhaps have seen in himself. The recognition within himself, by the reader, of what the book is saying, is the proof of its truthfulness, and vice versa, at least to a certain extent, it often being possible to impute the difference between the two texts not to the author but to the reader. In addition to this, the book may be too learned, too obscure, for the unsophisticated reader, and thus present him with a blurred lens, with which he will not be able to read. But other characteristics (such as inversion) may mean that the reader needs to read in a particular way in order to read properly; the author should not take offence at this, but instead should allow the reader the greatest possible freedom by saying to him: 'Look for yourself, try whether you see better with this lens, or that one, or the other one.'

If I had always been so interested in the dreams we have while we are asleep, was it not because, making up in potency what they lack in duration, they help you better to understand the subjective element in, for instance, love, by the simple fact that they produce – but with amazing speed – the effect commonly known as being crazy about a woman, even making us, in the course of a few minutes' sleep, love an ugly woman passionately, something which in real life would have needed years of familiarity and cohabitation – and that they are like intravenous injections of love, the invention of some miracle-working doctor, even though they can also be injections of suffering? With equal rapidity the amorous suggestion which they have instilled in us vanishes, and sometimes not only has the nocturnal lover ceased to occupy that guise, becoming once more the ugly woman familiar to us, but something more precious has also vanished, a wonderful array of feelings of tenderness, of voluptuous pleasure, of vaguely blurred regrets, a whole *Embarquement pour Cythère*[87] of passion, of which we should like to record, for our waking state, the subtle gradations of a delicious truth to life, but which disappears like a canvas faded far beyond restoration. And it was perhaps also because of the extraordinary tricks it plays with Time that the Dream fascinated me. Had I not often seen in one night, in one minute of one night, remote periods of time, consigned to those vast distances at which we can no longer distinguish the feelings we had then, rushing to overwhelm us, blinding us with their clarity, as if they were giant aeroplanes rather than the pale stars we believed them to be, bringing back before our eyes everything they had ever held for us, giving us the emotion, the shock, the clarity of their immediate proximity, only to resume, the moment we awake, the distance they had miraculously overcome, to the point of making us believe, wrongly in fact, that they are one of the means of finding Lost Time again?

I had realized that it is only coarse and inaccurate perception which places everything in the object, when everything is in the mind; I had lost my grandmother in reality many months after having lost her in fact, I had seen people vary in appearance according to the idea that I or others had of them, a single person being several according to the people who were observing him (various Swanns in the opening volume, for example; the Princess of Luxembourg for the judge), even for the same person over the course of years (the name of Guermantes or the various Swanns, for me). I had seen love placing qualities in a person which are only in the person who loves. I had realized this all the more forcefully because I had seen stretched to the utmost the distance between objective reality and love (Rachel for Saint-Loup and for me, Albertine for me and Saint-Loup, Morel or the omnibus conductor for Charlus, and other people, despite which Charlus was still affectionate; verses by de Musset, etc.). Finally, the pro-Germanism of M. de Charlus, like the way Saint-Loup had looked at the photograph of Albertine, had to a certain extent helped me to detach myself for a moment, if not from my Germanophobia, at least from my belief in the pure objectivity of it, and made me think that perhaps the same applied to hatred as to love and that, in the terrible judgment which at this moment France pronounced on Germany, which she deemed to be beyond the bounds of humanity, the primary factor was an objectification of feelings like those which once made Rachel and Albertine seem so precious, the one to Saint-Loup, the other to me. What in fact made it possible that this perversity was not entirely intrinsic to Germany was that, just as I individually had had successive love affairs, after the end of which the object of that love would seem valueless to me, I had already seen in my country successive hatreds which had, for example, made traitors – a thousand times worse than the Germans to whom they delivered France – of Dreyfusards such as Reinach[88] with whom today patriots were collaborating against a country every member of which was by definition a liar, a wild animal, or a fool, exceptions being made for those Germans who had embraced the French cause, like the King of Romania, the King of the Belgians or the Empress of Russia. The anti-Dreyfusards, it is true, might have replied: 'It's not the same thing.' But in fact it never is the same thing, any more than it is the same person: if it were not for that, anyone faced with the same phenomenon and taken in again by it would have only his subjective state to blame and would be able to believe that the qualities or failings were inherent in the object. The intellect, therefore, has no difficulty at all in basing a theory on this difference (church schools against nature according to the Radicals, impossibility of assimilation for the Jewish race, perpetual hatred of the Germanic race for the Latin race, the yellow race being temporarily rehabilitated[89]). This subjective aspect was also evident in the conversation of neutrals, where the pro-Germans, for example, had the capacity to stop understanding for a moment, even to stop listening, when one was talking to them about German atrocities in Belgium. (And yet they were quite real: the subjective element that I had observed in hatred, as in sight itself, did not mean that the object could not possess real qualities and defects, and did not in any way cause reality to vanish into a pure relativism.) And if after so many years had passed and so much time had been lost, I was aware of the crucial influence of this inner reality even in international relations, had I not suspected it at the very beginning of my life, when I was reading in the garden at Combray one of those novels by Bergotte which, even today, if I flick through a few forgotten pages of it and come across a villain's cunning plans, I cannot put down again until I have assured myself, by skipping a hundred pages, that as the end approaches this villain is duly humiliated and lives long enough to learn that his shady plans have failed? Because I never really remembered what happened to these characters, although in this they were no different from the people present at Mme de Guermantes's this afternoon and whose past lives, in a number of cases at least, were as vague for me as if I had read them in a half-forgotten novel. Had the Prince d'Agrigente ended up marrying Mlle X——? Or was it not rather Mlle X——'s brother who was to have married the Duc d'Agrigente? Or else was I confusing it with something I had read a long time ago, or with a recent dream? Dreams were another, very striking, fact of my life, and had probably done more than anything else to convince me of the purely mental nature of reality, and I did not spurn their help in the composition of my work. When I was living, in a somewhat less disinterested manner, for the sake of a love affair, a dream would come to me bringing strangely close, across vast distances of lost time, my grandmother, or Albertine, whom I had started to love again because she had provided me in a dream with a rather toned-down version of the affair with the laundry-girl. I thought that in this way they would sometimes bring closer to me truths or impressions which my efforts alone or even the chances of nature did not provide; that they would awaken in me the desire or the regret for certain non-existent things which is the condition for working, for being cut off from habit, for detaching oneself from the concrete. So I would not disregard this second muse, this nocturnal muse which sometimes compensated for the other one.

I had seen members of the nobility become common when their minds, like that of the Duc de Guermantes for example, were common ('Don't stand on ceremony,' as Cottard would have said). During the Dreyfus Affair, during the war, in medicine, I had seen people believe truth to be a kind of fact, believe that ministers or doctors possess a yes or no which requires no interpretation, and which ordains that an X-ray photograph indicate what the patient has without interpretation, believe that the men in power *knew* whether Dreyfus was guilty, *knew* (without needing to send Roques to make enquiries on the spot) whether Sarrail did or did not have the means to mobilize at the same time as the Russians.[90] There is no moment in my life which would not have served to teach me that only coarse and inaccurate perception places everything in the object when the opposite is true: everything is in the mind.

In short, when I thought about it, the raw material of my experience, which was to be the raw material of my book, came to me from Swann, and not merely because of everything that concerned him and Gilberte.

It was also he who, ever since the Combray days, had given me the wish to go to Balbec, where without that my parents would never have thought of sending me, and without which I would never have known Albertine, or even the Guermantes, since my grandmother would not have rediscovered Mme de Villeparisis nor I have made the acquaint- ance of Saint-Loup and M. de Charlus, who had introduced me to the Duchesse de Guermantes, and through her, her cousin, the result of which was that my very presence at this moment in the house of the Prince de Guermantes, where the idea for my work had just suddenly come to me (which meant that I owed Swann not just the material but the decision, too), also came to me from Swann. Rather a slender stem, perhaps, to support in this way the whole span of my life (the 'Guermantes way' thus being seen to derive from the 'way by Swann's'). But this source of the different aspects of our life is fre- quently a person much inferior to Swann, somebody of complete insignificance. Would it not have been enough for any school-friend to have told me about a good-looking girl to be had there (whom I would probably not have met) for me to have gone to Balbec? Thus it often happens that later in life one encounters some dislikable school-mate and scarcely even shakes his hand, whereas if one ever thought about it, it is from some passing comment he made to us, like 'You ought to come to Balbec,' that our whole life and our whole work have sprung. We make no recognition of this to him, but that does not constitute proof of ingratitude. For when he said those words he did not for a moment think of the tremendous consequences they would have for us. It is our sensibility and our intellect which have exploited the circumstances which, once the primary impetus has been given, have generated themselves, one after another, without his ever having been able to foresee anything, whether my living with Albertine, or the masked ball at the Guermantes'. No doubt his impetus was necessary, and in that sense the external form of our life and the very material of our work derive from him. Without Swann, it would never have occurred to my parents to send me to Balbec. Yet he was not responsible for the sufferings which he himself had indirectly caused me. They were due to my weakness. His had caused sufferings of his own through Odette. But by determining in this way the life that we have led, he has thereby excluded all the lives that we might have led in place of this one. If Swann had not talked to me about Balbec, I would not have known Albertine, the dining-room in the hotel, the Guermantes. But I would have gone somewhere else, met different people, and my memory, like my books, would be full of quite other pictures which I cannot even imagine, and the novelty of which, in its unfamiliarity, is appealing enough to make me regret not having gone in that direction instead, and regret too that Albertine and the beach at Balbec and Rivebelle and the Guermantes had not remained for ever unknown to me.

Of course, it is with that face, as I had seen it for the first time by the sea, that I associated certain things which I should no doubt be writing about. In a sense, I was right to associate them with her, because if I had not walked along the sea front that day, if I had not met her, all these ideas would not have been developed (unless they had been developed by another woman). I was also wrong, though, because this generative pleasure which we try retrospectively to situate in a beautiful feminine face comes from our own senses: it was actually quite clear that the pages I would write were something that Albertine, especially the Albertine of those days, would not have understood. That is precisely why (and this is a recommendation not to live in too intellectual an atmosphere), because she was so different from me, that she had fertilized me through grief, and even at the beginning through the sheer effort of imagining something different from oneself. If she had been capable of understanding these pages then, for that very reason, she would not have inspired them.

Jealousy is a good recruiting officer who, when there is a gap in our picture, goes searching through the streets for the beautiful girl we needed. If she is no longer beautiful, she regains her looks because we are jealous of her, and she will fill the empty space.

Once we are dead, we shall feel no joy at the picture being completed in this way. But there is nothing at all discouraging about that thought. Because we sense that life is a little more complicated than people say, and circumstances likewise. And there is an urgent necessity to demonstrate this complexity. Jealousy, for all its usefulness, does not necessarily arise from a look, or from a tale, or from a backward glance. It can turn up, ready to sting us, between the pages of a directory – the ones called *Tout-Paris* for Paris, and the *Annuaire des châteaux* for the country.⁹¹ We had absent-mindedly heard the girl we are no longer interested in saying she had to go and see her sister for a few days in the Pas-de-Calais, near Dunkirk; we had also at one time vaguely thought that M. E—— had perhaps made advances to the girl, though now she never saw him, as she never went to the bar where she used to meet him. What could her sister be? Maybe a housemaid? Being discreet, we had never asked. And now, opening the *Annuaire des châteaux* at random, we discover that M. E—— has a country place in the Pas-de-Calais, near Dunkirk. Suddenly everything becomes clear, to please the girl he has taken her sister on as a housemaid, and if the girl no longer meets him in the bar, it is because he has had her come to his house, living as he does in Paris almost all of the year, but unable to do without her even for the period he is in the Pas-de-Calais. The brushes, drunk with rage and love, continue to paint it all in. And yet, what if it was not like that? If M. E—— really was not seeing the girl any longer but, out of a wish to be helpful, had recommended her sister to one of his brothers who lives all the year round in the Pas-de-Calais? So that she goes, perhaps even quite by chance, to see her sister at a time when M. E—— is not there, as they no longer have any interest in each other? Or again perhaps the sister is not a housemaid in that country house or anywhere else but has relatives in the Pas-de-Calais. Our initial grief subsides in the face of these latter conjectures and jealousy is allayed. But what difference does it make? Hidden among the pages of the *Annuaire des châteaux*, it came at the right time, because now the empty space that was there in the canvas has been filled in. And the whole design comes together thanks to the presence, created by jealousy, of the beautiful girl of whom already we are no longer jealous and whom we no longer love.

*

At that moment the butler came to tell me that, the first piece having ended, I could leave the library and enter the drawing-rooms. This made me recollect where I was. But I was not at all disturbed in the train of thought which I had just begun by the fact that a fashionable party, my return to society, had provided me with my point of departure for a new life which I had not been able to find in solitude. There was nothing extraordinary about this fact, an impression capable of resuscitating the eternal man in me not necessarily being linked to solitude any more than to society (as I had once thought it was, as had perhaps once been the case for me, as ought still perhaps to be the case if I had developed harmoniously, instead of experiencing this long intermission, which seemed only now to be ending). For experiencing this impression of beauty only when, in the grip of some immediate sensation, however insignificant, a similar sensation, spontaneously re-arising within me, had just extended the first over several periods of time at once, and filled my soul, where individual sensations usually left so much emptiness, with a general essence, there was no reason why I should not receive sensations of this kind in society as much as in the natural world, since they are produced by chance, helped doubtless by the particular excitement which, on the days when one finds oneself outside the regular tenor of life, makes even the simplest things start to give us sensations which habit usually makes us spare our nervous system. I was going to try to find the objective reason why it should be precisely and uniquely this kind of sensation which led to the work of art, by continuing the thoughts which had come to me in such rapid sequence in the library; for I felt that the impetus given to my intellectual life was now strong enough for me to be able to continue as successfully in the drawing-room, among all the guests, as alone in the library; it seemed that, from this point of view, even in the midst of this large gathering I should be able to retain my solitude. Because for the same reason that great events do not impinge from outside on our mental powers, and that a third-rate writer living in an epic epoch will remain just as poor a writer, what was really dangerous in society was the socialite attitude one brings to it. By itself it was no more capable of rendering you third-rate than a heroic war was capable of making a third-rate poet sublime.

In any case, whether it was theoretically useful or not that the work of art was constituted in this fashion, and while I was waiting until I had examined this point as fully as I was intending to, I could not deny that so far as I was concerned, whenever truly aesthetic impressions had come to me, it had always been after sensations of this kind. They had, admittedly, been rather rare in my life, but they dominated it, and I was able to rediscover in the past some of those peaks which I had made the mistake of losing sight of (something I was intending not to do from now on). And already I could say that, although this characteristic might in my case, by the exclusive importance it assumed, have appeared personal to me, I had been reassured to discover that it was related to other, less marked but discernible characteristics, at bottom quite similar, in certain other writers. Is it not from a sensation of the same sort as that of the madeleine that the finest part of the *Mémoires d'outre-tombe* depends: 'Yesterday in the evening I was walking alone . . . I was roused from my reflections by the twittering of a thrush perched in the highest branch of a birch tree. Instantly, the magical sound made my father's estate reappear before my eyes; I forgot the catastrophes I had just witnessed, and, transported suddenly into the past, saw once again the countryside where so often I heard the thrush's piping song.' And is not this one of the two or three most beautiful passages in those memoirs: 'A delicate, sweet scent of heliotrope wafted from a little patch of beans in full flower; it was brought to us not by a breeze from our own land, but by a wild wind from Newfoundland, unconnected to the exiled plant, without congenial reminiscence and pleasure. In this perfume not breathed by beauty, not purified in her bosom, not scattered in her path, in this perfume of a new dawn, new cultivation and new world, there was all the melancholy of regret, of absence and of youth.'[92] One of the masterpieces of French literature, Gérard de Nerval's *Sylvie*, just like the book of *Mémoires d'outre-tombe* which deals with Combourg, contains a sensation of the same sort as the taste of the madeleine and the 'twittering of the thrush'. And above all in Baudelaire these reminiscences, more numerous still, are clearly less fortuitous and therefore, in my opinion, conclusive. Here it is the poet himself who with a more indolent resolution seeks deliberately, in the scent of a woman, for instance, of her hair and her breast, the analogies which will inspire him and evoke for him '*l'azur du ciel immense et rond*' and '*un port rempli de flammes et de mâts*'.[93] I was about to try to remember the passages in Baudelaire at the heart of which there is this sort of transposed sensation, in order finally to establish a place for myself in such a noble tradition, and thereby to give myself the assurance that the work which I no longer had the slightest hesitation in undertaking was worth the effort I was going to devote to it, when having arrived at the foot of the staircase leading down from the library, I found myself suddenly in the great drawing-room and in the midst of a party which was going to seem very different from any I had been present at before, and for me was going to take an unusual turn and assume a new meaning. In fact, as soon as I entered the great drawing-room, although my mind was still firmly fixed on the plan I had just reached the point of formulating, a dramatic turn of events occurred which seemed to raise the gravest of objections to my undertaking. An objection which I would probably overcome but which, as I continued to reflect inwardly on the conditions necessary for the work of art, was at any moment, through the hundredfold repetition of instances of the one consideration most likely to make me hesitate, about to interrupt the course of my thinking.

To begin with I did not understand why I was so slow to recognize the master of the house and the guests nor why everybody seemed to have put on make-up, in most cases with powdered hair which changed them completely. The Prince, as he received his guests, still had that air of a genial, fairy-tale king which I had noticed the first time I met him, but this time, as if he had submitted himself to the stipulations of dress he had imposed on his guests, he had decked himself out in a white beard and, dragging his feet along as though they were weighing him down like lead boots, seemed to have taken on the task of representing one of the 'Ages of Man'. His moustaches were white, too, as though still dusted with the frost of Hop o' my Thumb's forest. They seemed uncomfortable for his tightening mouth and, once the effect had been achieved, as if they ought to have been taken off. To be quite honest, I recognized him only by a process of logical deduction, by deciding on the identity of the person on the simple basis of a few recognizable features. I do not know what young Fezensac had put on his face, but while others had whitened, in some cases half their beard, in others just their moustache, he had not bothered himself with dyes of that sort, but had found a way of covering his face with wrinkles, his eyebrows with bristling hairs, although that did not suit him in the least, making his face look as if it had been hardened, rigidified, made solemn, ageing him so much that no one could possibly have taken him for a young man. I was even more astonished a moment later when I heard somebody address as Duc de Châtellerault a little old man with a silvery, ambassadorial moustache, in whom only some lingering remnant of the way he glanced around enabled me to recognize him as the young man whom I had met once when I had called on Mme de Villeparisis. In the case of the first person whom I thus succeeded in identifying, by trying to forget the disguise and then, by an effort of memory, adding to the features which were still unchanged, my first thought ought to have been, and for less than a second perhaps was, to congratulate him on being so marvellously made up that one felt at first, before recognizing him, the same hesitancy that great actors, appearing in a role in which they are very different from their usual selves, as they make their first entry, create in the audience, who, despite being forewarned by the programme, remain for a moment dumbfounded before bursting into applause.

Most extraordinary of all, from this standpoint, was my personal enemy, M. d'Argencourt, the real star of the party. Not only, in place of his scarcely even pepper-and-salt beard, had he donned an extraordinary beard of improbable whiteness, but additionally (so much can little physical changes shrink or enlarge a person and, more broadly, change their apparent character, their personality) the man had become an old beggar, no longer commanding the slightest respect, although his solemn appearance, and starchy inflexibility, were still fresh in my memory, who brought to the part of decrepit old man such credibility that his limbs were quivering, and the slack lines of his face, which always used to be so haughty, were set in a permanent smile of beatific inanity. Taken to this extreme, the art of disguise becomes something more than that, it becomes a complete transformation of the personality. And indeed, although a few little details confirmed that it really was Argencourt who was putting on this hilarious and colourful show, I would have had to work back through I do not know how many successive states of that face if I wanted to rediscover that of the Argencourt I had known, who, with nothing but his own body to work with, had become so different from himself! This was evidently the furthest extremity to which he had been able to bring it without its collapsing entirely: the proudest face and the most jutting chest were now no more than a bunch of disintegrating rags, shaken in every direction. Only by recalling, with some difficulty, the occasional smile which in the past had for a moment tempered his aloofness, could one find in the living Argencourt the man whom I had seen so often, and understand how this daft old-clothes-merchant's smile might have existed within the correct gentleman of earlier days. But, even supposing that a similar intention to Argencourt's lay behind this smile, the very substance of the eye through which he expressed the smile was so changed, because of the extraordinary transformation of his face, that the expression itself became quite different and even appeared to belong to a different person. I was seized by giggles at the sight of this sublime dodderer, rendered as affable in this benevolent caricature of himself as was, in more tragic mode, the stricken and well-mannered M. de Charlus. M. d'Argencourt, in his incarnation as a comic ancient in a play by Regnard, exaggeratedly reworked by Labiche,[94] was as approachable and as courteous as the King Lear version of M. de Charlus, who carefully doffed his hat to even the most obsequious of those he encountered. None the less it did not occur to me to tell him how much I admired the extraordinary sight he presented. It was not my old antipathy that held me back, for he had contrived to look so different from himself that I had the illusion of being in the presence of another person altogether, as kindly, helpless and inoffensive as the usual Argencourt was contemptuous, hostile and dangerous. So different a person that the sight of this ludicrously grimacing, white, comical character, this snowman looking like a childlike Général Dourakine,[95] made me reflect that the human being could go through metamorphoses as total as those of some insects. I had a sense that I was looking through the plate glass of a natural history museum display at an example of what the speediest and surest insect may turn into, and standing in front of this limp chrysalis, vibratile rather than capable of movement, I was unable to experience any of the feelings that M. d'Argencourt had always inspired in me. But I said nothing, I did not congratulate M. d'Argencourt on putting on a show that seemed to extend the possibilities available for the transformation of the human body.

Backstage at the theatre, of course, or at a fancy-dress ball, politeness tends to make one exaggerate the difficulty, almost to affirm the impossibility, of recognizing the person in their costume. Here, on the contrary, some instinct had warned me to conceal this as far as possible; I felt that there was nothing flattering about it, because the transformation was not voluntary, and finally realized something I had not suspected when I walked into this drawing-room, namely that any party, however simple, which takes place a long time after one has stopped going into society, so long as it brings together some of the people one knew in the past, produces the same effect as a masked ball, of the most successful kind imaginable, where one is quite genuinely *intrigué*[96] by the other guests, but where the disguises, which have long been set in their unintentional shape, cannot be removed with a wash once the party is over. Intrigued by other people? Also, alas, intriguing them ourselves. Because the same difficulty that I was experiencing in putting the right names to faces seemed to be shared by all the people who, seeing mine, took no more notice of it than if they had never seen it before, or else tried to release from my present appearance the memory of a different face.

If M. d'Argencourt had just performed this extraordinary 'number', which in its extravagant parody provided certainly the most striking vision that I would retain of him, he was like an actor coming out on to the stage for one last time before the curtain finally falls amidst gales of laughter. If I was no longer hostile to him, it was because he, having re-entered his childhood innocence, no longer had the slightest recollection of the scathing notions he might once have had about me, no memory of seeing M. de Charlus suddenly let go of my arm, either because he no longer had any such feelings, or because to get as far as me they were obliged to pass through physical refractors so distorting that they completely altered their meaning along the way, so that M. d'Argencourt seemed good in the absence of physical means of expressing the fact that he was still disagreeable, or of repressing his permanently engaging mirth. In fact to call him an actor would be an overstatement, unencumbered as he was by any kind of conscious spirit, it is more as a jigging puppet, with a beard made of white wool, that I saw him twitched about and walked up and down in the drawing-room, as if he were in a scientific and philosophical puppet-show, in which he served, as in a funeral address or a lecture at the Sorbonne, both as a reminder of the vanity of all things and as a specimen of natural history.

Puppets then, but puppets which, if one were to identify them with someone one had known, needed to be read on several levels at once, levels that underlay them and gave them depth and, when faced with one of these old marionettes, forced one to make an intellectual effort, because one was obliged to look at them with the memory at the same time as with the eyes; puppets steeped in the intangible colours of the years, puppets which were an expression of Time, Time which is normally not visible, which seeks out bodies in order to become so and wherever it finds them seizes upon them for its magic lantern show. As intangible as Golo had once been on my bedroom doorknob in Combray, the new, almost unrecognizable d'Argencourt stood there as the revelation of Time, which he rendered partially visible. In the new elements which made up the face and character of M. d'Argencourt one could read a certain tally of years, one could recognize the symbolic form of life not as it appears to us, that is as permanent, but in its reality, in such a shifting atmosphere that by evening the proud nobleman is depicted there in caricature, as an old-clothes-merchant.

In other people, too, these changes, these genuine estrangements seemed to go beyond the realm of natural history, and one was astonished, hearing a name, to find that the same individual might present, not like M. d'Argencourt the characteristics of a new species, but the external traits of some other personality. As in the case of M. d'Argencourt, many were the unsuspected possibilities that time had wrought with some young girl, but these possibilities, although entirely physiognomic or corporeal, seemed to have something moral about them, too. The facial features, if they change, if they form a different ensemble, if their expression habitually alters more slowly, take on a different meaning with their different appearance. In the case of a woman whom one had known as narrow-minded and unsympathetic, an unrecognizable relaxation of the cheeks, an unpredictable curving of the nose, caused the same surprise, often the same pleasant surprise, as some sensitive and profound remark or some noble and courageous deed that one would never have expected of her. All around this nose, this new nose, one could see opening up horizons which one could never have dared hope for. With those cheeks a kindness and affection once inconceivable became possible. One could make explicit in the presence of this chin, things that one would never have dreamed of intimating in front of its predecessor. All these new facial features implied different character traits, the unsympathetic, scrawny young woman turned into a large and indulgent dowager. It is no longer in a zoological sense, as in the case of M. d'Argencourt, so much as in a moral and social sense that one could say that this was a different person.

From all these aspects, a party like the one at which I found myself was something much more valuable than an image of the past, as it offered me, as it were, all the successive images, ones I had previously never seen, which separated the past from the present and, better still, the relationship that existed between the present and the past; it was like what we used to call an optical viewer, but giving an optical view of years, a view not of one moment, but of one person set in the distorting perspective of Time.

As for the woman whose lover M. d'Argencourt had been, she had not changed much, *if one took account of the time that had passed*, that is to say her face had not been completely ruined, at least for the face of a being which loses its shape progressively during the journey into the abyss towards which it has been hurled, the abyss whose direction we can express only by comparisons that are all equally pointless, since we can borrow them only from the spatial world, and whose only benefit, whether we define them by height, length or depth, is to make us feel that this inconceivable yet tangible dimension exists. The need, in order to put a name to the faces, to trace the years backwards, in effect, forced me then, in turn, to reinstate, by allowing them their real place, the years to which I had given no thought. From this point of view, and in order to prevent myself from being misled by the apparent identity of space, the entirely new appearance of an individual such as M. d'Argencourt was a striking revelation of this chronological reality, which normally remains an abstraction for us, just as the appearance of certain dwarf trees or giant baobabs tells us that we are in a different latitude.

Thus life begins to seem like a pantomime in which, from act to act, we watch a baby becoming an adolescent, then a grown man, then old and bent as he approaches the grave. And as one feels that it is by a permanent process of change that these individuals, encountered only at fairly long intervals, have become so different, one feels that one has followed the same law as these creatures, who are now so transformed that, although they have not ceased to exist, indeed precisely because they have not ceased to exist, they no longer resemble the appearance they presented to us in the past.

A young woman whom I had known long ago, now turned white and compacted into the form of a baleful little old woman, seemed to suggest that, in a theatrical finale, individuals need to be so disguised as to be unrecognizable. Her brother, however, had remained so upright, so like himself, that it was a complete surprise to see that he had whitened the elegantly curled moustache on his youthful face. The patches of white in beards hitherto entirely black rendered the human landscape of the party somewhat melancholy, like the first yellow leaves on the trees when one is still thinking one can count on a long summer, when before one has started to enjoy it one sees that it has already turned to autumn. So I, having lived from one day to the next since my childhood, and having also formed definitive impressions of myself and of others, became aware for the first time, as a result of the metamorphoses that had been produced in all these people, of all the time that had passed in their lives, an idea which overwhelmed me with the revelation that it had passed equally for me. And while irrelevant in itself, their old age devastated me by its announcing the approach of my own. This was, anyway, proclaimed by successive remarks which every few minutes assailed my ears like the trumpets of Judgment Day. The first was made by the Duchesse de Guermantes; I had just seen her, passing between a double line of onlookers who, unaware of the wonderful artifices of dress and aesthetic which created this effect, yet moved by the presence of this reddish head, this salmon-pink body barely emerging from its fins of black lace and stifled with jewels, gazed at it, at the hereditary sinuosity of its lines, as they might have gazed at some ancient sacred fish, encrusted with precious stones, in which was incarnate the tutelary spirit of the Guermantes. 'Ah! she said to me, how wonderful to see you, my oldest friend.' And although the vanity of the erstwhile young man of Combray, who never for a moment thought I might be one of her friends, actually sharing in the actual mysterious life she led among the Guermantes, one of her friends on the same footing as M. de Bréauté, as M. de Forestelle, as Swann, as all those who were dead, might have been flattered by these words, I was mainly saddened by them. 'Her oldest friend! I said to myself, she is exaggerating; perhaps one of the oldest, but am I really . . .' At that moment a nephew of the Prince came up to me: 'As an old Parisian, you . . . ,' he began. Only a few seconds later, I was handed a note. Just as I arrived I had encountered a young Létourville, whose exact relationship to the Duchesse I had forgotten, but who knew me slightly. He had just left Saint-Cyr and, telling myself that he would be a nice friend for me to have, as Saint-Loup had been, able to initiate me into army affairs, and all the changes they had undergone, I had told him that I would find him later and that we might arrange to have dinner together, for which he had thanked me warmly. But I had stayed too long dreaming in the library and the note he had left for me was to say that he had not been able to wait, and to leave me his address. The letter from this imagined friend ended thus: 'Most respectfully, your young friend, Létourville.' 'Young friend!' That was how I used to write to people who were thirty years older than myself, like Legrandin. And now this second lieutenant, whom I was imagining as a companion like Saint-Loup, called himself my young friend. So it was clearly not just military tactics that had changed since those days, and for M. de Létourville I was not a companion but an old gentleman; and from M. de Létourville, in whose company I was picturing myself, as I imagined myself, as a friend and companion, I was separated by the division of an invisible pair of compasses I had never dreamed of, which set me so far away from the young second lieutenant that, to somebody who described himself as my 'young friend', it seemed that I was an old gentleman.

Almost immediately afterwards somebody mentioned Bloch, and I asked whether they meant the young man or the father (unaware of his death during the war, from shock, it was said, at seeing France invaded). 'I didn't know he had children, I didn't even know he was married, said the Prince to me. But clearly we are talking about the father, because there's nothing of the young man about him, he added with a laugh. If he had sons they'd be grown-up themselves by now.' And I realized they were talking about my school-friend. Then a minute later, he came into the room. And superimposed on Bloch's features, too, I saw that daft, acquiescent expression, those feeble nods of the head which so quickly find their stop-notch, and in which I would have recognized the learned weariness of an amiable old man if I had not at the same time recognized my friend standing before me, and if my memories were not animating him with that uninterrupted youthful energy of which he now seemed bereft. For me, who had known him on the threshold of his life and always pictured him thus, he was my school-friend, an adolescent whose youth I measured by that which, thinking myself to have carried on at the age I was then, I unconsciously attributed to myself. I heard somebody say that he certainly looked his age, and was astonished to notice on his face some of the signs generally thought to be more characteristic of men who are old. Then I understood that this was because he really was old, and that it is out of adolescents who last a sufficient number of years that life makes old men.

As somebody, hearing that I had been unwell, asked whether I was not afraid of catching the flu which was so prevalent at that time, another well-meaning person reassured me by saying: 'No, it usually attacks younger people. Someone of your age is not really at risk.' I was also assured that the servants of the house had recognized me. They had whispered my name, and even, one lady told me, 'in the way they put it' she had them say 'There's old father . . .' (this expression was followed by my surname). And as I did not have any children, it could only be an allusion to my age.

'What! did I know the Maréchal? said the Duchesse to me. But I knew people who were even more typical, the Duchesse de Galliera, Pauline de Périgord, or Monsignor Dupanloup.' Hearing her, I naïvely regretted not having known what she called a relic of the old order. I ought to have thought that we call it the old order because we were able only to see the tail end of it; in the same way, what we see on the horizon takes on a mysterious grandeur and seems to close the door on a world we shall never see again; yet we continue to go forward, and soon it is we ourselves who are on the horizon for the generations who come after us; meanwhile the horizon retreats, and the world, which seemed to be finished, begins again. 'When I was a girl, added Mme de Guermantes, I even saw the Duchesse de Dino. My word, I'm not as young as I used to be.' That last remark annoyed me: 'She shouldn't have said that, that's how old ladies talk.' And immediately I remembered that she was in fact an old lady. 'As for you, she went on, you don't ever change. Yes, she told me, you're astonishing, you always look so young,' a saddening remark, because, however we may look, it only means anything if we have in fact grown old. She delivered the final blow by adding: 'I've always thought it was such a pity you didn't marry. But perhaps, who knows, it is all for the best. You would have been of an age to have sons in the war, and if they had been killed, like poor Robert (I still often think of him), you with your sensitivity would never have survived the loss.' I could see myself, as though in the first truthful glass I had ever encountered, reflected in the eyes of old men, who in their opinion were still young, just as I was in mine, and who when I described myself as an old man, hoping to hear a denial, showed in the way they looked at me, seeing me not as they saw themselves but as I saw them, no glimmer of protestation. Because we did not see our own true appearance, or age, and each of us, as though in a facing mirror, saw those of the others. And I am sure that many people confront the discovery that they have grown old with less sadness than I did. But old age, to begin with, has something in common with death. Some face it with indifference, not because they have more courage than others, but because they have less imagination. And then, a man who since his childhood has had one single idea in his mind, but who has been forced by idleness and his state of health continuously to put off its realization, each evening to write off the day that has been lost, so that the illness which hastens the ageing of his body retards that of his mind, is more surprised and overwhelmed to see that he has never ceased living in Time than somebody who has little interior life, organizes his life by the calendar, and does not all at once discover the total of the years whose increasing tally he has followed daily. But a more serious reason underlay my anxiety; I discovered this destructive action of Time at the very moment when I wanted to begin to clarify, to intellectualize within a work of art, realities whose nature was extra-temporal.

With some people the gradual replacement, achieved in my absence, of each cell by new ones, had brought about such a complete change, such a total metamorphosis, that I could have dined opposite them in a restaurant a hundred times without suspecting I had once known them, any more than I would have been able to guess the royal identity of a sovereign going incognito or the vices of a stranger. In fact even this comparison does not apply to the cases where I heard their names, because it is quite possible that the person sitting opposite you might be a criminal or a king, whereas these were people I had known, or rather I had known people of the same name but who were so different that I was unable to believe that they could be the same. However, just as I would have done with the idea of royalty or vice, which lose no time in giving a new face to the stranger, with whom one might, while one's eyes were still blindfolded, have committed the gaffe of being insolent or pleasant, and in whose same features one now discerns something distinguished or suspicious, I set about introducing into the face of one unknown, completely unknown woman, the idea that she was Mme Sazerat, and eventually restored the once familiar meaning of her face, which would, however, have remained truly alienated for me, utterly that of another person, as lacking now in all the human attributes I had once known as that of a man who has reverted to being a monkey, if the name and the affirmation of identity had not set me, despite the arduousness of the problem, on the track of the solution. Sometimes, though, the old face reappeared with enough precision for me to be able to try a confrontation; and then, like a witness brought face to face with a suspect he has seen, the difference was so great that I was forced to say: 'No . . . I don't recognize her.'

Gilberte de Saint-Loup said to me: 'Shall we go and dine, just the two of us, at a restaurant?' As I replied: 'So long as you don't think it compromising to dine alone with a young man,' I heard everybody round me laughing, and hastily added: 'or rather, with an old man.' I felt that the phrase which had caused the laughter was one that my mother might have used when speaking of me, my mother for whom I was always a child. Now I noticed that in matters of self-examination, I looked at things from the same point of view as she did. If I had finally taken in, like her, certain changes which had occurred since my early childhood, these were nevertheless now very old changes. I had stopped at the one which once made someone say, almost before it was true: 'He's almost a grown-up young man now.' I still thought this, but these days it was vastly out of date. I was not fully aware how much I had changed. But what, in fact, had those people who had just burst out laughing really noticed? I had not a single grey hair, my moustache was black. I would like to have been able to ask them what it was that revealed the evidence of this terrible thing.

And now it dawned upon me what old age was – old age, which of all realities is perhaps the one we continue longest to think of in purely abstract terms, looking at calendars, dating our letters, seeing our friends marry, and then our friends' children, without understanding, whether out of fear or laziness, what it all means, until the day when we see a silhouette we do not recognize, like that of M. d'Argencourt, which makes us realize that we are living in a new world; until the day when the grandson of one of our friends, a young man whom we instinctively treat as an equal, smiles as if we were making fun of him, as to him we have always seemed like a grandfather; now I understood the meaning of death, loves, the pleasures of the mind, the use of suffering, a vocation, etc. For while names had lost their individuality for me, words were yielding up their full meaning. The beauty of images lies behind things, the beauty of ideas in front of them. So that the former cease to impress us when we reach them, whereas we have to go beyond the latter in order to understand them.

The cruel discovery which I had just made could not but be of use to me as far as the raw material of my book was concerned. Since I had decided that it could not be constituted solely out of genuinely full impressions, impressions which exist outside time, of the other truths among which I was planning to set these, those which related to time, time, in which men, societies and nations are immersed and in which they change, would play an important part. I would not be concerned only to find a place for the alterations which the features of human beings undergo, and of which I was noticing new examples each minute, because, while I was thinking about my work, now definitively enough under way not to let itself be stalled by temporary distractions, I continued to greet people whom I knew and to chat with them. Ageing, it was clear, did not show itself in the same way for all of them.

I saw someone who was asking my name, and was told that it was M. de Cambremer. And then to show that he had recognized me: 'Do you still have your attacks of breathlessness?' he asked me; and, at my reply in the affirmative: 'You see that it's no barrier to longevity,' he said, as though I were a hundred years old. While I talked to him, I kept a close eye on two or three characteristics which I was able by an effort of thought to reintroduce into this synthesis, different though it was from my recollections, which I called his identity. Then for a moment he turned his head to one side. And I saw that what had made him so difficult to recognize was the addition of great red pouches to his cheeks which prevented him from fully opening his mouth and his eyes, so much so that I stood there stupefied, not daring to look at these carbuncular growths, which it seemed more polite not to mention until he did. But like a brave invalid, he made no allusion to them, laughed, and I was afraid of seeming heartless if I did not ask, and tactless if I did ask, what they were. 'But don't you get them less often with age?' he asked, continuing to talk about my breathlessness. I said not. 'No, no, my sister definitely has fewer than she used to,' he told me, in a contradictory tone of voice, as though it were impossible for my situation to be any different from his sister's, and as though old age were one of those remedies which, since they had been beneficial for Mme de Gaucourt, he could not believe might not be helpful to me. Mme de Cambremer-Legrandin having joined us, I grew increasingly anxious about appearing insensitive for not giving some expression of concern about what I had observed on her husband's face, yet did not dare mention it first myself. 'Are you pleased to see him? she said to me – He's in good health? I replied, hesitantly. – Heavens yes, pretty good, as you can see.' She had not noticed the affliction which I found so difficult to look at and which was no more than one of Time's masks which Time had fastened to the face of the Marquis, but only little by little, thickening it so gradually that the Marquise had been unaware of it. When M. de Cambremer had finished his questions about my breathlessness, it was my turn to ask somebody in a low voice whether the Marquis's mother was still alive. When one is estimating the passage of time, it is actually only the first step that is difficult. It is very hard at first to imagine that so much time could have passed, and then after a while it seems strange that even more has not passed. One had never dreamed that the thirteenth century was so distant, but then it seems almost impossible to believe that thirteenth-century churches might still exist, although there are countless examples of them in France. In the space of a few moments I had gone through the same process as happens more slowly to those people who, having had difficulty in believing that somebody they knew as a child is still alive at sixty, find it even harder fifteen years later to learn that they are still living and are still only seventy-five. I asked M. de Cambremer how his mother was. 'She is still wonderful,' he told me, using an adjective which, in contrast to those tribes where aged parents are treated mercilessly, is applied in certain families to old people whose command of the most basic faculties, such as hearing, walking to Mass and being impervious to bereavements, are imbued in the eyes of their children with a strange moral beauty.

With others whose faces were still intact, the only thing that seemed to worry them was having to walk; at first one imagined there was something wrong with their legs; only later did one realize that age had fastened its leaden soles to their feet. Some, like the Prince d'Agrigente, seemed to be made more attractive by age. The tall, thin man with the lacklustre eyes and hair that seemed destined to stay red for ever, had given place, through a metamorphosis analogous to that of insects, to an old man whose red hair, too long exposed to view, had been whipped away like an over-used table-cloth and replaced with white. His chest had taken on an unexpected, robust, almost warlike burliness, which must have required a positive rupture of the fragile chrysalis I had known; a conscious gravity lighted his eyes, tinged with a new kindness which seemed to be directed to everybody.

And since, despite everything, some points of resemblance still persisted between the mighty prince of the present and the portrait lodged in my memory, I was lost in admiration of the original powers of revitalization possessed by Time, which, while continuing to respect the unity of the individual and the laws of life, can thus do so much to change the outward finish and to introduce bold contrasts between two successive aspects of a single character. For many of these people were immediately identifiable, but rather as if they were bad portraits of themselves brought together at an exhibition where an inaccurate and malicious artist has hardened the features of one, removed the fresh complexion or the slender figure of another, and dulled her eyes. Comparing these images with the ones that answered to the eye of memory, I was less taken with the more recent ones. Just as one often finds less good, and rejects, one of the photographs between which a friend has asked one to choose, as I looked at the image of themselves that each person presented, I would have liked to say to them: 'No, not this one, you're not so good in this one, it isn't you.' I would not have dared add: 'Instead of your lovely straight nose, somebody's given you your father's hooked nose, which I've never seen on you before.' And it was in fact a new nose, but it was also the family nose. Briefly put, Time, the artist, had 'rendered' all these models in such a way that they were still recognizable but they were not likenesses, not because he had flattered them, but because he had aged them. He is also an artist who works extremely slowly. That replica of Odette's face, for example, the first outline sketch for which I had glimpsed in Gilberte's face on the day I saw Bergotte for the first time, Time had now finally taken to the most perfect likeness, in the same way that some painters keep a work for a long time, finishing it gradually, year by year.

If some women acknowledged their old age by using make-up, it became visible in contrasting fashion through an absence of make-up in the case of certain men on whose faces I had never particularly noticed it, and who yet struck me as greatly changed since, having lost heart in the attempt to please, they had stopped using it. Among these was Legrandin. The removal of the pink, which I had never suspected of being artificial, from his lips and his cheeks, gave his face the greyish look, as well as the sculptural precision, of stone, sculpted his doleful, elongated features to look like those of some Egyptian gods. Gods? Ghosts would be more appropriate. He had lost the courage not only to paint himself, but to smile, to make his eyes sparkle, to say clever things. One was astonished to see him so pale, so demoralized, uttering only occasional words which were as insignificant as those of the invoked dead. One wondered what cause was preventing him being lively, eloquent and charming, just as one asks the same thing about the nondescript 'double' of a man, brilliant in his lifetime, when a medium puts questions to it which ought to give rise to engaging and extensive answers. And one told oneself that this cause, which had substituted for the quick-thinking, brightly coloured Legrandin a pallid, pensive phantom of himself, was old age.

In several guests I eventually recognized not only themselves but them as they once used to be, Ski, for example, who was no more altered than a flower or a fruit which had been dried. He was a rough draft, confirming my theories about art. Others were not in the least interested in art, being society people. But they had not been ripened by old age either and their chubby faces, even if surrounded with a first circle of wrinkles and an arc of white hair, retained the cheerfulness of an eighteen-year-old. They were not old men, just extremely faded young people of eighteen. It would have taken very little to efface life's signs of wear, and death would find it no harder to restore youth to these faces than it is to clean a portrait which only a thin coating of dirt prevents from shining in the way it used to. I also thought about the illusion we fall victim to when, listening to some famous old man speaking, we are immediately ready to trust his goodness, his fairness and his generosity of spirit; because I felt that, forty years earlier, these people had been dreadful young men, and there was no reason to suppose that they had not kept that vanity, duplicity, arrogance and cunning.

Yet in complete contrast to these, I was surprised, when I was talking to men and women who used to be unbearable, to find that they had lost almost all their faults, perhaps because life, by disappointing or fulfilling their desires, had rid them of their pretension or their bitterness. A rich marriage putting an end to the need for struggle and ostentation, or the influence of the wife herself, and the slowly acquired awareness of values other than those that comprised the credo of a frivolous youth, had allowed their temperament to unbend and reveal their better qualities. These people, as they had grown old, seemed to have taken on a different personality, just as trees, as they change colour in the autumn, seem to change their essential nature. In them the essence of old age was indeed visible, but as something moral. In others it was primarily physical, and so new that the person (Mme d'Arpajon, for example) seemed both unfamiliar and familiar. Unfamiliar because it was impossible to suspect that it was she, and despite all I did I could not, as I returned her greeting, prevent myself revealing the mental effort which was causing me to hesitate between three or four individuals (among whom Mme d'Arpajon was not included) in my attempt to work out whose greeting I was returning, with a warmth which must have astonished her, for in my state of uncertainty, afraid of seeming too cool if she were a close friend, I had compensated for the vagueness of my gaze by the warmth of my handshake and my smile. On the other hand, though, her new appearance was not unfamiliar to me. It was the one I had often seen in the course of my life on the faces of stout, elderly ladies, but without ever suspecting that they could, many years before, have looked like Mme d'Arpajon. Her appearance was so different from the Marquise I had known that one might have taken her for a damned soul, a character out of a play, appearing first as a young girl, then as a sturdy matron, and soon no doubt to return as a bent and doddering old woman. She seemed, like an exhausted swimmer for whom the shore appears a long way away, to be scarcely able to rise above the waves of time that were submerging her. Gradually, though, by dint of studying her face, hesitant and uncertain like an unreliable memory which can no longer retain the shapes of earlier times, I finally managed to retrieve something of it by playing a little game of eliminating the squares and hexagons which age had added to her cheeks. Of course, it was not always merely geometric shapes that age combined with women's faces. In the cheeks of the Duchesse de Guermantes, still very recognizable but now as variegated as nougat, I could make out a trace of verdigris, a small pink patch of crushed shell, and a little lump, hard to define, smaller than a mistletoe berry and less transparent than a glass pearl.

Some men walked with a limp which one knew was not the result of a motor accident but was caused by a first stroke and by the fact that they already had, as they say, one foot in the grave. Almost at the mouth of theirs, half-paralysed, some women seemed unable fully to free their dress, which remained caught on the stone of the vault, and could not stand up, bent as they were, head lowered, in a curve which echoed their current descent between life and death, awaiting the final fall. Nothing could counter the movement of this parabola which was sweeping them away, and when they tried to rise they shook, and their fingers could not hold on to anything.

Some did not even have white hair. Thus, when he came over to pass a message to his master, I recognized the Prince de Guermantes's old valet. The shaggy whiskers that bristled on his cheeks, as well as the hair on his head, were still an almost pinkish red, and nobody could suspect him of using dye like the Duchesse de Guermantes. Nevertheless, he looked old. One simply felt that there are some kinds of men, as in the vegetable kingdom there are some kinds of mosses, lichens and the like, which do not change at the approach of winter.

These changes were usually, in fact, atavistic, and the family – often even – especially among Jews – the race – filled up the gaps left by the passing of time. After all, ought I to tell myself that these characteristics would die? I had always thought of the self, at any given moment, as a colony of polyps, where the eye, an independent but associated organism, blinks when a particle passes by without the intelligence ordering it to do so, or where the intestine, with a buried parasite, is infected without the intelligence learning of it; similarly for the soul, but over the duration of a life, as a sequence of selves which die one after another, or even alternate between themselves, like those at Combray which took one another's place within me when evening came. But I had also seen that these moral cells which make up an individual are more durable than he is. I had seen the vices and the courage of the Guermantes recur in Saint-Loup, as also his own strange and short-lived character defects, and in Swann's case his Semitism. I could see it again in Bloch. He had lost his father some years ago and, when I had written to him then, had not at first been able to reply to me, because in addition to the powerful family feeling that often exists in Jewish families, the idea that his father was a man utterly superior to all others had turned his love for him into worship. He had not been able to bear losing him and had to retreat to a sanatorium for almost a year. He had replied to my condolences in a tone both deeply felt and almost aloof, so enviable he thought my having been able to approach this superior being, whose two-horse carriage he would have liked to give to some museum of history. And now, at his family table, the same anger which animated M. Bloch against M. Nissim Bernard animated Bloch against his father-in-law. He made the same attacks on him at table. In the same way that I, listening to Cottard, Brichot and many other people talking, had felt that a single undulation uses culture and fashion to propagate identical patterns of speech and thinking throughout the whole expanse of space, so throughout the length of time a mighty ground-swell stirs up from the depths of the ages the same angers, the same sorrows, the same acts of bravery, the same obsessions, which rise through generation after superimposed generation, so that any section taken through a few of the same series will show the repetition, like shadows on successive screens, of a scene identical to, although frequently less insignificant than, the one that shows Bloch and his father-in-law battling against each other like M. Bloch senior and M. Nissim Bernard, and like other people whom I never knew.

Some faces under their cowl of white hair already had the rigidity, the sealed eyelids, of those about to die, and their lips, shaking with a permanent tremor, seemed to be mumbling the prayer of the dying. A face whose lines were still unchanged needed nothing for its appearance to be altered except white hair in place of black or blond. Theatrical costumiers know that a powdered wig is enough to disguise someone quite adequately and render them unrecognizable. The young Comte de ——, whom I had seen in Mme de Cambremer's box when he was still a lieutenant, the day when Mme de Cambremer was in the box below with her cousin, still had features as perfectly regular, in fact more so, the physiological rigidity of arteriosclerosis exaggerating further the impassive rectitude of his dandy's physiognomy, and giving his features the intense definition, which immobility turned almost to a grimace, which they would have had in a study by Mantegna or Michelangelo. His complexion, once a louche red, now had a funereal pallor; some silver hairs, a slight stoutness, a Doge-like nobility, a weariness that approached somnolence, all combined in him to give the novel and prophetic impression of doomed majesty. In place of his rectangle of blond beard, the equal rectangle of his white beard transformed him so perfectly that, noticing that the second lieutenant I had known now had five rings of braid, my first thought was to congratulate him, not on having been promoted colonel, but on looking so good as a colonel, a disguise for which he seemed to have borrowed both the uniform and the mournful gravity of the superior officer that his father had been. On another figure, the substitution of a white for a blond beard, while the face remained lively, smiling and young, simply made him appear ruddier and more militant, augmented the sparkle of the eyes and gave the still youthful socialite the inspired air of a prophet.

The transformation which white hair and other factors had effected, especially among the women, would have impressed me less forcefully had it been no more than a change of colour, which can be a pleasure to the eye, rather than a change of character, which is intellectually disturbing. To 'recognize' somebody, after all, even more, to identify somebody after not being able to recognize them, is to think two contradictory things under a single heading, to admit that what was here, the individual one remembers, no longer exists, and that what is here is a being one did not formerly know; it is to have to think about a mystery almost as disturbing as that of death, of which it is effectively the preface and the herald. Because I knew what these changes meant, what they were a prelude to. So that these women's white hair disturbed me, combined as it was with so many other changes. I was told a name and I was stunned by the thought that it applied both to the fair-haired woman I remembered waltzing long ago and the large lady with white hair ponderously crossing the room near me. Beyond a slight pinkness of complexion, the name might perhaps be the only thing these two women had in common, each – the one in my memory and the one at the Guermantes' party – more unlike the other than an innocent young girl and a dowager in a play. For life to have succeeded in giving the waltzing girl this enormous body, in slowing down her ungainly movements as if in response to some metronome, for it to have substituted, with perhaps as the one common factor the cheeks, broader now admittedly but rosaceous since youth, this portly old campaigner for that slender blonde, it must have had to carry through more demolition and reconstruction than replacing a steeple with a dome, and when one thought that this operation was conducted not on inert matter but on only imperceptibly changing flesh, the staggering contrast between the present apparition and the being whom I remembered drove the latter into a past that was more than distant, that was almost unbelievable. It was difficult to reconcile the two appearances, to think of the two people under a single heading; for just as it is hard to imagine that a dead person used to be alive, or that somebody who was alive is now dead, it is almost as difficult, and of the same order of difficulty (for the annihilation of youth, the destruction of a person full of energy and light-heartedness, is already a form of oblivion), to conceive that she who was young is now old, when the juxtaposition of the appearance of this old woman with that of the young one seems so strongly to exclude it that old and young and old again seem to be taking it in turns, alternating as in a dream, so that one would never have believed that this one had ever been that one, that they are made of the same material, that the original stuff did not take refuge elsewhere, but through the cunning manipulation of time has become this, that it really is the same material, never having left the one body – without the clue of the identical name and the positive testimony of friends, and the one appearance of verisimilitude provided by the rosacea, once a small patch among clusters of golden corn, now broadly spread beneath the snow.

And as with snow, too, the degree of whiteness of the hair seemed generally to be a sign of the depth of time lived, like those mountain-tops which, even when they seem to the naked eye to be at the same level as others, nevertheless reveal their altitude by their degree of snowy whiteness. Yet this is not universally true, especially among women. Thus the locks of the Princesse de Guermantes, which when they were grey and lustrous as silk looked like silver around her domed forehead, now that they had become white had taken on a tow-coloured, woolly mattness, which had the opposite effect of making them look as grey as dirty snow that has lost its sheen.

And in many case those fair-haired dancers had not only appropriated, along with a wig of white hair, the friendship of duchesses whom they never used to know. Having done nothing in the past but dance, they had been touched by art, as if by grace. And just as illustrious ladies in the seventeenth century would enter a religious order, they lived in apartments filled with Cubist paintings, each one with a Cubist painter working for her alone and she living only for him. As for the old men whose features had changed, they still tried to keep permanently fixed on their faces one of those fleeting expressions one adopts for a second in front of a camera in an attempt either to make the most of one's best features or else to compensate for some defect; they looked rather as if they had finally become immutable snapshots of themselves.

All these people had spent so much *time* putting on their disguises that these generally went unnoticed by those who lived with them. In many cases they were allowed an extension during which they could continue to remain themselves until quite late on. But then the deferred disguise was adopted more rapidly; whichever way it happened, it was unavoidable. I had never found any resemblance between Mme X—— and her mother, whom I had known only as an old woman, when she looked like a shrunken little Turk. Mme X—— herself I had always known as charming and upright, and for a long time that was how she remained, in fact for too long because, like someone who has to remember to put on her Turkish disguise before night falls, she had left it to the very last minute and had therefore been forced very hastily, almost suddenly, to shrink herself down and faithfully to reproduce the old Turkish woman's appearance adopted long ago by her mother.

There were some men whom I knew to be related to others without ever having thought that they might have features in common; in admiring the old recluse with white hair whom Legrandin had become I suddenly discerned, I may say I discovered with the satisfaction of a zoologist, in the different planes of his cheeks, the same construction as in those of his young nephew, Louis de Cambremer, who yet appeared to look nothing like him; then to this first common feature I added another which I had never noticed on Léonor de Cambremer, then others again, none of which were ones usually presented to me by my synthesis of the young man, so that I soon had a caricature of him which was truer and more profound than any literal likeness; his uncle now seemed merely the young Cambremer after entertaining himself by putting on the appearance of the old man which he would in reality one day become, so that now it was not only what had become of the young people of the past, but what would become of the young people of today, that was giving me such a strong sensation of time.

The features in which are graven if not their youth at least their beauty having vanished, the women had tried to discover whether, out of the face that was left, they could possibly make another. Displacing the centre, if not of gravity then at least, perspectively speaking, of their face and grouping the features around it on a different principle, at the age of fifty they began a new kind of beauty, as one might take up a new career late in life, or as ground that is no longer any good for vines can be used for growing beet. Around these new features a new youthfulness started to flourish. The only women who could not make use of these transformations were those who were too beautiful or too ugly. The former, sculpted like a piece of marble with permanent lines, nothing of which could be changed, would crumble away like a statue. The second group, those who had some deformity of the face, actually had some advantages over the beautiful ones. To begin with, they were the only ones who were instantly recognizable. One knows that there are no two mouths alike in Paris, and each one of this group demanded my recognition, even at this party where I did not recognize anybody else. And on top of that, they did not really look as if they had aged. Old age is something human; they were monsters, and they no more seemed to have 'changed' than whales do.

Some men, and some women, did seem not to have aged, their figures were still as slender, their faces as young as ever. But if, in order to speak to them, one leaned closer to the smooth-skinned face, with its fine contours, it suddenly appeared quite different, like the surface of a plant, or a drop of water or blood, when they are placed under a microscope. I could then make out numerous greasy patches on the skin which I had thought was smooth, which filled me with disgust. The lines could not sustain this enlargement either. Close up, the line of the nose broke down, filled out, was prey to the same oily circles as the rest of the face; and seen at close quarters the eyes retreated into bags which destroyed the resemblance between this current face and the face of the past which I thought I had rediscovered. So that these particular guests were young when seen from a distance, but their age increased with the enlargement of the face and the possibility of observing it from different angles; but it remained dependent on the spectator, who had to position himself carefully if he wanted to see these faces, and apply to them only the sort of distant looks which diminish the object, like the lens the optician chooses for a presbyopic patient; for them old age, like the presence of infusoria in a drop of water, was brought about less by the progress of the years than by the place on the scale occupied by the vision of the observer.

I met one of my oldest friends there, someone whom I had seen almost every day for ten years. Somebody asked if they could reintroduce us. So I went over to him, and he said in a voice that was immediately familiar to me: 'This is a great pleasure for me after all these years!' But what a surprise this was for me! The voice seemed to be emitted by an advanced phonograph, for while it was that of my friend, it emanated from a stout, grey-haired old fellow whom I did not know, and after that it seemed to me that it could only be artificially, by a mechanical trick, that my friend's voice could have been placed inside this stout old man who might have been anybody. Yet I knew it was he, and the person who had introduced us after so long was not given to playing practical jokes. My friend himself declared that I had not changed, and I realized he did not think that he had changed either. Then I looked at him more closely. And, in fact, although he had become very stout, he had kept many things from the old days. Yet I still could not grasp the fact that it was he. So I tried to remember. When he was young he had had blue eyes, always laughing, perpetually in motion, clearly in quest of something I had never thought about and which was likely to be very unselfish, the truth probably, pursued in perpetual uncertainty, with a sort of childishness but with an errant respect for all the friends of his family. Now a capable, influential and despotic politician, those blue eyes of his, which had never actually found what they were looking for, had lost their mobility, which gave them a pointed look, as if from beneath a frowning eyebrow. And the expression of gaiety, freedom and innocence had turned to one of cunning and dissimulation. I was on the point of deciding that this must indeed be another man when I suddenly heard, at something I said, his laugh, his old uncontrolled laughter, the laughter that went with the gay, perpetual mobility of his eyes. Some music-lovers find that, orchestrated by X——, the music of Z—— becomes absolutely different. These are nuances that ordinary people do not grasp. But a stifled, wild, boyish laugh coming from beneath an eye as pointed as a well-sharpened blue pencil is more than a difference of orchestration. Then the laugh stopped; and although I would very much like to have recognized my friend, like Ulysses in the *Odyssey* attempting to embrace his dead mother, like a medium trying unsuccessfully to obtain from an apparition a response which would identify it, like a visitor to an exhibition of electricity who cannot help believing that the voice which the phonograph restores unaltered is, all the same, spontaneously emitted by a person, I stopped recognizing him.

There is, however, one important qualification to all this, namely that the tempo of time itself may for certain people be accelerated or slowed down. Four or five years ago I happened, for instance, to encounter the Vicomtesse de Saint-Fiacre in the street (the daughter-in-law of the friend of the Guermantes). Her sculptured features seemed to assure her of eternal youth. Besides which, she was still young. Now, in spite of her smiles and her greetings, I simply could not recognize her in a lady with features so ravaged that the lines of her face were beyond reconstruction. This was because for three years she had been taking cocaine and other drugs. Her eyes, deeply ringed with black, looked almost wild. Her mouth was fixed in a strange rictus. She had got up, I was told, especially for the party, having spent months without leaving her bed or her chaise-longue. Time, therefore, has its special express trains which take you rapidly to a premature old age. But on the parallel track, trains run almost as quickly in the opposite direction. I mistook M. de Courgivaux for his son, because he looked the younger (he must have been over fifty, and looked younger than he had when he was thirty). He had found an intelligent doctor, and cut out alcohol and salt; he had gone back to being about thirty and in fact on this particular day seemed not yet to have reached that age. This was because, only that morning, he had had his hair cut. There was still one man, though, whom I could not recognize, even when I was told his name; I thought it must be someone with the same name, because there could be absolutely no connection between this man and the one whom I not only knew in the past, but had met again only a few years ago. Yet it was he, only white-haired and fatter, but he had shaved off his moustache and that had been enough to strip him of his personality.

Strangely enough, the phenomenon of old age seemed in the way it operated to take account of some social customs. There were great noblemen, for instance, who had always been dressed in the plainest alpaca and worn old straw hats which an ordinary middle-class man would not have been seen dead in, who had aged in the same way as the gardeners and the countrymen among whom they had spent their lives. Patches of brown had appeared on their cheeks, and their faces had yellowed and darkened like the pages of a book.

I also thought about all the people who were not there, because they were unable to be, and whose secretaries, trying give the illusion that they were surviving, had excused by one of those telegrams which the Princesse was handed from time to time, those invalids who have been dying for years, who never get up, never go out and, even in the midst of the shallow attentiveness of visitors drawn there by tourist curiosity or pilgrim piety, lie with their eyes closed, clutching their rosary, feebly pushing away their sheet which is already more like a pall, looking like effigies, carved into skeletal thinness by illness out of flesh stiff and white as marble, recumbent on their tomb.

The women attempted to keep in contact with what had been most individual in their charm, but often the new material of their faces no longer lent itself to this. One was afraid, thinking of the periods of time which must have elapsed before being accompanied by a parallel revolution in the geology of a face, to see what erosion had occurred along the nose, what great alluvia at the edge of the cheeks now surrounded the whole face with their opaque and refractory masses.

Some women, of course, were still eminently recognizable, their faces remaining almost the same, and all they had done, as if in harmony with the season, was to put on their autumn accessory of grey hair. But for others, and for some men, too, the transformation was so complete, the continued identity so impossible to establish – for example between the evil womanizer one remembered and the old monk before one's eyes – that even more than the actor's art, it was the skill of some of the best mime-artists, Fregoli[97] being the greatest, that these fabulous transformations reminded one of. The old woman had wanted to cry when she realized that the indefinable, melancholy smile which had been her main charm was no longer capable of radiating as far as the surface of the plaster mask that old age had applied to her face. Then suddenly deterred from crying, deciding that it showed more mental character to put up with things, she used it like a theatrical mask to provoke laughter! But for nearly all the women there was no respite in their attempt to fight against old age, and they were always holding out towards the beauty which was retreating, like a setting sun whose last rays they passionately wanted to conserve, the mirror of their face. To succeed in this, some of them tried to smooth it down, to enlarge the white surface, renouncing the lure of already threatened dimples and the roguishness of a smile condemned and already half disarmed; while others, seeing beauty finally vanished and obliged to take refuge in facial expression, like someone compensating for the loss of their voice with skilful diction, they clung on to a pout, or to a way of wrinkling their eyes, to a dreamy look, or sometimes to a smile which, because of the lack of coordination between no longer obedient muscles, made them look as if they were crying.

Furthermore, even among the men who had undergone only slight alteration, whose moustaches had turned white, etc., one felt that the change was not strictly speaking material. It was as if one had seen them through a mist of dye or a painted lens which changed the appearance of their faces, but also, more than that, by adding this blurring factor to our vision, showed that what we were being enabled to see 'life-size' was in reality very far away from us, within a different sort of distance, admittedly, from that of space, but at the far end of which, as from another shore, we felt that they were having as much difficulty in recognizing us as we were in recognizing them. Only perhaps Mme de Forcheville, as if she had been injected with a liquid, something like paraffin, which soaks into the skin and prevents it changing, still looked like a cocotte from the old days, now permanently 'stuffed'.

'You think I'm my mother,' Gilberte had said to me. It was true. Yet it was also almost kind: one starts off with the idea that people are the same and one finds them old. But if one starts with the idea that they are old, one rediscovers them, one finds that they don't seem so bad after all. In the case of Odette it was not only that; her appearance, once one knew her age and anticipated seeing an old woman, seemed a more miraculous defiance of the laws of chronology than the conservation of radium was of the laws of nature. If at first I had not recognized her, this was not because she had, but because she had not changed. Having become aware during the last hour of time's new additions to people and my need to subtract again in order to rediscover people as I had known them, I now rapidly made that calculation, adding to the former Odette the number of years which had passed over her, the result of which turned out to be a person who it seemed to me could not possibly be the one I was looking at, precisely because she was so like her old self. What part did make-up and dye play in this? Under her flat golden hair – a bit like the tousled chignon of a large mechanical doll, over a face set in an expression of surprise as immutable as a doll's – on which was superimposed an equally flat straw hat, she looked like the spirit of the 1878 Exhibition[98] (at which she might indeed easily have been, even more so if she were as old then as she was today, the most extraordinary attraction) coming to deliver her party-piece in an end-of-year revue, but the 1878 Exhibition played by a woman who was still young.

Close beside us passed a minister from before the Boulangist[99] period, now a minister once again, throwing a distant and tremulous smile to the ladies, looking as if he were imprisoned in the myriad ties of the past, like a little ghost led about by an invisible hand, reduced in stature, altered in substance and looking like a little version of himself made out of pumice-stone. This former Prime Minister, so welcome in the Faubourg Saint-Germain, had once been the subject of criminal proceedings, vilified by society and by the people. But thanks to the replacement of the individuals constituting each of these entities and, among those individuals who still survived, the replacement of their strong feelings and even their memories, nobody any longer knew about it, and he was honoured and respected. It seems therefore that there is no humiliation so great that one should not put up with it easily, in the knowledge that after a few years our buried faults will be no more than an invisible dust over which will smile the smiling and blossoming peace of nature. An individual who has momentarily strayed will find himself, thanks to the equilibrium effect of time, caught between two new social strata, both of which feel nothing but deference and admiration for him, in which he will strut and bask very comfortably. Nothing but time can achieve this; and while his troubles are still continuing nothing can console him for the fact that the young dairy-maid over the road has heard the shouts of 'sleaze' from the crowd, shaking their fists as he climbed into the 'Black Maria', the young dairy-maid who does not see things in the perspective of time, and who does not know that the men lauded in the morning newspaper were previously discredited, and that the man on the brink of a prison sentence at this moment yet, perhaps thinking of the dairy-maid, unable to utter the words of humility which might win her sympathy for him, will one day be celebrated by the press and sought after by duchesses. In a similar way time distances family quarrels. At the Princesse de Guermantes's party there was a couple, husband and wife, who had as uncles two men, dead now, one of whom, not content with their having come to blows with each other, and wanting further to humiliate the other, had sent his porter and butler as his seconds, as if he deemed gentlemen too good for him. These stories, though, were buried in the newspapers of thirty years ago, and nobody any longer remembered them. And thus the Princesse de Guermantes's drawing-room was illuminated, forgetful, and flowery, like a peaceful cemetery. There, time had not only brought about the ruin of the creatures of a former epoch, it had made possible, had indeed created, new associations.

To return to that politician, despite the changes in his physical substance, every bit as far-reaching as the transformation of the moral ideas which he now evoked in the public mind, in a word despite all the years that had passed since he had been Prime Minister, he became a member of the new cabinet, the leader of which had given him a portfolio, rather as a theatre director gives a part to one of his old friends, long retired, whom he deems still to be more capable than younger actresses of playing the part with subtlety, and whose difficult financial situation he is also aware of, and who, at almost eighty, still shows the public the whole of her talent almost at the height of its powers, along with that continuing vitality which people were subsequently amazed to have seen so vividly just a few days before her death.

The case of Mme de Forcheville, on the other hand, was so miraculous that one could not even say that she was rejuvenated, more that, with all her carmines and her russets, she had come back into flower again. More even than the incarnation of the 1878 Universal Exhibition, she might have been the chief curiosity and star attraction in a modern horticultural exhibition. To me, she did not seem to say: 'I am the 1878 Exhibition' so much as: 'I am the Allée des Acacias, 1892.' She looked as if she might still have been there. And precisely because she had not changed, she hardly seemed to be alive. She was like a sterilized rose. I said good-afternoon to her, she tried for a long time to discover my name from my face, like a pupil looking at the examiner's face for an answer he could more easily have found in his own head. I mentioned my name and immediately, as if the name had powers of enchantment thanks to which I stopped looking like an arbutus tree or a kangaroo or whatever appearance old age must have given me, she recognized me and started to talk in that intensely individual voice which those people who had applauded her in little theatres were so impressed, when they were invited to lunch with her 'in town', to hear again in everything she said, throughout the conversation, for as long as they liked to listen. The voice had stayed the same, needlessly warm, captivating, with a very slight English accent. And yet, just as her eyes seemed to be looking at me from a distant shore, her voice was sad, almost pleading, like that of the dead in the *Odyssey*. Odette was still capable of acting. I complimented her on her youthfulness. She said: 'You're very kind, *my dear*, thank you,' and, as she found it hard to express even the truest feelings in a manner unaffected by her need to seem what she took to be smart, she repeated several times: 'Thank you so much, thank you so much.' But I, who had long ago walked so far to catch sight of her in the Bois, who, the first time I went to see her, had listened for the sound of her voice falling from her lips as if it were treasure, now found the minutes spent in her company interminable because it was impossible to know what to say to her, and I moved on, telling myself that Gilberte's words 'You think I'm my mother' were not only true, but also that they could only be flattering for the daughter.

Besides, Gilberte was not the only one on whom family traits had appeared which had previously remained as invisible on their face as those parts of a seed, coiled up inside it, whose sudden eruption up out of it is completely unpredictable. Thus a great maternal beak appeared on this or that person at about the age of fifty, transforming a nose that until then had been straight and pure. Another woman, the daughter of a banker, found that her complexion, once fresh as a daisy, turned red and leathery and started to look as if it were a reflection of the gold her father had spent so much time handling. Some even ended up looking like the part of town they lived in, somehow bearing in their faces a reflection of the rue de l'Arcade, the avenue de Bois or the rue de l'Élysée. For the most part, though, they reproduced the characteristics of their parents.

She was not, alas, always to remain as unchanged as this. Less than three years later I was to see her, not in her second childhood, but not quite all there, at an evening party given by Gilberte; she had become incapable of concealing beneath a mask of impassivity what she was thinking, or rather – thinking puts it too high – what was going through her mind, nodding her head, pursing her lips, shrugging her shoulders at every impression she was feeling like a drunk does, or a small child, or poets who, sensing inspiration and oblivious to their surroundings, start composing a poem at a social gathering, furrowing their eyebrows and distorting their features, to the astonishment of the woman on their arm whom they are taking in to dinner. These impressions of Mme de Forcheville – all except one, which was actually the cause of her presence at the party, her affection for her beloved daughter and her pride that she should be giving such a glittering party, a pride which could not mask the mother's sadness at not being anything herself any more – these impressions were not joyful, they simply required a permanent defence in the face of the snubs she received, a defence as timorous as a child's. All one heard was people saying: 'I don't know if Mme de Forcheville knew who I was, perhaps I ought to get someone to introduce me again. – Oh, there's no point in doing that,' somebody else would say, at the top of their voice, not thinking that Gilberte's mother could hear every word (either not thinking or not caring). 'It's quite useless. You won't get anything out of it. Best leave her alone. She's a bit gaga, you know.' Furtively, Mme de Forcheville would dart a glance out of her still beautiful eyes towards those talking so offensively about her, then quickly withdraw the look, afraid of having been rude; although keeping her feeble indignation to herself, she was still upset by the insult, and one saw her head nodding and her breast heaving as she cast a fresh glance at another equally discourteous guest, and yet she was not particularly surprised because, having felt very ill for some days, she had guardedly suggested that her daughter should rearrange the party, but her daughter had refused. Mme de Forcheville did not love her any the less for it; all the duchesses arriving, and everybody's admiration of the new mansion, flooded her heart with joy; and when the Marquise de Sabran came in, who at the time was the lady whose salon was the very pinnacle of the social ladder, Mme de Forcheville felt that she had been a good and foresightful mother and that her maternal task had been accomplished. More sniggering guests made her look up again and talk to herself, if you can call it talking when the language is dumb and expressed solely through movement and gesture. Although still beautiful, she had become – something she had never been before – an object of infinite sympathy; because she who had betrayed Swann and everybody else was now being betrayed by the entire universe; and she had become so weak that she no longer even dared, now the roles were reversed, to defend herself against men. And soon she would not defend herself against death. But all this is to anticipate: we must go back three years, to the afternoon party we are attending at the house of the Princesse de Guermantes.

I had some difficulty recognizing my friend Bloch, who in fact had now permanently adopted his pseudonym of Jacques du Rozier as his own name, behind which it would have needed my grandfather's flair to detect the 'sweet valley' of Hebron and the 'bonds of Israel' which my friend seemed definitively to have broken. His face had been completely transformed in accordance with the latest English fashion, and every unevenness seemed to have been smoothed away, as with a plane. His once curly hair was brushed flat, with a centre parting, and gleamed with brilliantine. His nose was still large and red, but now seemed swollen by a sort of permanent cold, which also explained the nasal drawl in which he produced his languid sentences, for he had found, not only a hair-style appropriate to his complexion, but an intonation that suited his pronunciation, in which the old twang took on an air of disdain for full articulation which went well with his inflamed nostrils. And thanks to the haircut, to the removal of his moustache, to the general air of elegance, to the whole impression, and to sheer will-power, his Jewish nose had disappeared, in the way that a hunchback, if she presents herself well, can seem to stand almost straight. But as soon as Bloch appeared, the one thing that altered the significance of his physiognomy more than any other was a formidable monocle. By introducing a mechanistic element into Bloch's face this monocle exempted him from all the difficult duties the human face is subject to, the duty to be beautiful, to express intellect, kindness or effort. The mere presence of this monocle on Bloch's face exempted people, first of all, from wondering whether or not he was good-looking, just like looking over some English things in a shop which the assistant has said 'are the latest thing', after which one does not dare wonder whether one actually likes it. Also he was able to take up a position behind the glass of the monocle where he was as aloof, distant and comfortable as if it had been the glass window of an elegant, well-sprung carriage, and his other features, in keeping with the flattened hair and the monocle, never expressed anything now at all.

Bloch asked me to introduce him to the Prince de Guermantes; I did not even feel a hint of the difficulties I had found in my way on the day when I went first went to an evening party at his house and which had seemed quite natural to me then, whereas now it seemed perfectly simple to introduce to him one of his guests, and it would even have seemed simple for me to have led over to him, and unexpectedly introduced to him, somebody whom he had not invited. Was this because, since that distant epoch, I had become an 'intimate', although for some time now one of the 'forgotten', of that world in which I was then so new; or was it, on the contrary, because, not really being a member of fashionable society, all the things which they find so difficult no longer had any reality for me, once I had overcome my shyness; or was it because, people having gradually dropped for me their outward (and often their second and third) masks, I sensed behind the disdainful haughtiness of the Prince a great human avidity to know people, even to get to know those he affected to despise? Was it also because the Prince had changed, like all those who are overbearing in their youth and their maturity, but to whom old age brings a more measured nature (particularly as the coming men and the unknown ideas at which they used to balk have now long been recognized and accepted by those around them), and especially if old age brings with it some virtue or vice which extends his acquaintance, or the revolution caused by a political conversion, like the Prince's conversion to Dreyfusism?

Bloch questioned me, as I used to question people when I first entered society, and as I still occasionally did, about people I had once known socially, and who were now as distant, as far removed from everything, as those people in Combray I had so often found myself wanting to 'place' exactly. But I had thought of Combray as having such a different shape from anywhere else, one so impossible to confuse with all the others, that I could never manage to fit it into the jigsaw-map of France. 'So the Prince de Guermantes won't be able to tell me anything about Swann, nor about M. de Charlus?' asked Bloch, whose manner of speaking I had borrowed for so long and who now often imitated mine. 'Nothing at all. – But what made them so different? – You would have had to talk to them, but that's impossible now, Swann's dead and M. de Charlus is not far off it. But the differences were enormous.' And while Bloch's eyes shone with the thought of what these two wonderful individuals must have been like, I thought that I was probably exaggerating the pleasure I had taken in their company, it being something I had only ever felt when I was alone, and the impression of real differentiation taking place only in our imaginations. Did Bloch realize this? 'Perhaps you're giving me an idealized picture, he said to me; the lady of the house here, for instance, the Princesse de Guermantes, I know she's no longer young, but it's not so very long since you were going on to me about her incomparable charm, her marvellous beauty. Of course, I can see she's terrifically grand, and she's certainly got those extraordinary eyes you told me about, but in the end I don't find her quite as incredible as you said. And obviously she's aristocratic, but still . . .' I had to tell Bloch that he was not talking about the same person. The Princesse de Guermantes had died and it was the former Mme Verdurin whom the Prince, ruined by the defeat of Germany, had married. 'No, you're wrong, I looked in this year's *Gotha*,[100] confessed Bloch to me naïvely, and I found the Prince de Guermantes, living in this mansion where we are now, and married to somebody terribly grand, hang on a minute while I remember, married to Sidonie, Duchesse de Duras, née des Baux.' And this was right, Mme Verdurin, shortly after the death of her husband, had married the penniless old Duc de Duras, who had made her a cousin of the Prince de Guermantes and had died after two years of marriage. It had been a very useful transition for Mme Verdurin, and now by a third marriage she was Princesse de Guermantes and occupied an elevated position in the Faubourg Saint-Germain, which would have caused great astonishment at Combray, where the ladies of the rue de l'Oiseau, Mme Goupil's daughter and Mme Sazerat's step-daughter, before Mme Verdurin became Princesse de Guermantes, had pronounced the title 'the Duchesse de Duras' with snide giggles, as if Mme Verdurin were playing a role on the stage. In fact, their system of caste requiring that she should die Mme Verdurin, this title, which nobody imagined conferred any new social powers upon her, had rather a deleterious impact. 'Getting herself talked about,' the expression which, in all walks of life, is applied to a woman who has a lover, could also be applied in the Faubourg Saint-Germain to those who publish books, and among the respectable middle class of Combray to those who make marriages which, in one way or another, are 'unequal'. After she had married the Prince de Guermantes, they had to say that he could not be a real Guermantes, and must be an impostor. Myself, I thought that there was something as distressing in this continuity of name and title, which meant that there was a Princesse de Guermantes once again, and that she had nothing to do with the one who had so cast her spell on me and who was no longer here and who, a defenceless corpse, had been robbed of her name, as seeing Princesse Hedwige's[101] possessions, like her country house, and everything she had owned, being enjoyed by another woman. Succession to a name is sad, like all succession, like all usurpation of property; yet wave after wave of new Princesses de Guermantes would continue to come for ever, uninterruptedly, or perhaps better, replaced in the job from one age to the next by a different woman, a single Princesse de Guermantes, timeless, unaware of death, indifferent to everything that changes and wounds our hearts, the name closing over those who from time to time sink beneath its always unchanging, immemorial placidity.

Of course, even the outward changes to the faces that I had known were no more than the symbols of an interior change which had been going on from day to day; these people may have continued doing the same things, but as the idea they had of themselves and the people they saw shifted slightly from day to day, after a few years, while the names were still the same, the objects and people they loved were different, and they having become different people themselves it would have been very surprising if they had not had new faces.

Among the people present there was a man of some distinction who had just given evidence in a famous trial, the only value of which lay in his high moral standards, which the judges and lawyers had unanimously accepted and which had resulted in the conviction of two people. So there was a stir of deferential curiosity when he entered. It was Morel. I was perhaps the only person there who knew that he had been kept simultaneously both by Saint-Loup and by a friend of Saint-Loup's. Despite these memories, he greeted me with pleasure, if somewhat reservedly. He recalled the time when we had met at Balbec, memories which for him were full of the poetry and melancholy of youth.

But there were also people there whom I could not recognize, for the reason that I had never met them before, for time had been working its chemistry in this drawing-room upon society as well as upon individuals themselves. This little world, in whose specific nature, defined by certain affinities which attracted to it all the great princely names of Europe and its power to keep all non-aristocratic elements at a distance, in which I thought I had found a tangible refuge for the Guermantes name, one which in the end gave it its reality, this little world, in its inner composition which I had believed was stable, had itself undergone profound alteration. The presence of people whom I had seen in quite different social settings, and who seemed destined never to penetrate into this one, was still not quite so surprising as the intimate familiarity with which they were received and addressed by their first names. A certain concatenation of aristocratic prejudices and snobberies, which had once kept at a distance anything that was not in harmony with the Guermantes name, had ceased to function.

Some people (Tossizza, Kleinmichel) who, when I first started going into society, used to give grand dinners to which they invited only the Princesse de Guermantes, the Duchesse de Guermantes, the Princess of Parma, and who had an honoured place in those ladies' houses, and were generally regarded as, and indeed quite possibly were, among the most firmly established members of society at that time, had disappeared without trace. Had they all been foreign members of diplomatic missions who had gone back to their countries? Perhaps a scandal, a suicide, an abduction had prevented them from reappearing in society, or they may even have been Germans. But their names owed their lustre only to their situation then and were no longer borne by anybody, nobody would even know whom I was talking about if I mentioned them, and if I did ever start to spell out a name, it merely made people think of flashy foreigners on the make. The people who, according to the old code, ought not to have been there turned out, to my great astonishment, to be close friends of others from extremely good families who had only come to be bored at the Princesse de Guermantes's party because of their new friends. For if there was one thing which really characterized this social milieu, it was its prodigious capacity for coming down in the world.

Whether relaxed or broken, the springs of the machine that kept people out no longer worked, and a thousand foreign bodies found their way in, removing all homogeneity, all standards and decorum, and all colour from society. The Faubourg Saint-Germain, like a senile dowager, made no response beyond a timid smile to the insolent servants who invaded her drawing-rooms, drank her orangeade and introduced her to their mistresses. Once again, the sensation of time's slipping away, and a little part of my past disappearing with it, was aroused less vividly by the destruction of this coherent whole (which the Guermantes salon had been) than by the very annihilation of the awareness of the thousand reasons, the thousand social gradations, why one man present today was naturally in his approved place, while another, rubbing shoulders with him, presented a suspicious appearance of novelty. This ignorance was not restricted to society, but encompassed politics and everything else. For memory is less long-lasting in individuals than life, in addition to which the very young, never having had the memories which their elders have lost, and now constituting a part of society, entirely legitimately, even in the genealogical sense, and people's origins being forgotten or ignored, they accept them at the point in their elevation or descent where they happen to be, believing this to be how it has always been, that Mme Swann and the Princesse de Guermantes and Bloch had always been in the most elevated social position, that Clemenceau and Viviani had always been conservatives.[102] And as some facts survive longer than others, and as the detested memory of the Dreyfus Affair enjoyed a vague persistence in their minds by virtue of what their fathers had told them about it, if one said that Clemenceau had been a Dreyfusard, they would say: 'That's not possible, you're getting confused, he's on completely the opposite side.' Ministers with tarnished reputations and former prostitutes were now regarded as paragons of virtue. Someone having asked a young man from one of the best families if there was not some story about Gilberte's mother, the young nobleman replied that it was true that in the first part of her life she had been married to an adventurer named Swann, but that she had subsequently married one of the most prominent men in society, the Comte de Forcheville. No doubt there were still several people in that drawing-room, the

Duchesse de Guermantes, for instance, who would have smiled at that assertion (which in its denial of Swann's social position seemed outrageous to me, even though I myself had in the past, at Combray, shared my great-aunt's belief that Swann could not know 'princesses'), and also some others who might have been there except that they hardly went out any more, the Duchesses de Montmorency, de Mouchy and de Sagan, who had been intimate friends of Swann's and had never set eyes on this Forcheville, who was not received in society at the time when they still went out to parties. But the fact is that the society of those days, like the faces which are now altered, and the blonde hair replaced with white, no longer had any existence outside the memory of a few individuals, whose number was diminishing every day.

During the war Bloch had stopped 'going out', stopped frequenting his old pre-war haunts, where he had cut such a sorry figure. On the other hand, he had not left off publishing those books of his, the absurd sophistry of which I was today doing my best to demolish so as not to be bogged down by it, works without originality but which provided young people, and a large number of fashionable women, with the impression of an unusually rarefied intellect, a sort of genius. It was thus after a complete break between his old and new social self, and in keeping with this new phase of his life, honoured and glorious, in a reconstituted society, that he had created the appearance of a great man. Young people naturally did not know that he was making his first entry into society at this advanced age, especially since the few names he had retained from his acquaintance with Saint-Loup enabled him to give his current prestige the illusion of infinite regress. At all events, he seemed to be one of those men of talent who have flourished in fashionable society in all epochs, and nobody dreamed that he had ever lived in any other way.

The old assured me that everything about society had changed, that people were being received who would never have been received in their day, and, as people say, this was true and it was not. It was not true because they did not take account of the curve of time, which meant that those today saw new people at their point of arrival while the older generation remembered them at their point of departure. And when they, the old, had entered society, there were people who had just arrived there whose first steps on the ladder others again could remember. One generation is long enough to encompass the change, which in former times took centuries, by which a middle-class name like Colbert became an aristocratic one. And on the other hand it could be true, because when people's social position changes, the most deeply rooted ideas and customs (as well as the fortunes and alliances of countries, and the hatreds between them) also change, and this includes even the principle of receiving only people who are chic. Snobbery not only changes its form, it could even disappear like the war, and radicals and Jews become members of the Jockey Club.

If the new generations regarded the Duchesse de Guermantes as unimportant because of her friendship with actresses, etc., the now old ladies of her family still considered her an extraordinary individual, on the one hand because they knew everything about her birth, her heraldic primacy, her being on intimate terms with what Mme de Forcheville would have called *royalties*, but also because she did not bother to come to family gatherings, was bored by them, and they knew that they could never expect her at any of them. Her theatrical and political connections, which nobody knew very much about anyway, only increased her rarity, and therefore her prestige. So that while in artistic and political circles she was regarded as hard to define, a sort of defrocked member of the Faubourg Saint-Germain who associated with under-secretaries of state and stars of the stage, in the Faubourg Saint-Germain itself, if one were giving an evening party, one would say: 'Is it even worth asking Oriane? She won't come. We'd better, for form's sake, I suppose, but we mustn't expect anything.' And if, at around half past ten, in a dazzling dress, a hard gleam in her eyes seeming to express her scorn for all her cousins, Oriane entered, pausing on the threshold with a sort of majestic disdain, and if she stayed for an hour, it was a greater occasion for the grand old lady who was giving the party than it would once have been for a theatre manager had Sarah Bernhardt, having made a vague promise of support which nobody thought would materialize, turned up and recited, with infinitely obliging kindness and a complete lack of affectation, not the one piece promised, but twenty others instead. Even though it was attended only by the most fashionable women, it was the presence of this Oriane, to whom private secretaries spoke condescendingly but who continued none the less (intellect rules the world) to try to make the acquaintance of more and more of them, which meant that this dowager's party would be ranked over and above all the other dowagers' parties of that *season* (as, again, Mme de Forcheville would have said), the ones which Oriane had not taken the trouble to attend.

As soon as I had finished talking to the Prince de Guermantes, Bloch seized hold of me and introduced me to a young woman who had heard a great deal about me from the Duchesse de Guermantes, and who was one of the smartest women of the day. Her name was completely unknown to me, and those of the various Guermantes must not have been familiar to her, as she asked an American woman why it was that Mme de Saint-Loup seemed on such intimate terms with all the most glittering members of society in the room. Now this American was married to the Comte de Farcy, an obscure relation of the Forchevilles, for whom they represented all that was grandest in the world. She therefore replied, unaffectedly: 'Wouldn't it be because she is a Forcheville by birth? There's nothing grander than that.' But Mme de Farcy, although she naïvely thought the name of Forcheville was superior to that of Saint-Loup, at least knew what the latter meant. But the charming friend of Bloch and of the Duchesse de Guermantes was completely unaware of it and, being rather hare-brained, replied quite sincerely to a young girl who asked her how Mme de Saint-Loup was related to the master of the house, the Prince de Guermantes: 'Through the Forchevilles', information which the young girl passed on, as if she had always known it, to one of her friends, who, being nervy and cantankerous, turned as red as a turkey-cock the first time a gentleman told her that Gilberte was not related to the Guermantes through the Forchevilles, with the result that the gentleman thought he must be wrong, adopted the erroneous idea and lost no time in propagating it. Dinner-parties and fashionable gatherings were a sort of Berlitz school for the American woman. She heard the names and repeated them without having first understood their value, and their precise significance. Somebody explained to another person, who asked whether Tansonville came to Gilberte from her father M. de Forcheville, that it did not come from him at all, that it was an estate belonging to her husband's family, that Tansonville was close to Guermantes, and had belonged to Mme de Marsantes but, being heavily mortgaged, had been redeemed out of Gilberte's dowry. Finally an elderly man, one of the old guard, having recalled the time when Swann was a friend of the Sagans and the Mouchys, and Bloch's American friend having asked how I had known him, declared that I had met him in the house of Mme de Guermantes, not for a moment imagining that it was the country neighbour, the young friend of my grandfather, that he represented for me. Misapprehensions of this nature have been committed by the most famous men, and are regarded as particularly serious in all conservative circles. Saint-Simon, wishing to show that Louis XIV's ignorance was such as to 'make him fall sometimes, in public, into the most glaring absurdities', gives us just two examples of this ignorance, to wit, first, that the King, not knowing that Renel was from the family of Clermont-Gallerande, nor that Saint-Herem was a Montmorin, treated the men as if they were of humble birth. As far as Saint-Herem is concerned we at least have the consolation of knowing that the sovereign did not die in that error, for he was disabused 'very late in the day' by M. de La Rochefoucauld. 'Even then, adds Saint-Simon slightly pityingly, it had to be explained to him what these houses were, as their names meant nothing to him.'

One repercussion of this perennial forgetting, which so rapidly covers over the most recent past, of this invasive ignorance, is the creation of a minor branch of knowledge, all the more valuable for being seldom encountered, concerning itself with people's genealogies, their true situation, the reasons of love, money or whatever for which they became allied, or misallied, with this or that family, knowledge prized in all societies where a conservative spirit rules, knowledge which my grandfather possessed in the highest degree, as it concerned the middle class of Combray and Paris, knowledge which Saint-Simon prized so much that at the point where he celebrates the wonderful intelligence of the Prince de Conti, before he even mentions learning, or rather as if this were its finest form, he praises him for having been 'a very fine mind, luminous, just, precise, extensive, of infinite reading, who forgot nothing, and knew the genealogies, their chimeras and their realities, of a discriminating politeness that recognized rank and merit, doing everything that the princes of the blood should do, and no longer do; he even explained himself, and what he thought about their assumption of extra powers. The history he learned from books and from conversation provided him with the material to contribute the most helpful comments he could on matters of birth, offices, etc.' As applied to a less glittering world, to everything pertaining to the middle class of Combray and Paris, my grandfather was no less precisely knowledgeable about the subject, and relished it no less eagerly. Connoisseurs and enthusiasts of this sort, who knew that Gilberte was not a Forcheville, nor Mme de Cambremer a Méséglise, nor the younger Mme de Cambremer a Valentinois, had become very few in number. Very few, perhaps not even recruited from the upper ranks of the aristocracy (it is not necessarily the devout, nor even Catholics, who are best-informed about the *Golden Legend*[103] or thirteenth-century stained-glass windows), but often from a minor aristocracy, more keenly interested in something with which they have scarcely any contact, and which they have all the more leisure to study as they spend less time in it, but fond of getting together, meeting one another, giving delicious group dinners, like those of the Society of Bibliophiles or the Friends of Rheims Cathedral, dinners at which genealogies are savoured and appreciated. Wives are not admitted, but the husbands, when they get home, all say to their wives: 'That was a most interesting dinner. There was a M. de La Raspelière there who kept us all spellbound as he explained how Mme de Saint-Loup, the one with the pretty daughter, is not a Forcheville at all. It's just like a novel.'

The friend of Bloch and of the Duchesse de Guermantes was not only smart and charming, she was also intelligent, and conversation with her was enjoyable, but it was made difficult for me because it was not only my interlocutress herself whose name was new to me, but those of a great number of the people she was talking about and who currently made up the core of society. It is true, on the other hand, as she wanted to listen to what I had to say, that many of the names I mentioned will have meant absolutely nothing to her, they were all sunk in oblivion, or at least those who had shone only with the light of their own individual celebrity and were not the permanent, generic name of some famous aristocratic family (whose exact title the young woman seldom knew, making mistaken assumptions about birth or descent on the basis of names misheard at dinner the previous evening), and she had never, in most instances, heard them pronounced, having started moving in society (not only because she was still young, but because she had not long lived in France, and had not been received immediately) only some years after I myself had withdrawn from it. The name of Mme Leroi happened to fall from my lips, I do not know how, and by chance my interlocutress, thanks to some elderly friend of Mme de Guermantes who was an admirer of hers, had heard of her. But inaccurately, as I saw from the disdainful tone with which this snobbish young woman replied: 'Yes, I know who Mme Leroi is, she's an old friend of Bergotte,' a tone which meant 'a person whom I should never have wished to have under my roof'. I understood at once that the old friend of Mme de Guermantes, as a perfect gentleman, imbued with the Guermantes ethos, one of the characteristics of which was not to seem to attach any importance to aristocratic connections, had thought it too silly and too anti-Guermantes to say: 'Mme Leroi, who was a friend of all royalty and of every duchess', and had preferred to say: 'She was very entertaining. Do you know what she said to Bergotte one day?' Only, for people who do not have the requisite knowledge, information drawn from conversation like this is the equivalent of the stuff fed by the press to the people, so that they believe in turn, according to their newspaper, either that M. Loubet and M. Reinach are thieves or that they are great citizens. For my interlocutress, Mme Leroi had been a kind of Mme Verdurin, in her first manifestation, with less brilliance and with her little set limited to Bergotte alone. That young woman is, though, one of the last to have heard, by pure chance, the name of Mme Leroi. Nobody today any longer knows who she is, which is really as it should be. Her name does not even figure in the index to the posthumous memoirs of Mme de Villeparisis, whose thoughts were so often occupied with Mme Leroi. The Marquise did not talk about Mme Leroi, less because the latter had not been very well disposed towards her while she was alive than because nobody could be interested in her after her death, and her silence was dictated less by feminine social resentment than by the literary tact of the writer. My conversation with Bloch's smart friend was charming, because the young woman was intelligent, but this difference between our two vocabularies made it both uneasy and instructive. It is in vain that we know that the years pass, that youth gives way to age, that the most solid of thrones and fortunes crumble, that fame is ephemeral, the manner by which we become aware, and so to speak take a snapshot of this moving universe, swept along by Time, contradictorily, immobilizes it. With the result that we see as still young the people whom we knew when they were young, while those who were old when we met them we retrospectively adorn in the past with the virtues of old age, that we trust unreservedly in the credit of a millionaire and in the support of a sovereign, understanding rationally, but not actually believing, that they may tomorrow be fugitives, stripped of power. In a more restricted field, one purely social, as in the case of a simple problem which leads on to difficulties more complex but still of the same order, the lack of intelligibility which resulted, in my conversation with the young woman, from the fact that we had lived in a certain society at twenty-five years' distance from each other, gave me the impression, and might have strengthened within me the sense, of History.

Moreover, it must be said that this ignorance of the true situation which every ten years makes individuals suddenly emerge in their current guise, as if the past never existed, which prevents a newly disembarked American woman from seeing that M. de Charlus had held the highest social position in Paris at a time when Bloch had had none, and that Swann, who put himself to such trouble for M. Bontemps, had been treated with the greatest friendship by the Prince of Wales,[104] this ignorance does not exist only among the newcomers, but among those who have always frequented adjacent sections of society, and this ignorance, in the latter as in the others, is also an effect (but this time operating upon the individual rather than the social stratum) of Time. There would doubtless be no point in our changing our social circle or our way of life, as our memory, by retaining the thread of our personal identity, attaches to it at successive periods the memory of the societies in which we have lived, even if forty years earlier. Bloch in the house of the Prince de Guermantes was perfectly aware of the modest Jewish surroundings in which he had lived at the age of eighteen, and Swann, when he no longer loved Mme Swann but a woman who served tea at the same Colombin's where Mme Swann had for a while believed that it was chic to go, as she had of the tea-room in the rue Royale, Swann knew perfectly well his own social standing, remembered Twickenham;[105] he was in no doubt at all about his reasons for going to Colombin's rather than to the Duchesse de Broglie's, and was perfectly aware that, had he himself been a thousand times less 'chic', whether he went to Colombin's or to the Ritz would not have made him one iota more fashionable, as anyone who can pay may go to either. And Bloch's friends or Swann's probably also remembered the little Jewish circle or the invitations to Twickenham, and so friends, like the slightly distinct 'selves' of Swann and Bloch, did not separate in their memories the sordid Bloch of the past from the smart Bloch of today, or the Swann of Buckingham Palace from the Swann in his latter days at the Colombin. These friends though were, in a way, Swann's neighbours in life; their own had developed on a line sufficiently close to his for their memory to be fairly full of him; but in the case of others less close to Swann, at a greater distance from him not so much socially as in terms of intimacy, who knew him more vaguely and met him less often, the less numerous memories had rendered their conception of him more wavering. Now, when it comes to comparative strangers like this, after thirty years one hardly remembers anything specific enough to extend back into the past and alter the worth of the person standing in front of one's eyes. I had heard, during the last years of Swann's life, even society people, when his name was mentioned say, as if it were his claim to notoriety: 'You're speaking of the Swann of Colombin's?' And I now heard even people who ought to have known better saying, when they were speaking of Bloch: 'The Guermantes Bloch? The close friend of the Guermantes?' These errors, which divide up a life and, by isolating its present, turn the man spoken of into another man, a different man, a creation of the day before, a man who is no more than the condensation of his current habits (although he carries within himself the continuity of his life which links him to the past), these errors too are dependent on Time, but they are not a social phenomenon but a phenomenon of memory. An example occurred at that very moment, not quite of the same sort of thing admittedly but all the more striking for that, of the way this forgetting modifies the way individuals appear to us. A long time ago, a young nephew of Mme de Guermantes, the Marquis de Villemandois, had been persistently insolent towards me, which had obliged me by way of reprisal to adopt an attitude in respect of him so insulting that we had tacitly become as it were enemies. While I was reflecting on Time at this party at the Princesse de Guermantes's, he introduced himself to me, saying that he believed I had known his parents, that he had read articles by me and that he wished to make, or renew, my acquaintance. It is true that with age he had, like many others, lost his impertinence and become more serious, that he no longer had the same arrogance, and also that people were talking about me, though only on the strength of some rather slight articles, in the social circles in which he moved. But these reasons for his cordiality and his advances were only secondary. The principal reason, or at least the one which allowed the others to come into play, is that, either having a worse memory than me, or having paid less sustained attention to my retorts that I once did to his attacks, I then being a less important person in his eyes than he was in mine, he had entirely forgotten our hostilities. At the most, my name reminded him that he must have seen me, or some member of my family, at the house of one of his aunts. And being uncertain whether to introduce or to re-introduce himself, he hastened to mention his aunt, in whose house he was sure that he must have met me, recalling that people there often spoke of me, but not of our quarrels. A name, that is very often all that remains for us of an individual, not when he is dead even, but while he is still alive. And our conceptions of him are so vague and so bizarre, and correspond so little to those which we had of him in the past, that we have entirely forgotten that we came very close to fighting a duel with him, whereas we do remember that, as a child, he wore strange yellow leggings in the Champs-Élysées, where he, on the other hand, despite our assurances of it, has no memory of having played with us.

Bloch had come bounding into the room like a hyena. I thought: 'He is welcome in drawing-rooms he could never have got into twenty years ago.' But he was also twenty years older. He was nearer his death. So what benefit was it to him? Close up, in the translucency of a face in which, from further away and in poor light I had seen nothing but youthful gaiety (whether it actually still survived there or because I was evoking it), was visible the almost frightening, deeply anxious face of an old Shylock, waiting, with his make-up on, in the wings, just about to go on stage, already reciting his first line under his breath. In ten years, in drawing-rooms like this whose inertia will have made him a leading light, he will enter on crutches, people will address him as Maître, he will find it a chore to be obliged to go the La Trémoïlles. What benefit would this be to him?

From changes brought about in society I could all the more easily extract truths which were important and worthy to hold one part of my book together, as they were not in any way, as I would have been tempted to believe at the outset, peculiar to our time. At the time when, scarcely arrived in society myself, I first entered, even more of a newcomer than Bloch himself today, the Guermantes' social circle, I must have regarded as an integral part of that circle elements absolutely different, recently incorporated, and which would have seemed curiously new to older members from whom I did not differentiate them, who in turn, believed by the dukes of that period always to have been members of the Faubourg, had either themselves been, or their fathers or their grandfathers had once been, newly elevated to their position. So much so that it was not the quality of men in the best society which rendered this society so glittering, but the fact of having been assimilated more or less completely by this society which made people, who fifty years later would all appear similar in standing, into society people. Even in the past to which I had traced the Guermantes name in order to give it its full grandeur, quite rightly, incidentally, as under Louis XIV the Guermantes, being practically royal, were much grander figures than they are today, the same phenomenon which I was noticing now used also to arise. Did they not then ally themselves with the Colbert family, for example, a family which today, it is true, seems very noble to us since to marry a Colbert seems a good match even for a La Rochefoucauld? Yet it is not because the Colberts, then ordinary middle-class folk, were noble that the

Guermantes allied themselves with them, it is because the Guermantes allied themselves with them that they were ennobled. If the name of Haussonville dies with the present representative of that house, it will perhaps owe its lustre to its descent from Mme de Staël, although before the Revolution M. d'Haussonville, one of the first lords of the kingdom, regarded it as a source of pride that he could tell M. de Broglie that he was not acquainted with Mme de Staël's father and was therefore no more able than M. de Broglie himself to introduce him, never for a moment imagining that their sons would one day marry, one the daughter and the other the grand-daughter of the authoress of *Corinne*. I realized, after what the Duchesse de Guermantes had said to me, that in those circles I might have played the part of an untitled man about town, whom people readily assume always to have had links with the aristocracy, such as Swann had at one time been, and before him M. Lebrun, M. Ampère, and all those friends of the Duchesse de Broglie, who herself, at the outset, was very far from being a member of the best society. The first times I dined with Mme de Guermantes how I must have shocked men like M. de Beauserfeuil, not so much by my mere presence, as by the remarks I made, indicating that I was entirely ignorant of the memories which constituted his past and which shaped the image he had of society! One day, when Bloch, grown very old, has a fairly long-standing memory of the Guermantes drawing-room as it presented itself to his eyes at this moment, he will feel just the same astonishment, just the same ill-humour at the presence of certain intrusions and certain displays of ignorance. Yet on the other hand, he would doubtless have acquired, and would dispense to those around him, those qualities of tact and discretion which I had thought the prerogative of men such as M. de Norpois, but which take fresh shape and become incarnate in those who seem to us more than anybody else to preclude them.

Again, the opportunity which had arisen for me to be admitted into the Guermantes circle had seemed something exceptional to me. But if I looked outside myself and my immediate social surroundings, I saw that this social phenomenon was not so isolated as had at first appeared to me, and that from the fountain-basin of Combray where I was born quite a number of water-jets turned out to have been raised in symmetry with me above the liquid mass which had fed them all. No doubt, circumstances always having something particular about them, and characters something individual, it was in a quite different manner that Legrandin, in his turn (through the curious marriage of his nephew), had penetrated into these circles, or that Odette's daughter had married into them, or that Swann himself, and then finally I had come to them. For me, who had always been wrapped up in my own life, and seen it from within, Legrandin's seemed to have no connection with mine, seemed to have followed quite opposite paths, in the same way as a stream in a deep valley does not see a divergent stream, even though, despite the deviations of its course, it issues into the same river. But taking a bird's-eye view, as does the statistician, who disregards the reasons of sentiment or the unavoidable acts of imprudence which may lead to the death of any individual, and counts only the number of people who die per year, one would see that a number of individuals who shared the same social background, the depiction of which occupied the first part of this narrative, had ended up in a completely different one, and it is probable that, since an average number of marriages takes place each year in Paris, every other rich and cultivated middle-class circle would have contributed an approximately equal proportion of people like Swann, like Legrandin, like me and like Bloch, all of whom would be found flowing into the ocean of 'high society'. Moreover, they recognized one another there, for if the young Comte de Cambremer astonished the whole of society with his distinction, his refinement, his sober elegance, I recognized in these – at the same time as in his winning looks and his burning desire to succeed – the same characteristics as those of his uncle Legrandin, that is, of an old friend, supremely middle-class for all his aristocratic appearance, of my parents.

Kindness, a simple process of maturation which has succeeded eventually in sweetening natures more initially acidic than Bloch's, is as widespread as the feeling of justice which makes us believe that if our cause is good we can have no more to fear from a prejudiced judge than from a friendly one. And Bloch's grandchildren will be good and unassuming almost from birth. Bloch was perhaps not quite there yet. But I observed that he, who once pretended to believe himself obliged to undertake a two-hour railway journey to go to see someone who had only quite casually asked him, now that he received so many invitations not only to lunch and to dinner, but also to spend a fortnight here and a fortnight there, declined many of them, without mentioning them, without boasting of having received them, nor of having declined them. Discretion, discretion in actions and in words, had come to him with social position and with age, with a sort of social age, if one can say that. No doubt Bloch was once as indiscreet as he was incapable of benevolence or thoughtfulness. But certain defects, certain qualities, are not so much attached to this or that individual as to this or that moment of existence considered from the social point of view. They are almost external to individuals, who move in their light as if beneath a variety of solstices, pre-existent, general, unavoidable. Doctors who are trying to discover whether some medicament diminishes or increases the acidity of the stomach, stimulates or slows down its secretions, obtain differing results, not in relation to the stomach from whose secretions they have taken a small amount of gastric juice, but in relation to whether they take it earlier or later in the process of ingesting the remedy.

Thus at all moments in its history, the name of Guermantes, considered as an agglomeration of all the names which it admitted into itself, around itself, suffered decline, recruited new elements, like those gardens in which, at any moment, flowers scarcely in bud and the ones already beginning to wither which they are preparing to replace, all blend into a single mass which looks the same, save to those who have not yet seen the new arrivals and retain in their memory the precise image of the ones that no longer exist.

More than one of the individuals assembled at this afternoon party, or whose memory was evoked by it, by making me remember the aspects he or she had in turn presented to me through the different, or opposite, circumstances from which they had, one after the other, arisen before me, caused the varied aspects of my life to emerge in my mind's eye, the differences of perspective, just as a feature in the landscape, a chateau or a hill, appearing sometimes on the right, sometimes on the left, seems first to look down over a forest, then to emerge from a valley, and thereby reveals to the traveller the changes of direction and the differences in altitude along the road he is following. As I went further and further back, I eventually came across images of the same person separated by such a long interval of time, retained by such distinct selves, and themselves having such different meanings, that I habitually omitted them when I believed I was considering the whole past course of my relations with them, that I had even ceased to think of them as the same people I had once known, and that it needed a chance flash of attention to reconnect them, etymologically as it were, to the original meaning they had had for me. Mlle Swann threw me, from the other side of the pink hawthorn hedge, a look the significance of which I would later, in fact, have retrospectively to retouch, it being a look of desire. Mme Swann's lover, as all Combray regarded him, looked at me behind the same hedge with an unfriendly stare which equally did not have the meaning I then attributed to it, and subsequently changed so much that I had completely failed to recognize him at Balbec as the gentleman perusing a poster by the casino, a look which I would perhaps recall once every ten years and say to myself: 'And that was M. de Charlus, even then! It's very strange!' Mme de Guermantes at Dr Percepied's wedding; Mme Swann wearing pink at my great-uncle's; Mme de Cambremer, Legrandin's sister, so smart that he was terrified we were going to ask him to give us an introduction to her, these, as well as a number of others concerning Swann, Saint-Loup, etc., were just so many images which I sometimes amused myself with, when I came across them, in setting up as frontispieces at the threshold of my relations with different individuals, but which did in fact seem no more than images, not something lodged within me by the individuals themselves, to whom nothing any longer connected them. Not only do some people have good memories and others bad (without going as far as the constant forgetfulness in which the Turkish Ambassadress lives, and others like her, which enables them always to find – since recent news evaporates after a week, and fresh reports have the knack of exorcizing it – always to find room for the contradictory news people tell them), but two people with equally good memories do not even remember the same things. One will have paid little attention to an act for which the other will always retain a feeling of great remorse, and he, conversely, will have instantly seized upon some remark which the other just let fall almost without thinking, and elevated it as a characteristic sign of congeniality. One's investment in not having been wrong when one has issued a mistaken forecast shortens the lifetime of one's memory of it, and allows one very quickly to affirm that one did not issue it. Lastly, a deeper and more disinterested investment diversifies people's memories, so that the poet who has almost forgotten almost all the facts which one is recalling to him still retains a fleeting impression of them. All this shows why it is that, after an absence of twenty years, where one had expected bitterness one finds involuntary and unconscious forgiveness, while on the other hand one encounters numerous instances of hatred for which (because one has forgotten in one's turn the bad impression one once made) one can find no explanatory reason. When it comes to the sequence of events in the lives even of those one has known best, one has forgotten the dates. And because it was at least twenty years since she had met Bloch for the first time, Mme de Guermantes would have been prepared to swear that he had been born into her world and been dandled on the knee of the Duchesse de Chartres when he was two years old.

And how many times these people had reappeared before me in the course of their lives, the diverse circumstances of which seemed to present me with the same individuals, but in various forms and for various ends; and the diversity of the points of my life through which had passed the thread of the life of each of these characters had ended up mingling those which seemed furthest apart, as if life possessed only a limited number of threads with which to achieve the most widely differing patterns. What could be more separate, for example, in my various pasts, than my visits to my uncle Adolphe, the nephew of Mme de Villeparisis, the Maréchal's cousin, Legrandin and his sister, and Françoise's friend, the old waistcoat-maker in the courtyard? And today all those different threads had come together to create the web, here of the Saint-Loup household, there of the young Cambremer couple, not to mention Morel, and so many others whose conjunction had combined to create a set of circumstances that it seemed to me that the circumstances were the complete unity, and the characters merely component parts. And my life was already sufficiently long that, for more than one of the individuals that it presented me with, I could find in opposite regions of my memories, to complete him or her, another being. Even to the Elstirs which I saw here hung in positions which were an indication of his fame, I was able to add very old memories of the Verdurins, the Cottards, the conversation in the Rivebelle restaurant, the reception at which I had met Albertine, and numerous other things. In the same way a connoisseur of art, shown one wing of an altarpiece, remembers in which church, what museums, what private collection, the others are dispersed (just as by keeping abreast of the sale catalogues or by regularly visiting the antique shops he will eventually find the object that is twin to the one he possesses and which forms its pair); he is able to reconstitute the predella, and the entire altar, in his head. Just as a bucket being hauled up on a pulley swings around and knocks into the rope here and there on different sides, there was no character with a place in my life, and hardly even any things, that had not in their turn played different roles. A simple social relationship, even a material object, if I rediscovered it in my memory after a few years, I saw that life had gone on weaving different threads around it which eventually became dense enough to form that inimitable, lovely, velvety bloom on the years, like the accretion which in old parks shrouds a simple water-pipe in a sheath of emerald.

It was not only the appearance of these characters that made one think of them as people in a dream. They themselves were finding that life, already drowsy in youth and in love, had become more and more of a dream. They had even forgotten their resentments and their hatreds, and in order to be certain that it was the person now in front of them with whom they had not been on speaking terms ten years ago, they would have had to consult a register, which, however, would have been just as vague as a dream in which one had been insulted, without it being clear by whom. All these dreams helped to shape the contradictory appearances of political life, with men who had accused each other of murder or treason being members of the same government. And the dream became as murky as death in some old men on the days after those on which they had made love. On those days, there was no point in asking any questions of the President of the

Republic, he forgot everything. Then, if one left him in peace for a few days, his memory of public affairs returned, as fortuitously as the memory of a dream.

Sometimes it was not in a single image that this individual, so very different from the person I had subsequently come to know, appeared. For years I had imagined Bergotte as a gentle, godlike old man, I had felt paralysed as if by a ghost at the sight of Swann's grey hat or his wife's violet cloak, or the mystery in which the family name shrouded the Duchesse de Guermantes, even in a drawing-room; almost legendary origins, a fascinating mythology of relations which subsequently became so banal, but which are thus extended back into the past as if into the depths of the sky, with a brilliance equal to the light emanating from the glittering tail of a comet. And even the ones which had not begun in mystery, like my relations with Mme de Souvré, so dry and purely social these days, still retained from their earliest phase that first smile, calmer, sweeter and so smoothly traced in the fullness of an afternoon by the sea, or the close of a spring day in Paris, with the noise of carriages, dust in the air, and sunlight rippling like water. And while Mme de Souvré might not, perhaps, have been worth very much if taken out of this frame, like those monuments – the Salute,[106] for example – which, while having no great beauty of their own, do admirably in their place, she was part and parcel of a whole bundle of memories which I valued at a certain price as a 'job lot', without asking myself exactly how much of it the person of Mme de Souvré accounted for.

One thing about all these beings which struck me even more forcibly than the social and physical changes they had undergone, and that was the change in the different ideas they all had about each other. Legrandin used to despise Bloch and would never speak to him. Now he was on the best of terms with him. This was not entirely due to the more elevated position that Bloch had taken, which in this instance would not be worth noting, because social changes necessarily lead to alterations in the respective positions of those concerned. No: it was because in our memories people – and by people I mean as they are for us – do not have the same uniformity as a picture. Their development is subject to the arbitrary whims of our forgetting. Sometimes we go so far as to confuse them with other people: 'Bloch, that's somebody who used to come to Combray', saying Bloch, when in fact it was me they meant. Conversely, Mme Sazerat was convinced that I was the author of a certain historical treatise about Philip II (which was actually by Bloch). Without going to these extremes of transposition, one does forget the dirty tricks which somebody has played on you, his defects, and how the last time you met you left without shaking hands, and one remembers instead an earlier occasion when you got on very well together. And it is to that earlier occasion that Legrandin's manners were responding, in his friendliness towards Bloch, either because he had lost the memory of some part of the past, or because he judged it taboo, from a mixture of forgiveness, forgetting and indifference, which is another of the effects of Time. Nor are the memories we all have of one another, even in love, the same. I had known Albertine recall in extraordinary detail some remark I had made to her at one of our first meetings, and which I had completely forgotten. Yet of another incident, permanently settled deep in my mind like a pebble, she would have no memory at all. Our parallel lives seemed like those garden walks where, at regularly positioned intervals, tubs of flowers are placed symmetrically but never opposite each other. This makes it all the more understandable that when it comes to people with whom we have only a slight acquaintance we should have difficulty remembering who they are, or else that we should remember something different from how we used to think of them, something from an earlier time, something suggested by the people amongst whom we meet them again, who have only known them for a short while, adorned with qualities and a social position which they used not to have, but which we, oblivious, instantly accept.

No doubt life, by setting these people in my path on a number of occasions, had presented them to me in particular circumstances which, by surrounding them on all sides, had limited the view I had had of them and had prevented me from knowing their essence. Even those Guermantes, who had been the focus of such elaborate dreams for me, had appeared to me, when I had first come close to any of them, under the aspect, one of an old friend of my grandmother, the other of a gentleman who had looked at me in an unpleasantly forbidding way one morning in the gardens of the casino. (Because between us and other beings there is a margin of contingencies, just as I had understood in my readings at Combray that there is a margin in perception which prevents absolute contact taking place between reality and the mind.) So that it was only ever after the event, by relating them to a name, that my acquaintance with them became an acquaintance with the Guermantes. But perhaps that may even have made my life seem more poetic, the thought that this mysterious family with the piercing eyes, the beak of a bird, this rose-coloured, golden, unapproachable family, had so often, and so naturally, as a consequence of blind and varied circumstance, offered itself to my contemplation, to my society and even to my friendship, to the point that, when I had wanted to meet Mlle de Stermaria or to have dresses made for Albertine, it was to the Guermantes that I turned, as being the most helpful of all my friends. Certainly I was sometimes bored by having to go to their houses, as I was in the houses of other society people whom I had later come to know. Even with the Duchesse de Guermantes, as with certain pages of Bergotte, her charm was visible to me only at a distance and vanished when I was close to her, for it all lay in my memory and my imagination. But in the end the Guermantes, and Gilberte too, differed from the other people in society in that they thrust their roots further down into a past time of my life in which I dreamed more and believed more strongly in individuals. What at least I had before me, bored as I was chatting away first with one then with the other Guermantes, were those of my childhood imaginings whom I had found the most beautiful and believed the most inaccessible, and I consoled myself, like a shop-keeper whose book-keeping has become muddled, by confusing the value of having them there with the price my desire had once put on them.

In the case of some other people, though, my relations with them in the past had been inflated with more ardent dreams, conceived without hope, in which my life of that time blossomed so richly, and was so entirely dedicated to them, that I could scarcely comprehend how their fulfilment could have been that narrow, thin and lustreless ribbon of indifferent and disdainful intimacy, in which I was never afterwards able to rediscover anything of their old mystery, their fever and their sweetness. Not all had been 'received', or been decorated, for some the adjective was different, though not more important: they were recently dead.

'How is the Marquise d'Arpajon? asked Mme de Cambremer. − Oh, she's dead, replied Bloch. − You're confusing her with the Comtesse d'Arpajon, who died last year.' The Princesse d'Agrigente joined the discussion; the young widow of a very rich old husband and bearer of a great name, she was much sought after in marriage and this had greatly increased her self-assurance. 'The Marquise d'Arpajon died too, about a year ago. − A year? Oh, surely it can't be, replied Mme de Cambremer, I was at a musical evening in her house less than a year ago.' Bloch was no more capable of making a useful contribution to the discussion than any of the elegant young men in society, for the deaths of all these old people were too distant from them, either by virtue of the enormous difference in years, or by recent arrival (as in the case of Bloch) in a changing society which he approached indirectly, at the moment when it was starting to decline into a twilight where the memory of a past that was unfamiliar to him could provide no illumination. And for people of the same age and social background death had lost some of its strange significance. Every day they would send out for news of so many people who were at the point of death, of whom some would have rallied while others would have 'succumbed', that they could no longer remember with any accuracy whether somebody who no longer ever appeared anywhere had recovered from their pneumonia or had expired. Death became much more active and more indeterminate in these aged regions. At this crossroads of two generations and of two societies which, ill-placed for different reasons to distinguish death, almost confused it with life, the former had been socialized, had become an incident which more or less described a person but without the tone of voice seeming to signify that this incident put an end to everything for him or her. People said: 'But you're forgetting, so and so is dead,' in the same way as they might say: 'He's been decorated' or 'he's a member of the Academy', or − and this came to the same thing since it also prevented their presence at parties − 'he's gone south for the winter', 'he's been ordered to get some mountain air'. And in the case of well-known men, what they left behind them when they died helped to remind people that their existence was over. But with ordinary, very old, society people, one got confused about whether they were dead or not, not only because one knew little about, or had forgotten, their past, but because they had no connection of any sort with the future. And the difficulty each of them had in selecting one from among the illness, absence, retirement to the country, or death of old society people, made the insignificance of the departed quite as acceptable as the indifference of the hesitant.

'But if she's not dead, why don't we see her any more, or her husband? asked a spinster who liked trying to be witty. 'Well, I'll tell you,' replied her mother who, although in her fifties, never missed a party, 'It's because they're old: people of that age don't go out any more.' Before one reached the cemetery it seemed there was a whole self-contained city of the old, its lamps permanently lit in the mist. Mme de Saint-Euverte put an end to the argument by saying that the Comtesse d'Arpajon had died a year ago, after a long illness, but that the Marquise d'Arpajon had also died since then, very quickly, 'of something very ordinary'. A death which thereby resembled all these lives, and also thereby explained why it passed unnoticed, excused those who were confused. When she heard that Mme d'Arpajon really was dead, the spinster looked towards her mother with alarm, for she was afraid that learning of the death of one of her 'contemporaries' might 'come as a blow'; in her mind she could already hear talk of her own mother's death, with this explanation: 'The death of Mme d'Arpajon had come as a *great blow* to her.' But the spinster's mother, on the contrary, felt as if she had won a victory in a competition against distinguished competitors every time that a person her age 'disappeared'. Their deaths were the sole means by which she could still become pleasantly aware of her own life. The spinster noticed that her mother, who had not seemed sorry to say that Mme d'Arpajon was shut away in the sort of residence from which tired old people scarcely ever re-emerge, had been even less so to learn that the Marquise had entered the city after that, the one from which no traveller returns. This display of indifference on the part of her mother amused the spinster's caustic mind. And later to entertain her girl-friends she told them a hilarious story of the light-hearted manner in which, as she claimed, her mother had rubbed her hands and said: 'Well, goodness me, poor Mme d'Arpajon really does seem to be dead then.' So even those who did not need this death in order to feel glad to be alive were made happy by it. For every death is a simplification of existence for the others, removes the necessity to show gratitude, the obligation to pay visits. This was not, though, how the death of M. Verdurin had been received by Elstir.

A lady left, because she had other parties to attend and had to go and have tea with two queens. It was that great society cocotte, whom I had known in the past, the Princess of Nassau. If it were not that she had lost some of her height, which gave her, her head now being less loftily poised than formerly, an air of having *one foot in the grave*, one could scarcely have said that she looked any older. She remained a Marie-Antoinette with her Austrian nose, her enchanting glance, well-preserved, embalmed by a thousand kinds of make-up adorably combined to give her face a tint of lilac. Hovering over her features was that confused and affectionate expression which indicated that she was obliged to leave, that she promised fondly to return, that she was slipping away quietly, but also that she was expected at a host of parties given by the best people. Born almost on the steps of a throne, married three times, kept for long periods and in luxury by great bankers, to say nothing of the countless fancies with which she had indulged herself, she bore lightly beneath her gown, mauve like her wonderful, round eyes and her painted face, the slightly confused memories of this crowded past. As she passed by me, slipping discreetly away, I greeted her. She recognized me, clasped me by the hand and fixed me with those round, mauve eyes which seemed to say: 'How long it is since we saw one another! We must talk about it all another time.' She gave my hand a forceful squeeze, not quite able to remember whether, one evening in her carriage as she was taking me back from the Duchesse de Guermantes's house, there had not been some flirtation between us. She seemed, just to be on the safe side, to be alluding to something that had not happened, not a difficulty for her since she could appear deeply affected by a strawberry tart, and if ever she had to leave before the end of a piece of music, adopted an expression of despairing yet not final withdrawal. Uncertain, anyway, about the flirtation with me, her furtive squeeze of my hand did not delay her long and she spoke not a word to me. She merely looked at me, as I say, in a manner that signified: 'It's been so long!' and in which one could see the succession of husbands and men who had kept her, and two wars, as her stellar eyes, like an astronomical clock carved into an opal, marked one after another all those solemn hours of the distant past which she rediscovered each time she meant to bid you a good-afternoon that was always in fact an apology. Then, leaving me, she started to trot towards the door, so that nobody would have to put themselves out for her and to show me that if she had not stopped to talk to me, it was because she was in a hurry, as well as to make up for the minute lost squeezing my hand and thus be on time for the Queen of Spain, with whom she was going to have tea alone. As she drew near to the door, I even thought she was going to break into a run. And she was, in fact, running towards her grave.

A stout lady greeted me, and during the short time she was speaking the most varied thoughts thronged my mind. I hesitated for a moment before replying to her, afraid that, recognizing people no better than I did, she might have thought that I was somebody else, then her confidence made me, on the contrary, out of fear that this might be somebody whom I had known extremely well, exaggerate the friendliness of my smile, while my looks continued to search her features for the name I could not find. As a candidate for the baccalaureate, in his uncertainty, fixes his eyes on the examiner's face and hopes in vain to find there the answer for which he would do better to look in his own memory, I fixed my eyes on the features of the stout lady. They seemed to be those of Mme Swann, so my smile took on a more respectful quality, while my indecision began to diminish. Then a second later I heard the stout lady say: 'You thought I was Mama, it's true I am beginning to look very like her.' And I recognized Gilberte.

We talked a great deal about Robert, Gilberte speaking of him in a deferential tone of voice, as if he had been a superior being whom she was anxious to show me she had admired and understood. We reminded one another how the ideas he used to expound in the old days about the art of warfare (for he had often repeated to her at Tansonville the same arguments that I had heard him expound at Doncières and after) had frequently, and on a great number of points, been proved right by the last war.

'I can't tell you how forcefully the slightest things he said to me at Doncières strike me now, as they did during the war. The last words of his that I heard, as we parted for the last time, were that he was expecting Hindenburg, as a Napoleonic general, to adopt one of the typically Napoleonic battle-plans, the one whose aim is to separate two enemies, perhaps, he added, the English and us. Now, scarcely a year after Robert's death, a commentator for whom he had a profound admiration and who visibly exercised a major influence upon his military ideas, M. Henri Bidou,[107] said that Hindenburg's offensive in March 1918 was "the battle of separation of one concentrated army against two adversaries in linear formation, a manœuvre which the Emperor carried though successfully in 1796 in the Apennines, but which failed in Belgium in 1815". A few minutes before, Robert had for my benefit compared battles to plays in which it is not always easy to see what the author meant, or where he may have changed his plan at some point along the way. If Robert had interpreted that German offensive of 1918 in this way, of course, he would not have been in agreement with M. Bidou. But other commentators think that it was Hindenburg's success in the direction of Amiens, followed by his enforced halt, then his success in Flanders, then another halt, which made Amiens, and then Boulogne, accidental objectives that had not been designated in advance. And since anybody can reshape a play or a campaign, there are those who see in this offensive the beginnings of a lightning-like march on Paris, while others see it as a series of disorganized attacks designed to destroy the English army. And even if the orders given by the commander conflict with this or that conception, critics and commentators will always be free to say, as Mounet-Sully said to Coquelin[108] when he tried to persuade him that *Le Misanthrope* was not the melancholy drama he wanted to make it (for Molière, as his contemporaries attested, gave the part a comic interpretation and made audiences laugh at it): 'Well, Molière was wrong then.'

'And about aeroplanes, do you remember when he said (he always had such a good way of putting things): "Each army has to be a hundred-eyed Argus"? What a pity he wasn't able to see his assertions proved true. – But he did, I replied, he knew that at the Battle of the Somme they started by blinding the enemy by putting his eyes out, destroying his aeroplanes and captive balloons. – Oh yes! that's right.' And since she lived now only for things of the mind, and as a result had become a bit pedantic: 'And he used to claim that people would return to the ancient methods. Do you know that the Mesopotamian expeditions in this war' (she must have read this, at the time, in Brichot's articles) 'are exactly the same, no changes at all, as the retreat in Xenophon? And that to move from the Tigris to the Euphrates, the English command used bullums, long, narrow boats, the local equivalent of gondolas, which the earliest Chaldeans also used?' These words gave me a powerful sense of that stagnation of the past which in certain places is frozen indefinitely, through a kind of specific gravity, so that one can rediscover it exactly as it was.

'There is one aspect of the war which he was beginning, I believe, to grasp, I said to her, that it is human, it has to be lived like love or hatred, it could be narrated like a novel, and that consequently if somebody goes round repeating that strategy is a science, it does nothing to help them understand war, because war is not strategic. The enemy has no more knowledge of our plans than we have of the ultimate intentions of the woman we love, and we may perhaps not even know these plans ourselves. Was it the Germans' aim, in the March 1918 offensive, to take Amiens? We just don't know. Perhaps they didn't know themselves, and it was the way that events turned out, their advance in the west towards Amiens, that determined their plan. Even assuming that war were scientific, it would still have to be painted as Elstir painted the sea, the other way round, starting with illusions and beliefs which are then gradually rectified, in the same way as Dostoyevsky would tell the story of a life. But anyway war is quite definitely more medical than strategic, including unforeseen accidents the clinician was hoping to avoid, like the Russian Revolution.'

But I must admit that because of the books I had been reading at Balbec, not far from Robert, I was more impressed, during the fighting in France, to rediscover the word *trenches* in Mme de Sévigné, or in the Middle East, in connection with the siege of Kut-el-Amara (meaning Kut-the-emir, 'just as we say Vaux-le-Vicomte and Bailleau-l'Évêque,' the curé of Combray would have said, if he had extended his thirst for etymologies as far as Oriental languages), to see recurring, close to the name of Baghdad, the town of Basra, or Bassorah, mentioned so often in the *Arabian Nights* and which, each time he left Baghdad or before he returned there, was the port used for embarkation or disembarkation, long before General Townshend and General Gorringe, at the time of the Caliphs, by Sindbad the Sailor.

Throughout this conversation Gilberte had talked to me about Robert with a degree of deference which seemed directed more towards my former friend than towards her deceased husband. It was if she were saying: 'I know how much you admired him. Please believe that I was capable of understanding what a superior being he was.' And yet the love which she certainly no longer had for his memory was perhaps the distant cause of certain features of her present life. For example, Gilberte now had an inseparable friend in Andrée. And although the latter was beginning, thanks largely to her husband's talent and her own intelligence, to penetrate, not of course into the Guermantes' circle, but into a level of society infinitely smarter than the one she used to move in, people were very surprised that the Marquise de Saint-Loup should condescend to be her best friend. The fact that she was seemed to be a sign, on Gilberte's part, of her fondness for what she took to be an artistic existence, and for what was undeniably a social decline. This explanation may be the true one. Another one, however, does come to my mind, always very much aware of the extent to which the images we see assembled somewhere are generally the reflection, or in some way or other the effect, of an earlier somewhat different but symmetrical grouping of other images, far removed from the second. My thought was that if Andrée, her husband and Gilberte were seen together every evening, it was perhaps because, so many years earlier, one might have seen Andrée's future husband living with Rachel, then leaving her for Andrée. It is unlikely that Gilberte knew anything about it then, living as she did in a social world too remote and too elevated. But she must have found out about it later, when Andrée had risen and she herself had descended far enough for them to be able to notice one another. Then she must have been powerfully aware of the prestige of the woman for whom Rachel had been left by the man, no doubt extremely seductive, whom she had preferred to Robert. (The Princesse de Guermantes could be heard excitedly repeating, in a voice with a tinny rattle because of her false teeth: 'Yes, that's it, let's get together, let's make a set! I love these young people, so intelligent, so ready to join in! Oh, what a mushishian you are!' And she stuck her great monocle in her round eye, half amused, half apologetic for not being able to sustain the gaiety for long, though she was determined to 'join in', to 'make a set', right to the bitter end.)

So perhaps the sight of Andrée reminded Gilberte of the youthful romance that her love for Robert had been, and also inspired in her a great respect for Andrée, who was still so deeply loved by a man who had been so much loved by Rachel, whom in turn Gilberte felt to have been more deeply loved by Robert than she herself had ever been. Or perhaps on the contrary those memories had nothing to do with Gilberte's fondness for this artistic couple, and one had to look at it quite simply, as many did, as an illustration of two enthusiasms customarily inseparable among society women, for culture and for slumming. Gilberte perhaps had forgotten Robert as completely as I had forgotten Albertine, and even if she did know that it was Rachel whom the artist had left for Andrée she may never have thought, when she saw them, about something which never played any part in her liking for them. Whether my first explanation was not merely possible but true could have been discovered only through the testimony of those involved, the only recourse remaining in such cases, so long as they could bring to their confidences both insight and sincerity. But the first is rarely met with, and the second never. At all events, the sight of Rachel, now a celebrated actress, could not be very pleasant for Gilberte. I was therefore annoyed to learn that she was going to be reciting some verses in the course of the party, namely, it was announced, Musset's 'Le Souvenir', and some fables by La Fontaine.

'But what brings you to a crowded party like this?' Gilberte asked me. It's not at all how I think of you, running into you in this sort of shambles. In fact I'd expect to see you anywhere but at one of my aunt's do's. Because I'm afraid she is my aunt,' she added pointedly, for having been Mme de Saint-Loup since slightly earlier than Mme Verdurin entered the family, she considered herself always to have been a Guermantes and to have been dishonoured by the misalliance her uncle had contracted by marrying Mme Verdurin and which, it is true, she had heard the family make fun of countless times in her presence, whereas it was naturally only behind her back that people talked about the misalliance Saint-Loup had contracted when he married her. Moreover she affected all the more disdain for this aunt with no breeding since, by one of those perverse impulses which make intelligent people want to escape their conventional manners, and also because of old people's need for reminiscences, and lastly in an attempt to provide a past for her new smartness, the Princesse de Guermantes liked to say, talking about Gilberte: 'Of course, it isn't as if she was someone new to me, I knew the child's mother very well, why, she was a great friend of my cousin Marsantes. It was in my house that she met Gilberte's father. As for poor Saint-Loup, I knew all his family long ago, his uncle was a very close friend in the old days at La Raspalière.' 'You see, the Verdurins weren't bohemians at all,' I would be told by people who had heard the Princesse de Guermantes saying things like this, 'they've always been friends of de Saint-Loup's family.' I was probably the only person to know, through my grandfather, that the Verdurins were indeed not bohemians. But this was hardly because they had known Odette. But it is always easy to put together stories about a past which nobody any longer remembers, like those about journeys to countries where nobody has ever been. 'So, concluded Gilberte, since you do come down from your ivory tower sometimes, wouldn't you prefer intimate little gatherings at my house, with just a few agreeable and intelligent people invited? Great soulless affairs like this one are not really designed for you. I saw you talking to my aunt Oriane, who has plenty of good qualities, but I don't think it would be unfair, do you, to say that she's hardly one of the intellectual elite.'

I could not tell Gilberte about the thoughts I had been having for the last hour, but I did think that, purely in terms of entertainment, she might provide me with some pleasure, which in fact seemed unlikely to come from having to talk about literature with the Duchesse de Guermantes any more than with Mme de Saint-Loup. Certainly I intended to resume living in solitude from the next day onward, but this time with a specific purpose. Even at home I would not let people come to see me during my working moments, for the duty to write my book took precedence over that of being polite or even good-natured. They would probably insist, those who had not seen me for such a long time, coming to see me in the belief that I was cured, coming when the labour of their day or of their life was finished or interrupted, and having then the same need of me as I had once had of Saint-Loup; and because, as I had already noticed at Combray when my parents reprimanded me at the moment when, unknown to them, I had made the most praiseworthy resolutions, the internal clocks which are allocated to human beings are not all set to the same time. One strikes the hour of repose at the same time as another is striking that of work, one that of punishment by the judge when within the culprit the hour of repentance and self-improvement has long since struck. But I would have the courage to reply to those who came to see me, or who sent for me, that, because of essential matters which I needed to get abreast of immediately, I had an urgent, a crucially important meeting with myself. And yet, even though there is little relation between our true self and the other one, none the less, because they are homonymous and because they share a body, the abnegation which makes you sacrifice your simpler duties, even pleasures, appears to other people as selfishness.

And anyway was it not so that I could be occupied by them that I was living apart from those people who would complain about not seeing me, so that I could be more deeply occupied by them than I could ever have been with them, in order to try to reveal them to themselves, to make them real? What use would it have been if I had continued for yet more years to waste whole evenings bouncing my equally vain remarks off the hardly defunct echo of theirs, all for the sterile pleasure of a social contact which excludes everything that is not superficial? Was it not better that I should take these gestures they made, these things they said, their lives, their natures, and attempt to describe the curve they made and to isolate and define their laws? I would unfortunately have to struggle against that habit of putting oneself in another person's place which, although it may help the conception of a work, is a hindrance to its execution. For, through a kind of superior politeness, it impels one to sacrifice to others not only one's pleasure but one's duty because, looking at it from somebody else's standpoint, this duty, whatever it may be, even if it is just somebody who can do nothing useful at the front staying behind the lines where he is useful, will look like our pleasure, when in reality it is not.

And far indeed from thinking myself unfortunate, as even the greatest sometimes have, in this life without friends, without conversation, I realized that the forces of elation expended in friendship are so to speak out of true, aiming at one particular friendship which leads to nothing and deflecting us from a truth towards which they were capable of leading us. But in the end, when intervals of rest and society became necessary, I felt that, rather than the intellectual conversations which society people thought useful for writers, a few light love affairs with young girls in flower would be a select nutrient which, if I had to, I might allow my imagination, like the famous horse that was fed on nothing but roses. What suddenly I hoped for again was what I had dreamed of at Balbec when, before I had yet met them, I had seen Albertine, Andrée and their friends walking beside the sea. But alas! I could no longer hope to rediscover those girls whom at that moment I desired so strongly. The action of the years which had transformed all the individuals I had seen today, including Gilberte herself, had certainly turned all those who still survived, as they would have done Albertine if she had not been killed, into women very different from my recollections of them. It was painful for me to have to retrieve these for myself, for time, which changes individuals, does not modify the image we have of them. Nothing is sadder than this contrast between the way individuals change and the fixity of memory, when we understand that what we have kept so fresh in our memory no longer has any of that freshness in real life, and that we cannot find a way to come close, on the outside, to that which appears so beautiful within us, which arouses in us a desire, seemingly so personal, to see it again, except by looking for it in a person of the same age, that is to say in another being. It is simply, as I had often had reason to suspect, that what seems unique in a person whom one desires does not in fact belong to her. But the passage of time was giving me a more complete proof of this since, after twenty years, spontaneously, I was trying to find, not the girls whom I had known, but those who now possessed the youth that the others had had then. (Nor is it only the re-awakening of our physical desires which corresponds to no reality because it fails to take account of lost time. I sometimes used to find myself wishing that, by a miracle, still alive contrary to what I had believed, my grandmother or Albertine might just walk into the room where I was. I imagined I could see them, my heart shot towards them. I forgot only one thing, which was that if they really were still living, Albertine would now have something like the appearance that Mme Cottard had presented at Balbec, and that my grandmother, being over ninety-five years old, would show me nothing of that beautiful, calm, smiling face with which I still imagined her now, as arbitrarily as one might give a beard to God the Father, or as in the seventeenth century Homeric heroes were depicted in all the accoutrements of gentlemen, without any attention paid to their antiquity.)

I looked at Gilberte and I did not think: 'I'd like to see her again,' but I did tell her that she would always be giving me pleasure if she invited me to meet very young girls, preferably poor, so that I could give them pleasure by giving them little gifts, without asking anything of them except a revival of the reveries and sorrows of earlier times and perhaps, one unlikely day, a chaste kiss. Gilberte smiled and then seemed to be giving the idea her serious consideration.

In the same way that Elstir liked to see incarnate before him, in his wife, the Venetian beauty he had often painted in his works, I gave myself the excuse that there was a degree of aesthetic selfishness in my attraction towards beautiful women who could cause me pain, and I felt something close to idolatry for the future Gilbertes, the future Duchesses de Guermantes, the future Albertines whom I might meet and who, it seemed to me, might inspire me, as if I were a sculptor walking among fine classical marbles. I ought, though, to have realized that even earlier than this attraction to each of them was my sense of the mystery surrounding them and that therefore, rather than asking

Gilberte to introduce me to young girls, I would do better to go out to places where we have no connection with them, where between them and oneself one feels something unbridgeable, where two steps away, on the beach, going for a bathe, one feels separated from them by impossibility. That is how my sense of mystery had been able to attach itself in turn to Gilberte, to the Duchesse de Guermantes, to Albertine and to so many others. No doubt in due course the unknown, and almost the unknowable, had become the known, familiar, indifferent or painful, yet it always retained something of the charm it had once possessed.

And to tell the truth, like those calendars the postman brings to get his Christmas box, there was not one of my years which might not have had as its frontispiece, or intercalated between its days, the image of a woman I had desired; an image made even more arbitrary by the fact that sometimes I had never seen the woman, as for example when it was Mme Putbus's maid, or Mlle d'Orgeville, or some girl whose name I had glimpsed in the society page of a newspaper, among 'the bevy of charming waltzers'. I would imagine her as beautiful, fall in love with her, and create for her an ideal body, its height dominating a landscape in the part of the country where, as I had read in the *Annuaire des châteaux*, her family estates were to be found. For the women whom I had known, this landscape was at least twofold. Each woman arose, at a different point in my life, towering up like a local tutelary deity, first in the middle of one of these dream landscapes the juxtapositions of which chequered my life, the landscape in which I had first wanted to imagine her, then seen from the viewpoint of memory, surrounded by the places where I had known her and of which she reminded me, remaining attached to them, for although our lives are vagabond, our memories are sedentary and although we may move endlessly on, our memories, fastened to the places from which we free ourselves, continue to lead their unadventurous lives there, like the friends which a traveller makes briefly in a town and whom he is forced to abandon when he leaves it, because it is there that they who are not leaving will end that day and their lives as if he were still there, in front of the church, down by the harbour and beneath the trees of the promenade. So that the shadow of Gilberte, for instance, lay not only in front of a church in the Île-de-France where I had imagined her, but also across the path of a park on the Méséglise way, the shadow of Mme de Guermantes on a wet road where violet and reddish clusters rose in spikes, or on the morning gold of a Paris pavement. And this second person, born not of desire but of memory, was not for any of these women a single figure. For I had known each of them more than once, at different times, when each was a different woman for me, or I myself was different, steeped in dreams of a different colour. And the law which had governed the dreams of each year kept gathered around them the memories of a woman I had known, so that everything relating, for example, to the Duchesse de Guermantes at the time of my childhood was concentrated by a magnetic force around Combray, and everything which had to do with the Duchesse de Guermantes, when she was about to invite me to lunch, around a quite different sensitive entity; there were several Duchesses de Guermantes, as there had been several Mme Swanns since the lady in pink, separated by the colourless ether of the years, and from one to the other of whom I could no more jump than if I had to leave one planet and travel to another across the intervening ether. Not only separated, but different, adorned by dreams which I had at very different times, as with a particular flora not found on any other planet; to the extent that after having decided that I would lunch neither at Mme de Forcheville's nor at Mme de Guermantes's, I was able to tell myself only, so much had I been transported into a different world, that the one was not a different person from the Duchesse de Guermantes who was descended from Geneviève de Brabant, and the other from the lady in pink, because a knowledgeable man within me told me so with the same authority as a scientist might have told me that a Milky Way of nebulae was the result of the disintegration of one single star. In the same way Gilberte, whom none the less I was asking, without quite realizing that this was what I was doing, to enable me to have friends who would be like she had once been, was no longer anything to me but Mme de Saint-Loup. I no longer thought, when I saw her, of the part played in my love for her, which she had also forgotten about, by my admiration for Bergotte, for Bergotte once again simply the author of his books, without my remembering (save in rare and entirely distinct moments of recollection) the emotion of having been presented to the man, the disappointment, the astonishment at the conversation, in the drawing-room with the white fur rugs, filled with violets, where so many lamps were brought in so early, and set on so many consoles. All the memories which composed the original Mlle Swann had in effect been subtracted from the Gilberte of today, kept at a distance by the powers of attraction of another universe, grouped around a phrase of Bergotte's with which they fused into a unity, and steeped in the scent of hawthorn.

The fragmentary Gilberte of today listened to my request with a smile. Then, as she began to think about it, her face took on a more serious expression. And I was glad about this, as it prevented her from paying attention to a group the sight of which could certainly not have pleased her. The Duchesse de Guermantes could be seen deep in conversation with a frightful old woman, whom I looked at without being able even to guess who she was: I had absolutely no idea about her. It turned out to be Rachel, that is the actress, now famous, who in the course of the party was going to recite verses by Victor Hugo and La Fontaine, whom Gilberte's aunt, Mme de Guermantes, was speaking to. For the Duchesse, aware for too long of occupying the foremost position in Paris society (unaware that such a position exists only in the minds of those who believe in it, and that many newcomers, if they never saw her anywhere, if they never read her name in the accounts of any smart functions, would think in fact that she occupied no position at all), no longer went, save for calls as few and infrequent as possible, and then with a yawn, to the Faubourg Saint-Germain, which, she said, bored her to death, and instead indulged herself by having lunch with this or that actress whom she thought exquisite. In the new circles she moved in, having remained more like her old self than she thought, she continued to believe that being easily bored was a sign of intellectual superiority, but she expressed this with a sort of violence which gave her voice rather a harsh tone. When I mentioned Brichot to her: 'He bored me so much for twenty years,' and when Mme de Cambremer said: 'You should reread what Schopenhauer says about music,' she drew everyone's attention to the phrase by saying, forcefully: 'Re-read, that's wonderful! Who does she think she's taking in?' Old M. d'Albon smiled at what he took to be a manifestation of the Guermantes wit. Gilberte, more up-to-date, remained impassive. Although Swann's daughter, like a duckling hatched by a hen, she was more of a romanticist than he had been, and would say: 'I think that's so touching; or, he is delightfully sensitive.'

I told Mme de Guermantes that I had run into M. de Charlus. She seemed to think he had 'declined' more than was in fact the case, people in society making distinctions, where intelligence is concerned, not only between different members of society amongst all of whom it is pretty much the same, but even within a single person at different points in their life. Then she added: 'He has always been the image of my mother-in-law; but it's more striking than ever now.' There was nothing out of the ordinary in this resemblance. It is well known, in fact, that certain women as it were project themselves into another individual in perfect detail, the one error being in the matter of sex. An error of which one cannot say *felix culpa*, for the sex has implications for the personality, and in a man femininity becomes affectation, shyness becomes touchiness, and so on. It does not matter if the face is bearded or if the cheeks are heavily whiskered, they still have certain lines that could be superimposed on to a maternal portrait. There is scarcely an old Charlus who is not a ruin within which one can recognize with surprise under all the impasto of powder and paint a few fragments of a beautiful woman in her eternal youth. At that moment Morel entered the room; the Duchesse greeted him with a politeness which I found a little disconcerting. 'Oh, I never take sides in family quarrels, she said. Don't you find them boring, family quarrels?'

And if over periods of twenty years conglomerations of coteries disintegrated and re-formed in accordance with the magnetic force of new stars, themselves also destined to fade away, then to reappear, a similar process of crystallization, then fragmentation, followed by fresh crystallization took place in the minds of individuals. If for me Mme de Guermantes had been a number of people, for Mme de Guermantes, for Mme Swann, etc., a given person had been a favourite in a era that preceded the Dreyfus Affair, then a fanatic or a fool after the Affair had broken and had changed the value of individuals for them and reclassified the parties, which since then had again disintegrated and re-formed. The most powerful effect on this, adding its own influence to purely intellectual affinities, is the passage of time, which makes us forget our antipathies, our disdains, the very reasons that explain our antipathies and our disdains. If one had scrutinized the fashionable young Mme de Cambremer closely, one would have found that she was the daughter of Jupien, the tradesman from our building, and that the additional factor which had enabled her to become a glittering success was that her father procured men for M. de Charlus. But the combination of those things had produced dazzling effects, while the causes, already distant, not only were unknown to most of the newcomers, but most of those who had known them had forgotten them, being much more concerned with current brilliance than with past embarrassments, for a name is always taken at its current valuation. And the interesting thing about these drawing-room transformations was that they too were an effect of lost time, and a phenomenon of memory.

The Duchesse still hesitated, for fear of a scene with M. de Guermantes, to approach Balthy and Mistinguett,[109] whom she thought adorable, but had definitely taken Rachel as her friend. The new generations concluded from this that Mme de Guermantes, despite her name, must be some demi-rep who had never really been properly upper-crust. It is true that in the case of a few sovereigns for whose close friendship two other great ladies were mounting a challenge, Mme de Guermantes still went to the trouble of having them to lunch. But, on the one hand, they do not come very often, and tend to know people of little social standing, and also the Duchesse, out of the Guermantes' superstitious adherence to old-fashioned protocol (because well-bred people *bored her to tears* while at the same time she insisted on good manners), always had her invitations read: 'Her Majesty has commanded the Duchesse de Guermantes, has deigned', etc. And the new strata, ignorant of these formulas, concluded from them that the position of the Duchesse was all the less elevated. From the point of view of Mme de Guermantes, close friendship with Rachel might indicate that we were mistaken when we thought her hypocritical and dishonest in her condemnations of smart society, when we thought that when she refused to go to Mme de Saint-Euverte's she was acting not in the name of intelligence but of snobbery, thinking her stupid only because the Marquise allowed her snobbery to show, not yet having achieved her goal. But this intimacy with Rachel could also signify that the Duchesse's intelligence was ordinary, unsatisfied and belatedly desirous, now she was tired of society, of some kind of fulfilment, though with a total ignorance of the true realities of intellectual life, and a touch of that fanciful spirit which makes quite respectable ladies think: 'What fun that will be!' and then end their evening in what turns out to be a very boring way, by going through the farce of waking somebody up, not in the end knowing what to say to them, standing by their bed for a little while in their evening cloak, after which, having noticed that it is very late, they finally go home to bed.

It must be added that the antipathy which the unpredictable Duchesse had recently developed towards Gilberte may have meant that she took a certain pleasure in receiving Rachel, which also allowed her to proclaim one of the Guermantes maxims, namely that they were too many to take sides in one another's quarrels (almost too many to take notice of each other's bereavements), an independence of the 'I don't see why I should have to' sort, which had been reinforced by the policy they had been obliged to adopt in relation to M. de Charlus, who, if you had followed him, would have involved you in hostilities with the whole of society.

As for Rachel, if she had in reality gone to considerable lengths to establish a connection with the Duchesse de Guermantes (lengths which the Duchesse had not been able to discern beneath the affected disdain, the deliberate impoliteness, which had whetted her appetite and given her an inflated idea of an actress so little given to snobbery), that was doubtless something, in a general way, to do with the fascination which people in society begin after a certain time to exert over the most hardened bohemians, parallel to the one that bohemians themselves exercise over people in society, a double reflux corresponding in the political order to the reciprocal curiosity and the desire to form an alliance between nations which have recently been at war. But there may have been a more specific reason for Rachel's desire. It was in the house of Mme de Guermantes, from Mme de Guermantes herself, that she had, long ago, received her most terrible humiliation. Rachel had gradually, not forgotten, but forgiven, but the singular prestige which the Duchesse had, in her eyes, thereby received could never be effaced. The conversation from which I was wanting to distract Gilberte's attention was interrupted, anyway, because the mistress of the house came looking for the actress as it was time for the recitation, and a few moments later, having left the Duchesse, she appeared on the platform.

Meanwhile, at the other end of Paris, a very different spectacle was taking place. La Berma, as I said, had invited a few people to come and take tea in honour of her son and daughter-in-law.[110] But the guests were in no hurry to arrive. Having learned that Rachel was reciting poetry at the Princesse de Guermantes's (which deeply scandalized La Berma, the great artist who still regarded Rachel as a tart who had been allowed to appear in dramas in which she, La Berma, was playing the leading role, because Saint-Loup paid for the dresses she wore on stage – and scandalized her the more because there was a rumour current in Paris that, although the invitations were in the name of the Princesse de Guermantes, it was Rachel who in reality was the hostess in the Princesse's house), La Berma had written for a second time insistently to a few loyal friends, asking them not to miss her tea-party, for she knew that they were also friends of Mme de Guermantes, whom they had known when she was Mme Verdurin. Now the hours were passing and nobody arrived at La Berma's. Bloch, on being asked whether he wanted to come, had artlessly replied: 'No, I'd rather go to the Princesse de Guermantes's.' Unfortunately, this was what everybody else had privately decided to do. La Berma, suffering from a fatal illness which meant that she saw only very few people, had seen her condition worsen when, to pay for the luxury her daughter needed and which her son-in-law, idle and with poor health, was unable to provide, she had returned to acting. She knew that she was shortening her life, but she wanted to give pleasure to her daughter, to whom she gave her large fees, and to her son-in-law, whom she hated but flattered, for knowing how her daughter adored him, she was afraid that if she failed to please him he might, out of spite, prevent her from seeing her daughter. This daughter, secretly loved by the doctor who attended her husband, had let herself be persuaded that these performances of *Phèdre* were not dangerous to her mother. She had in a sense forced the doctor to tell her this, in that she had retained nothing else but this from his reply, or from his objections, which had made no impression on her; and in fact the doctor had said that he could not see any great risk in La Berma's performances. He had said this out of a feeling that he would thereby be pleasing the young woman he loved, and perhaps also out of ignorance, and because he also knew that the disease was, in any case, incurable, and that we are happy to resign ourselves to cutting short the suffering of somebody who is ill when that which is fated to cut it short benefits us, and perhaps also out of some stupid idea that it would please La Berma and was therefore bound to be good for her, a stupid idea which may have seemed justified when, having been given a box by La Berma's children, and having left all his patients for the occasion, he had found her as overflowing with life on the stage as she seemed close to death when she was at home. And in fact our habits do to a very great extent allow us, allow even our organs, to adapt to an existence which would seem at first sight to be quite impossible. Who has not seen an elderly riding-master with a weak heart go through a whole range of acrobatics which one would not have believed his heart could sustain for a minute? La Berma was no less of an old stalwart of the stage, to the demands of which her organs were so perfectly adapted that she was able, by husbanding her energies with a caution invisible to the public, to give the illusion of good health disturbed only by a purely nervous and imaginary ailment. After the scene in which she declares herself to Hippolyte, La Berma may well have been aware of nothing but the dreadful night she was about to have, but her admirers applauded her with all their might, declaring her more beautiful than ever. She went back home in terrible pain, but glad that she was able to bring her daughter the large banknotes which, in the girlish way of an actress brought up on the boards, she still used to stuff into her stockings, whence she would proudly produce them in the hope of a smile and a kiss. Sadly, all these banknotes merely enabled new embellishments to their *hôtel*, adjacent to the mother's: whence incessant hammering, which interrupted the sleep of which the great actress was in such great need. In accordance with changes in fashion, and to conform to the taste of M. de X—— or Mme de Y—— whom they hoped to entertain, they made alterations to every room. And La Berma, sensing that sleep, which alone could ease her pain, had fled, resigned herself to not sleeping again, although not without a secret contempt for these refinements which were hastening her death and making her last days so excruciating. This, in part at least, was no doubt why she despised them, a natural vengeance upon whatever harms us and that we are powerless to prevent. But it is also because being aware of the genius that was in her, having learned very early in life the meaninglessness of these edicts of fashion, she had herself remained faithful to the tradition she had always respected, of which she was the incarnation, which led her to judge things and people as she had done thirty years earlier, and for instance to judge Rachel not as the fashionable actress she was today, but as the little tart she had once known. La Berma was not actually any better than her daughter, who had got from her, by heredity and the contagious effects of example that an all too natural admiration made the more efficacious, her selfishness, her pitiless mockery, her unconscious cruelty. Save that all this La Berma had sacrificed to her daughter and thus been freed from it herself. Moreover, even if the daughter had not had workmen in her house all the time, she would still have worn out her mother, as the thoughtless and ferocious attractive powers of youth wear out age and illness, which exhaust themselves trying to keep up with it. Every day there was another lunch party, and people would have thought La Berma selfish to have deprived her daughter of them, or even not to have been present at lunches where the prestige of the famous mother's company was relied upon to mitigate the difficulty of attracting recalcitrant recent acquaintances to the house. They would 'promise' her to the same acquaintances for a party away from home, just to be civil. And the poor mother, gravely occupied with her private converse with the death installed within her, would be obliged to get up early, and go out. Worse still, as this was the time when Réjane,[111] at the dazzling peak of her talent, was giving performances abroad which were enormously successful, the son-in-law decided that La Berma must not let herself be eclipsed, wanted the family to pick up some of the same abundant glory, and forced La Berma on tours where she had to be given injections of morphine which, because of the state of her kidneys, might easily have caused her death. The same appeal of smartness, of social prestige, of life, had worked on the day of the Princesse de Guermantes's party like a suction-pump to attract, as if with some pneumatic machine, all La Berma's most loyal friends so that, in consequence and by contrast, there was absolute, deathlike emptiness in her house. One young man, uncertain whether La Berma's party might not also be a glittering affair, had come. When La Berma saw the appointed time pass, and realized that everybody had abandoned her, she ordered tea to be served, and they sat down at the table, but rather as if it were a funeral repast. Nothing about La Berma's face any longer recalled the face whose photograph had disturbed me so much one evening in mid-Lent.[112] La Berma, as people say, had death written all over her face. This time she really did look like one of the marble figures in the Erechtheum.[113] Her hardened arteries were already semi-petrified, the long sculptural ribbons visibly stretching across her cheeks, with a mineral rigidity. The dying eyes seemed relatively alive by contrast with this terrible ossified mask, and gleamed palely like a snake asleep in a heap of stones. But the young man, who had sat down at the table out of politeness, could hardly keep his eyes off the clock, drawn as he was by the glittering party at the Guermantes'.

La Berma did not utter a word of reproach about the friends who had abandoned her, and who naïvely hoped that she would not notice that they had gone to the Guermantes'. She merely murmured: 'A Rachel giving a party in the Princesse de Guermantes's house. It could only happen in Paris.' And, silently and with a solemn slowness, she ate forbidden cakes, as if taking part in some funerary ritual. The 'tea-party' was all the more gloomy as the son-in-law was furious that Rachel, whom he and his wife knew very well, had not invited them. His anguish was intensified when the young guest had told him that he knew Rachel so well that if he left at once for the Guermantes' he could ask her, even at this late stage, to invite the shallow couple. But

La Berma's daughter was too well aware what a very low estimation her mother had of Rachel, and knew that she would make her die of despair if she solicited an invitation from that former tart. So she had told the young man and her husband that it was quite impossible. But she got her own back throughout the tea by making expressive little facial gestures indicative of the desire for pleasure and of annoyance at being deprived of it by her spoil-sport of a mother. The latter pretended not to notice her daughter's sulky expression, and from time to time addressed a few amiable words, in a dying voice, to the young man, the sole guest to have come. But soon the blast of air which was sweeping everything towards the Guermantes, and which had swept me there myself, was too strong, and he rose and left, leaving Phèdre, or death, it was not very clear any longer which of the two it was, with her daughter and her son-in-law, to finish eating the funeral cakes.

We were interrupted by the voice of the actress gradually becoming audible. This was a clever ploy on her part, for it presupposed that the poetry which the actress was in the process of speaking was part of a whole that existed prior to this recitation, and that we were only hearing a fragment of it, as if the artist, on her way along a road, had happened for a few moments to be within our earshot.

The announcement of poems that almost everybody knew had met with approval. But when people saw the actress, before she began, gazing in all directions, wild-eyed and questioning, raising her hands in the air in supplication and almost groaning out each word, they all started to feel embarrassed, almost shocked, by this display of feeling. Nobody had imagined that the recital of poetry could be anything like that. Gradually, people become accustomed to it, that is to say they forget the original sensation of unease, they sift out the good, they compare different methods of recitation in their minds, in order to tell themselves: this is better, this is less good. But the first time, in the same way as when, in a simple case, one sees the barrister step forward, raise a robed arm and begin declaiming in an ominous voice, nobody dares look at their neighbours. Because to begin with one thinks it is grotesque, but then it seems it might be wonderful, and one waits to make up one's mind.

Nevertheless, the audience was amazed when they saw this woman, before she had uttered a single sound, bend her knees, stretch out her arms to cradle some invisible body, become knock-kneed and then suddenly, in order to speak lines which were very well known, adopt an imploring tone of voice. Everybody looked at one another, not quite knowing what expression to assume, a few ill-mannered young people stifled giggles, each person cast furtive glances at his neighbour, the sort that at smart dinner-parties, when there is a new implement in front of you, a lobster-fork, a sugar-grater, etc., whose purpose and use you do not know, you cast at some more authoritative guest who, you hope, will be served before you are and thus give you the opportunity to copy what they do. You do the same, too, when somebody quotes a line of poetry you do not know, but which you want to look as if you do know, when, as if pausing to permit somebody to enter a door first, you allow another, better-informed person, as if it were a favour, to have the pleasure of saying where it comes from. In this way, while they listened to the actress, everyone waited, heads lowered and eyes enquiring, for other people to take the initiative by laughing, or criticizing, or weeping, or applauding.

Mme de Forcheville, who had returned expressly from Guermantes, whence the Duchesse had been almost expelled, had adopted a taut, attentive, almost pained expression, either to show that she was a connoisseur and not merely there for social reasons, or as a form of hostility towards people less well versed in literature who might have talked to her about other things, or else by the exertion of her whole being to discover whether she 'liked' or did not like a piece, or perhaps because, while finding one 'interesting', she certainly did not 'like' the manner in which certain lines were spoken. It might seem that this attitude would have been better adopted by the Princesse de Guermantes. But as this was taking place in her house, and as, having become as miserly as she was rich, she had decided to give Rachel nothing but five roses, she was acting as a claque. She was whipping up enthusiasm and creating favourable impressions by constantly giving voice to exclamations of delight. Here alone her Verdurin nature could still be seen, for she seemed to be listening to the poems for her own pleasure, to have wanted someone to come and speak them to *her* and her alone, while it was only by chance that there should have happened to be five hundred people there, her friends, whom she had allowed to come as it were secretly to witness her private pleasure.

Meanwhile I observed, without any gratification of my vanity, for she was old and ugly, that the actress was giving me the eye, though in a somewhat restrained manner. During the whole of the recitation she allowed a repressed but penetrating smile to flicker in her eyes as if it were the first sign of an acquiescence she might have wished to see coming from me. At the same time, some elderly ladies, not used to poetry recitals, were saying to their neighbours: 'Did you see that?' alluding to the actress's solemn, tragic gestures, not knowing what to make of them. The Duchesse de Guermantes sensed the slight wavering and ensured a victory by exclaiming: 'Wonderful!' right in the middle of a poem which she thought had perhaps just ended. More than one guest was then anxious to accentuate this exclamation with a look of approbation and a nod of the head, less perhaps to show their understanding of the performance than to show off their relationship with the Duchesse. When the poem was finished, as we were near the actress I heard her thank Mme de Guermantes, and at the same time, taking advantage of the fact that I was standing beside the Duchesse, she turned to me with some gracious greeting. I realized then that this was somebody whom I ought to recognize, and that unlike the passionate glances of M. de Vaugoubert's son, which I had mistaken for the greeting of a person who thought I was somebody else, what I had taken as a look of desire on the part of the actress was merely a reserved attempt to get me to recognize her and greet her. I responded with a bow and a smile. 'I'm sure he doesn't recognize me, the reciter said to the Duchesse. – Of course I do, I said confidently, I recognize you perfectly. – Who am I, then?' I had absolutely no idea who she was, and my position was becoming awkward. Fortunately for me, while, during the loveliest lines of La Fontaine, this woman reciting them with so much assurance had been thinking mainly, either out of kindness or stupidity, about the difficulty of saying good-afternoon to me, during the same lovely lines Bloch's thoughts had been exclusively occupied with making preparations, as soon as the poetry ended, to dash forward as if attempting an escape from some beleaguered position, treading on the feet, if not the bodies, of his neighbours, to come and congratulate the reciter, either out of a misplaced sense of duty or else out of a desire for ostentation. 'Isn't it funny to see Rachel here!' he whispered in my ear. The magic name instantly shattered the enchantment which had given Saint-Loup's mistress the unknown form of this disgusting old woman. As soon as I knew who she was I recognized her perfectly. 'That was wonderful,' he said to Rachel, and having spoken these simple words, his desire satisfied, he went back and had so much difficulty and made so much noise regaining his place that Rachel had to wait more than five minutes before reciting her second poem. When she had finished this one, 'Les Deux Pigeons', Mme de Morienval came up to Mme de Saint-Loup, whom she knew to be very well-read, while not remembering that she also had her father's subtle and sarcastic wit: 'That's the La Fontaine fable, isn't it?' she asked, thinking she recognized it but not being absolutely certain, for she did not know La Fontaine's fables well at all, and indeed believed them to be childish things, not for recitation in fashionable society. To have had a success like that, the artist must surely have been doing a pastiche of the fables of La Fontaine, the dear good woman thought. Now Gilberte unintentionally strengthened her in that idea for, not liking Rachel, and wanting to say that there was almost nothing left of the fables after a delivery like hers, she said so in that over-subtle manner which had been her father's, and which used to leave unsophisticated people in doubt as to what he meant: 'It was a quarter the invention of the performer, a quarter complete lunacy, a quarter made no sense at all, and the rest was La Fontaine,' which enabled Mme de Morienval to continue to believe that what they had just heard was not 'Les Deux Pigeons' by La Fontaine, but a new version, a quarter of which at the most was by La Fontaine, which news, owing to these people's extraordinary ignorance, came as a surprise to nobody.

But one of Bloch's friends having arrived late, Bloch had the pleasure of asking him whether he had ever heard Rachel, giving him an extraordinary account of her delivery, exaggerating it, and suddenly discovering, as he spoke, a curious pleasure in revealing this modernist diction to another person which he had not experienced at all in hearing it. Then Bloch, with exaggerated feeling, congratulated Rachel in his high-pitched voice and introduced his friend, who declared that he admired her above all others; and Rachel, who now knew ladies from the highest ranks of society, and unconsciously copied them, replied: 'Oh, I'm terribly flattered, so honoured by your appreciation.' Bloch's friend asked her what she thought of La Berma. 'Poor woman, it seems she's in complete poverty. She wasn't without, I won't say talent, because at bottom she didn't possess true talent, she only liked the most horrible things, but she had skill; her acting was more alive than other actresses', and personally she was very decent, generous, ruined herself for other people, and now of course it's been a long time since she's earned anything at all, because for years the public hasn't liked the sort of things she does . . . But anyway, she added with a laugh, I'm not really old enough to have heard her, naturally, except right at the end of her career when I was too young myself to form a judgment. – But wasn't she a particularly good speaker of verse?' ventured Bloch's friend to flatter Rachel, who replied: 'Oh, she couldn't do it to save her life; it always came out sounding like prose, or Chinese, or Volapük, or anything except like a line of verse.'

But I was becoming aware that the passing of time does not necessarily bring about progress in the arts. Just as some author of the seventeenth century, who knew nothing of the French Revolution, or the discoveries of science, or the war, may be better than some writers of today, and just as even Fagon[114] may have been as great a doctor as du Boulbon (superior genius compensating here for the shortfall in knowledge), so La Berma was, as they say, head and shoulders above Rachel, and time, by making Rachel a star at the same time as Elstir, had overrated a mediocrity and consecrated a genius.

It should come as no surprise that Saint-Loup's former mistress should run La Berma down. She would have done it when she was young. Even if she would not have done it then, she certainly would now. If a society woman of the highest intelligence and with the kindest of natures becomes an actress, displays great talent in her new occupation, and meets with unalloyed success, one will be surprised, finding oneself in her company after some long time, to hear not her own way of speaking but the language of actresses, the special cattiness with which they refer to their colleagues, everything that rubs off on to a human being from the experience of 'thirty years in the theatre'. Rachel had all this, and she did not start off in society.

'Say what you like, it is wonderful, it has shape, it has character, it's intelligent, nobody has ever spoken the lines like that,' said the Duchesse, anxious in case Gilberte should start running it down. But she moved away towards another group to avoid a conflict with her aunt, who, none the less, went on to make a series of quite banal remarks to me about Rachel. Mme de Guermantes, in her declining years, had felt a new awakening of curiosity within her. She had nothing more to learn from society. The idea that she occupied the foremost position in it was as evident to her as the height of the blue sky above the earth. She did not believe there was any need to consolidate a position she deemed unshakeable. On the other hand, reading, going to the theatre, she would have wished each activity to go on for longer than it did; just as in the past, in the narrow little garden where one would drink orangeade, all that was most exquisite in the best society would come informally, among the scented breezes of evening and the haze of pollen, to sustain in her the taste for grand society, so now a different appetite made her want to know the reasons for this or that literary controversy, to know authors, even to know actresses. Her jaded mind demanded a new kind of nourishment. In order to get to know authors and actresses, she approached women with whom in the past she would not have wished to exchange cards, and who now turned their friendship with the editor of some review to good account in the hope of attracting the Duchesse to their houses. The first actress to be a guest thought that she was the only one in a remarkable setting, a setting which seemed less impressive to the second when she saw who had preceded her. The Duchesse, because on some evenings she received sovereigns, thought that her social position continued unchanged. In reality she, the only one who was truly of unalloyed blood, she who, having been born a Guermantes could sign herself 'Guermantes-Guermantes' when she did not sign herself 'The Duchesse de Guermantes', she who seemed something unusually precious even to her sisters-in-law, like a Moses saved from the waters, a Christ escaped into Egypt, a Louis XVII freed from the Temple, the purest of the pure, she had now, sacrificing no doubt to that hereditary need for spiritual nourishment which had brought about the social decline of Mme de Villeparisis, become herself a Mme de Villeparisis, at whose house snobbish women were afraid they might meet some unsuitable man or woman, and whom the younger people, seeing her present situation without knowing what had preceded it, imagined her to be a Guermantes from an inferior vintage, from an inferior year, a declassified Guermantes.

But since the best writers often cease, as old age approaches, or after an excess of production, to have any talent, society women may certainly be excused for no longer being witty after a certain time. Swann could no longer recognize in the harsh wit of the Duchesse de Guermantes the gentle humour of the Princesse de Laumes. Late in life, tiredness or even the least exertion made Mme de Guermantes say a huge number of silly things. Of course she was capable at any moment, as happened several times in the course of this party, of becoming once more the woman I had known and of making witty social observations. But alongside that, it frequently happened that, sparkling beneath the beautiful eyes, this conversation, which for so long had held intellectual sway over the most eminent men in Paris, still shone but, so to speak, emptily, to no effect. When the moment came for her to make a witty remark, she would pause for the same number of seconds as before, seemed to be hesitating, to be on the verge of production, but the joke that then appeared would be completely flat. Yet how few people noticed this! The continuity of the procedure made them believe in the continued survival of the wit, in the same way as people sometimes, superstitiously attached to some brand of pâtisserie, continue to order their petits fours from the same firm without noticing that they have become revolting. During the war, the Duchesse had already shown some signs of this diminution of her powers. If somebody said the word culture, she would stop him, smile, her eyes would light up, and she would come out with: 'K-k-k-kultur', which made her friends laugh, thinking this to be another illustration of the Guermantes wit. And indeed it was the same mould, the same intonation, the same smile as had delighted Bergotte, who for his part had also kept his characteristic sentence rhythms, his interjections, his ellipses, his epithets, though all in order to say nothing. But the newcomers were surprised and would sometimes say, if they had not chanced upon a day when she was funny and 'in full possession of her faculties', 'How stupid she is!'

The Duchesse, it should be said, arranged matters so as to contain her slumming and not allow it to affect those members of her family from whom she derived her aristocratic aura. If, in order to fulfil her role as patroness of the arts, she had invited a minister or a painter to the theatre, and one or other had naïvely asked whether her husband or sister-in-law were not in the audience, the Duchesse, covering her nervousness with a bold show of hauteur, would arrogantly reply: 'I have no idea. Once I leave my house, I have no knowledge of what my family does. As far as any politicians or artists are concerned, I am a widow.' In this way she prevented over-attentive social climbers from being rebuffed – and herself from being reprimanded – by Mme de Marsantes and by Basin.

'I can't tell you what a tremendous pleasure it is to see you. Good heavens, when was the last time I saw you? . . . – I was calling on Mme d'Agrigente, I often used to see you there. Naturally I used to go there often, dear boy, as Basin was in love with her at the time. You were always most likely to find me at the house of his most recent sweetheart, because he would say: "You must go and visit her, without fail." Actually, I thought there was something a little inappropriate about the kind of "thank-you" calls he sent me to make once he had achieved his aim. I got used to it quite quickly, but the most boring thing about it was that I had to keep up the friendship after he had broken off the relationship. It always made me think of that line by Victor Hugo:

Emporte le bonheur and laisse-moi *l'ennui*[115]

'Of course, as the poem goes on to say, I still entered with a smile, but really it wasn't fair, he ought to have left me the right to be fickle where his mistresses were concerned, because once I had accumulated all of his rejects, I ended up not having an afternoon to myself. All the same, that seems a relatively pleasant period compared with the present. Of course, the fact that he has started deceiving me again can only be flattering, because it makes me feel younger. But I preferred his old way of doing it. You know, it's been such a long time since he was last unfaithful to me that he couldn't remember how to do it. Still, we get on all right together, we talk to each other, we're even fond of each other, up to a point,' the Duchesse said to me, fearful in case I should think that they had separated completely, rather as one says of somebody who is very ill: 'But he can still speak quite well, I read to him for an hour this morning.' She added: 'I'll go and tell him you're here, he'd like to see you.' And she went over to the Duc, who was sitting beside a lady on a sofa, deep in conversation. I was surprised to see that he was almost the same, merely with whiter hair, being still as majestic and as handsome as ever. But when he saw his wife coming to talk to him, he looked so furious that all she could do was retreat. 'He is busy, I don't know what he's doing, you'll see in a minute,' Mme de Guermantes said to me, preferring to leave me to work things out for myself.

Bloch having come up to us and asked, on behalf of his American lady, the identity of a young duchess who was among the guests, I replied that she was the niece of M. de Bréauté, at which, as the name meant nothing to him, Bloch asked for further explanation. 'Oh, Bréauté!' exclaimed Mme de Guermantes, turning to me, 'you remember all that, how ancient it all seems, how long ago! Well, he was a snob. These were people who lived near my mother-in-law's house. Not of any interest to you, M. Bloch; though our friend here may be amused by it, since he knew all those people long ago, at the same time as I did,' added Mme de Guermantes, gesturing towards me, and demonstrating by these words, in a number of ways, just how long a period of time had elapsed. Mme de Guermantes's friendships and opinions had been so often renewed since then that she retrospectively thought of her charming Babal as a snob. In another connection, not only was he now a thing of the past, but, something I had never realized when in my first days in society I had taken him for one of the essential notables of Paris, someone who would always be associated with its social history, like Colbert with that of the reign of Louis

XIV, he too bore the mark of his provincial origins, having been a country neighbour of the old Duchesse, which was the guise in which the Princesse de Laumes had made his acquaintance. Yet now Bréauté, stripped of his wit, and relegated to years so long ago that he dated them (which proved that he had since been entirely forgotten by the Duchesse) and to the neighbourhood of the Guermantes, was, which I could never have believed on that first evening at the Opéra-Comique when he had appeared to me like a god of the sea inhabiting his underwater lair, a link between the Duchesse and me, because she recalled that I had known him, therefore that I was a friend of hers, if not sprung from the same social world as her at least an inhabitant of the same social world as her for much longer than many of the people present, she recalled this, but so inaccurately as to have forgotten certain details which had seemed to me then to be essential, namely that I did not go to Guermantes, and was only a middle-class boy from Combray at the time when she came to Mlle Percepied's nuptial mass, and that for the whole year after her appearance at the Opéra-Comique, despite all Saint-Loup's entreaties she never invited me to her house. To me this seemed terribly important, because it was precisely at this point that the life of the Duchesse de Guermantes appeared to me to be a paradise I would never enter. But to her it just seemed to be a part of the same ordinary life as always and, since after a certain point I had dined with her often and had also, even before that, been a friend of her aunt and her nephew, she was not entirely clear at what period our friendship had begun, and was unaware of the serious anachronism she was committing by making this friendship begin several years too soon. For this meant that I would have known the Mme de Guermantes of the name of Guermantes, which it was impossible to know, and that I would have been received within the name with the golden syllables, in the Faubourg Saint-Germain, whereas I had quite simply been to dinner in the house of a lady who already by then meant nothing more to me than any other, and who had occasionally invited me, not to descend into the underwater kingdom of the Nereids, but to spend the evening in her cousin's box at the theatre. 'If you want to know about Bréauté, and it's not really worth the bother, she added, turning to Bloch, ask our friend here (who is a hundred times more worth knowing): he must have dined at my house with him at least fifty times. Wasn't it in my house that you met him? At any rate, that's where you met Swann.' I was as much surprised that she could have thought that I might have met M. de Bréauté anywhere else, and therefore that I might have moved in those circles before I met her, as I was to realize that she thought that it was in her house that I had met Swann. Less untruthfully than Gilberte, when she said of Bréauté: 'He is an old country neighbour of mine, I do enjoy talking about Tansonville with him' when in the past he never visited them at Tansonville, I could have said: 'He was a country neighbour of ours who often used to come and see us in the evening' of Swann, who in fact reminded me of things quite other than the Guermantes.

'I don't know what to tell you. He was a man who talked about nothing but royalty. He had a stock of odd anecdotes about some of the Guermantes, and my mother-in-law, and Mme de Varambon before she joined the Princess of Parma's household. But who remembers Mme de Varambon these days? Our friend here, yes, he knew all those people, but all that's gone now, they are not even names any longer, and what's more they didn't deserve to be remembered.' And I realized, despite the unity which society appears to be, and in which in fact social relations reach their maximum concentration and everything is interconnected, that provinces remain within it, or at least that Time creates provinces, the names of which change, and which are no longer comprehensible to those who arrive there only when the pattern has altered. 'She was a good lady who said things of unbelievable silliness,' went on the Duchesse, who, insensitive to that poetry of the incomprehensible which is one of the effects of time, drew out the comic element in everything, anything that resembled the Meilhac[116] type of literature, or that nourished the Guermantes wit. 'There was a time when she had an obsession with taking a kind of cough drop they used to have then, which was called' (she continued, laughing herself at the name once so special, so widely known, and now so unfamiliar to the people around her) 'Géraudel pastilles. "Mme de Varambon, my mother-in-law, said to her, if you carry on wolfing those Géraudel pastilles like that you'll give yourself a stomach ache. – But Mme la Duchesse, replied Mme de Varambon, how could they possibly give me a stomach ache when they go straight to the bronchial tubes?" And she's also the one who said: "The Duchesse has a beautiful cow, so beautiful that people are always thinking it's a bull."' And Mme de Guermantes would happily have carried on telling stories about Mme de Varambon, of which we knew hundreds, but we realized that in Bloch's ill-informed memory her name did not evoke any of the images which rose up for us as soon as Mme de Varambon or M. de Bréauté or the Prince d'Agrigente were mentioned, and for that very reason, perhaps became endowed in his mind with a glamour which I knew to be exaggerated but which I could understand, although not because I had felt it myself, our own mistakes and our own absurdities rarely having the effect, even when we have seen through them, of making us more indulgent to those of others.

The reality, which was really quite insignificant, of this distant time was so lost that when somebody not far away from me asked whether the Tansonville estate had come to Gilberte from her father M. de Forcheville, somebody else replied: 'Oh, no! It comes from her husband's family. It's all on the Guermantes side. Tansonville is very close to Guermantes. It belonged to Mme de Marsantes, the mother of the Marquis de Saint-Loup. Only it was very heavily mortgaged. So it was given to him as a wedding present and redeemed out of Mlle de Forcheville's fortune.' And another time, somebody to whom I mentioned Swann, trying to find a way of explaining what it meant to be a man of wit in that period, said: 'Oh yes, the Duchesse de Guermantes told me some witticisms of his; he was an old gentleman whom you met at her house, I think?'[117]

The past had been so transformed in the Duchesse's mind (or the demarcations which existed in mine had always been so absent from hers that things which had constituted events for me had passed unnoticed by her) that she could imagine that I had met Swann in her house and M. de Bréauté elsewhere, thus constructing for me a past as a figure in society which she extended back too far. For this sense of the passage of time that I had just acquired was one the Duchesse also possessed, in her case with an opposite illusion to mine of believing it to be shorter than it was, she, on the contrary, exaggerating it, making it go too far back, most notably in respect of that immeasurable line

of demarcation between the time when she became first a name for
me, then the object of my love – and the time when she had been no
more to me than any other society woman. I went to her house only
in this second period, when for me she was a different person. But in
her own eyes, these differences did not exist, and she would not have
thought it at all odd that I might have been in her house two years
earlier, not knowing that she was a different person, even with a
different door-mat, and her personality not revealing to her, as it did
to me, any discontinuity.

I said to the Duchesse de Guermantes: 'That reminds me of the first
evening I went to the Princesse de Guermantes's, when I thought I
might not have been invited and that they would show me the door,
and when you wore a red dress and red shoes. – Good heavens,
that was all so long ago,' said the Duchesse de Guermantes, thus
accentuating my impression of the passage of time. She gazed melancholically into the middle distance, yet dwelt particularly on the red
dress. I asked her to describe it for me, which she was glad to do. 'You
couldn't wear something like that now. But it was the sort of dress we
used to wear in those days. – But surely it was very pretty, wasn't it?'
I said. She was always afraid of giving herself away by what she said,
of saying something which might diminish her in other people's eyes.
'Oh, yes, I thought it was very pretty, myself. People don't wear that
sort of thing now because it isn't done at present. But it'll come back,
all fashions come round again, in dresses, in music, in painting,' she
added forcefully, for she thought there was something rather original
about this philosophy. But the sadness of growing old brought with it
a sense of tiredness which her smile struggled to overcome: 'Are you
sure about the red shoes? I thought that they were gold.' I assured her
that they were for ever fixed in my mind, without saying anything
about the circumstances which enabled me to be so certain. 'It is very
kind of you to remember that,' she said to me fondly, for women refer
to any recollection of their beauty as kindness, as artists do when you
admire their work. Besides, however distant the past may be, when
one is as capable a woman as the Duchesse, it need not have been
forgotten. 'Do you remember', she said to me, as a way of thanking
me for my memory of her dress and her shoes, 'that we brought you

home, Basin and I? You had a girl who was coming to see you after midnight. Basin laughed so much at the thought of somebody calling on you at that time of night.' Albertine had indeed come to see me after the Princesse de Guermantes's party. I remembered it as clearly as the Duchesse, although Albertine was as unimportant to me now as she would have been to Mme de Guermantes, if Mme de Guermantes had known that the girl because of whom I had not been able to go in was Albertine. Long after the poor departed have gone from our hearts, their insignificant dust continues to be mingled, to be used as an alloy, with the events of the past. And although we no longer love them, it sometimes happens that when we are describing a room, or a garden path, or a road, where at a certain time they once were, we are obliged, in order to fill the gap they occupied, to mention them, but without missing them, without naming them even, and without enabling anybody else to identify them. (Mme de Guermantes was hardly likely to have identified the girl who was due to visit me that evening, had never known who she was and only mentioned her because of the eccentricity of the time and the circumstances.) Such are the final, and unenviable, forms in which we survive.

If the judgments pronounced by the Duchesse on Rachel were, in themselves, ordinary, they none the less interested me in that they too marked a new hour on the dial. For the Duchesse had not forgotten, any more than had Rachel, the evening which the latter had spent in her house, but her memory had undergone no less of a transformation. 'I must say, she told me, I'm all the more interested to hear her, and to hear her recite, because it was I who discovered her, saw how good she was, sang her praises and made people take notice of her at a time when she had no reputation and everybody thought she was ridiculous. Yes, my dear friend, it may come as a surprise to you, but the first place she ever performed in public was in my house! Oh yes, while all the so-called avant-garde, like my new cousin,' pointing ironically towards the Princesse de Guermantes, who, in Oriane's eyes, was still Mme Verdurin, 'would have left her to die of hunger without condescending to hear her, I had decided that she was interesting, and I had offered her a fee to come and perform in my house in front of the most distinguished and influential audience I could get. I may say, though the phrase is a bit silly and pretentious, for in the end real talent doesn't need any help, that I launched her. But of course she didn't need me.' I made a vague gesture of protest, and saw that Mme de Guermantes was quite ready to accept the opposite argument: 'You disagree? You think talent needs supporting, needs someone to put it under the spotlight? You may be right, you know. It's funny, Dumas used to tell me exactly the same thing, years ago. In this case I'm extremely flattered if I've been able to do anything, however small, obviously not to improve her talent, but to promote the reputation of an artist like her.' Mme de Guermantes preferred to abandon her idea that talent will break through on its own, like an abscess, because the alternative was more flattering for her, but also because for some time now, receiving newcomers to society, and being generally tired, she had become almost humble, questioning other people and asking their opinions before forming one of her own. 'I don't need to tell you, she went on, that the intelligent public that calls itself society did not understand a word of what she did. They complained, they laughed. It was no good my saying to them: "This is new, this is interesting, it's something that's never been done before," they didn't believe me, as nobody has ever believed me about anything. It was just the same with the piece she gave, it was something by Maeterlinck, terribly well-known now, but then everybody thought it was absurd, except me, I thought it was wonderful. It does strike me as surprising, when I think about it, that a country girl like me, with only the same education as the other provincial girls, should have had such an instant affinity for things like that. I couldn't have told you why, of course, but I liked it, it moved me; and Basin, who is not a sensitive soul, was struck by the effect that it had on me. He said to me: "I don't want you listening to this nonsense any more, it's making you ill." And it was true, people think I'm an unfeeling woman, when really I'm just a bundle of nerves.'

At this moment an unexpected incident occurred. A footman came to tell Rachel that La Berma's daughter and son-in-law were asking to speak to her. We have seen how La Berma's daughter had resisted her husband's wish that Rachel should be asked to invite them. But after the departure of the one guest, the young couple had grown increasingly annoyed as they sat with their mother, the thought that other people were enjoying themselves tormented them, and so, taking advantage of a moment when La Berma had retired to her room, spitting a little blood, they had hastily thrown on some smarter clothes, called a cab and come to the Princesse de Guermantes's without an invitation. Rachel, surmising what had happened and secretly flattered, put on an arrogant tone of voice and told the footman that she could not be disturbed, that they should write a note to explain the purpose of their unusual approach. The footman returned bearing a card on which La Berma's daughter had scribbled that she and her husband had been unable to resist their desire to hear Rachel, and begged to be allowed to enter. Rachel smiled at the transparency of their pretext and at her own triumph. She sent back word that she was very sorry but that she had finished her recital. The footmen in the ante-room, where the couple's wait still continued, were already beginning to snigger at the two rejected supplicants. The shame of being snubbed, and her recollection of Rachel's insignificance in comparison to her mother, drove La Berma's daughter to pursue to its ultimate conclusion a process on which she had originally only ventured in a search for entertainment. She sent to ask whether Rachel, as a favour, might allow her, even though she had not been able to hear her, to shake her hand. Rachel was at that moment talking to an Italian prince, said to be fascinated by the attraction of her large fortune, the origin of which was somewhat concealed by her social connections; she summed up the reversal of position which now put the children of La Berma at her feet. After giving a comic account of the incident to everybody, she asked that the young couple be allowed to enter, which they did without needing to be asked twice, ruining at a stroke La Berma's position in society, as they had destroyed her health. Rachel understood this, and also realized that gracious civility would give her a reputation in society for kindness and them a reputation for craven self-abasement, something which a denial would not have achieved. So she received them with exaggeratedly open arms, saying in the manner of an admired patroness able, for a moment, to ignore her grandeur: 'Oh, you're here, I'm so glad. The Princesse will be delighted.' Unaware that in theatrical circles it was believed that the invitations came from her, she may perhaps have been afraid that by denying entry to La Berma's children she might make them doubt, not her good-will, which would not have bothered her, but her influence. The Duchesse de Guermantes moved away instinctively, for the more anyone seemed to be striving for social acceptance, the more they sank in her esteem. She found nothing to respect in the present situation except Rachel's kindness, and would have turned her back on La Berma's children if they had been introduced to her. Rachel however was already composing in her head the gracious phrases with which she would crush La Berma backstage the following day: 'I was heartbroken, mortified, that your daughter had to wait so long outside the door. If I had only realized! She sent me in card after card.' She was delighted to deal La Berma this blow. Yet she might have shrunk from delivering it if she had known that it would be fatal. People like to have victims, but they like to let them stay alive, not put themselves in the wrong instead. Besides, what had she done that was wrong? A few days later she was to say, with a laugh: 'It's all a bit much, I wanted to be nicer to her children than she ever was to me, and because of that they're practically saying I murdered her. The Duchesse will be my witness.' It seems that, all the unpleasant emotions and all the artificiality of the theatrical life descending to their children without the concomitant relief of passionate work that the mothers had, the great actresses often die victims of domestic conspiracies woven around them, as happened to them so many times at the end of the plays in which they acted.

The Duchesse's life, nevertheless, was very unhappy, and for a reason one incidental consequence of which was that the Duc, likewise, had started to move in lower social circles. Long tamed now by his advancing years, though still robust, he had ceased to be unfaithful to Mme de Guermantes, but had suddenly fallen in love with Mme de Forcheville, without anyone quite knowing how or when the liaison had started. (When one considered how old Mme de Forcheville must now be, it seemed extraordinary. But she may perhaps have started her life of affairs very young. And then there are women whom one sees each decade in a new incarnation, having new love affairs, sometimes when one had thought that they were dead, causing the despair of young wives who are abandoned for them by their husbands.)

But this liaison had assumed such proportions that the old man, imitating in this latest affair the manner in which he had conducted his earlier ones, sequestrated his mistress to the point that, if my love for Albertine had repeated, with major variations, Swann's love of Odette, M. de Guermantes's love for her recalled my love for Albertine. She was required to lunch and dine with him, he was always at her house; she paraded him in front of her friends, who without her would never have come into contact with the Duc de Guermantes, and who came there in order to meet him, somewhat as one might go to the house of a courtesan to meet a sovereign, her lover. Mme de Forcheville, of course, had long been part of society. But reverting late in life to being a kept woman, and kept by such a proud old man, who was nevertheless the person of importance in her household, she minimized her own position, trying to have only wraps which he liked and food which he liked, and flattering her friends by telling them that she had been talking to him about them, as if she were telling my great-uncle that she had been speaking about him to the Grand-Duc, who was sending him some cigarettes; in a word, she was tending, despite everything she had attained by achieving her social position, under the pressure of these new circumstances, to become once more, just as she had appeared to me in my childhood, the lady in pink. My uncle Adolphe, of course, had been dead for many years. But does the substitution around us of new people for those who were formerly there prevent us from starting the same life over again? She had doubtless adapted to the new circumstances out of cupidity, and also because having been much sought after in society as the mother of a marriageable daughter, and then dropped as soon as Gilberte had married Saint-Loup, she thought that the Duc de Guermantes, who would have done anything for her, would enlist a number of duchesses who would be delighted to do their friend Oriane a bad turn; and lastly perhaps because she was stimulated by the distress of the Duchesse, over whom a feminine feeling of rivalry made her glad to prevail.

The liaison with Mme de Forcheville, a liaison which was merely an imitation of his previous relationships, had just for the second time lost the Duc de Guermantes the presidency of the Jockey Club and a vacant seat in the Académie des Beaux-arts, just as the way of life of M. de Charlus, publicly linked with that of Jupien, had cost him the presidency of the Union, as well as that of the Société des amis du vieux Paris. The two brothers, so different in their tastes, had therefore come into disrepute through the same indolence, and the same lack of will, which were observable, but in a less unprepossessing fashion, in the Duc de Guermantes their grandfather, a member of the Académie française, but which, in the two grandsons, had allowed a natural taste in one, and what is regarded as not being such in the other, to damage their position in society.

Up until his death, Saint-Loup used faithfully to bring his wife to see her.[118] Were the two of them not the heirs both of M. de Guermantes and of Odette, who would herself moreover be the principal heir of the Duc? Even the fastidious Courvoisier nephews, and Mme de Marsantes, the Princesse de Trania, came there in the hope of a legacy, without worrying about the pain that might cause to Mme de Guermantes, of whom of Odette, stung by her contempt, spoke very ill.

The old Duc de Guermantes no longer went out, for he spent all his days and his evenings with her. But today he did come for a moment to see her, despite the irritation of meeting his wife. I had not noticed him, and probably would not have recognized him if he had not been clearly pointed out to me. He was little more than a ruin, but a superb one, or perhaps not even a ruin so much as that most romantic of beautiful objects, a rock in a storm. Lashed on all sides by the waves of suffering, of anger at suffering, and of the rising tide of death, by which he was surrounded, his face, crumbling like a block of stone, still kept the style, the hauteur I had always admired; it was worn away like one of those beautiful but half-obliterated classical heads with which we are still always glad to ornament a study. Only it seemed to belong to a period more ancient than before, not only because of the way in which its once more lustrous material had become rough and broken, but because an expression of subtlety and playfulness had been succeeded by an involuntary, an unconscious expression, constructed out of illness, the struggle against death, mere resistance and the difficulty of living. The arteries, all their suppleness gone, had given his once beaming face a sculptural rigidity. And although the Duc had no inkling of this, his neck, his cheeks, his forehead all displayed indications that the human being within, as if obliged to cling tenaciously to each minute, seemed to be buffeted by a tragic gale, while the white strands of his thinner but still magnificent hair lashed with their spume the flooded promontory of his face. And I realized that, like the strange, unique glints which only the approach of an all-engulfing storm gives to rocks normally a different colour, the leaden grey of the stiff, worn cheeks, the almost white, foam-flecked grey of the swelling locks, the weak light still emanating from the scarcely seeing eyes, were not unreal colours, far from it, all too real, but uncanny, and borrowed from the palette and the lighting, inimitable in its terrifying and prophetic shades of darkness, of old age, and of the proximity of death.

The Duc stayed no more than a few minutes, long enough for me to have understood that Odette, attentive to her younger suitors, was treating him with contempt. But the strange thing was that he who in the past had been almost ridiculous when he behaved like a stage-king had taken on a genuinely grand appearance, rather like his brother, whom old age, by stripping him of all inessentials, made him resemble. And he, once proud, like his brother although in a different way, seemed almost deferential, although also in a different way. For he had never undergone the same decline as his brother, reduced by forgetfulness brought on by illness to greeting with politeness people whom he would once have scorned to know. But he was very old, and as he tried painfully to pass through the door and descend the staircase on his way out, old age, which is really the most wretched human state and which hurls people from their life's eminence as if they were kings in Greek tragedies, old age, by forcing him to stop on the *via dolorosa* that life becomes for the impotent and endangered, to wipe his dripping brow, to grope around as his eyes searched for a step which eluded him, because he really needed support for his faltering steps, and for his clouded eyes, giving him without his knowing it an air of gently and timidly imploring it from other people, more than august, old age had made him suppliant.

Unable to do without Odette, in whose house he was always installed in the same armchair, from which old age and gout made it difficult to extricate himself, M. de Guermantes allowed her to receive friends who were only too happy to be presented to the Duc, to leave the conversation to him, to hear him talking about society in the old days, about the Marquise of Villeparisis, and the Duc de Chartres.

Thus in the Faubourg Saint-Germain, the apparently impregnable positions of the Duc and the Duchesse de Guermantes and of Baron de Charlus had lost their inviolability, as all things change in this world, by the action of an internal principle which nobody had ever thought about: in the case of M. de Charlus this was his love for Charlie, which had made him a slave of the Verdurins, and led to the softening of his brain; in Mme de Guermantes, a taste for novelty and for art; in M. de Guermantes an exclusive love affair, like several similar ones he had already had in his life, but which the weakness of age rendered more tyrannical, and to the weaknesses of which the strict standards of the Duchesse's salon, where the Duc no longer appeared and which anyway had almost ceased to function socially, could no longer oppose their denial, or work their social redemption. This is how the pattern of things changes in this world; how the focus of empires, registers of wealth, and titles to social positions, everything that seemed permanent is perpetually recast, and the eyes of a man may over the course of a lifetime contemplate the most complete change precisely in those places where it had appeared most impossible.

From time to time, under the gaze of the old paintings assembled by Swann in a 'collector's' arrangement which added a finishing touch to the antiquated, old-fashioned nature of this scene, with this very 'Restoration' Duc and this perfectly 'Second Empire' courtesan in one of the wraps he liked so much, the lady in pink would interrupt him with her bright chatter; he would stop dead and glare at her, fiercely. Perhaps he had come to realize that she too, like the Duchesse, sometimes said silly things; perhaps, in an old man's hallucination, he thought that it was a badly timed witticism from Mme de Guermantes that had interrupted him, believing himself to be in the Guermantes *hôtel*, as chained animals might imagine for a moment that they are free in the deserts of Africa again. And brusquely lifting his head, with his little round yellow eyes, which had a wild animal gleam to them, he would fix her with one of the looks which had sometimes, when I was visiting Mme de Guermantes, and he thought she was talking too much, made me tremble. Thus the Duc stared for moment at the audacious lady in pink. But she stared back, her gaze not leaving his eyes, and at the end of a few moments which seemed very long to those watching, the vanquished old beast, remembering that he was not free at home with the Duchesse, in that Sahara whose entrance is marked by the door-mat at the top of the stairs, but in his cage in the Zoological Gardens at Mme de Forcheville's, sank his head, from which still hung a thick mane, which might equally have been blond or white, back between his shoulders, and went on with his story. He seemed not to have taken in what Mme de Forcheville had tried to say, which usually did not make much sense anyway. He allowed her to have friends to dinner with him; but, out of a habit derived from his earlier affairs, which would have come as no surprise to Odette, used to the same thing from Swann, and which struck a sympathetic chord in me, as it reminded me of my life with Albertine, always insisted that these persons should leave early so that he might be the last to say good-night to Odette. Needless to say, he had scarcely left before she would go out to meet other people. But the Duc never suspected this, or preferred not to seem to suspect it: the eyesight of old men weakens as their hearing becomes less acute, their acumen grows dull, and tiredness itself causes them to relax their vigilance. At a certain age Jupiter is ineluctably transformed into a character out of Molière – not the Olympian lover of Alcmene, either, but a laughable Géronte.[119] Moreover, Odette deceived M. de Guermantes, as she looked after him, without charm and without nobility. She was indifferent in this role as in all her others. Not because life had not frequently given her leading roles, but because she did not know how to play them.

And in fact each time I tried to see her in the days following the party I was unsuccessful, for M. de Guermantes, in an attempt to satisfy the demands both of his health and of his jealousy, permitted her to attend only daytime parties, with the further condition that no dances were allowed. She frankly admitted to me the confinement in which she was kept, for several reasons. The principal one was that, although I had written only a few articles and published some essays, she had the idea that I was a well-known author, which even caused her naïvely to say, recalling the time when I used to go to the Allée des Acacias to see her pass by, and later when I used to go to her house: 'Oh, if only I'd known that one day you'd be a great writer!' Now, having heard that writers enjoy being with women because they can gather material, getting them to recount their love affairs, she now reverted, in order to interest me, to being a mere cocotte. She would tell me stories: 'Well, once there was a man who was crazy about me and whom I was desperately in love with, too. We led a heavenly life. He had to travel to America, I was to be going with him. The day before the departure I decided it was better not to let a love which couldn't always remain so perfect just slowly fade away. We had a last evening together, when he still thought I was going with him, then a night of mad passion; in his arms I felt infinite joy, and despair at the thought that I would never see him again. In the morning I went and gave my ticket to a traveller I didn't know. He wanted me to let him pay for it at least. I replied: "No, you're doing me such a favour by taking it, I don't want any money."' Then there was another story: 'One day I was in the Champs-Élysées and M. de Bréauté, whom I'd only ever met once, started staring at me so insistently that I stopped and asked him why he thought he was looking at me like that. He replied: "I'm looking at you because you've got a ridiculous hat." It was true. It was a little hat with pansies, fashions were ghastly then. But I was furious, I said to him: "I won't allow you to speak to me like that." It started to rain. I said to him: "I would only forgive you if you had a carriage. – Well, it happens that I do have one, and I shall accompany you. – No, I'll be pleased to take your carriage, but I don't want you." I climbed into the carriage, he went off in the rain. But in the evening he turns up at my house. We had two years of wild love. Come and have tea with me some time and I'll tell you how I met M. de Forcheville. In point of fact, she said with a melancholy expression, I have spent my life cloistered away, because all my great love affairs have been with men who were terribly jealous. I'm not talking about M. de Forcheville, as he was basically commonplace, and I have only

ever really been able to love intelligent men. But, you see, M. Swann
was as jealous as the poor Duc is; and I do without everything for his
sake because I know that he's not happy at home. With M. Swann, I
was madly in love with him, and I think it is fair enough to sacrifice
dancing and society and everything else if it gives pleasure to the man
you love, or even if it stops him worrying. Poor Charles, he was so
intelligent, so fascinating, exactly the kind of man I liked best.' And
perhaps this was true. There had been a time when she had liked
Swann, precisely the time when she was not 'his type'. Indeed, to tell
the truth, 'his type' was something that, even later, she had never been.
Yet he had loved her so much then, and so painfully. He had been
surprised, later, by that contradiction. But it need not be a contradiction
if we think what a large proportion of the suffering in men's lives is
caused by women 'who were not their type'. Perhaps there are a
number of reasons for this; first, because they are not 'your type' one
allows oneself, at the beginning, to be loved without loving, as a result
of which one lets habit get a hold on one's life which it would not
have done with a woman who was 'our type' who, feeling herself
desired, would have put up some resistance, would have agreed to
meet only occasionally, and would not have made herself so much at
home in every hour of our day that later, if love does come and we
suddenly start to miss her, because of a quarrel or because she is
travelling and has sent us no news, the pain of her absence tugs not at
one bond but a thousand. Then, this habit is sentimental because there
is no great physical desire at its heart, and if love does develop the
mind works much harder: there is a romance instead of a need. We do
not mistrust women who are not 'our type', we let them love us, and
if we then come to love them, we love them a hundred times more
than the others, without ever experiencing in their arms the satisfaction
of gratified desire. For these reasons and many others, the fact that we
have our greatest moments of unhappiness with women who are not
'our type' is not simply a product of that mocking destiny which brings
our happiness into being only in the form which pleases us least. A
woman who is 'our type' is rarely dangerous, for she wants nothing
from us, she makes us content, rapidly leaves us, does not install
herself in our lives, and what is dangerous and liable to create suffering

in love is not the woman herself, it is her continuous daily presence, our constant curiosity about what she is doing; it is not the woman, it is habit.

I was cowardly enough to say that it was kind and generous of her, but I knew how false this was, and how much of her openness was mingled with lies. I thought with horror, as she told me more and more of her adventures, of all that Swann had been unaware of, which would have made him suffer so much because he had made this one person the focus of his sensitivity, and which he almost certainly guessed, merely from the look in her eyes when she saw an unknown man, or woman, who attracted her. She did it, in the end, simply to give me what she thought were subjects for novels. She was wrong, not because she had not provided the reserves of my imagination with an abundance of material, but because this had been done in a much more involuntary fashion and by an act that I initiated myself as I drew out from her, without her knowledge, the laws of her life.

M. de Guermantes kept his thunders solely for the Duchesse, to whose easy-going friendships Mme de Forcheville had not failed to draw his angry attention. So the Duchesse was very unhappy. It is true that M. de Charlus, with whom I discussed it once, claimed that the original faults had not been on his brother's part, that the legend of the Duchesse's purity had in reality been constructed over an incalculable number of cunningly dissimulated intrigues. I had never heard anybody else say that. In the eyes of almost everybody, Mme de Guermantes was a totally different woman. The universally accepted idea was that she had always been irreproachable. I was unable to decide which of these two ideas conformed to the truth, the truth which three out of four people are almost always unaware of. I remembered very clearly some blue-eyed roving glances from the Duchesse de Guermantes in the nave at Combray. But in truth neither of the ideas was refuted by these, each position being capable of giving them a different and equally acceptable meaning. In my foolishness, as a boy, I had taken them for a moment as looks of love aimed at me. Since then I had come to realize that they were merely the benevolent looks of a sovereign lady, like the one in the stained-glass windows of the church, towards her vassals. Had I now to believe that my first idea had been the right one, and that if the Duchesse had never subsequently spoken to me of love, this was because she was afraid of compromising herself with a friend of her aunt and her nephew rather than with an unknown boy encountered by chance in Saint-Hilaire de Combray?

The Duchesse may have felt glad for a moment to feel that her past was more firmly grounded for being shared with me, but in answer to some questions which I put to her about the provincial background of M. de Bréauté, whom at the time I had scarcely distinguished from M. de Sagan or M. de Guermantes, she resumed her society woman stance, namely a scornful attitude towards society. While we were talking, the Duchesse showed me round the house. In the smaller sitting rooms we found more intimate friends, who had preferred to get away from the throng in order to listen to the music. In a little Empire[120] sitting-room, where a few men in black evening clothes were listening, sitting on sofas, there was, beside a cheval-glass supported by a figure of Minerva, a chaise longue, set at a right angle, but with a hollow interior, like a cradle, on which a young woman was stretched at full length. Her relaxed pose, which the entry of the Duchesse did not induce her to alter, contrasted with the wonderful brilliance of her Empire dress in a nacarat silk beside which the reddest fuchsias would have paled and on whose pearly fabric emblems and flowers seemed long ago to have been pressed, for their traces were still etched deep within it. She greeted the Duchesse with a slight inclination of her beautiful dark head. Although it was broad daylight, as she had requested that the tall curtains be drawn, in order to facilitate contemplation of the music, and so that people did not twist their ankles, an urn had been lighted on a tripod, and from it came a faint, iridescent gleam. In response to my question, the Duchesse de Guermantes told me this was Mme de Saint-Euverte. I then wanted to know what relation she was to the Mme de Saint-Euverte whom I had known. Mme de Guermantes told me that she was the wife of one of her great-nephews, seemed to think she might have been born a La Rochefoucauld, but denied ever having known the Saint-Euvertes herself. I reminded her of the evening party (which admittedly I only knew about from hearsay) at which, as the Princesse de Laumes, she had come upon Swann, but Mme de Guermantes swore that she had never been at that party. The Duchesse had always been a little untruthful, and was now much more so. Mme de Saint-Euverte, to her, was a social figure – now much diminished with time – whom she enjoyed repudiating. I did not press my case. 'No, who you may have seen at my house, because he had a degree of wit, was the husband of the person you are talking about, whom I never had anything to do with. – But she didn't have a husband. – You probably thought that because they were separated, but he was a great deal nicer than she was.' It finally hit me that an enormous man, very tall, very strong, with completely white hair, whom I used to meet all over the place and whose name I had never known, was Mme de Saint-Euverte's husband. He had died the previous year. As for the niece, I do not know whether it was because of a stomach complaint, or nerves, or phlebitis, or an imminent, recent or miscarried confinement, that she was listening to the music lying down and not moving for anybody. In all probability, proud of her gorgeous red silks, she thought that by lying on the chaise longue she would look rather like Mme Récamier.[121] She had no idea that she was giving birth for me to a new blossoming of the Saint-Euverte name, which, after such a long interval, marked both the distance and the continuity of Time. It was Time that she was rocking in that hollow cradle, where the name of Saint-Euverte and Empire style were bursting into flower in red fuchsia silks. The Empire style was something that Mme de Guermantes declared she had always detested; that meant that she detested it now, which was true, for she followed fashion, although with some delay. Without complicating matters by talking about David, whom she knew very little about, when she was very young she had thought M. Ingres the most boring conventional painter, then suddenly the most delectable of those revered by Art Nouveau, to the point that she began to detest Delacroix. By what stages she had retreated from worship to reprobation it does not really matter, since these are shifts in taste which are reflected by art critics ten years before they become topics of conversation among clever women. After having censured the Empire style, she apologized for talking to me about people as insignificant as the Saint-Euvertes and about silly issues like the provincial side of Bréauté, for she was as far from imagining why I was interested in these matters as Mme de Saint-Euverte-La Rochefoucauld, seeking the good of her stomach or an Ingres-like effect, was far from suspecting that her name had captivated me, her husband's name, not the more glorious name of her parents, and that I saw it as her function, in this room full of symbols, to beguile and cradle Time.

'But why am I talking to you about this nonsense? It can't possibly interest you,' exclaimed the Duchesse. She had spoken this sentence under her breath and nobody could have heard what she said. But one young man (who subsequently interested me as bearing a name once much more familiar to me than that of Saint-Euverte) got up with an expression of exasperation and moved further away in order to listen more intensely. For they were playing the Kreutzer Sonata,[122] although having misread the programme, he thought that it was a piece by Ravel which somebody had told him was as beautiful as Palestrina, but hard to understand. In his impatient rush to change his place, he bumped in the semi-darkness into an escritoire, which did not pass without several people turning their heads, the simple exercise of looking over their shoulders providing a momentary interruption to the torture of 'religiously' listening to the Kreutzer Sonata. And Mme de Guermantes and I, the causes of this little scandal, quickly moved to another room. 'Yes, how can these dreary little details interest a man of your calibre? It's like just now, when I saw you talking to Gilberte de Saint-Loup. She's not worth your attention. In my view that woman is just nothing, she's not even a woman, she's the most artificial, the most bourgeois thing I've ever seen' (for the Duchesse's aristocratic prejudices tinged even her defence of intellectuality). 'Anyway, are you sure you ought you to be coming to places like this? Today I suppose I can understand, because there was the recitation by Rachel which probably interested you. But lovely as it was, she doesn't give of her best in front of all these people. I'll have you to lunch alone with her. Then you'll see what she's really like. She's a hundred times better than anybody here. And after lunch she will recite some Verlaine for you. You'll be astonished by it. But no, I can't understand why you come to great soulless affairs like this. Unless of course you're gathering material . . .' she added dubiously, with a slight air of mistrust, but without risking anything further, as she was not very clear about what sort of thing constituted the improbable operation to which she was alluding.

She told me with particular pride about her afternoon gatherings where every day X—— and Y—— would be present. For she had acquired the notion, common to all the women with 'salons' whom in the past she used to despise (though these days she denied this), that real superiority, the sign of election as she saw it, was to have 'all the men' at one's house. If I chanced to say that some great lady with a salon had spoken ill of Mme Howland, when she was still alive, the Duchesse burst out laughing at my naïvety: 'Of course she did, she had all the men coming to her and that woman was trying to lure them away.'

'Don't you think, I said to the Duchesse, that it might be distressing for Mme de Saint-Loup to have to listen, as she just has, to her husband's former mistress?' I saw forming itself in Mme de Guermantes's face the blank expression behind which an oblique process of thought links what one has just heard to some rather unpleasant thoughts. An unexpressed process of thought, admittedly, but not all the serious things we say receive a verbal or a written response. Only a fool asks ten times in vain for a reply to a letter which was a mistake and which should never have been written; for letters like that only ever receive a response in the form of deeds, while the woman you imagined was merely slow in replying to your letters, addresses you as Monsieur when you next meet, instead of calling you by your first name. There was nothing of an unpleasant nature about my allusion to the relationship between Saint-Loup and Rachel, and at most it might annoy her for a moment by reminding her that I had been Robert's friend and perhaps his confidant on the subject of the rebuff that Rachel's performance at the Duchesse's party had resulted in. But she did not persist in those thoughts, the stormy expression vanished, and Mme de Guermantes replied to my question about Mme de Saint-Loup: 'If you ask me, I don't think it matters to her at all, Gilberte never loved her husband. She is a dreadful little thing. She loved the social position, the name, being my niece, and getting out of the gutter where she belonged, but since then she seems to have been doing her best to get back into it. I tell you, it distressed me very much for poor Robert's sake, because he may not have been a genius, but he could see it very well, and a whole lot of other things too. I shouldn't say anything because she is my niece, after all, and I don't have any positive proof that she was unfaithful to him, but there were an awful lot of stories. No, I'm wrong, there was one I do know about, with an officer from Méséglise, Robert wanted to challenge him. It was because of all that that Robert joined up, the war seemed liked a deliverance from his family worries; if you want to know what I think, he wasn't killed, he got himself killed. She never showed the slightest grief, she even astonished me by the unusually cynical way she affected indifference, which upset me a great deal because I was very fond of poor Robert. This may surprise you, because people don't know me very well, but I still often think about him; I never forget anyone. He never spoke to me about it, but he understood that I guessed everything. But just think about it, if she had loved her husband even a little bit, could she endure to be in the same drawing-room, unperturbed, as the woman with whom he had been so desperately in love for so many years? You could say for ever, even, because I'm quite certain it never stopped, even during the war. Heavens, she'd have had her by the throat!' exclaimed the Duchesse, forgetting that she herself, by arranging for Rachel to be invited and thereby making possible the scene she deemed to be inevitable if Gilberte had loved Robert, was perhaps acting cruelly. 'No, you know, she concluded, she is a slut.' Such an expression from Mme de Guermantes was rendered possible by her descent from the pleasant social circles of the Guermantes to socializing with actresses, and also because she grafted it on to an eighteenth-century manner which she thought full of vitality, and then also because she thought she could do whatever she liked. But the word itself was the product of the hatred she felt for Gilberte, by a need to hit her, if not physically then in effigy. At the same time, the Duchesse thought by this to justify the whole of her behaviour towards Gilberte, or rather against her, in society and within the family, where Robert's interests and his estate were concerned.

But as sometimes one's judgments receive apparent justification from facts of which one was unaware and could not have imagined,

Gilberte, who had no doubt inherited some of the characteristics of her mother's family (and it may well be this accommodating attitude which I had unconsciously relied upon when I asked her to introduce me to very young girls), after some thought, from the request I had made, and doubtless so that the profit would stay in the family, drew a conclusion bolder than any I could have imagined. She said: 'If you'll allow me, I'm going to go and find my daughter to introduce to you. She is over there chatting to the Mortemart boy and other young things of no interest. I'm sure she'll be a nice friend for you.'

I asked her if Robert had been happy about having a daughter: 'Oh, he was very proud of her. Though of course given his tastes, Gilberte went on naïvely, I think he would have preferred a boy.' This daughter, whose name and fortune might have given her mother hope that she would marry a royal prince and crown the whole work of social ascendance begun by Swann and his wife, later chose to marry an obscure literary figure, for she was devoid of snobbery, and brought her family down to a level below that from which it had started. It was therefore extremely difficult to make subsequent generations believe that the parents of this obscure couple had held such an elevated position in society. The names of Swann and Odette de Crécy were miraculously revived to enable people to tell you that you were wrong, and that there was nothing so very extraordinary about the family; and people in the end thought that Mlle de Saint-Loup had made the best marriage she could, that her grandfather's with Odette de Crécy (he having no standing) had been made in a vain attempt to better himself, whereas on the contrary, at least from the point of view of love, his marriage had inspired theories like those which in the eighteenth century drove great aristocrats, under the spell of Rousseau, and other forerunners of the Revolution, to live a life of nature and to abandon their privileges.

My astonishment at her words and my pleasure at hearing them were rapidly replaced, as Mme de Saint-Loup disappeared in the direction of another sitting-room, by the idea of Past Time, which was also, in its way, prompted, without my having even seen her, by Mlle de Saint-Loup. Was she not, as indeed most human beings are, like one of those 'stars' in forests, cross-roads where roads converge which have come, as they do in our lives, from the most diverse starting-points? They were numerous enough, in my case, the roads leading to Mlle de Saint-Loup and radiating out again from her. Above all it was the two great 'ways' which had led to her, along which I had had so many walks and so many dreams – through her father, Robert de Saint-Loup, the Guermantes way, through her mother, Gilberte, the Méséglise way which was the 'way by Swann's'. One, through the little girl's mother and the Champs-Élysées, led me to Swann, to my evenings at Combray, to the Méséglise way; the other, through her father, to my afternoons at Balbec, where I could visualize him close to the sunlit sea. Already some connecting roads were establishing themselves between these two main routes. For the actual Balbec, where I had met Saint-Loup, was a place that I had so much wanted to go to very largely because of what Swann had told me about the churches there, especially about the Persian church, and then again, through Robert de Saint-Loup, the nephew of the Duchesse de Guermantes, I came back, in Combray once more, to the Guermantes way. But there were still many other points in my life to which Mlle de Saint-Loup led, to the lady in pink, who was her grandmother and whom I had met at my great-uncle's house. A new connecting road here, because this great-uncle's manservant, who let me in that day and who later, through the gift of a photograph, enabled me to identify the Lady in Pink, was the father of the young man whom not only M. de Charlus but the father of Mlle de Saint-Loup himself had been in love with, on whose account he had made her mother so unhappy. And was it not the grandfather of Mlle de Saint-Loup, Swann, who had first mentioned the music of Vinteuil to me, just as it was Gilberte who had first spoken to me of Albertine? And it was by talking about the music of Vinteuil to Albertine that I had discovered who her great friend was and thus had begun that part of my life with her which led to her death and caused me so much pain. And it was also Mlle de Saint-Loup's father who had set off to try to make Albertine come back. And even to my whole life in society, whether in Paris in the drawing-rooms of Swann or the Guermantes, or at the opposite extreme with the Verdurins, thus bringing into line, alongside the two ways of Combray, the Champs-Élysées and the beautiful terrace of La

Raspelière. In fact, what individuals have we known who, if we want
to tell the story of our friendship with them, do not oblige us to set
them successively in a series of quite different places in our lives? A
life of Saint-Loup as portrayed by me would unfold in every sort of
setting and involve the whole of my life, even those parts of it where
he was least familiar, like my grandmother or like Albertine. And the
Verdurins, even though at the opposite end of the scale, were connected
to Odette through her past, and to Robert de Saint-Loup through
Charlie; and think of the part played in their house by Vinteuil's music!
Finally, Swann had been in love with Legrandin's sister, who in turn
had known M. de Charlus, whose ward the young Cambremer had
married. If it were only a matter of our hearts, the poet would have
been right to speak of the 'mysterious threads' that are broken by
life.[123] But it is even more true to say that life is ceaselessly weaving
these threads between individuals and between events, that it inter-
weaves them, doubles them, to make the weave thicker, to such an
extent finally that between the least significant point in our past and
all the others a rich network of memories gives us in fact a choice
about which connection to make.

One might say that, if I tried not to make use of it unconsciously
but to remember what it had been, there was not a single one of the
things which were useful to us at that moment that had not been a
living thing, something for us alive with its own life, subsequently
transformed for our use into simple industrial raw material. My introduction to Mlle de Saint-Loup was about to take place in Mme
Verdurin's house: spellbound, I thought over all the journeys I had
made with the Albertine for whom I was going to ask Mlle de
Saint-Loup to be a substitute – in the little tram, to Doville, to visit
Mme Verdurin, the same Mme Verdurin who had brought together in
love, and then forced apart, long before my love affair with Albertine,
the grandfather and grandmother of Mlle de Saint-Loup –! All round
us were paintings by Elstir, the man who had introduced me to
Albertine. And just to meld all my pasts together, Mme Verdurin, like
Gilberte, had married a Guermantes.

It would not be possible to recount our relationship, even with a
person we hardly knew, without recreating a succession of the most

diverse settings of our life. So each individual – and I was one of these individuals myself – became a measure of duration for me each time he completed a revolution not just around himself, but around other people, and in particular by the successive positions he occupied in relation to me. And no doubt all these different planes, in relation to which Time, as I had just grasped in the course of this party, arranged my life, by giving me the idea that in a book whose intention was to tell the story of a life it would be necessary to use, in contrast to the flat psychology people normally use, a sort of psychology in space, added a new beauty to the resurrections that had taken place in my memory while I was lost in my thoughts alone in the library, since memory, by bringing the past into the present without making any changes to it, just as it was at the moment when it was the present, suppresses precisely this great dimension of Time through which a life is given reality.

I saw Gilberte coming towards me. Saint-Loup's marriage, and the thoughts which had preoccupied me then and were still the same this morning, were as fresh in my mind as if they were yesterday's, so I was astonished to see beside her a young girl of about sixteen, whose tall figure was a visible measure of the distance I had not wanted to see. Time, colourless and intangible, had been materialized in her so that I could, so to speak, see it and touch it, it had shaped her into a master-work, while at the same time on me, alas, it had merely done its work. Yet here was Mlle de Saint-Loup, in front of me. She had deep-set, piercing eyes and her delightful nose was slightly prominent, like a beak, and curved, not at all perhaps like Swann's, but more like Saint-Loup's. The spirit of that Guermantes had disappeared; but the enchanting head and piercing eyes of a bird in flight had taken up a new position on the shoulders of Mlle de Saint-Loup, likely for a long time to arouse dreams and reveries in those who had known her father.

I was struck by the way that her nose, constructed on the template of her mother's and grandmother's, stopped precisely at that perfect horizontal line beneath it, sublimely though perhaps a fraction late. Such an individual feature, even if it was the only one visible, would have made one statue recognizable among thousands of others, and I marvelled that nature should have returned at the appointed time to the granddaughter, as to the mother and to the grandmother, like a great and original sculptor, to perform this powerful and decisive stroke of the chisel. I thought she was very beautiful: still full of hopes, laughing, formed out of the very years that I had lost, she looked like my youth.

Finally, this idea of Time was valuable to me for one other reason, it was a spur, it told me that it was time to start, if I wanted to achieve what I had sometimes sensed during the course of my life, in brief flashes, on the Guermantes way, in my carriage-rides with Mme de Villeparisis, which had made me feel that life was worth living. How much better life seemed to me now that it seemed susceptible of being illuminated, taken out of the shadows, restored from our ceaseless falsification of it to the truth of what it was, in short, realized in a book! How happy the writer of a book like that would be, I thought, what a labour awaited him! To give some idea of it, one would have to go to the most elevated and divergent arts for comparisons; for this writer, who would also need to show the contrasting aspects of each character to create depth, would have to prepare his book scrupulously, perpetually regrouping his forces as in an offensive, and putting up with the work like tiredness, accepting it like a rule, constructing it like a church, following it like a regime, overcoming it like an obstacle, winning it like a friendship, feeding it up like a child, creating it like a world, without ever neglecting its mysteries, the explanations for which are probably to be found only in other worlds, while our occasional inklings of them are what, in life and in art, move us most deeply. In books of this scope, there are parts which have never had time to be more than sketched in and which will probably never be finished because of the very extent of the architect's plan. Think how many great cathedrals have been left unfinished! One feeds a book like that, one strengthens its weak parts, one looks after it, but eventually it grows up, it marks our tomb, and protects it from rumours and, for a time, from oblivion. But to return to myself, I was thinking about my book in more modest terms, and it would even be a mistake to say that I was thinking of those who would read it as my readers. For they were not, as I saw it, my readers, so much as readers of their own selves, my book being merely one of those magnifying glasses of the sort the optician at Combray used to offer his customers; my book, but a books thanks to which I would be providing them with the means of reading within themselves. With the result that I would not ask them to praise me or to denigrate me, only to tell me if it was right, if the words they were reading in themselves were really the ones I had written (possible divergences in this regard not necessarily always originating, it should be said, in my having been wrong, but sometimes in the fact that the reader's eyes might not be of a type for which my book was suitable as an aid for self-reading). And as every few moments I changed the comparison by which I could best and most materially represent the task on which I was embarking, I thought that at my big deal table, watched by Françoise, who, in the way that all unpretentious people who live alongside us do, had an intuitive understanding of my task (and I had sufficiently forgotten Albertine to have forgiven Françoise for any harm she had done her), I would work next to her, and work almost in the same way as her (at least in the way she used to in the past: she was now so old she could hardly see at all); for, pinning a supplementary page in place here and there, I should construct my book, I don't dare say, ambitiously, as if it were a cathedral, but simply as if it were a dress I was making. When I did not have all of what Françoise called my manuscribbles within reach, and could not find just the one that I wanted, Françoise would sympathize with my annoyance, as she always used to be saying how she could not sew if she did not have the right number thread and the proper buttons. And then through being so close to my life, she had developed a kind of instinctive understanding of literary work, more accurate than that of many intelligent people, let alone fools. Once, for example, when I had done my article for the *Figaro*, when the old butler, with the kind of commiseration which always slightly exaggerates the laborious nature of any alien task, like people who say: 'How it must tire you to sneeze like that,' expressed his pity for writers by saying: 'What a headache that must be,' Françoise, by contrast, sensed my happiness and respected my work. The only thing that angered her was when I told Bloch about the contents of my article in advance, as she was afraid he would write it first, and would say: 'You're too trusting, those people are all copifiers.' And indeed

Bloch did often give himself a retrospective alibi every time I had sketched out something he liked the sound of, by saying: 'That's a coincidence, I've just written something very similar myself, I must read it to you.' (He could not have read it to me then, but he would go and write it that evening.)

Because I often had to glue one piece on to another, the papers that Françoise called my manuscribbles kept getting torn. But Françoise would always be able to help me mend them, just as she put patches on the worn-out parts of her dresses or, while she was waiting for the glazier, as I was for the printer, she would stick a piece of newspaper over a broken pane in the kitchen window. Françoise would say to me, pointing to my note-books, eaten away like wood that insects have got into: 'It's all moth-eaten, look, that's a pity, there's a page here that looks like lace,' and examining it closely like a tailor: 'I don't think I can mend this, it's too far gone. It's a shame, those might have been your best ideas. You know what they used to say in Combray, even the best furriers don't know as much as the moths. They always get into the best material.'

But given that individual entities (whether human or not) in a book are made up of a large number of impressions which, taken from many girls, many churches, many sonatas, are then used to form a single sonata, a single church, a single girl, should I not make my book in the same way as Françoise made her braised beef in aspic, which M. de Norpois had so much liked, in which the jelly was enriched by so many carefully selected extra pieces of meat? And I was finally on the point of achieving what I had so longed for on my walks on the Guermantes way and believed impossible, as I had believed it to be impossible, when I got back home, ever to get used to going to sleep without kissing my mother or, later, to the idea that Albertine loved women, an idea with which in the end I lived without even noticing its presence; for our worst fears, like our greatest hopes, are not outside our powers, and we can come in the end to triumph over the former and to achieve the latter.

Yes, the idea of Time that I had just formed was telling me that it was time to apply myself to the work. It was high time; but, and this was the explanation for the anxiety which had beset me as soon as I entered the drawing-room, when the made-up faces had given me the idea of lost time, was there still time, and was I even still in a sufficiently fit condition? The mind has its landscapes and only a short time is allowed for their contemplation. My life had been like a painter who climbs up a road overhanging a lake that is hidden from view by a screen of rocks and trees. Through a gap he glimpses it, he has it all there in front of him, he takes up his brushes. But the night is already falling when there is no more painting, and after which no day will break. Only, one prerequisite of my work as I had just recently conceived it in the library was the thorough investigation of impressions which needed first to be recreated through memory. But that was threadbare.

First of all, nothing having yet been started, I might well feel anxious, even though I might think, on account of my age, that I still had a few years ahead of me, for my hour might strike at any moment. For I really had to start from the fact that I had a body, that is that I was perpetually under threat from a twofold danger, external and internal. Yet I spoke of it in those terms only as a convenience of language. For the internal danger, such as from a cerebral haemorrhage, is also external, as it threatens the body. And having a body is in itself the greatest threat to the mind. To human, thinking life, which should probably not be described as a miraculously perfected state of animal and physical life, so much as an imperfect state, still at the same rudimentary level as the communal existence of protozoa in polyparies or as the body of the whale, etc., in the organization of the life of the mind. The body encloses the mind in a fortress; before long the mind is besieged on all sides, and in the end the mind has to give itself up.

But accepting the distinction between the two sorts of danger threatening the mind, and beginning with the external one, I remembered that in my life so far, it had often happened in moments of intellectual excitement in situations where any physical movement on my part was suspended, as for example when I left the Rivebelle restaurant, half drunk, in a carriage to go to a nearby casino, that I felt the present object of my thought very clearly within myself, and understood how entirely dependent on chance it was, not only that this object had not entered my thoughts before, but also that, along with my body, it might be annihilated at any moment. I did not worry much about that then. My cheerfulness was not tempered by prudence or anxiety. I did not care if this joy ended after a second and became nothing. It was no longer like that now; because the happiness I experienced now was not merely the product of a purely subjective tension of the nerves, which isolates us from the past but, quite the opposite, came from an expansion of my mind in which this past was reshaped and re-actualized, and this gave me, though unfortunately only for a moment, something of permanent value. I would have liked to bequeath it to those whom I could have enriched with my treasure. Certainly what I had experienced in the library and was trying to protect was still pleasure, but it was no longer selfish pleasure, or at least its selfishness (for all the fruitful altruisms in nature develop in a selfish way, human altruism that is not selfish is sterile, like the altruism of a writer who breaks off his work to see a friend in trouble, or to accept a public office, or to write propaganda articles) is of a kind that is useful for other people. I no longer had the indifference I used to feel coming back from Rivebelle, I felt myself enhanced by the work I carried within me (as if by something precious and fragile that had been entrusted to me and which I would have wished to pass on intact to the hands for which it was destined, which were not my own). Now, feeling myself the bearer of a work of literature made the idea of an accident in which I might meet my death seem much more dreadful, even (to the extent that the work seemed necessary and lasting) absurd, in contrast with the scope of my wishes, with the impetus of my thoughts, but that did not make it any the less possible since (as the simplest incidents show us every day of our lives, as when, while one is trying very hard not to make a sound that might disturb a sleeping friend, a carafe placed too near the edge of the table falls off and wakes him) accidents, being products of material causes, can perfectly well occur at a moment when very different wishes, which they unwittingly destroy, make them quite appalling. I was well aware that my brain was a rich mining-basin, in which was a vast expanse and enormous diversity of valuable deposits. But would I have time to exploit them? I was the only person capable of doing it. For two reasons: my death would mean the disappearance not only of the one mineworker capable of extracting these minerals, but also of the mineral deposit itself; and when, in a little while, I left to go home, it needed only the car I would take to crash into another for my body to be destroyed and for my mind, from which life would be withdrawn, to be forced to abandon for ever the new ideas which at this very moment, not having had the time to put them in the securer surroundings of a book, it was anxiously keeping locked up within its quivering, protective, but fragile pulp. But by a bizarre coincidence this rational fear of danger emerged at a moment when I had recently become much less concerned about the idea of death. There had been a time when the fear of no longer being myself had horrified me, and similarly with each new love I felt (for Gilberte, for Albertine), because I could not bear the idea that one day the being who loved them would no longer exist, which seemed like a kind of death. But after so much repetition, this fear had by a natural process become transformed into a trustful equanimity.

An accident affecting the brain was not even necessary. Its symptoms, which I perceived as a feeling of emptiness in my head and a tendency to forget everything so that things only ever recurred by chance, as when in sorting out one's possessions one finds something one had forgotten or even had been searching for, were making me like a hoarder whose strong-box had a hole in it through which the wealth was progressively disappearing. For a while there existed a self which deplored the loss of these riches and tried to marshal the memory to resist it, but soon I felt that the memory, as it contracted, took this self with it.

If the idea of death during this period had, as we have seen, cast a gloom over love, the memory of love had for a long time now helped me not to be afraid of death. For I understood that dying was not something new but quite the reverse, that since my childhood I had already died a number of times. To take the most recent period, had I not been more attached to Albertine than to my life? Could I conceive of my personality, then, without my love for her continuing? Now that I no longer loved her, I was no longer the being who loved her, but a different being who did not love her, I had stopped loving her when I became somebody else. But there was no suffering involved in becoming this other person, in not loving Albertine any longer; and certainly some day not having my body any longer could not possibly seem as sad, from any point of view, as not loving Albertine one day had once seemed to be. And yet, how little I cared now about not loving her! These successive deaths, so feared by the self they were doomed to annihilate, so meaningless, so gentle after they had happened and when the person who was afraid of them was no longer there to feel them, had enabled me for some time now to understand how unwise it would be to be frightened of death. But it was now that I had been indifferent to it for a while that I was starting to fear it again, although in a different form, not for myself but for my book, for the birth of which this life of mine threatened by so many dangers was, for a time at least, indispensable. Victor Hugo says:

'Il faut que l'herbe pousse et que les enfants meurent.'[124]

Personally, I say that the cruel law of art is that human beings die and that we ourselves die after exhausting all the forms of suffering, so that not the grass of oblivion may grow, but the grass of eternal life, the vigorous grass of fruitful works of art, on which future generations will come, heedless of those asleep beneath it, to have their *déjeuner sur l'herbe*.[125]

I talked about external dangers; but there are internal dangers too. If I managed to escape an accident from without, who knows whether I might not be prevented from profiting from that grace by an accident supervening from within me, by some internal catastrophe, before the months needed to write this book had elapsed.

When in a few minutes I made my way home through the Champs-Élysées, who was to say that I would not be struck down by the same illness as my grandmother, one afternoon when she had gone there with me for a walk which was to be her last, although she had no suspicion, such is the ignorance in which we live, that the hand of the clock had, unawares, arrived at the point when the clenched spring of the clockwork was to strike the hour? Perhaps the fear of having already lived through almost the whole of the minute which precedes the first stroke of that hour, when it is already being prepared, perhaps this fear of the stroke that was about to toll in my brain, was like a

shadowy recognition of what was about to occur, like a reflection in
consciousness of the precarious state of the brain when its arteries are
about to give up, something which is no more impossible than the
sudden acceptance of death by men who have been wounded and who,
although still lucid, when both the doctor and their desire to live
attempt to mislead them, say, as they see what is about to happen: 'I'm
going to die, I'm ready,' and write their farewells to their wife.

And in fact something very like this happened to me before I started
my book, and happened in a guise I would never have suspected.
People were telling me, one evening when I went out, that I was
looking better than before, and expressing surprise that I still had all
my black hair. But I nearly fell three times as I was going down the
staircase. I had gone out for only two hours; but when I got back
home, I felt as if I no longer had any memory, any thoughts, any
strength, or even any existence. People might have come to see me,
to proclaim me king, to seize me, to arrest me, and I would have
allowed them to do it without uttering a word, without opening my
eyes, like those people suffering from extremely bad seasickness who,
in a boat crossing the Caspian sea, don't even put up a show of
resistance if they are told they are to be thrown overboard. I did not,
strictly speaking, have anything wrong with me, but I felt that I was
no longer capable of anything, as sometimes happens to old men, alert
the day before, who having broken their hip or suffering from a bout
of indigestion, take to their bed and adopt an existence which is nothing
but a more or less extended preparation for their now inevitable death.
One of the selves, the one which long ago used to take part in those
barbaric festivals called dining out, and where, for the men in white
tie, for the women half-naked and plumed, values are so reversed that
someone who fails to turn up to dinner after having accepted, or simply
does not arrive until the roast, commits an act more culpable than all
the immoral acts discussed casually during dinner, along with recent
deaths, and where death or life-threatening illness are the only excuses
for not coming, so long as warning be given, even if one were dying,
in sufficient time for another fourteenth guest to be invited, this one
of my selves had kept its scruples and lost its memory. The other
self, the one which had conceived his work, on the other hand still

349

remembered. I had received an invitation from Mme Molé, and learned
that Mme Sazerat's son was dead. I had decided to use one of the hours
after which I could no longer utter a word, my tongue being as tied
as my grandmother's had been when she was dying, nor even swallow
milk, to send my excuses to Mme Molé and my condolences to Mme
Sazerat. But after a few moments I forgot what I was meant to be
doing. A fortunate forgetfulness, for the memory of my work was
alert and ready to use the unexpected gift of the extra hour to lay the
first foundations. Unfortunately, as I took hold of my note-book to
start writing, Mme Molé's card slid out and caught my attention.
Immediately the forgetful self, which was able to dominate the other
one, as is always the case with scrupulous barbarians who have been
out to dinner, pushed away the note-book and wrote to Mme Molé
(who would no doubt have been very impressed, had she known it, at
my putting my reply to her invitation ahead of my architectural
labours). Then a word in my reply suddenly reminded me that Mme
Sazerat had lost her son, and I wrote to her too, then, having sacrificed
a genuine duty to the factitious obligation to show that I was sensitive
and polite, I fell back exhausted, closed my eyes and could do nothing
but vegetate for a week. Yet while all these pointless duties, to which
I was always ready to sacrifice the real one, had left my head after a
few minutes, the idea of my construction never left me for an instant.
I did not know if it would be a church in which the faithful would
gradually be able to learn truths and discover harmonies, the great
general plan, or if it would remain – like a druidic monument on the
high point of an island – something for ever unvisited. But I had
decided to devote all my powers to it, which seemed to be failing
regretfully and so as to leave me time, once the walls were up, to close
'the funerary gate'.[126] Soon I was able to show people a few sketches.
Nobody understood anything. Even those who were well disposed
towards my perception of the truths which I intended subsequently to
engrave within the temple congratulated me on having discovered
them with a 'microscope', when on the contrary I had used a telescope
to make out things which were indeed very small, but only because
they were situated a long way away, each of them a world in itself. In
the places where I was trying to find general laws, I was accused of

sifting through endless detail. So what was the point of all of it? I had had a certain facility when I was young, and Bergotte had thought the pages I had written as a student 'splendid'. But instead of working, I had lived a life of idleness, of dissipation and pleasure, of illness, anxieties and obsessions, and was undertaking my work on the eve of my death, without knowing anything about my craft. I no longer felt strong enough to face up to my obligations to other people, nor to my duties towards my thought and my work, still less to both of them. As far as the former were concerned, forgetting that there were letters to write, etc., simplified my task. But suddenly, after a month or so, the association of ideas caused me to remember them, with a twinge of conscience, and I was overwhelmed with the sense of my own impotence. I was surprised to discover that I did not really mind it, that since the day when my legs had trembled so badly while I was going down the staircase I had become indifferent to everything, I longed for nothing but rest, while I waited for the great repose which would finally come. It was not because I was postponing until after my death the admiration which, it seemed to me, people ought to have for my work that I was indifferent to the approbation of the current elite. The elite after my death could think what it liked, it would no longer be of any concern to me. In reality, if I thought about my work and not at all about the letters to which I ought to be replying, this was no longer because I was making any great distinction of importance between the two things, as I had done during my idleness and had continued to do after I had started work, until the day when I had had to catch hold of the staircase banister. The organization of my memory, of my preoccupations, was bound up with my work, perhaps because, whereas the letters were forgotten the moment after, the idea of my book was in my head, always the same, in a perpetual process of becoming. But it had also become tiresome. I felt like a son whose dying mother still feels the need to take care of him all the time, in between her injections and her cuppings. She may still love him, but knows this only through the exasperating sense of the duty she feels to look after him. In my case the powers of the writer were no longer up to the selfish demands made by the work. Since the day of the staircase nothing in the world, no happiness, whether it came from people's friendship, from the progress of my work, from the hope of glory, reached me except as very weak, pale sunshine, not strong enough to warm me, to bring me to life, to give me any kind of desire, and yet it was still too bright, wan as it was, for my eyes, which preferred to close, and I turned my face to the wall. It seemed, from the slight movement I felt in my lips, that I must have had a little smile right at the corner of my mouth when a lady wrote to me: 'I was *very surprised* to receive no reply to my letter.' None the less, that would remind me of her letter, and I would answer it. In order that people should not think me ungrateful, I wanted to try to show the same level of politeness as that which people must have shown to me. And I was overwhelmed by the imposition on my failing existence of the superhuman fatigues of life. The loss of my memory helped me somewhat by cutting out some of my obligations; my work replaced them.

This idea of death established itself permanently within me, in the way that love does. Not that I was in love with death, I hated it. But after having contemplated it from time to time, as one does a woman with whom one is not yet in love, the thought of it adhered to the deepest stratum of my brain so completely that I could not think about anything without its first passing through the idea of death, and even if I was doing nothing, remaining in a state of complete repose, the idea of death kept me company as ceaselessly as the idea of my self. I do not think that, on the day when I became half-dead, it was the accidents which characterized that state, the incapacity to descend a staircase, to recall a name, to get up, that had even unconsciously caused this idea of death, the idea that I was already practically dead, so much as that they had both come together and the great mirror of the mind had inevitably reflected a new reality. Yet I did not see how one could pass from the ailments that I had to total death without any warning. But then I thought about other people, about all the people who die every day without the hiatus between their illness and their death seeming at all extraordinary to us. I even thought that it was only because I was seeing them from within (even more than through the illusions of hope) that certain ailments, taken one by one, did not seem fatal, even though I believed that I was dying, just as those who are most convinced that their time has come are nevertheless easily persuaded that their inability to pronounce certain words has nothing at all to do with a stroke or aphasia but stems from a tiredness of the tongue, a nervous state akin to stammering, or exhaustion following a bout of indigestion.

For myself, what I had to write was something different from a dying man's farewell, longer, and for more than one person. Longer to write. In the daytime, at best, I could try to sleep. If I worked, it would be only at night. But I would need a good number of nights, perhaps a hundred, perhaps a thousand. And I would be living with the anxiety of not knowing whether the Master of my destiny, less indulgent than the Sultan Shahriyar, when I broke off my story each morning, would stay my death sentence, and permit me to take up the continuation again the following evening. Not that I was claiming in any way to be rewriting the *Arabian Nights*, any more than the *Mémoires* of Saint-Simon, both of them books written at night, nor any of the other books that I had loved in the naïvety of my childhood, when I had become as superstitiously attached to them as I would be to my loves, and was unable to imagine without horror any book that was different from them. But, as Elstir found with Chardin, one can remake something one loves only by renouncing it. No doubt my books too, like my mortal being, would eventually die, one day. But one has to resign oneself to dying. One accepts the thought that in ten years oneself, in a hundred years one's books, will not exist. Eternal duration is no more promised to books than it is to men.

It would be a book as long as the *Arabian Nights* perhaps, but quite different. It is probably true that when one is in love with a work of literature one wants to make something as like it as possible, but one needs to sacrifice one's love of the moment, think not of one's own taste, but of a truth which does not ask for your preferences and forbids you to think about them. And only if one follows it will one sometimes find that one has come upon what one abandoned, that, by forgetting them, one has written the *Arabian Nights* or the *Mémoires* of Saint-Simon for a new age. But was there still enough time for me? Was it not too late?

I asked myself not only 'Is there still enough time?' but also 'Am I still in a sufficiently fit condition?' The illness which, by compelling me, like a severe spiritual adviser, to die to the world, had done me a service for 'except a corn of wheat fall into the ground and die, it abideth alone; but if it die, it bringeth forth much fruit',[127] the illness which, after my idleness had protected me from my facility, was now perhaps going to protect me from idleness, had also exhausted my powers and, as I had long observed, particularly at the time when I stopped loving Albertine, my powers of memory. But was not the re-creation through memory of impressions, which then needed to be investigated, illuminated and transformed into intellectual equivalents, one of the preconditions, almost the very essence, of the work of art as I had conceived it just now in the library? Oh, if only I still had the powers that were still intact on the evening which had come back into my mind when I noticed *François le Champi*! It was that evening, when my mother abdicated her authority, that marked the beginning, along with the slow death of my grandmother, of the decline of my will and of my health. Everything had been decided at the moment when, unable to bear the idea of waiting until the next day to set my lips on my mother's face, I had made my resolution, jumped out of bed, and gone, in my nightshirt, to stay by the window through which the moonlight came, until I heard M. Swann go. My parents having gone with him, I heard the garden gate open, the bell ring, the gate close again . . .

Then I suddenly thought that, if I did still have the strength to complete my work, this afternoon party – like certain days long ago at Combray which had influenced me – which had, just today, given me both the idea of my work and the fear of not being able to accomplish it, would be bound to mark it more than anything else with the form that I had sensed long ago in the church at Combray, and which normally remains invisible to us, the form of Time.

There are, of course, many other errors of the senses, and we have seen how various episodes of this narrative had proved this to me, which falsify our perception of the real appearance of the world. But where necessary, by doing everything I could to give the most exact transcription, I would be able to keep the location of sounds unchanged, to abstain from detaching them from their cause, besides which the intellect situates them only after the event, even though to make the rain sing gently in the middle of the room and to make the bubbling of our tisane fall torrentially in the courtyard ought, after all, to be no more disconcerting than what painters have done so often when they have depicted, very close or very far away, depending on how the laws of perspective, the intensity of colour and our first illusory glance make them appear to us, a sail or a peak, which the rational mind will then relocate, sometimes across enormous distances. I might, even though the error would be more serious, continue the general practice of adding features to the face of a passer-by, although instead of a nose, cheeks and a chin, there should not really be anything except an empty space over which would flicker, at most, the reflection of our desires. And even if I did not have the leisure to prepare, and this was a much more important matter, the hundred masks which ought properly to be attached to a single face, if only because of all the eyes that see it and the different meanings they read into its features, as well as for the same eyes the effect of hope and fear or, on the contrary, of the love and habit which for thirty years can conceal the changes wrought by age; even if I was not in the end proposing, although my relationship with Albertine had been enough to show me that anything else is factitious and untruthful, to represent certain individuals not as outside but as inside us, where their least acts can entail fatal disturbances, and to vary the light of the moral sky, according to the differing pressures of our sensibility or when, disturbing the serene skies of our certainty beneath which an object is so small, the slightest cloud of danger multiplies its size in a moment; if I could not use these changes and many others (the necessity for which, if one intends to depict reality, has become apparent in the course of this narrative) in the transcription of a universe which had to be completely redesigned, at least I would not fail to describe man, within it, as possessing the length not of his body but of his years, and as being obliged, in a task that grows more and more enormous, and which in the end defeats him, to drag them with him whenever he moves.

Moreover, the fact that we occupy an ever larger place in Time is something that everybody feels, and this universality could only delight me, since this was the truth, the truth suspected by everybody, that it was my task to try to elucidate. Not only does everybody feel that we

occupy a place in Time, but the simplest measure it in approximately
the same way as they measure the place we occupy in space, so that
people of no special perspicacity, seeing two men whom they do not
know, both with black moustaches, or both clean-shaven, will say that
these are two men, one of about twenty and the other of about forty
years old. Of course they will often be wrong in their estimate, but
the fact that people think it possible at all shows that age is conceived
as something measurable. The second man with the black moustache
has effectively had twenty years added on to him.

It was this notion of embodied time, of past years not being separated
from us, that it was now my intention to make such a prominent
feature in my work, and it was at that very moment of decision, in the
hôtel of the Princesse de Guermantes, that I heard that sound of my
parents' footsteps as they led M. Swann to the gate, heard the tinkling
of the bell, resilient, ferruginous, inexhaustible, shrill and fresh, which
told me that M. Swann had gone and that Mama was on her way
upstairs, heard the very sounds themselves, heard them even though
they were situated so far away in the past. Then, as I thought of all
the events which had to be set in place between the moment when I
heard those sounds and this party at the Guermantes', I was frightened
to think that the bell could still be ringing in me without my being
able to do anything to alter the shrillness of its tinkling, since, no
longer remembering very clearly how it faded away, and wanting to
rediscover this, and to listen to it properly, I had to try to block out
the sound of the conversations which the masks were holding all
around me. In order to try to hear it at closer quarters, I was forced
to go back down into myself. It must therefore be that this tinkling
was always there, and also, between it and the present moment, the
whole of this past, unrolled indefinitely, which I did not know that I
was carrying. When it tinkled, I already existed, and for me still to be
able to hear the tinkling there must have been no break in continuity,
I must not have ceased for a moment, not taken a rest from existing,
from thinking, from being conscious of myself, because this moment
from long ago still stuck to me, so that I could still find it again, still
go back to it, simply by going more deeply back into myself. And it
is because they contain in this way every hour of the past that human

bodies can do so much damage to those who love them, because they contain so many memories of joys and desires already effaced from their minds, but cruel indeed for anyone who contemplates and projects back through the array of time the cherished body of which he is jealous, so jealous as to wish for its destruction. For, after death, Time leaves the body, and the memories – so indifferent, so pale now – are effaced from her who no longer exists and soon will be from him whom at present they still torture, but in whom they will eventually die, when the desire of a living body is no longer there to support them. The depths of Albertine, whom I saw sleeping, and who was dead.

I felt a sense of tiredness and fear at the thought that all this length of time had not only uninterruptedly been lived, thought, secreted by me, that it was my life, that it was myself, but also that I had to keep it attached to me at every moment, that it supported me, that I was perched on its vertiginous summit, and that I was unable to move without its collaboration, without taking it with me. The date at which I heard the sound of the garden bell at Combray, so distant and yet still within me, was a benchmark in that vast dimension which I did not know I had. I felt giddy at the sight of so many years below me, yet within me, as if I were miles high.

I finally understood why the Duc de Guermantes, who had caused me to wonder, seeing him sitting on a chair, how he could have aged so little when he had so many more years than I had below him, had, the moment he rose and tried to stand upright, wavered on trembling legs, like those of some ancient archbishop whose metal crucifix is the only solid thing about him, and towards whom hasten a few strapping young seminarists, and could not move forward without shaking like a leaf, on the scarcely manageable summit of his eighty-three years, as if all men are perched on top of living stilts which never stop growing, sometimes becoming taller than church steeples, until eventually they make walking difficult and dangerous, and down from which, all of a sudden, they fall. (Was this the reason why the faces of men over a certain age were, even to the least aware eyes, so impossible to confuse with those of young men, and were visible only through a sort of cloudy aura of seriousness?) I began to be afraid that the stilts on which I myself was standing had already reached that height, and it did not seem to me that I would for very long have the strength to keep this past attached to me which already stretched so far down. Therefore, if enough time was left to me to complete my work, my first concern would be to describe the people in it, even at the risk of making them seem colossal and unnatural creatures, as occupying a place far larger than the very limited one reserved for them in space, a place in fact almost infinitely extended, since they are in simultaneous contact, like giants immersed in the years, with such distant periods of their lives, between which so many days have taken up their place – in Time.

THE END

Notes

1. *Marienbad*: a popular spa town in what was then Bohemia. (This passage repeats almost verbatim the description of Legrandin, in *The Fugitive* pp. 629–30.)

2. *Theodora*: wife of the Emperor Justinian, and the eponymous heroine of a play (by Victorien Sardou) in which Sarah Bernhardt had a great success in 1885.

3. *the Faubourg Saint-Germain . . . Jardin des Plantes*: the former is a generic term for aristocratic society; the latter is the Paris zoo.

4. *as Balzac would say*: the word Balzac uses is 'tante' (aunt); other female family terms were apparently also current in the 1830s and after, depending on the age of the effeminate person in question. See Balzac, *Splendeurs et misères des courtisanes*, ed. P. G. Castex (Paris: Bibliothèque de la Pléiade, 1977), vol. 6, p. 840 and note.

5. *Fourier*: Charles Fourier, utopian theorist (1772–1837), enjoyed something of a vogue at the end of the nineteenth century.

6. *Tobolsk*: in Siberia, where Tsar Nicolas and his family were temporarily interned after the Russian Revolution of 1917.

7. *the Goncourts' Journal*: the *Journal* of the Goncourt brothers, Jules and Edmond, novelists and men of letters, spans the period between 1851 and 1896. The later volumes (such as the one pastiched here) are by Edmond alone, Jules having died in 1870. Partly published between 1887 and 1896, it was only finally published in complete form in 1956.

8. *Blanc . . . Burty*: Charles Blanc, art historian and art critic; Paul de Saint-Victor, man of letters and theatre critic; Charles-Augustin Sainte-Beuve, man of letters, literary critic, 'the father of modern criticism'; for Proust's disagreements with his judgments see *Against Sainte-Beuve and Other Essays*, translated by John Sturrock (Penguin Books, 1988); Philippe Burty, art critic.

9. *Maîtres d'autrefois*: a volume of art criticism by Eugène Fromentin.

10. *hôtel*: a large, private town house, often a mansion.

11. *La Fontaine*: a fictitious edition, a reference to the eighteenth-century

Fermiers Généraux edition of La Fontaine's *Contes et nouvelles en vers*, which the Goncourts greatly admired as an unparalleled example of book production.

12. *La Faustin*: one of Edmond Goncourt's later novels (1882).

13. *the Du Barry*: mistress of Louis XV, and an important patron of the arts in the later eighteenth century. (She was guillotined in 1793.)

14. *Jean d'Heurs*: a former abbey, the home of Goncourt's cousins, who kept an excellent kitchen.

15. *Et que . . . dans la nuit!* 'And that all this should make a star in the heavens!' Proust misquotes the last line of a poem by Victor Hugo, from his *Contemplations*: 'Et que tout cela fasse un astre dans les cieux!'

16. *One of Sainte-Beuve's prettiest poems*: 'La Fontaine de Boileau. Épitre à Mme la comtesse Molé'.

17. *Cot or Chaplin*: Pierre-Auguste Cot and Charles Chaplin were both successful nineteenth-century portrait painters.

18. *the Directory*: *le Directoire*, the form of revolutionary government in France between 1795 and 1799.

19. *Mme Tallien*: mistress of Barras, a member of the Directory; a leader of salon society, and a fashion-setter, best known for her introduction of Greek-style dresses.

20. *Talma's*: François-Joseph Talma, a famous tragic actor, a friend of Napoleon.

21. *the Three Years Law*: introduced in 1913, this law increased the period of military service from two to three years.

22. *Mémoires d'outre tombe*: Proust was particularly fond of Chateaubriand's *Memoirs*, not only for their style but because he found in Chateaubriand a similar attitude to memory and beauty.

23. *Sans-culotte . . . chouan . . . bleu*: terms from the French Revolution: *sans-culottes* was a term for Revolutionary patriots, *chouans* (literally 'owls') were Royalist insurgents in Brittany and Normandy, and *bleus* were members of the Republican army.

24. *M. de Haussonville was a member*: the Comte d'Haussonville, biographer and man of letters, was one of a group of seven or eight members of aristocratic families in the Académie française in the late nineteenth century, popularly known as the 'Ducs' Party' as they were thought to control a substantial number of votes.

25. *Gallifet*: Général Gallifet (1830–1909), hated by the left after his suppression of the 1871 Commune, was equally disliked by the right, later in his life, when he became Minister of War in the pro-Dreyfus cabinet of 1899.

26. *the 'also-ran'*: the baccarat player at the Balbec hotel, first encountered in *In the Shadow of Young Girls in Flower* (see p. 457).

27. *Russian Ballet . . . Bakst . . . Dubufe*: the Russian Ballet, under the direction of Serge Diaghilev, was extremely fashionable from its first appearance in France in 1909. Leon Bakst (of whom Proust was a great admirer) was one of many painters to design productions. Guillaume Dubufe (1853–1909) was a more conventional and extremely eminent designer of interiors, executing many major official commissions.

28. *Frenchman of Saint-André-des-Champs*: a conventionally admirable, patriotic Frenchman.

29. *de Beers*: diamond-mining shares.

30. *taubes*: the German word for pigeon, the general word applied in Paris to the German bombing planes.

31. *'poilu'*: the word generally used for common soldiers, as 'Tommy' was in English. It rapidly lost its initial vulgarity and assumed resonances of determination and courage.

32. *Rodin or Maillol*: Aristide Maillol, like Auguste Rodin, was a major French sculptor.

33. *Romain Rolland*: Rolland's *Above the Battle* (1915), a series of newspaper articles republished in book form, argued idealistically against chauvinism, against the 'moral epidemic' of war, and for a sympathetic recognition of German culture. The book was widely regarded as betraying French war aims.

34. *La Fille aux mains coupées*: Pierre Quillard, a keen supporter of Dreyfus, published this dramatic poem in 1886.

35. *Ferrari*: François Ferrari, gossip and society columnist for the *Figaro*.

36. *Feydeau's farce*: Georges Feydeau co-authored this 1894 farce with Maurice Desvallières. Typically, it is full of nocturnal encounters, mistaken rendezvous and other staples of his oeuvre.

37. *Bressant or Delaunay*: Bressant (1815–1886) and Delaunay (1826–1903) of the Comédie-Française were both actors famous for playing juvenile leads, even (in the case of the latter) when they were rather old for it.

38. *My uncle . . . à la Chambord*: this is a rather laboured joke, with extensive reference. Essentially, M. de Charlus would consort with Mme Molé and Arthur Meyer (a Catholic, Royalist journalist of dubious reliability) out of monarchist sentiment, the former because of her connection with the late pretender to the French throne, the Comte de Chambord. Carp à la Chambord was a very lavish way of cooking it (in champagne), with stuffed sweetbreads, truffles and foie gras. The implication is that Charlus will swallow anything as long as it is dished up as monarchism.

39. *Bonnet rouge*: 'Red Cap', a revolutionary pacifist paper.

40. 'from the unfathomable abyss./As every day renewed the sun shall climb

the sky/Washed clean within the deeps of the profoundest seas.' Baudelaire, 'Le Balcon' (slightly altered).

41. *Gothas*: these German aeroplanes made regular and damaging raids on Paris in the first months of 1918. In the first raid alone, forty-five people died and over two hundred were injured.

42. '*time change*': the French government introduced 'summer-time' for the first time in 1916.

43. *Zouaves*: colonial regiment whose soldiers wore colourful, Oriental uniforms.

44. *Anastasia*: for some unclear reason, this was the term in general use for the censorship.

45. *L'Île du rêve*: a light-operatic Polynesian idyll, based on a novel by Pierre Loti. The music was by Proust's friend, Reynaldo Hahn.

46. *fêtes galantes*: the best-known such painter was Watteau (whose painting *L'Embarquement pour Cythère*, an important example of this genre, is mentioned below, p. 220).

47. *a novel by a Swiss writer . . . militarists*: the book in question is *Die Mädchenfeinde* (1907), a short novel by Carl Spitteler, winner of the Nobel Prize for literature in 1920.

48. *General de Boisdeffre . . . Colonel du Paty de Clam . . . Colonel Henry's forgery*: three of the officers deeply involved in the fabrication of evidence against Dreyfus.

49. *Vauquois*: the 1915 battle for the village of Vauquois, twenty-five kilometres west of Verdun, though fiercely contested, was not a battle of world-historical significance.

50. *Caillaux*: leader of the Radical Party, imprisoned in 1918 for treating with the enemy and endangering state security.

51. *Giolitti*: a pro-German Italian politician, who opposed Italy's alliance with France and England.

52. *Diadoch*: heir to the Greek throne.

53. *Ferdinand of Coburg*: i.e. the Bulgarian Tsar.

54. *habent sua fata libelli*: 'books have their destinies.'

55. *self is always hateful*: see Pascal, *Pensées*, 136. Anatole France wrote a preface to Emile Combes's *Une campagne laïque 1902–1903*.

56. *Père Didon . . . a Duval Restaurant*: Father Henri Didon (1840–1900) was a famous Dominican preacher. The 'Duval Bouillons' were Paris restaurants serving cheap, nutritious food; they were clean, respectable, and the waitresses wore a severely unsexy uniform.

57. *Clarisse*: the first of the three novellas which make up Paul Morand's *Tendre stocks* (1921). An essay Proust wrote on Morand in 1920 was reprinted as that book's preface.

58. *as M. Barrès would call it*: the reference is to *Les Déracinés* (1897), the first volume of a trilogy of novels preaching a mystical French nationalism, by Maurice Barrès.

59. *Déroulède*: President of the League of Patriots.

60. *Dreyfus . . . murmur from anyone*: Picquart suffered for being one of the main defenders of Dreyfus, but was reinstated in the army, and became Minister of War in 1906.

61. *You once made me read . . . waged by the Empire*: Charles Maurras's elegant essay was collected in his *L'Avenir de l'intelligence* (1905). Aimée de Coigny's *Mémoires* were not published until 1902, although she died in 1820. What she wanted, in 1812, despite her earlier advocacy of revolutionary opinions, was the restoration of the monarchy, but she had not yet been persuaded of the desirability of a return to absolute monarchy and consequently supported the liberal Duc d'Orléans and the establishment of a bourgeois, constitutional monarchy.

62. *M. Syveton*: Gabriel Syveton, one of the founders of the 'Ligue de la patrie française', a Nationalist deputy, famously slapped the face of the War Minister in 1904.

63. *the heroines of M. Becque*: see Henry Becque's *La Parisienne* (1885), a novel with a cynically immoral heroine.

64. *the Duc d'Enghien*: in 1804, at the instigation of Napoleon, the Duc d'Enghien was first court-martialled and then shot in the moat of Vincennes Castle.

65. *Inculcabis super leonem et aspidem*: Psalm 91:13: 'Thou shalt tread upon the lion and adder: the young lion and dragon shalt thou trample under feet.'

66. *Action libérale*: a political party of the moderate Catholic Republican right.

67. *Action française*: a group centred upon the newspaper of that name, edited by Léon Daudet (son of Alphonse) and Charles Maurras, which began as a pamphlet in 1899, becoming a daily paper in 1908. Their politics were very right-wing, anti-Semitic, Royalist and Nationalist.

68. *the Capets*: the ruling house of France from 987 to 1328. By extending and consolidating their power, the Capetian kings laid the foundation of the French nation-state.

69. *a newspaper that was appearing at the time*: Clemenceau's paper *L'Homme libre* (The Freeman) had been rechristened *L'Homme enchaîné* in protest against wartime censorship.

70. *poutana*: whore.

71. *Boissier's . . . Gouache's*: Paris shops selling cakes, pastries and confectionery.

72. *it is the opposite of the Carmelites, it is the vice that takes care of virtue*: the

Carmelites used not only to pray for the sins of the world, but also to mortify their flesh, by means of flagellation among other methods.

73. *Phèdre . . . Les Saltimbanques*: Racine's greatest tragedy is contrasted with a contemporary operetta.

74. *Ruskin's Sesame and Lilies*: Proust's translation was published in 1906.

75. *Gilbert the Bad*: ancestor of the Guermantes, depicted on a stained-glass window at Combray.

76. *the rod of justice*: an iron bar to which prisoners who had been clapped in irons were fastened as a punishment on board French naval vessels.

77. *the 'expulsion of the nuns'*: one of the consequences of the law of 1 July 1901 was that many religious communities, especially teaching communities which ran their own schools, were disbanded. (See also below, p.222.)

78. *Lectures pour tous*: a popular magazine, which ran from 1898 until 1939.

79. *M. Arthur Meyer*: see note 38 above.

80. *Bossuet*: seventeenth-century cleric, preacher and writer, best known for the eloquence of his funeral orations.

81. *François le Champi by George Sand*: this, of course, is the novel which the narrator's mother reads to him at the beginning of the novel. Published in 1850, it deals with the love between the eponymous foundling child and the young woman, later a widow, who becomes his adoptive mother.

82. *Foucquet*: Jean Foucquet, a fifteenth-century illuminator of books.

83. *the Confédération Générale de Travail*: the General Confederation of Labour, to which trade unions were affiliated and through which they might speak with a collective voice.

84. *Port-Royalist*: the convent of Port-Royal gave its name in the seventeenth century to a spiritual and educational movement associated with Jansenist ideas (and hence anti-Jesuit) which laid considerable stress on logic and rigorous thinking as well as conscience. Pascal and Racine are the best-known names associated with Port-Royal; Sainte-Beuve devoted a major work to it.

85. *'Men often want . . . to remain free'*: La Bruyère, *Caractères*, 'Du Coeur', No. 16.

86. *Young Werther*: the quintessentially noble, Romantic lover in Goethe's *The Sorrows of Young Werther*.

87. *Embarquement pour Cythère*: the painting by Watteau (see note 45).

88. *Reinach*: Joseph Reinach (1856–1921), an outspoken supporter of Dreyfus and a leader of the campaign to prove his innocence.

89. *Church Schools against nature . . . temporarily rehabilitated*: all examples of current attitudes influential in one circle or another.

90. *knew . . . at the same time as the Russians*: the reference is to an enquiry

by Général Roques into the leadership methods of Sarrail, who commanded an allied expeditionary force to Salonika in 1915.

91. *Tout-Paris . . . Annuaire des châteaux*: *Tout-Paris* was a sort of cross between *Who's Who* and the telephone directory; the *Annuaire des châteaux* listed 40,000 owners of country houses, with their names and addresses.

92. *Yesterday . . , and of youth*: Chateaubriand's posthumously published *Memoirs*, one of the great works of French prose, contain passages (like these) which seem to anticipate Proust's understanding of spontaneous memory.

93. *L'azur . . . et de mâts*: 'The blue of heaven, spacious, curved' and 'A harbour thick with pennants and with masts' (from 'Parfum exotique', in Baudelaire's *Les Fleurs du mal*).

94. *Regnard . . . Labiche*: Jean-François Regnard (1655–1709), a comic drama tist sometimes regarded as the successor to Molière. The reference here is to *Le Légataire universel* in which a young man's valet impersonates an ancient uncle. Eugène Labiche (1815–88) was an immensely prolific comic playwright.

95. *Général Dourakine*: the Russian-born Comtesse de Ségur (1799–1874) was the author of quantities of children's books, of which *Général Dourakine* was one.

96. *intrigué*: there was, so far as I know, no equivalent English usage to this: to 'intrigue' somebody with whom you were enjoying yourself at a masked ball was to show them that you recognized them, without revealing your own identity.

97. *Fregoli*: Leopoldo Fregoli was best known as a virtuoso quick-change artist, so much so that his name became a synonym for rapid transformations.

98. *the 1878 Exhibition*: the Universal Exhibition of 1878 was one of the international fairs and exhibitions which became popular in the wake of the Great Exhibition of 1851 in London. It was actually personified by an actress, whose dress was decorated with lots of different national flags, in a revue on the Paris stage that year.

99. *Boulangist*: a short-lived political movement of national regeneration. Général Boulanger himself, a former war minister, was elected Deputy in 1889, but disappointed his followers by not attempting a coup, fled the country, was condemned for treason, and committed suicide in 1891. So this is another instance of Time's rehabilitation of the formerly discredited.

100. *Gotha*: the *Gotha Almanach* was the European equivalent of *Burke's Peerage*, the annual register of the aristocracy and its continuing pedigree.

101. *Hedwige's*: i.e. the first Princesse de Guermantes's.

102. *that Clemenceau and Viviani . . . conservatives*: Clemenceau was already a radical Republican at the time of the Paris Commune in 1871, the experience of which made him an extreme left-winger. His increasingly independent critical position, however, saw him move further and further rightwards. Viviani was a Socialist Deputy who became leader of the Nationalist coalition government for a while during the war.

103. *the Golden Legend*: the work of Jacob of Voragine (?1228–98), a collection of lives of the saints, and similar religious material, translated into all western European languages and very influential on medieval art and iconography.

104. *the Prince of Wales*: Proust does not actually say 'by the Prince of Wales' (or 'by the Duc d'Orléans', whom it might equally be), but this is generally thought to be an omission.

105. *Twickenham*: York House, Twickenham, was the home of the Comte de Paris, pretender to the French throne.

106. *the Salute*: the dome of the church of Santa Maria della Salute in Venice marks the beginning of the Grand Canal.

107. *M. Henri Bidou*: during the war, Henri Bidou wrote a regular column on military affairs for *Le Journal des Débats*. Proust was a keen reader of it.

108. *as Mounet-Sully said to Coquelin*: Jean Mounet-Sully (1841–1916), a famous tragic actor; Constant-Benoît Coquelin (1841–1909), an actor long associated with the Comédie-Française, wrote *Molière et le Misanthrope* in 1881.

109. *Balthy and Mistinguett*: Louise Balthy (1869–1925) was a singer in operetta and revue; Mistinguett (the stage name of Jeanne Bourgeois (1875–1956)) was a music-hall artiste.

110. *her son and daughter-in-law*: for some reason, Proust has got this the wrong way round: it is her daughter and son-in-law.

111. *Réjane*: (1857–1920), an internationally acclaimed actress. She retired in 1915.

112. *Mid-Lent*: actually it was New Year's Day: see *In the Shadow of Young Girls in Flower*, I, pp. 61–2).

113. *one of the marble figures in the Erechtheum*: see *In the Shadow of Young Girls in Flower*, I, p. 135, where Bergotte compares La Berma to one of these marble maidens.

114. *Fagon*: Guy-Crescent Fagon (1638–1718) was Louis XIV's doctor. He is eulogized by Saint-Simon in his *Mémoires*.

115. *Emporte le bonheur et laisse*-moi *l'ennui*: 'Take the happiness and leave the boredom to *me*' (Victor Hugo, from *Les Contemplations*, IV. ii).

116. *Meilhac*: Henri Meilhac wrote witty, amusing drawing-room comedies and operetta libretti, the latter (with Halévy) for Offenbach.

117. *The reality . . . I think?*: repetition, slightly rephrased, of a passage from pp. 269–70 above.

118. *to see her*: i.e. to see Odette.

119. *Géronte*: a stock comedy name for an old man: Molière has two characters so called.

120. *Empire*: Empire style (reflecting the period of the Napoleonic Empire between 1804 and 1815), in furniture as in architecture and painting, had a strong archaeological influence, derived from Egypt as well as from Greece and Rome. Mahogany veneers, ormolu mounts, winged-lion supports, pilasters headed with sphinxes, busts or palm leaves, were all popular. Contemporary designs were mingled with symbolic motifs, often referring to Napoleon's reign, such as winged victories and the laurel wreaths for triumph, bees, sheaves of grain and cornucopias for prosperity.

121. *Mme Récamier*: a beauty and intellectual, she had the most eminent literary and political salon in Paris during the Napoleonic and Restoration periods.

122. *the Kreutzer Sonata*: Beethoven's Violin Sonata Op. 47 is generally known as the Kreutzer Sonata.

123. *the poet . . . broken by life*: Proust is referring to Victor Hugo's 'Les Rayons et les ombres', 'How little time is needed for everything to change / Nature with skies serene, how you forget! / And how in your metamorphoses you break / The mysterious threads in which our hearts are bound!'

124. *'Il faut . . . et que les enfants meurent'*: 'Grass has to grow, and children have to die.'

125. *déjeuner sur l'herbe*: *Le Déjeuner sur l'herbe* is the painting by Manet, disrespectfully reworking a painting by Giorgione.

126. *'the funerary gate'*: 'And I shall follow those who love me, in my banishment. / Their fixed eyes draw me to the depths of the infinite / I run towards them. Close not the funerary gate' (Victor Hugo).

127. *'except a corn of wheat . . . much fruit'*: John 12: 24.

Synopsis

At Tansonville. Staying at the house of Gilberte de Saint-Loup at Tansonville; through the window of my bedroom I see the forest of Méséglise and the steeple of Combray (3). Under the influence of his vice, Robert de Saint-Loup, unlike M. de Charlus, has started to look like a cavalry officer (4). His lies (5). Françoise thinks highly of him because of his role as Morel's protector (7). Robert's feelings for Gilberte, and for Morel (10). Saint-Loup is coming to look more and more like all the other Guermantes (11). Homosexuality in the Guermantes and the Courvoisiers. My conversations with Saint-Loup never get beyond military strategy (11). And Gilberte is equally reluctant to talk about Albertine (13).

The Goncourts' 'Journal'. Instead of reading Balzac's *La Fille aux yeux d'or*, I read an extract from one of the Goncourts' recently published journals (15). The extract transcribed includes the description of a dinner at the Verdurins', their *hôtel*, Brichot, and their salon (18). The painter Elstir was discovered by them (20). Accounts of Swann and Cottard (22).

The magic of literature (23)! The Goncourt journal shows me that I am not fitted for looking and listening to surface details (24), but this is because I am more interested in psychology (25). Memoirs contain a different order of truth from art itself (29).

M. de Charlus during the war: his opinions and his pleasures. After years in a sanatorium I return to Paris in 1916 (30). Wartime Paris like Paris during the Directory, with Mme Verdurin and Mme de Bontemps as its queens (30). New fashions and new ways of behaving (32). The war, in the aftermath of the Dreyfus Affair, has created upheavals in society. The Verdurin salon, and its old and new adherents ('the faithful') (33): Morel, a deserter (37); Octave 'the Also-ran', now author of an admired book, has married Andrée (38). Mme de Verdurin's approaches to Odette (39). The Verdurins' new home (40).

Aeroplanes in the sky over the city at nightfall (41). My night-time walks in Paris remind me of Combray (42).

My earlier, brief, return to Paris in 1914 (44). I meet Saint-Loup just after war is declared (44). He conceals his attempts to get sent to the front (45). Bloch's pretence of patriotism (46); Saint-Loup's real patriotism, and that of his friends at Doncières (49). The ideal of masculinity among homosexuals, officers and diplomat-writers (53). The manager of the Grand Hotel at Balbec is in a concentration camp, the lift-boy wants to be an aviator (54). The butler torments Françoise with war news (56). Françoise has not lost any of her faults: indiscretion, bad faith, a fondness for turns of phrase which she then gets wrong (57). Back in my sanatorium I receive a letter from Gilberte, who has fled to Tansonville, now occupied by the Germans (59) In another letter, Saint-Loup talks about war and its laws, and the death of young Vaugoubert (60) His intellectual and artistic tastes (62).

My second return to Paris: another letter from Gilberte, explaining that she is in Tansonville to look after the house (63). Fighting around Combray (64). Recent visit from Saint-Loup, on leave (65). His thoughts on the war: the Wagnerian beauty of nocturnal air-raids (66). His reflections on strategy and diplomacy show him to be brilliant, but less original than his uncle Charlus (67). On foot to the Verdurins' (70). I admire the Oriental impression created by sunset over the city. I meet M. de Charlus (71). He now looks like all inverts; decline of his social position (72). Mme Verdurin's malevolence towards him (73). Not fashionable (74). Cruel treatment by Morel, author of scurrilous articles about him (75). Parallel between nations at war and the relations between individuals (79). Mme Verdurin's croissant and the sinking of the *Lusitania* (81). M. de Charlus's pro-Germanism (83). His sarcasm about Brichot's articles, which like the rest of the press have become militaristic (86). His on-off quarrel with Morel (88). Charlus enumerates the absurdities in articles by Norpois and Brichot, reveals his own childishness (90). Mme de Forcheville has updated her anglophile vocabulary (97). Annoyed by the success of his pedantic articles, Mme Verdurin makes Brichot the butt of her jokes (99). Charlus's conversation about the war completely betrays him; aestheticism and respect for tradition make him a defeatist (102). His dangerous harangue in the street, where he is followed by unsavoury individuals (108). The night sky full of circling aeroplanes; moonlight (109). M. de Charlus wants to make it up with Morel (112). Two years later, Morel will tell me he was afraid of Charlus (113). M. de Charlus compares Paris to Pompeii (114). His admiration for the soldiers of all the Allied armies; their classically inspired masculinity (115). His handshake as we part (117).

*

Jupien's hotel. Walking through a Paris which feels like something out of the *Arabian Nights* (118). I need a drink and a rest, so enter a hotel, in which I see an officer like Saint-Loup leaving (119). Conversation among patrons, soldiers and workers in the hotel; it takes a disturbing turn (120). I take a room (121); I see a man in chains, being whipped: M. de Charlus (123). Jupien appears; he runs the place, but Charlus is the owner (124). The young men recruited by Jupien, whom Charlus thinks are too soft, all look like Morel (126). Universality of the laws of love (127). A *croix de guerre* found on the ante-room floor (129). Two very elegant clients (130). How emotion affects what we say (130). Jupien hides me in a room off the hall where I can see and hear without being seen (132). Charlus and his harem of young men; disappointed by their normality (133). A rotten priest (137). After Charlus has left, Jupien makes a great effort to justify his position, ending up with my translation of Ruskin's *Sesame and Lilies* (138).

Back in the street, watching out for aeroplanes (141). The Pompeians in the subways of the Métro, all social classes mixed together (142). Our habits, independent of moral value, as with M. de Charlus, whose aberrations betray the universal poetic dream of love (146). After the all-clear, I go back home; Saint-Loup has been there, looking for his *croix de guerre*, which he has lost (149). Françoise and the war; tormented by the butler (150). The triumph of virtue: the Larivières, cousins of Françoise (153). Death of Saint-Loup, the day after his return to the front (155). Recollections of our friendship (156). The secret of his life, a parallel with Albertine's secret (156). Françoise mourns him (157). The laws of death (158). I write to Gilberte (159). Unexpected grief of the Duchesse de Guermantes (160). Another consequence of Saint-Loup's death: Morel, arrested as a deserter and unsettling M. de Charlus and M. d'Argencourt with his revelations, is sent to the front and wins the *croix de guerre*. If Saint-Loup had lived . . . (161).

The Princesse de Guermantes's afternoon party. Perpetual adoration. My third return to Paris, after the war (162). My train stops in open countryside, where a line of trees fails to arouse any emotion in me: confirmation that I am incapable of writing (163). Invitation to an afternoon party at the Princesse de Guermantes's (164); glad to embrace purely social pleasures again; recollections of the magic of the Guermantes' name (165). My short journey to the avenue des Bois is also a journey in time, towards the silent heights of memory (166). On the Champs-Elysées I meet M. de Charlus, white-haired and decayed but majestic, accompanied by Jupien (167). His greeting to Mme de Saint-Euverte, whom he has forgotten he used to despise (168). Signs of aphasia, but his memory still intact (170). Roll-call of dead friends and relations (171). Meets the Duchesse de Létourville, who loses patience with Charlus for his infirmity (171). According to Jupien, though, the Baron is still as randy as a young man; he is also still very pro-German (172). Frivolous pleasure of the Princesse de Guermantes's party, my sense that I am untalented (174). Bergotte was wrong, I did not know the joys of the minds (174). In the courtyard, I stumble over some unevenly laid paving-stones: I rediscover the same happiness as at other moments of my life, particularly the taste of the madeleine (175). Resurrection of the memory of Venice (175). Inside the house, more exhilarating sensations (176). Waiting in the library-cum-sitting-room for a piece of music to end before I go in, I rediscover the source of identical pleasures, the sound of a spoon, the stiffness of a napkin, which recall a moment of my past life (177). The only true paradise is a paradise that we have lost (178). These impressions, through an identity between the present and the past, enable us to enjoy the essence of things, outside of time (179). Whereas the intellectual observation of reality is disappointing (180). Fugitive nature of this optical illusion (181). But another echo of a past sensation shows me that the pleasure it gives is the only real and fertile one (183). Memory is the means by which we can reach this reality, whereas travel can never recreate lost time (185). The happiness offered to Swann by the sonata's little phrase and which had never been vouchsafed to him (186). Inadequacy of intelligence. The work of art the only means of interpreting sensations, signs of so many laws and ideas (187). Difficulty of deciphering this internal book (188). Art enables us to discover our real life; uselessness of literary theories, and their demands (189). Finding *François le Champi* in the Duc de Guermantes's library confirms my line of thought (191). The book summons up within me the child in Combray, because books remain linked to what we were when we read them (192). The kind of bibliophile I would have been, collecting the editions in which I first read a book (194). The idea of popular art, like that of patriotic art, seems laughable (196). Reality is a relationship between sensations and memories; the writer expresses them in a metaphor. The duty and task of a writer are those of a translator (197). The mistake of the celibates at the shrine of art, rough sketches for the artist (201). Constant aberrations of literary criticism; its verbiage (202). The best reader does no more than achieve complete consciousness of another person's thoughts (203). The literature of mere observation is valueless (203). The only life lived to the full is literature (204). Original artists put different worlds at our disposal (204). Making signs meaningful again after they have become meaningless through habit (205). The truths which the intelligence derives directly from reality are not to be despised (207). All these raw materials for a literary work were actually my past life (208). A vocation (208). I have created a sketch book without being aware of it (209). Extracting generalizable features from our grief (210). A book is a great cemetery (212). Why the work is a sign of happiness (213). Happiness alone is good for the body; whereas sorrow develops the strength of the mind (215). Ideas are substitutes for sorrows (215). Creative suffering leads us to truth and death (218). Meaning of the insignificant events in my life (219). Material of the book neutral, as shown by the phenomenon of sexual inversion (220). Dreams are another way of finding Lost Time again (221). Only coarse and inaccurate perception places everything in the object, when everything is in the mind (221). The subjective nature of love and hatred (222). Everything is in the mind (222). The raw material of my experience, which was to be the raw material of my book, came to me from Swann, and therefore excludes all other possible lives (223). Importance of jealousy (225).

The 'Bal de têtes' ('masked ball'). Back to the party (226). The butler tells me I can now enter the drawing-rooms (226). Chateaubriand, de Nerval and Baudelaire on aesthetic impressions (228). A dramatic turn of events raises serious objections to my undertaking (229). Difficulty in recognizing my host and fellow-guests, as all of them have been made up to look like old men and women (229). M. d'Argencourt as an old beggar (230). He is the revelation of Time, which he renders visible (233). Deeper changes to characters (234). Time has passed for me too (235). The Duchesse de Guermantes and young Létourville make me realize this (236). Bloch comes in, an old man: we are the same age (237). Anguish at discovering the destructive aspect of Time just as I have decided to depict extra-temporal realities in a work of art (239). Some people, like Mme Sazerat, completely changed (239). Realize that the discovery of old age will be the main subject matter of my book (240). M. de Cambremer disfigured by the mask of Time (241). Old age has improved the Prince d'Agrigente (242). Legrandin, sculpted like an Egyptian god (243). Old age has turned some people into faded adolescents, others have acquired new personalities (245). Bloch (246). To recognize somebody is to think about a mystery almost as disturbing as death (248). Young Cambremer's resemblance to his uncle prefigures the old man he will become (251). Unattractive features of old age (252). One friend so changed I only recognize his voice (252). In some cases, the tempo of time may be slowed down or accelerated (253). Both women and men altered by age; only Mme de Forcheville seems unchanged (256). How time rehabilitates disgraced politicians (256). Odette like a sterilized rose (258). Her company, so long sought, is now interminably dull (259). People think her a bit gaga; she has become an object of sympathy, no longer able to defend herself (260). Bloch now known permanently as Jacques du Rozier, and English fashion has transformed his appearance (261). I introduce him to the Prince de Guermantes (262). Bloch's confusion about who the Princesse is: Mme Verdurin's progress (263). Morel enters the room (264). Time works its chemistry upon society as well as upon individuals (265). Society has lost its standards and its homogeneity (265). Memory shorter than life (266). Misapprehensions of name and rank recall Saint-Simon's account of the ignorance of Louis XIV (270). The usefulness of genealogists (271). With the passing of time, people mistake the social status of men like Bloch and Swann; these errors too are dependent on Time, but they are a phenomenon of memory, not a social phenomenon (273). Close up, Bloch looks like an old Shylock (276). Even the most aristocratic names change their resonance over time: my understanding of the Faubourg is just as historically conditioned as any newcomer's (277). Bloch has lost his earlier indiscretion, in a process of social maturation (278). The different people at the party cause the varied aspects of my life to emerge in my mind's eye (279). Early memories of Mlle Swann, Charlus, the Duchesse de Guermantes (280). Importance of impressions for memory (282). Relativity of one individual's memories (example of Albertine) (284). The importance of death in the lives of older people; difficulty of remembering who has died (286). Death a cheering simplification of existence for those left alive (287). The Princesse de Nassau leaves (288). I mistake Gilberte for her mother (289). She talks to me about Robert and his ideas about the war (290).

Gilberte now has an inseparable friend in Andrée (292). Rachel to recite poetry at the party (293). My intention to resume a life of solitude while I write my book (295). I ask Gilberte to introduce me to some very young girls (297). The Duchesse de Guermantes in conversation with a frightful old woman, who turns out to be Rachel (300).

Meanwhile, across town, La Berma's tea-party is a failure (304). One young man is the only guest (307). La Berma's self-sacrifice for her ungrateful children (307).

Rachel's recitation, and the responses it evokes (308). Rachel disparages La Berma (312). I become aware that the passing of time does not necessarily bring about progress in the arts (312). The social decline of the Duchesse de Guermantes (313). Diminution of her powers (314). Her recollections of Bréauté very different from mine, illustrating 'that poetry of the incomprehensible which is one of the effects of time' (316). The Duchesse now claims to have discovered Rachel (321).

*

La Berma's son-in-law and daughter succeed in getting themselves admitted to the party in the belief that it is Rachel's (323). They thereby compound their destruction of La Berma's health by ruining her social reputation (324).

The Duc de Guermantes's love for Mme de Forcheville (324). He is a superb ruin (326). Odette makes fun of him (328). How the pattern of things changes in this world (328). His demands on Odette remind me of my life with Albertine (329). Odette's tales of love (330). Why a large proportion of the suffering in men's lives is caused by women 'who were not their type' (331). Another Mme de Saint-Euverte: a new blossoming of the Saint-Euverte name which marks both the distance and the continuity of Time (333). Mme de Guermantes's malicious remarks about Gilberte (335). Gilberte introduces me to her young daughter: the idea makes me think about the dense dimensionality of Time, as every thread of my life seems to meet in her (340). The idea of Time a spur to make me start my book (342). Importance of not leaving it unfinished (343). My methods, and Françoise's help (343). Danger of accidents (345). Yet I have become indifferent to the idea of my death, except for the sake of my book (346). One evening I go out and become unwell (349). Loss of capacity (350). Social self loses its memory; self that conceived the work still remembers (350). Nobody understands my first sketches (351). The idea of death establishes itself permanently within me, in the way that love does (352). I shall work at night, writing a book as long as the *Arabian Nights* or Saint-Simon's *Mémoires* (353). Is it too late? Illness, by compelling me to 'die to the world', has done me a service (354). The work will be marked by the form of Time (354). The garden bell at Combray (356). Remembering it at such a distance gives me a sense of giddiness (357). I imagine men as perched on living stilts, representing the length of time they have lived (357). My chief concern will be to describe people as they exist in Time (358).